Debian Perl

DIGITAL DETECTIVE

THE MEMORY THIEF

LAUREN DAVIS·MEL HILARIO·KATIE LONGUA
BRITTANY CURRIE · ANDWORLD DESIGN

Debian Perl
DIGITAL
DETECTIVE
—•THE MEMORY THIEF•—

CARACAL™   KNOWYOURSELF™

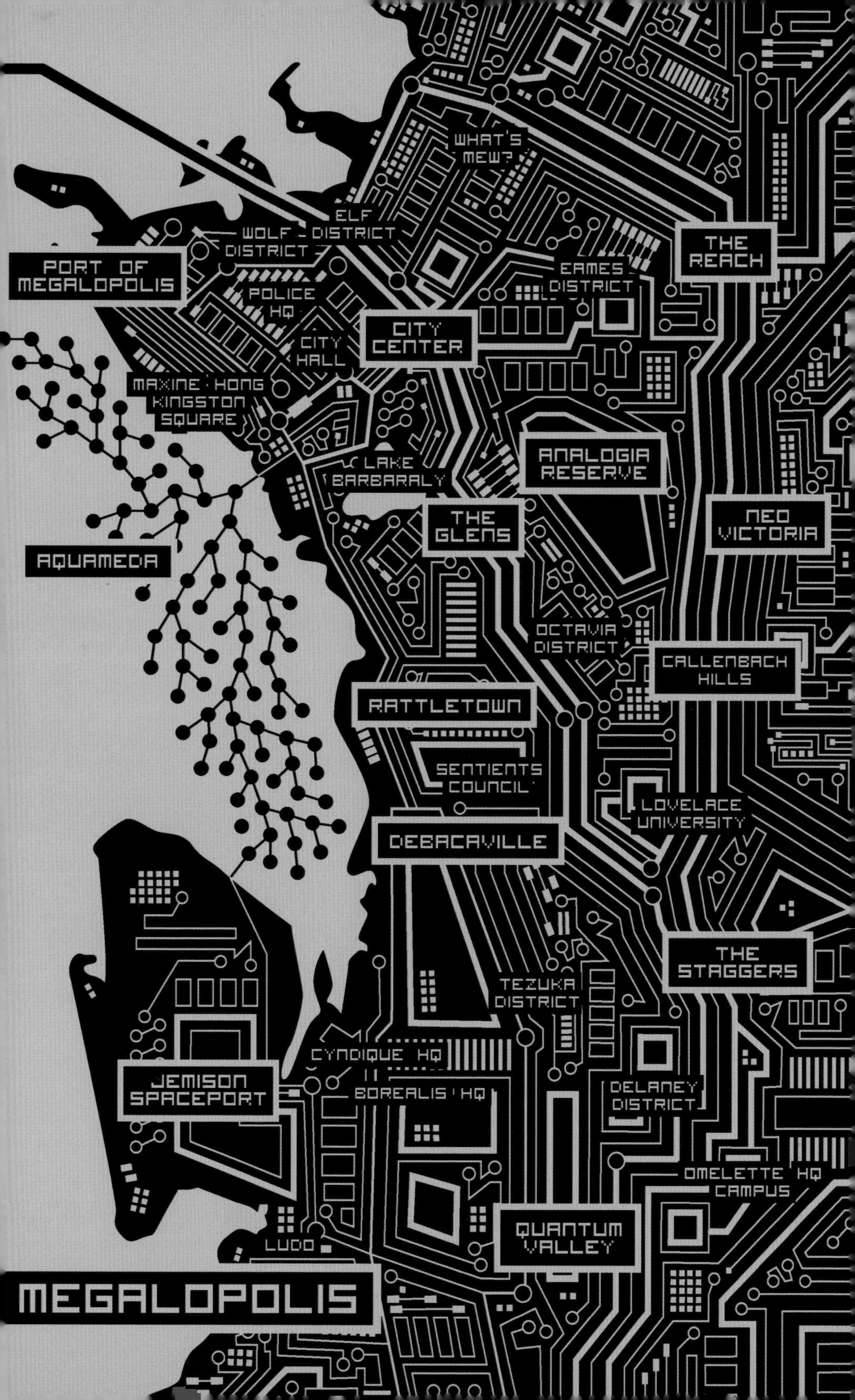

MEGALOPOLIS
WHAT'S MEW?
ELF DISTRICT
WOLF DISTRICT
PORT OF MEGALOPOLIS
THE REACH
EAMES DISTRICT
POLICE HQ
CITY CENTER
CITY HALL
MAXINE HONG KINGSTON SQUARE
ANALOGIA RESERVE
LAKE BARBARALY
THE GLENS
NEO VICTORIA
AQUAMEDA
OCTAVIA DISTRICT
CALLENBACH HILLS
RATTLETOWN
SENTIENTS COUNCIL
LOVELACE UNIVERSITY
DEBACAVILLE
THE STAGGERS
TEZUKA DISTRICT
CYNDIQUE HQ
JEMISON SPACEPORT
BOREALIS HQ
DELANEY DISTRICT
OMELETTE HQ CAMPUS
QUANTUM VALLEY
LUDO

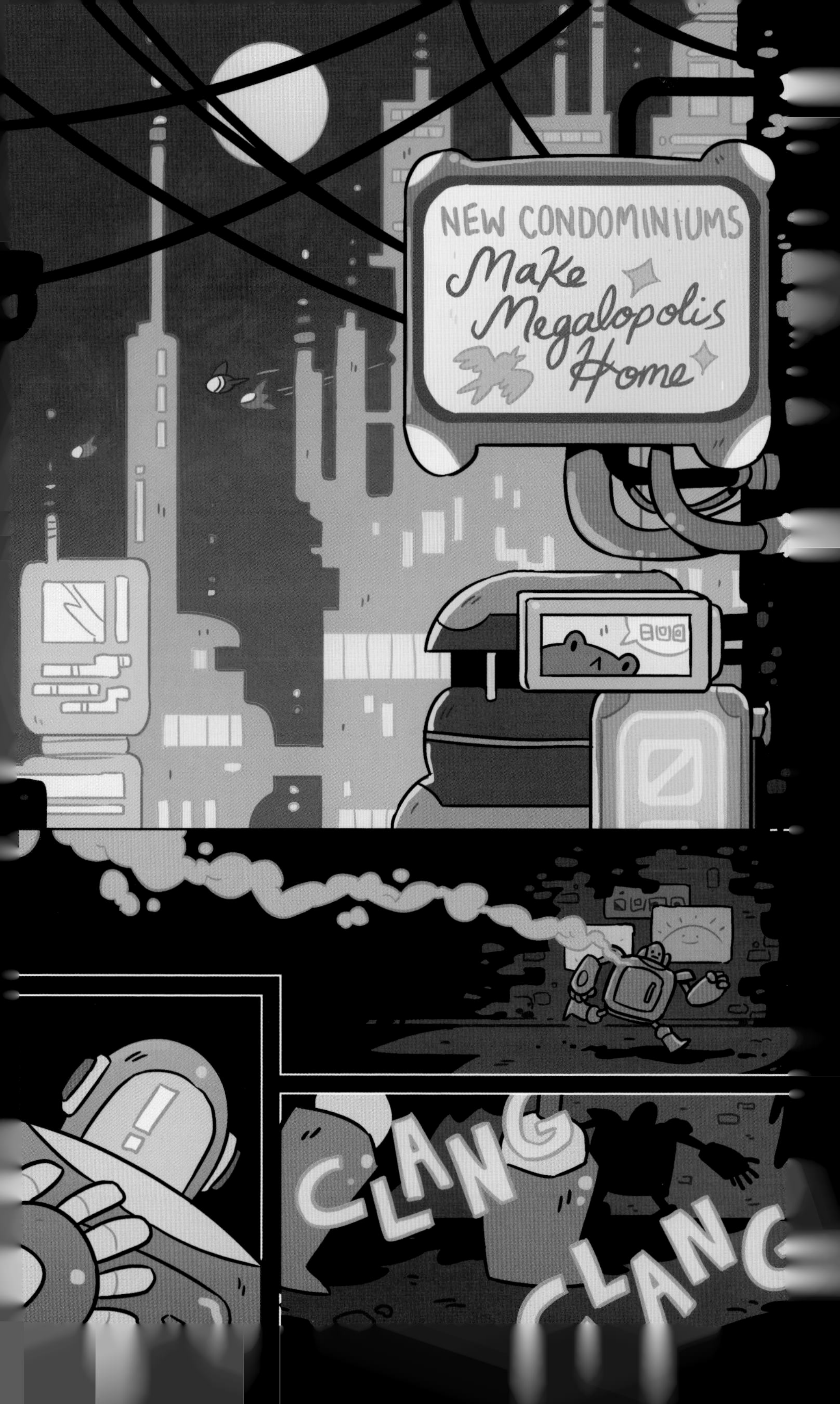
NEW CONDOMINIUMS
Make Megalopolis Home
CLANG
CLANG

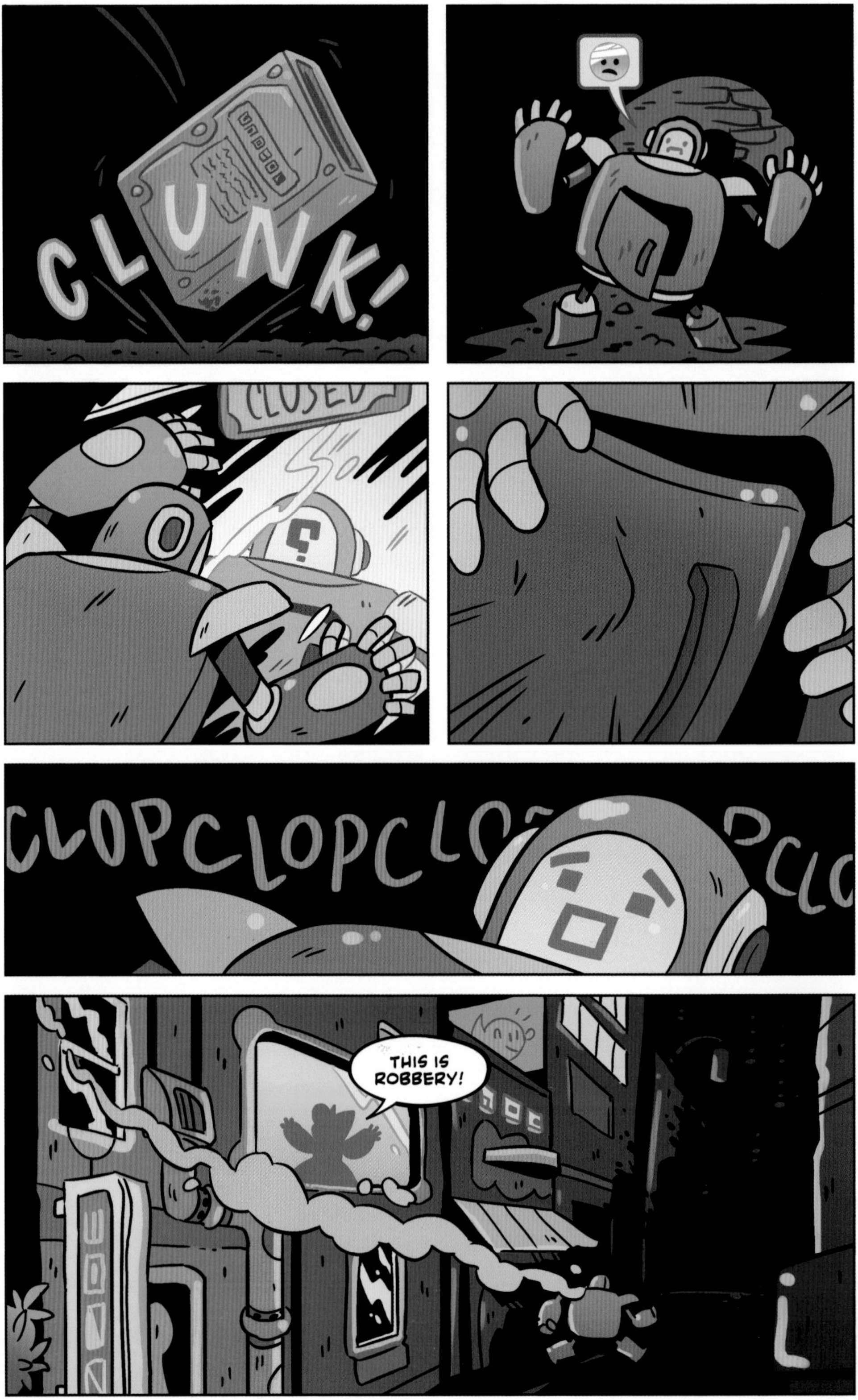
CLUNK!
CLOSED
CLOPCLOPCLOPCLO
THIS IS ROBBERY!

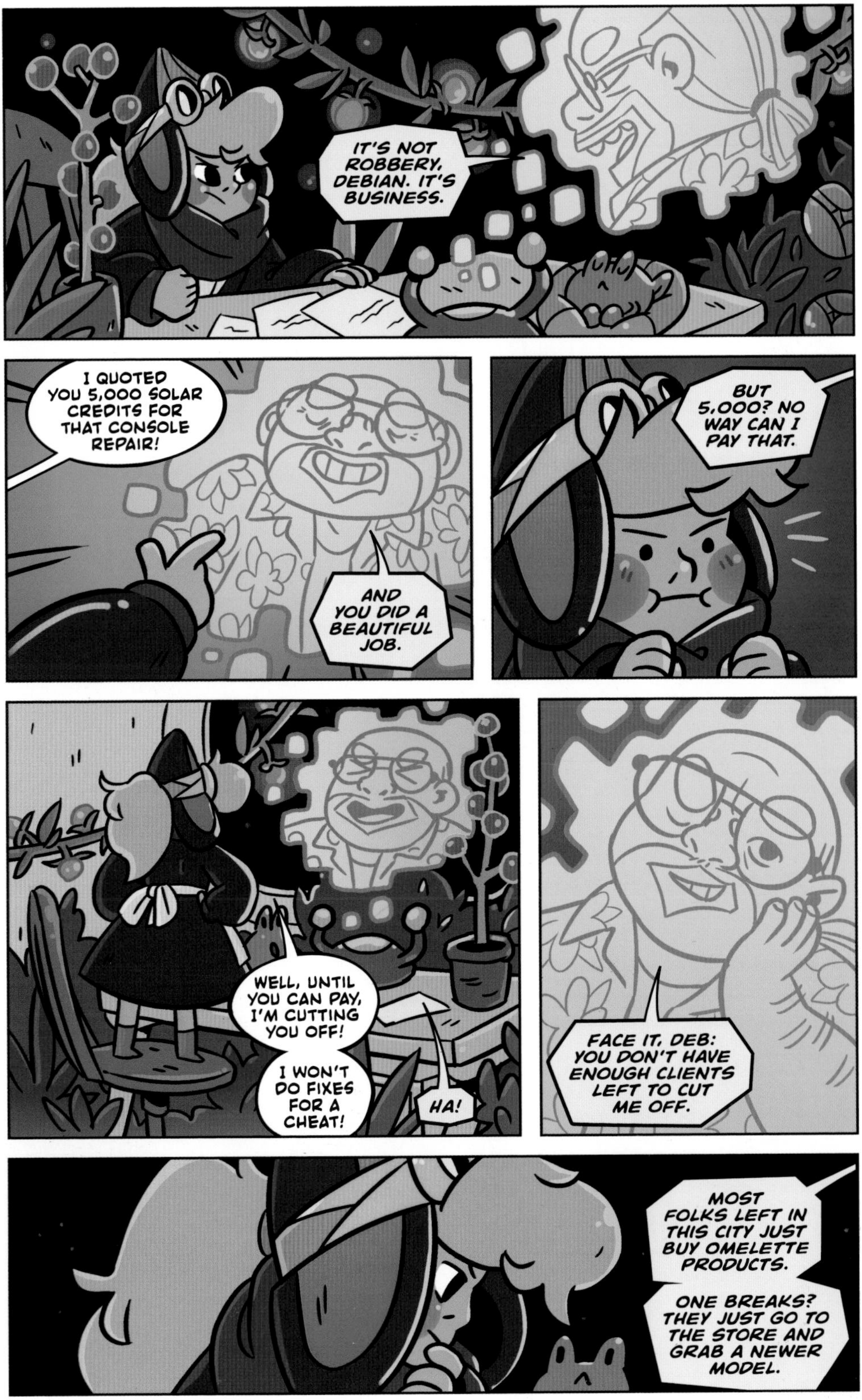
IT'S NOT ROBBERY, DEBIAN. IT'S BUSINESS.
I QUOTED YOU 5,000 SOLAR CREDITS FOR THAT CONSOLE REPAIR!
AND YOU DID A BEAUTIFUL JOB.
BUT 5,000? NO WAY CAN I PAY THAT.
WELL, UNTIL YOU CAN PAY, I'M CUTTING YOU OFF!
I WON'T DO FIXES FOR A CHEAT!
HA!
FACE IT, DEB: YOU DON'T HAVE ENOUGH CLIENTS LEFT TO CUT ME OFF.
MOST FOLKS LEFT IN THIS CITY JUST BUY OMELETTE PRODUCTS.
ONE BREAKS? THEY JUST GO TO THE STORE AND GRAB A NEWER MODEL.

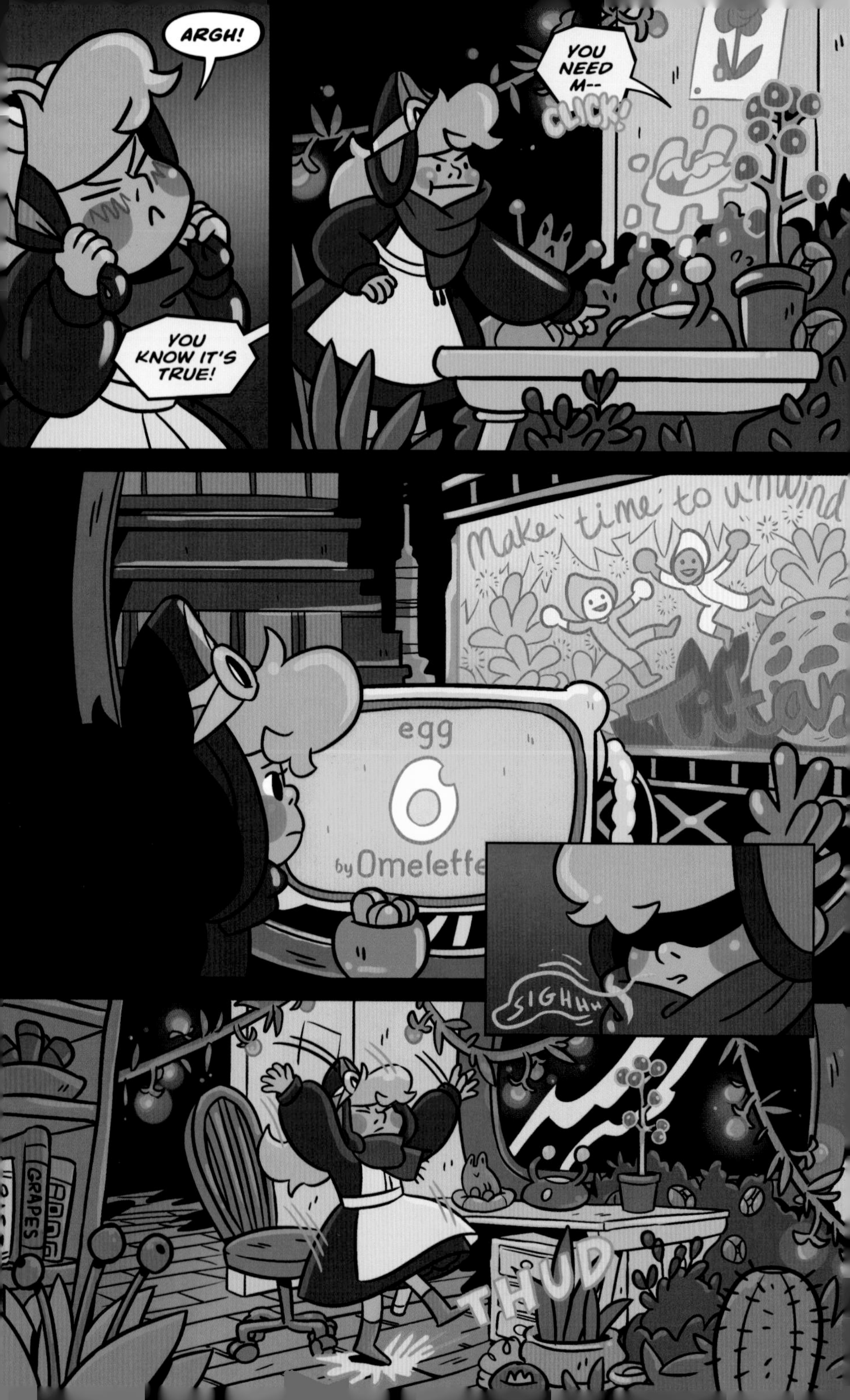

ARGH!
YOU KNOW IT'S TRUE!
YOU NEED M--
CLICK!
Make time to unwind
Titan
egg
by Omelette
SIGHHH
GRAPES
THUD

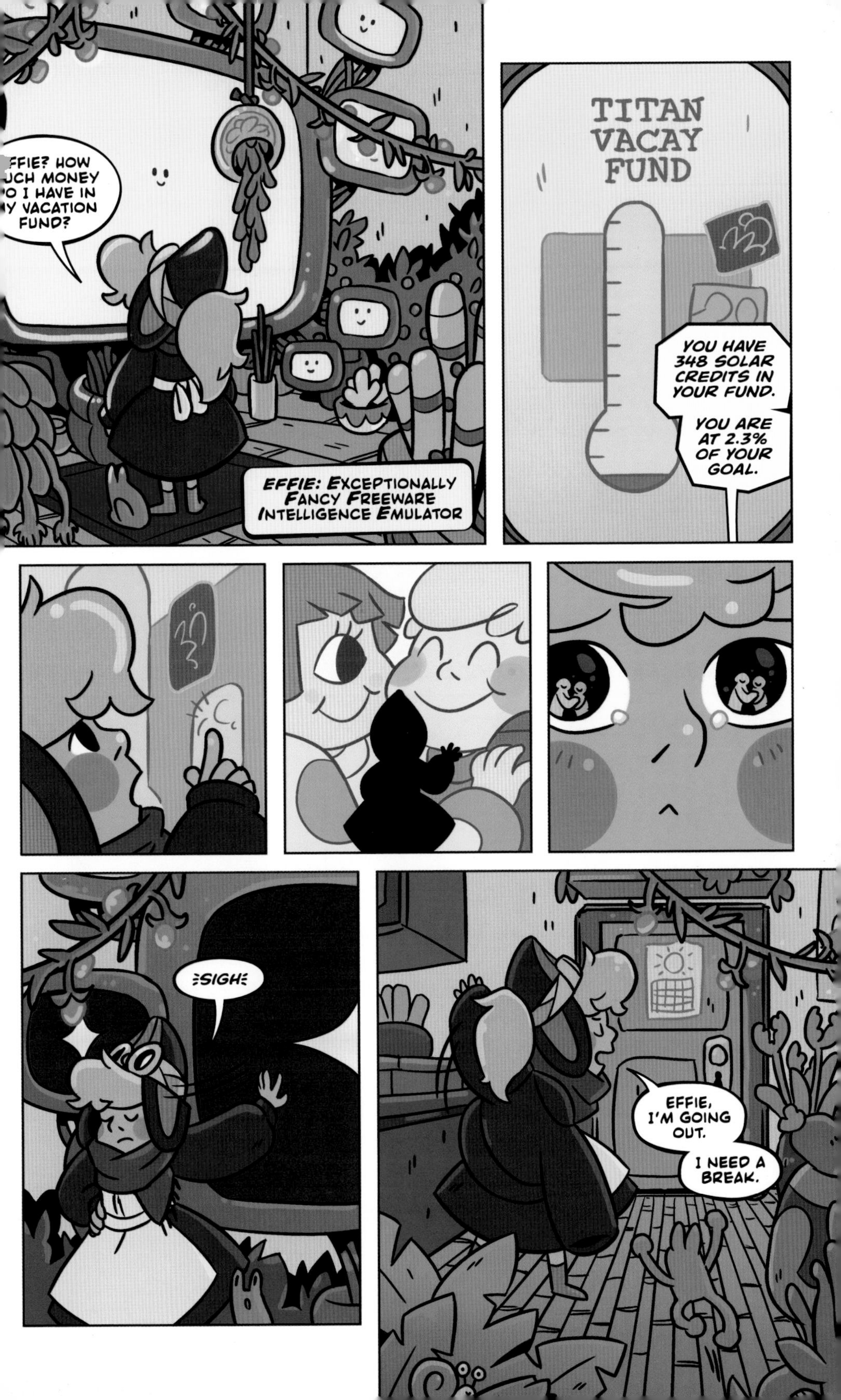
FFIE? HOW
UCH MONEY
O I HAVE IN
Y VACATION
FUND?
EFFIE: EXCEPTIONALLY FANCY FREEWARE INTELLIGENCE EMULATOR
TITAN VACAY FUND
YOU HAVE 348 SOLAR CREDITS IN YOUR FUND.
YOU ARE AT 2.3% OF YOUR GOAL.
SIGH
EFFIE, I'M GOING OUT.
I NEED A BREAK.

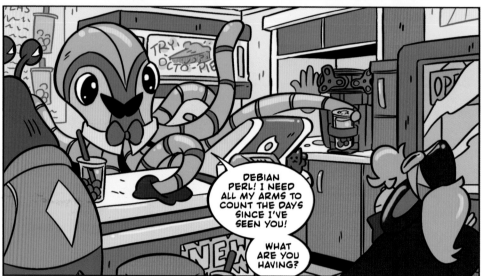

DEBIAN PERL! I NEED ALL MY ARMS TO COUNT THE DAYS SINCE I'VE SEEN YOU!

WHAT ARE YOU HAVING?

GIVE ME A GUAVA MILK TEA, EXTRA SWEET, NO ICE.

AND AN EXTRA SCOOP OF GRASS JELLY.

YOU DOING OKAY, DEB?

MMMFFFF.

SORRY, DEB. YOU'RE A HERO AROUND HERE--THIS ONE'S ON THE HOUSE.

JUST KEEP ON TECHNOMANCING FOR THE REST OF US! GREEN AND OTHERWISE...

THANKS, SAM. YOU'RE A PEACH.

DID YOU HEAR "AN ARM & A LEG" IS CLOSING?

WHAT? NO! I LOVE THOSE GUYS!

I MEAN, THEY WERE KIND OF MY COMPETITION, BUT NO ONE FABRICATES FINGERS LIKE LARRY AND HAROUN.

IT'S A BUMMER--CYNDIQUE OPENED ANOTHER PROSTHETICS SHOWROOM DOWN THE STREET. GUESS THERE'S NO STOPPING PROGRESS.

I GUESS NOT. I JUST WORRY I'M GONNA GET PROGRESSED RIGHT OUT OF THIS TOWN.

GOOD NIGHT, SAM.

CLOSED

FOR YOUR PATIENT IT IS THE LAW

CAT

SAM'S POTLUCK TEAS

7

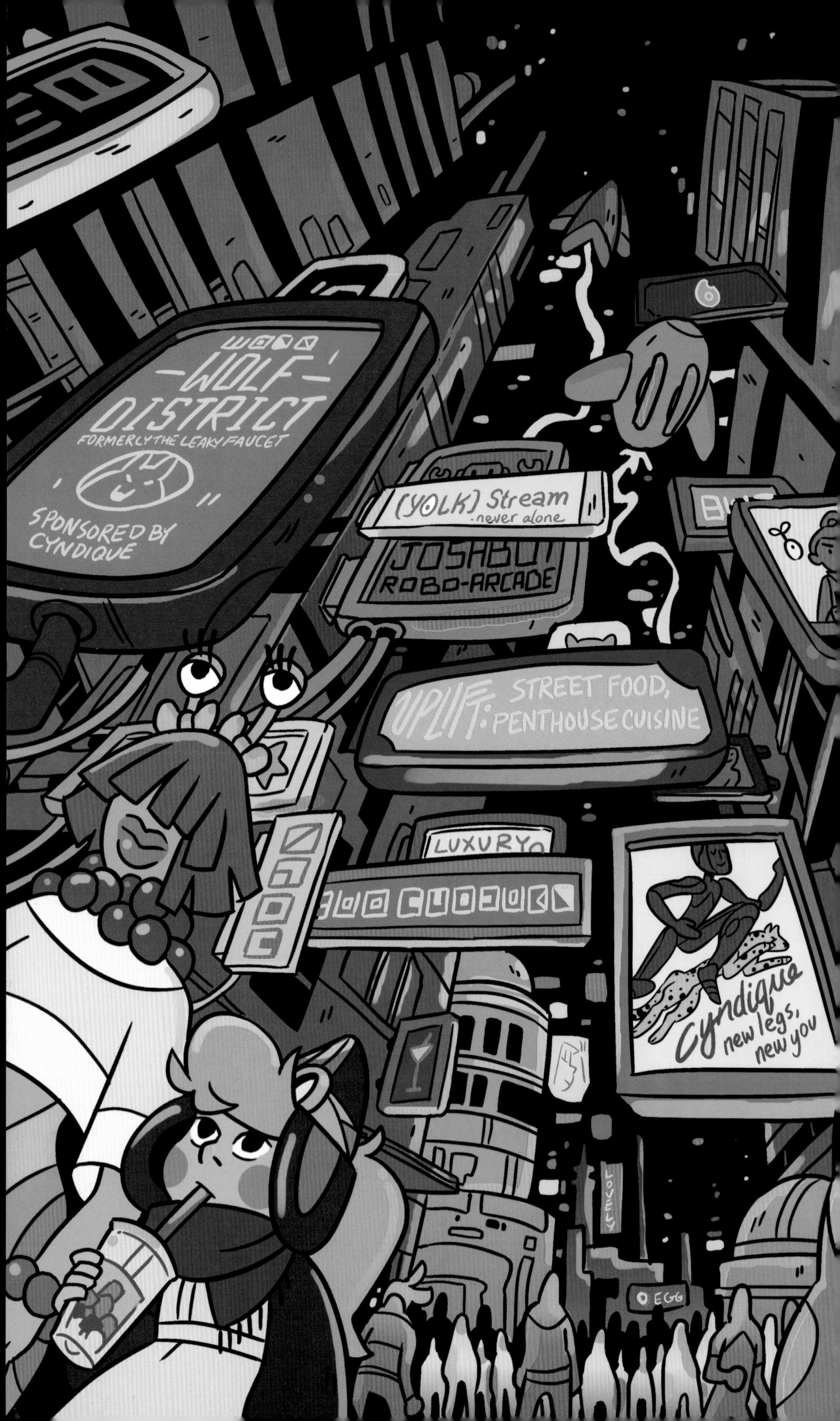

WOLF DISTRICT
FORMERLY THE LEAKY FAUCET
SPONSORED BY CYNDIQUE
[YOLK] Stream
-never alone
JOSHBOT ROBO-ARCADE
UPLIFT: STREET FOOD, PENTHOUSE CUISINE
LUXURY
Cyndique
new legs, new you
LOVELY
EGG

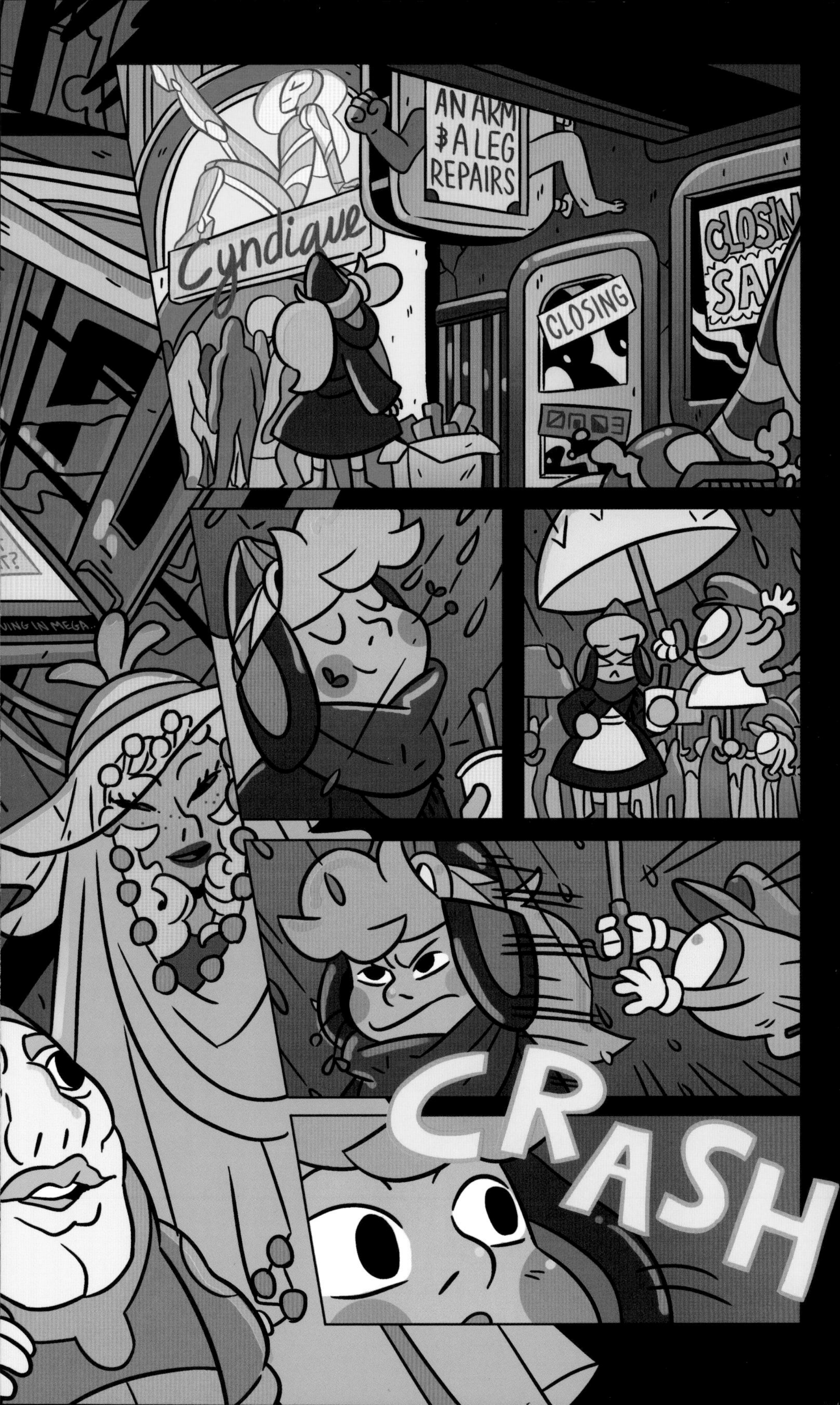
AN ARM & A LEG REPAIRS
Cyndique
CLOSING
CRASH

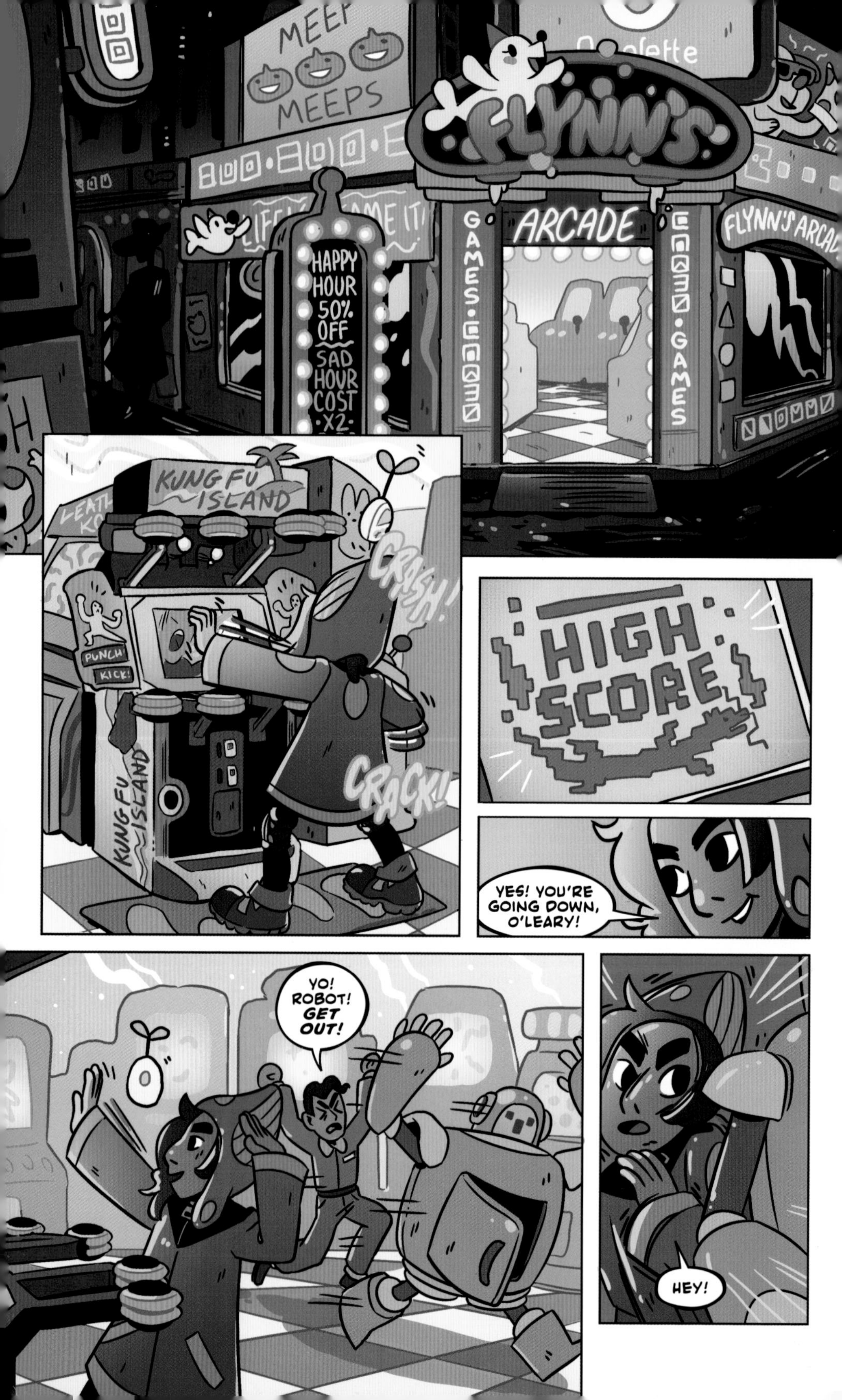
MEEP
MEEPS
ARCADE
GAMES
GAMES
FLYNN'S
FLYNN'S ARCADE
HAPPY HOUR 50% OFF
SAD HOUR COST ·X2·
KUNG FU ISLAND
PUNCH!
KICK!
CRASH!
CRACK!
KUNG FU ISLAND
HIGH SCORE
YES! YOU'RE GOING DOWN, O'LEARY!
YO! ROBOT! GET OUT!
HEY!

WHAT'S THE BIG...

...IDEA?

NO! NO! NO!

BETTER THAN LIFE!

GET OUT OF HERE!

THAT'S EXACTLY WHAT HE'S TRYING TO DO.

SANKAR

DEBIAN PERL, LICENSED TECHNOMANCER.

LOOKS LIKE YOU'RE HAVING ROBOT TROUBLE?

```
if(your need ==
    technomancer){
    the best =
    debian_perl;
}
```

THIS CLUNKER CRASHED IN HERE AND NOW HE WON'T LEAVE!

HUH!

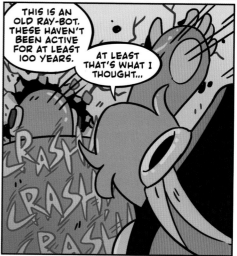

THIS IS AN OLD RAY-BOT. THESE HAVEN'T BEEN ACTIVE FOR AT LEAST 100 YEARS.

AT LEAST THAT'S WHAT I THOUGHT...

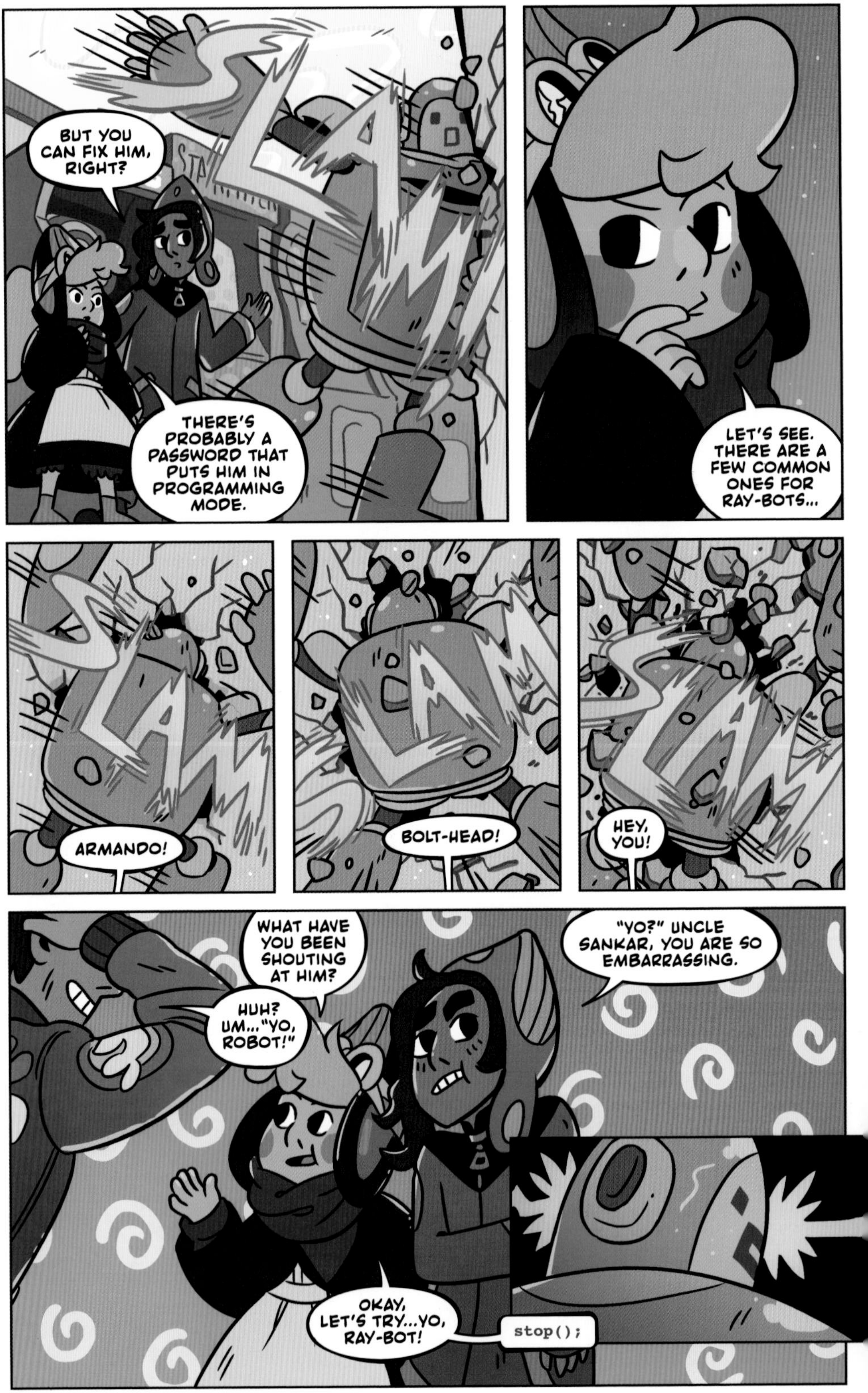
BUT YOU CAN FIX HIM, RIGHT?
THERE'S PROBABLY A PASSWORD THAT PUTS HIM IN PROGRAMMING MODE.
LET'S SEE. THERE ARE A FEW COMMON ONES FOR RAY-BOTS...
ARMANDO!
BOLT-HEAD!
HEY, YOU!
WHAT HAVE YOU BEEN SHOUTING AT HIM?
HUH? UM..."YO, ROBOT!"
"YO?" UNCLE SANKAR, YOU ARE SO EMBARRASSING.
OKAY, LET'S TRY...YO, RAY-BOT!
stop();

WELL, THAT WORKED.

HEY THERE, BUDDY. NOW WHERE DID YOU COME FROM?

HMM, WELL, WE'VE GOT A BIT OF A MYSTERY ON OUR HANDS.

AND I BET YOU'VE GOT A HUMDINGER OF A HEADACHE.

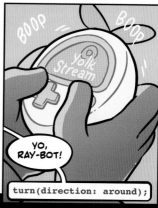

YO, RAY-BOT!

`turn(direction: around);`

(YOLK)Stream

DIGITS HERE, STREAMING LIVE FROM FLYNN'S ARCADE, WHERE SOMETHING REALLY WEIRD IS GOING DOWN.

THIS RANDO JUST STOPPED A MALFUNCTIONING ROBOT FROM CAUSING TOTAL DESTRUCTION!

STREAM CHAT

xX_bAd_Xx: clunkers should be put down

takmai: aww, he's kinda cute 🖤🖤🖤

dotdotdot_v: whoa! retro arcade!

NinjaKitty: flynn's isn't retro, just old

Trolltastic: butts🐱
Trolltastic: butts🐱
Trolltastic: butts🐱
Trolltastic: butts🐱

NinjaKitty: not again

Trolltastic: butts🐱
Trolltastic: butts🐱
Trolltastic: butts🐱

DIGITBOT: user Trolltastic has been temp banned for spamming

katogjohnson: nice

DIGITS@FLYNN'S ARCADE 👤 853 👁 11,235

HE'S NOT MALFUNCTIONING. HE JUST NEEDS PRECISE INSTRUCTIONS.

YO, RAY-BOT!

13

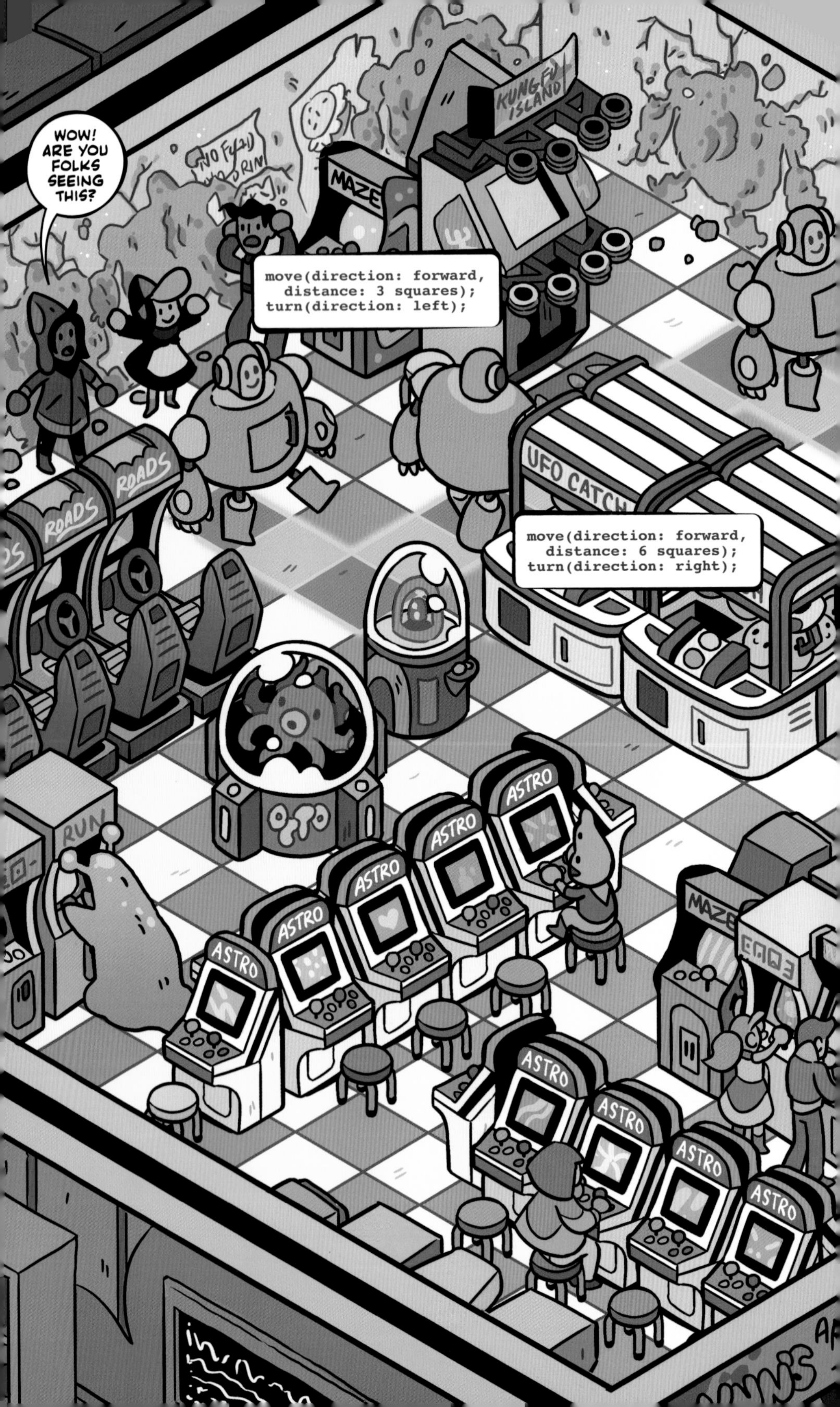

WOW! ARE YOU FOLKS SEEING THIS?
KUNG FU ISLAND
MAZE
move(direction: forward, distance: 3 squares); turn(direction: left);
ROADS
ROADS
UFO CATCH
move(direction: forward, distance: 6 squares); turn(direction: right);
OCTO
RUN
ASTRO
ASTRO
ASTRO
ASTRO
ASTRO
MAZE
ASTRO
ASTRO
ASTRO
ASTRO

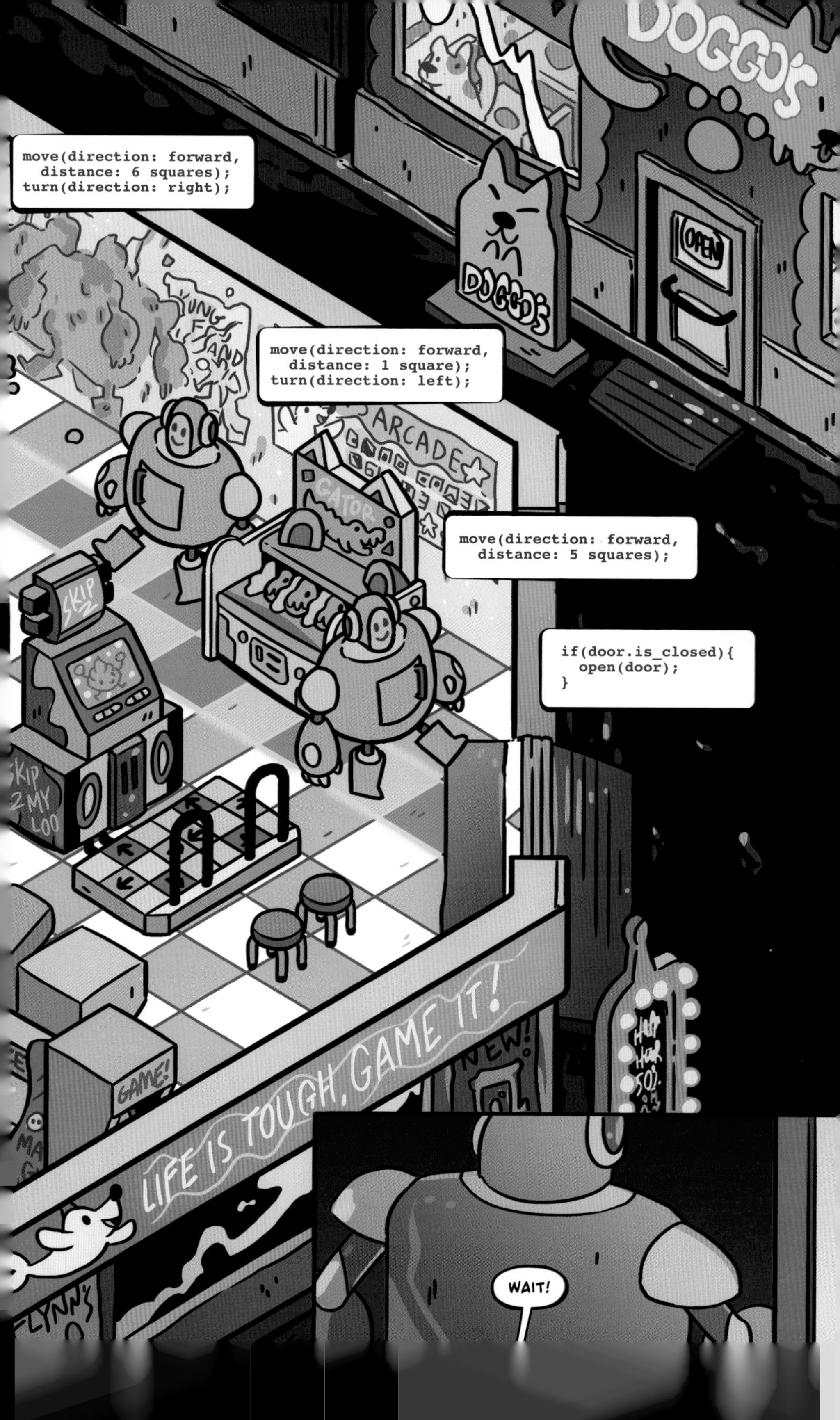
DOGGO'S
OPEN
DOGGO'S
move(direction: forward,
distance: 6 squares);
turn(direction: right);
move(direction: forward,
distance: 1 square);
turn(direction: left);
ARCADE
GATOR
move(direction: forward,
distance: 5 squares);
if(door.is_closed){
open(door);
}
SKIP 2
SKIP 2 MY LOO
NEW!
GAME!
LIFE IS TOUGH, GAME IT!
FLYNN'S
WAIT!

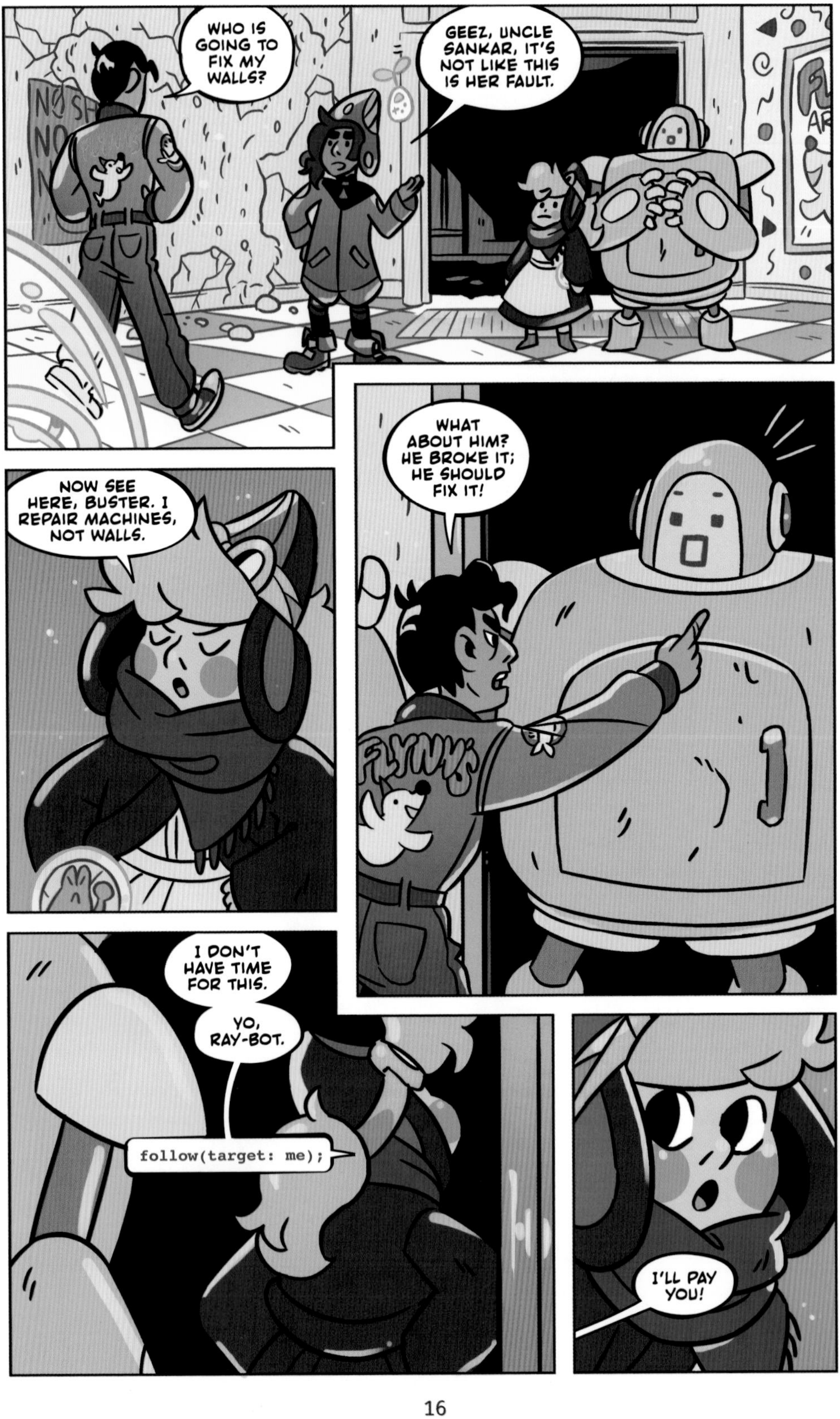
WHO IS GOING TO FIX MY WALLS?
GEEZ, UNCLE SANKAR, IT'S NOT LIKE THIS IS HER FAULT.
WHAT ABOUT HIM? HE BROKE IT; HE SHOULD FIX IT!
NOW SEE HERE, BUSTER. I REPAIR MACHINES, NOT WALLS.
I DON'T HAVE TIME FOR THIS.
YO, RAY-BOT.
follow(target: me);
I'LL PAY YOU!

WELL, IN THAT CASE... TITAN, HERE I COME!

CRRK CRRK

ALL RIGHT, BUDDY. LET'S SEE WHAT YOU'VE GOT KNOCKING AROUND IN THERE.

ARE YOU GOING TO GIVE HIM A SET OF COMMANDS TO FIX THE WALL?

I'M ACTUALLY HOPING HE ALREADY HAS A FUNCTION FOR THAT.

A FUNCTION? WHAT'S THAT?

A **FUNCTION** IS A SERIES OF INSTRUCTIONS THAT GETS A MACHINE TO PERFORM A CERTAIN TASK.

IF MEMORY SERVES ME CORRECTLY, RAY-BOTS WERE OFTEN PROGRAMMED TO WORK IN CONSTRUCTION.

YO, RAY-BOT.

```
repair(wall);
```

WHOA.

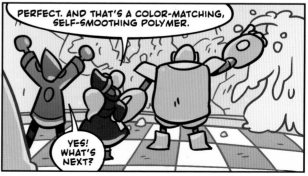

PERFECT. AND THAT'S A COLOR-MATCHING, SELF-SMOOTHING POLYMER.

YES! WHAT'S NEXT?

17

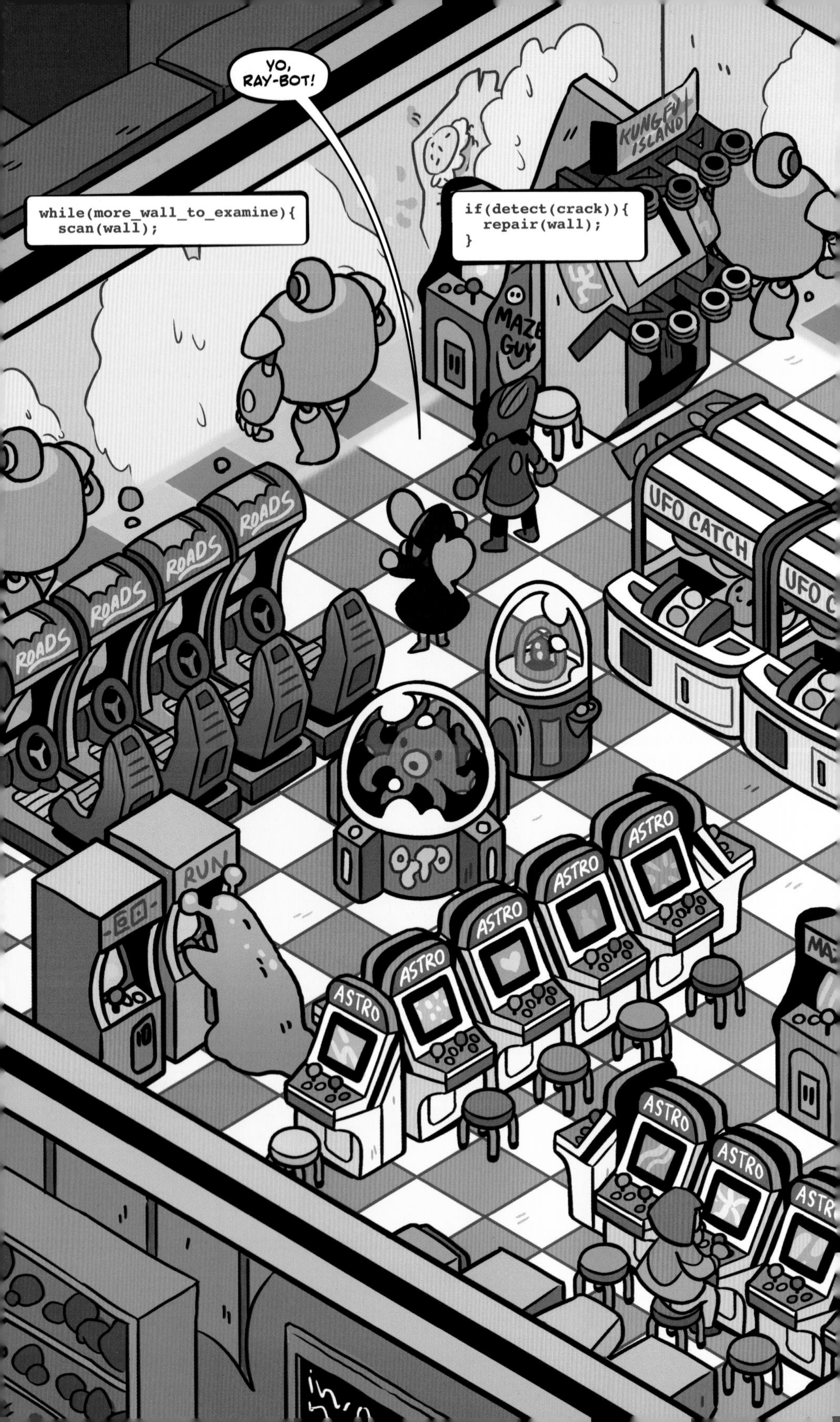
while(more_wall_to_examine){
scan(wall);
YO, RAY-BOT!
if(detect(crack)){
repair(wall);
}
KUNG FU ISLAND
MAZE GUY
UFO CATCH
UFO C
ROADS
ROADS
ROADS
ROADS
RUN
ASTRO
ASTRO
ASTRO
ASTRO
ASTRO
ASTRO
ASTRO
ASTRO

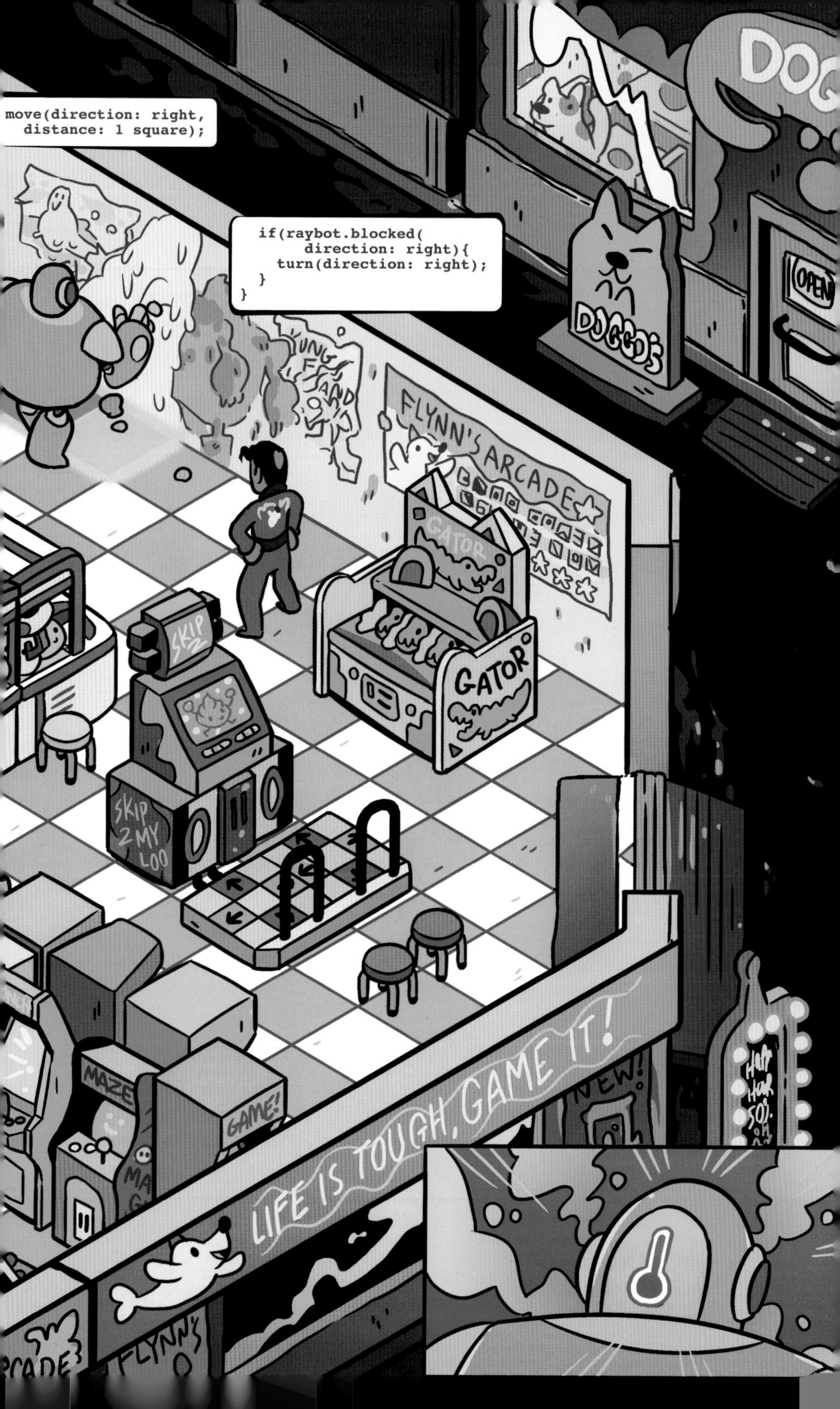

move(direction: right,
  distance: 1 square);
if(raybot.blocked(
     direction: right){
   turn(direction: right);
 }
}
OPEN
DOGGO'S
FLYNN'S ARCADE
GATOR
GATOR
SKIP 2
SKIP 2 MY LOO
MAZE
GAME!
LIFE IS TOUGH, GAME IT!
NEW!

OH NO! HE'S OVERHEATING.

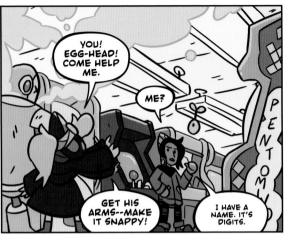

YOU! EGG-HEAD! COME HELP ME.

ME?

GET HIS ARMS--MAKE IT SNAPPY!

I HAVE A NAME. IT'S DIGITS.

WE'VE GOTTA GET HIM OUT OF HERE...

I'LL SEND YOU A BILL FOR MY SERVICES!

AND TELL MOM I WON'T BE HOME FOR DINNER!

NOT SO FAST, DEBIAN.

WE GOT A CALL ABOUT A ROGUE ROBOT.

SHOULD'VE KNOWN WE'D FIND DEBIAN PERL HERE.

WHO, ME?

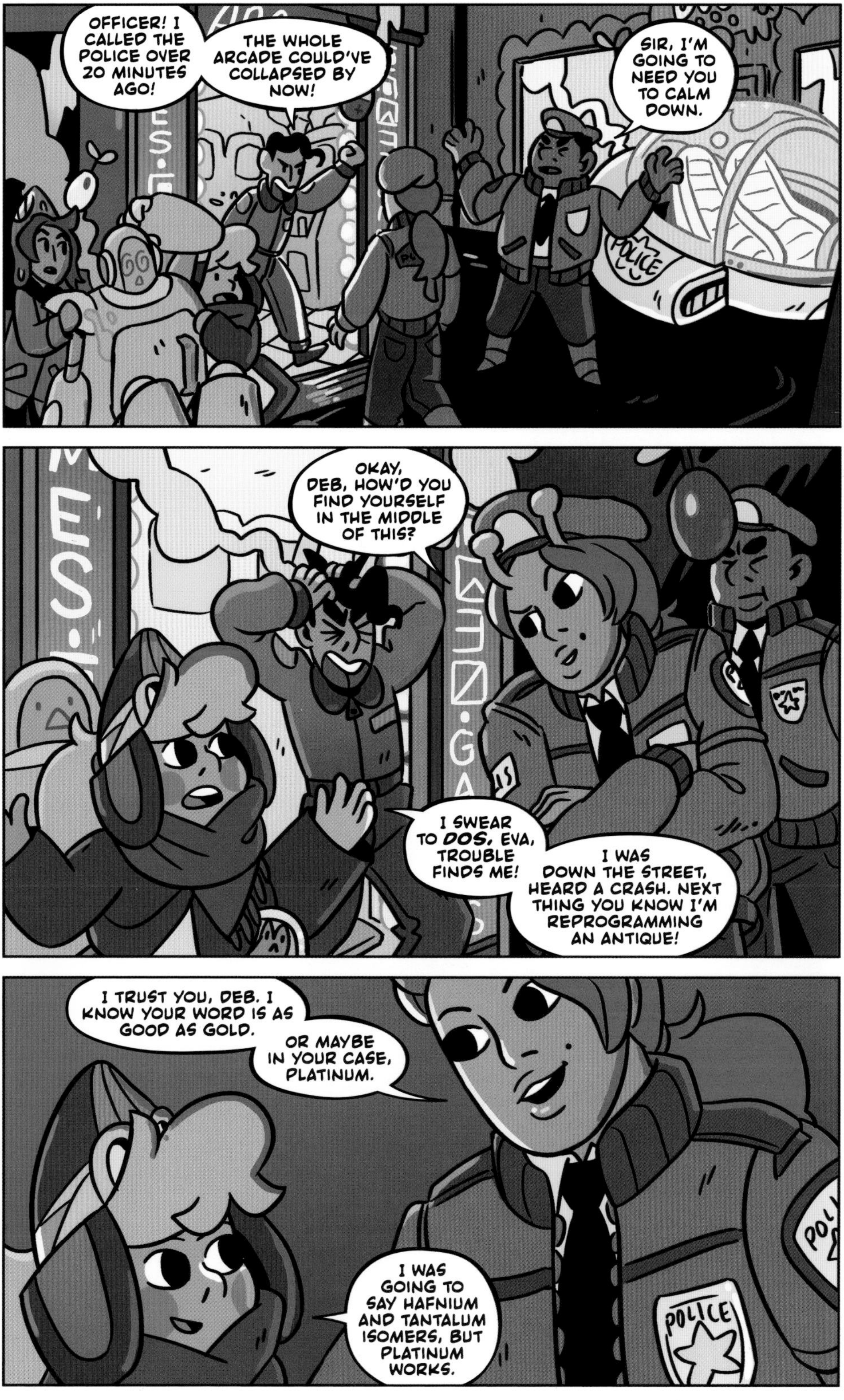
OFFICER! I CALLED THE POLICE OVER 20 MINUTES AGO!
THE WHOLE ARCADE COULD'VE COLLAPSED BY NOW!
SIR, I'M GOING TO NEED YOU TO CALM DOWN.
POLICE
OKAY, DEB, HOW'D YOU FIND YOURSELF IN THE MIDDLE OF THIS?
I SWEAR TO DOS, EVA, TROUBLE FINDS ME!
I WAS DOWN THE STREET, HEARD A CRASH. NEXT THING YOU KNOW I'M REPROGRAMMING AN ANTIQUE!
I TRUST YOU, DEB. I KNOW YOUR WORD IS AS GOOD AS GOLD.
OR MAYBE IN YOUR CASE, PLATINUM.
I WAS GOING TO SAY HAFNIUM AND TANTALUM ISOMERS, BUT PLATINUM WORKS.
POLICE

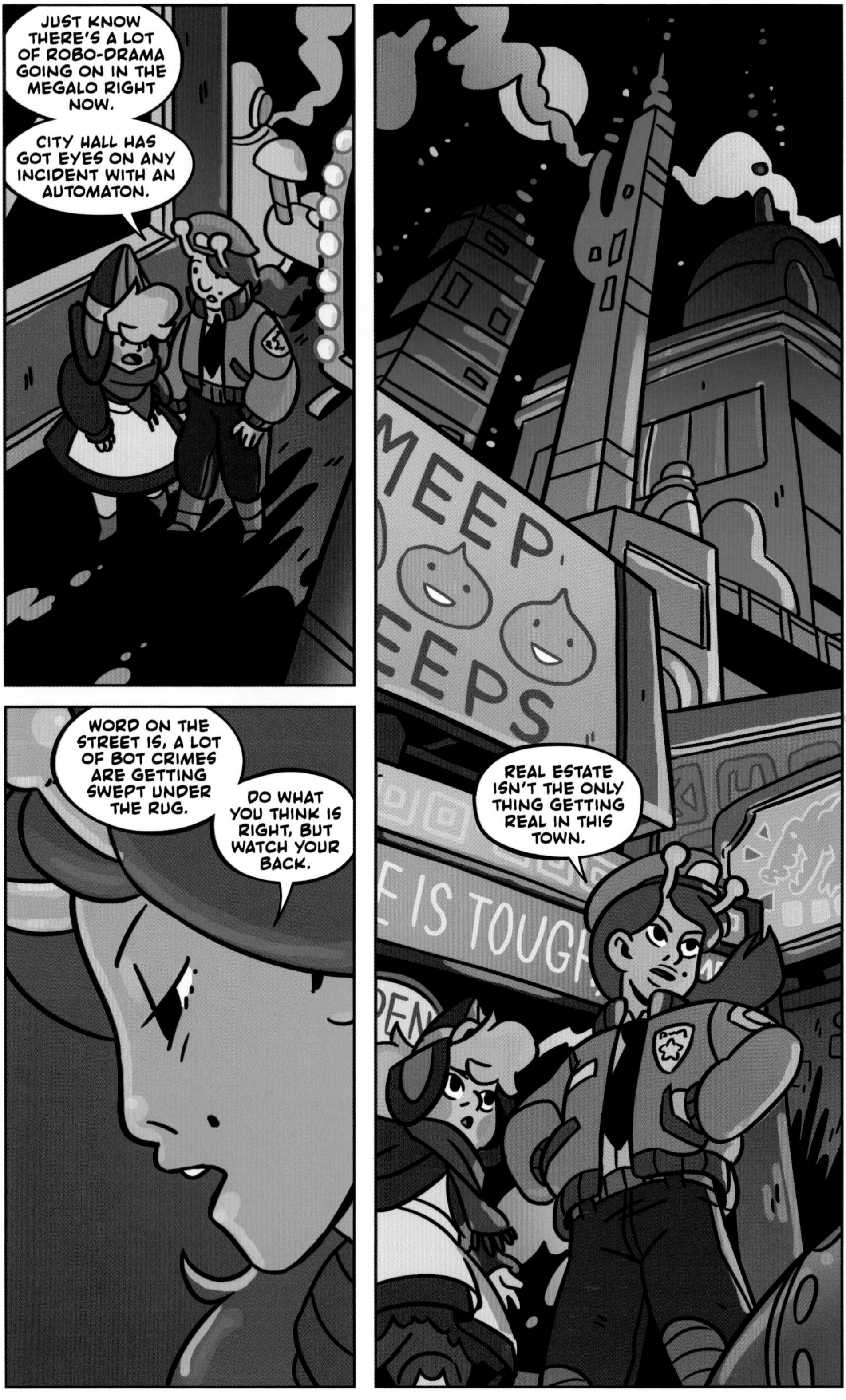
JUST KNOW THERE'S A LOT OF ROBO-DRAMA GOING ON IN THE MEGALO RIGHT NOW.
CITY HALL HAS GOT EYES ON ANY INCIDENT WITH AN AUTOMATON.
MEEP MEEPS
REAL ESTATE ISN'T THE ONLY THING GETTING REAL IN THIS TOWN.
E IS TOUGH
WORD ON THE STREET IS, A LOT OF BOT CRIMES ARE GETTING SWEPT UNDER THE RUG.
DO WHAT YOU THINK IS RIGHT, BUT WATCH YOUR BACK.

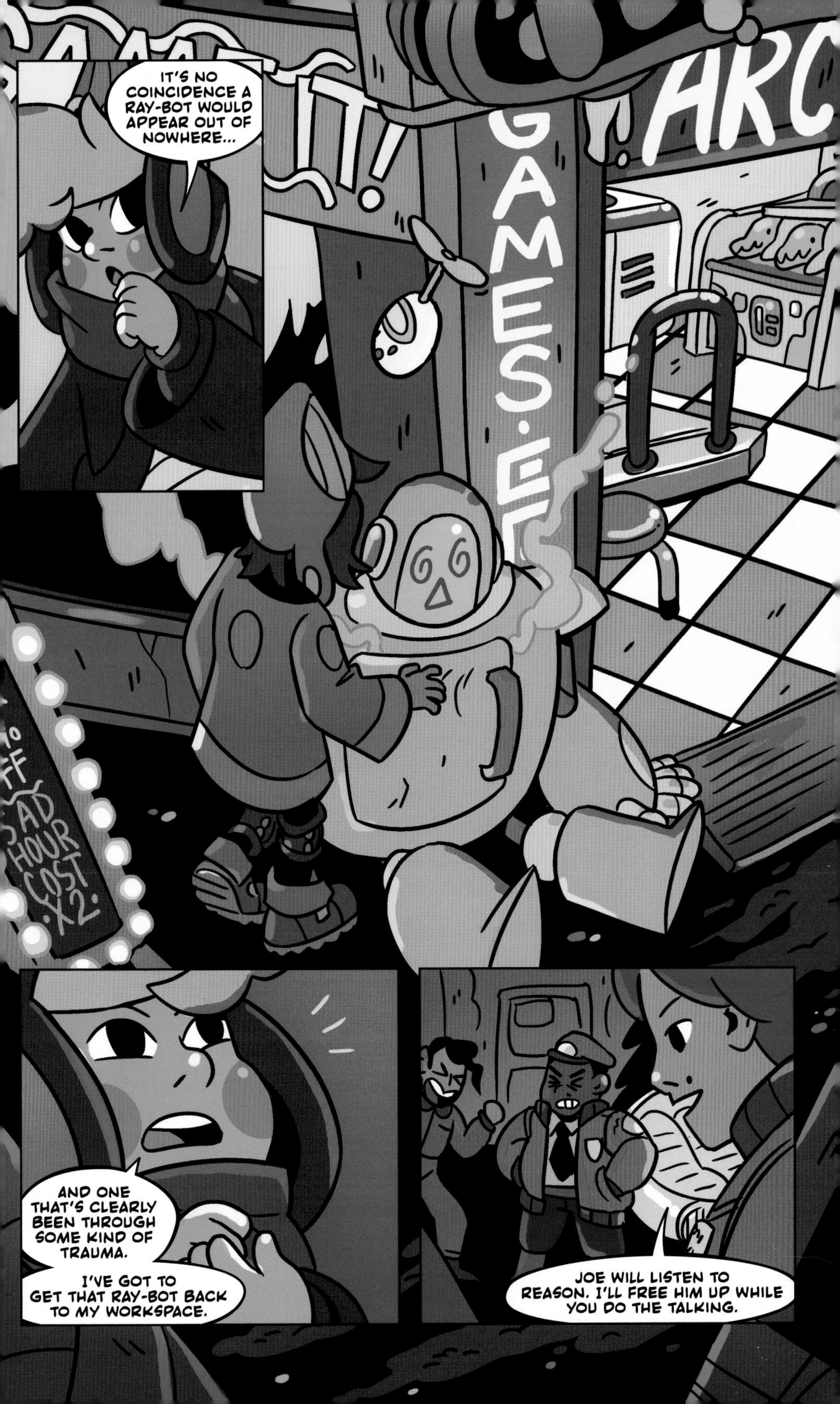
IT'S NO COINCIDENCE A RAY-BOT WOULD APPEAR OUT OF NOWHERE...
GAMES
ARC
SAD HOUR COST X2
AND ONE THAT'S CLEARLY BEEN THROUGH SOME KIND OF TRAUMA.
I'VE GOT TO GET THAT RAY-BOT BACK TO MY WORKSPACE.
JOE WILL LISTEN TO REASON. I'LL FREE HIM UP WHILE YOU DO THE TALKING.

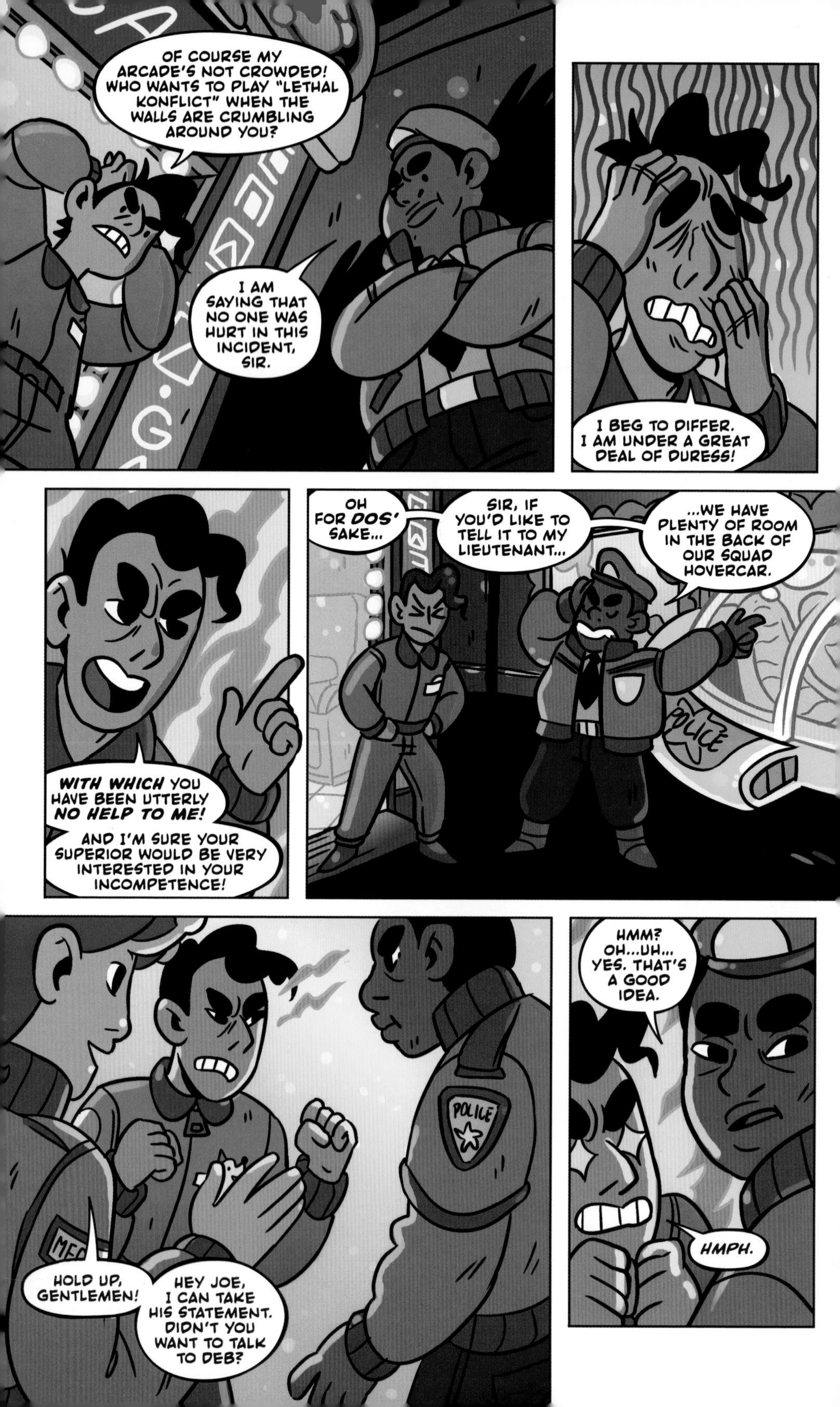
OF COURSE MY ARCADE'S NOT CROWDED! WHO WANTS TO PLAY "LETHAL KONFLICT" WHEN THE WALLS ARE CRUMBLING AROUND YOU?
I AM SAYING THAT NO ONE WAS HURT IN THIS INCIDENT, SIR.
I BEG TO DIFFER. I AM UNDER A GREAT DEAL OF DURESS!
WITH WHICH YOU HAVE BEEN UTTERLY NO HELP TO ME!
AND I'M SURE YOUR SUPERIOR WOULD BE VERY INTERESTED IN YOUR INCOMPETENCE!
OH FOR DOS' SAKE...
SIR, IF YOU'D LIKE TO TELL IT TO MY LIEUTENANT...
...WE HAVE PLENTY OF ROOM IN THE BACK OF OUR SQUAD HOVERCAR.
POLICE
HOLD UP, GENTLEMEN!
HEY JOE, I CAN TAKE HIS STATEMENT. DIDN'T YOU WANT TO TALK TO DEB?
POLICE
HMM? OH...UH... YES. THAT'S A GOOD IDEA.
HMPH.

CAN YOU TELL ME WHAT HAPPENED HERE, SIR?

REC

THAT CRAZY ROBOT CAME IN HERE AND STARTED SMASHING UP THE PLACE!

OFFICER ADEBAYO. AS YOU CAN SEE, I'VE CLEANED UP A MESS THAT WASN'T EVEN MINE!

YOU'RE WELCOME!

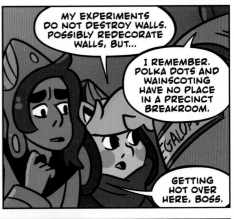

MMM-HMM.

I DON'T SUPPOSE ANYONE HAS REPORTED A MISSING RAY-BOT?

THERE HASN'T BEEN A *RAY-BOT* REGISTERED IN MEGALOPOLIS IN DECADES.

IF THIS IS ONE OF YOUR MADCAP EXPERIMENTS...

MY EXPERIMENTS DO NOT DESTROY WALLS. POSSIBLY REDECORATE WALLS, BUT...

I REMEMBER. POLKA DOTS AND WAINSCOTING HAVE NO PLACE IN A PRECINCT BREAKROOM.

GETTING HOT OVER HERE, BOSS.

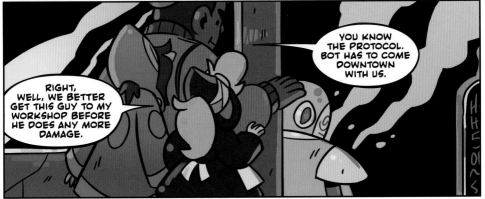

YOU KNOW THE PROTOCOL. BOT HAS TO COME DOWNTOWN WITH US.

RIGHT, WELL, WE BETTER GET THIS GUY TO MY WORKSHOP BEFORE HE DOES ANY MORE DAMAGE.

WAIT, DID *MPD* HIRE A TECHNOMANCER I DON'T KNOW ABOUT?

WELL, OUR MECHANIC...

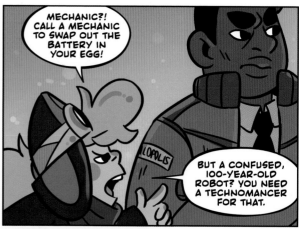

MECHANIC?! CALL A MECHANIC TO SWAP OUT THE BATTERY IN YOUR EGG!

BUT A CONFUSED, 100-YEAR-OLD ROBOT? YOU NEED A TECHNOMANCER FOR THAT.

I DON'T MAKE THE RULES--

IF HE OVERHEATS AND SHUTS DOWN, HIS RANDOM-ACCESS MEMORY IS GONE. POOF!

WHEN HE REBOOTS, HE WON'T REMEMBER ME OR THE EGG-HEAD--

DIGITS!

LOOK, BEHIND EVERY UNREGISTERED ROBOT IS A LAW-BREAKING HUMAN...

YOU WANT TO LOSE EVIDENCE AND LET THAT SLIDE?

OKAY, WE'LL DO IT YOUR WAY, DEBIAN.

BUT WHEN HE'S FIXED UP I WANT A FULL REPORT.

YOU'LL BE THE FIRST TO KNOW, ADEBAYO.

HEY! THE CRACKS THAT BOT DIDN'T FIX ARE COMING OUT OF YOUR PAYCHECK!

RUM BLEE

CR ASH!

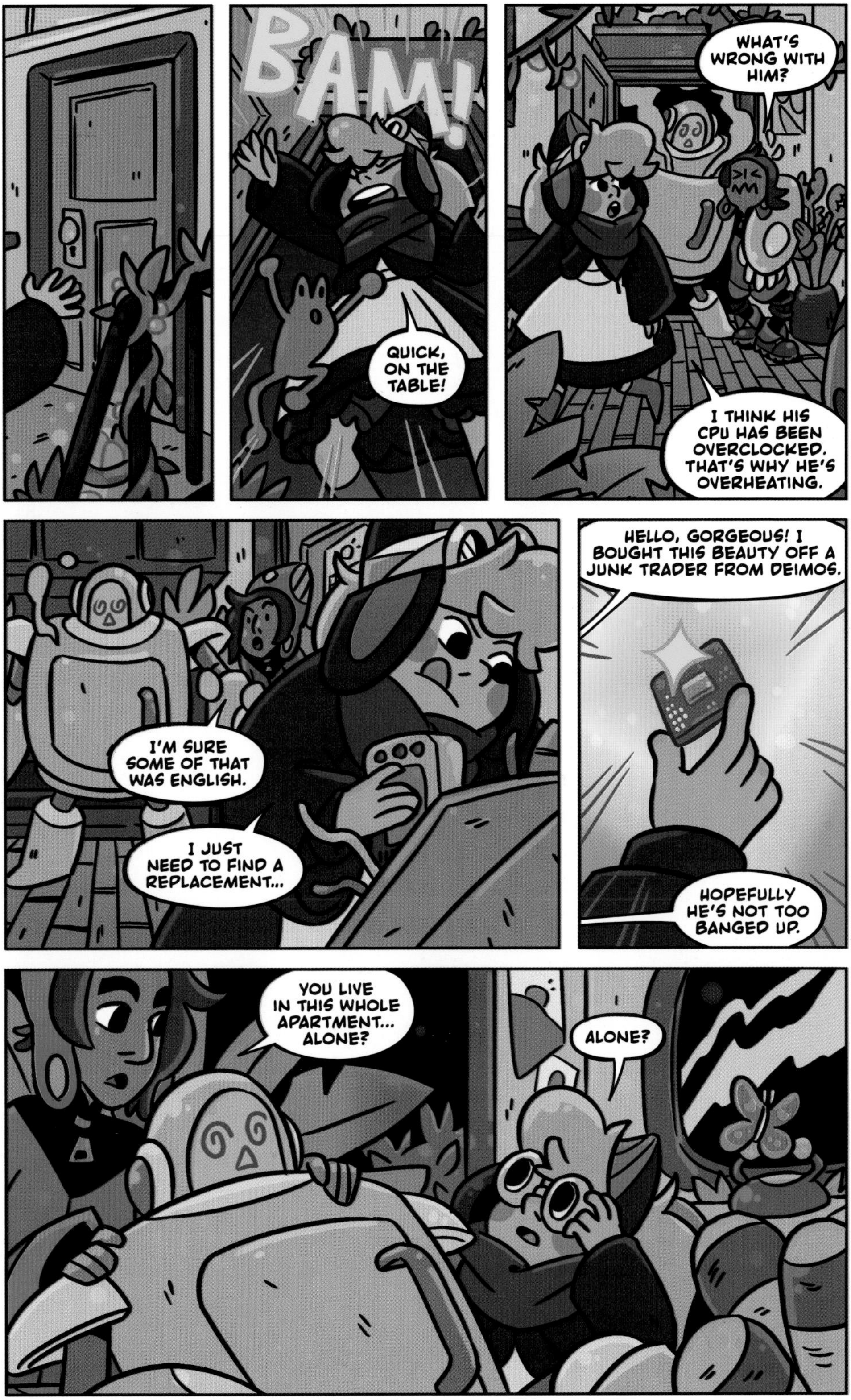
BAM!
QUICK, ON THE TABLE!
WHAT'S WRONG WITH HIM?
I THINK HIS CPU HAS BEEN OVERCLOCKED. THAT'S WHY HE'S OVERHEATING.
I'M SURE SOME OF THAT WAS ENGLISH.
I JUST NEED TO FIND A REPLACEMENT...
HELLO, GORGEOUS! I BOUGHT THIS BEAUTY OFF A JUNK TRADER FROM DEIMOS.
HOPEFULLY HE'S NOT TOO BANGED UP.
YOU LIVE IN THIS WHOLE APARTMENT... ALONE?
ALONE?

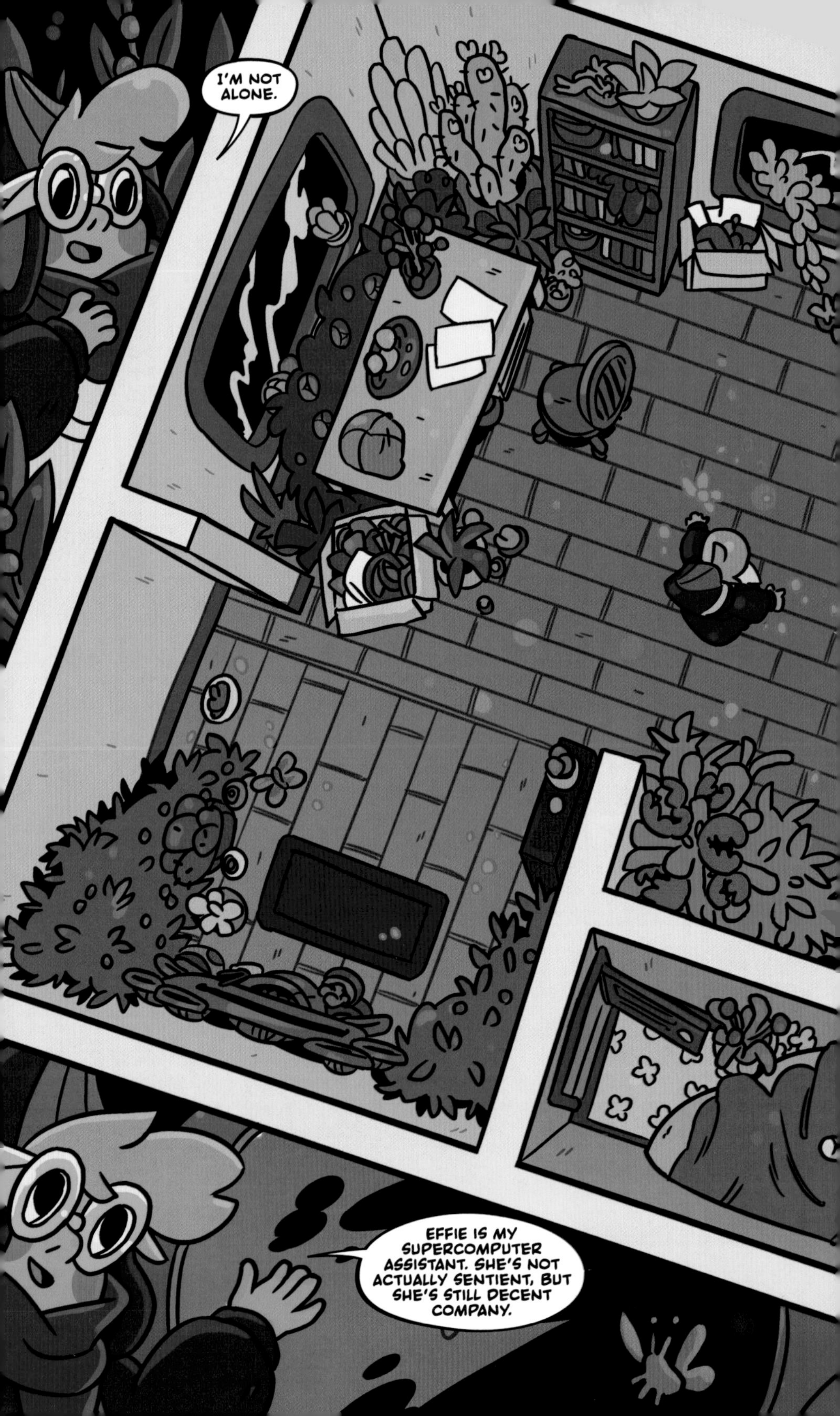
I'M NOT ALONE.
EFFIE IS MY SUPERCOMPUTER ASSISTANT. SHE'S NOT ACTUALLY SENTIENT, BUT SHE'S STILL DECENT COMPANY.

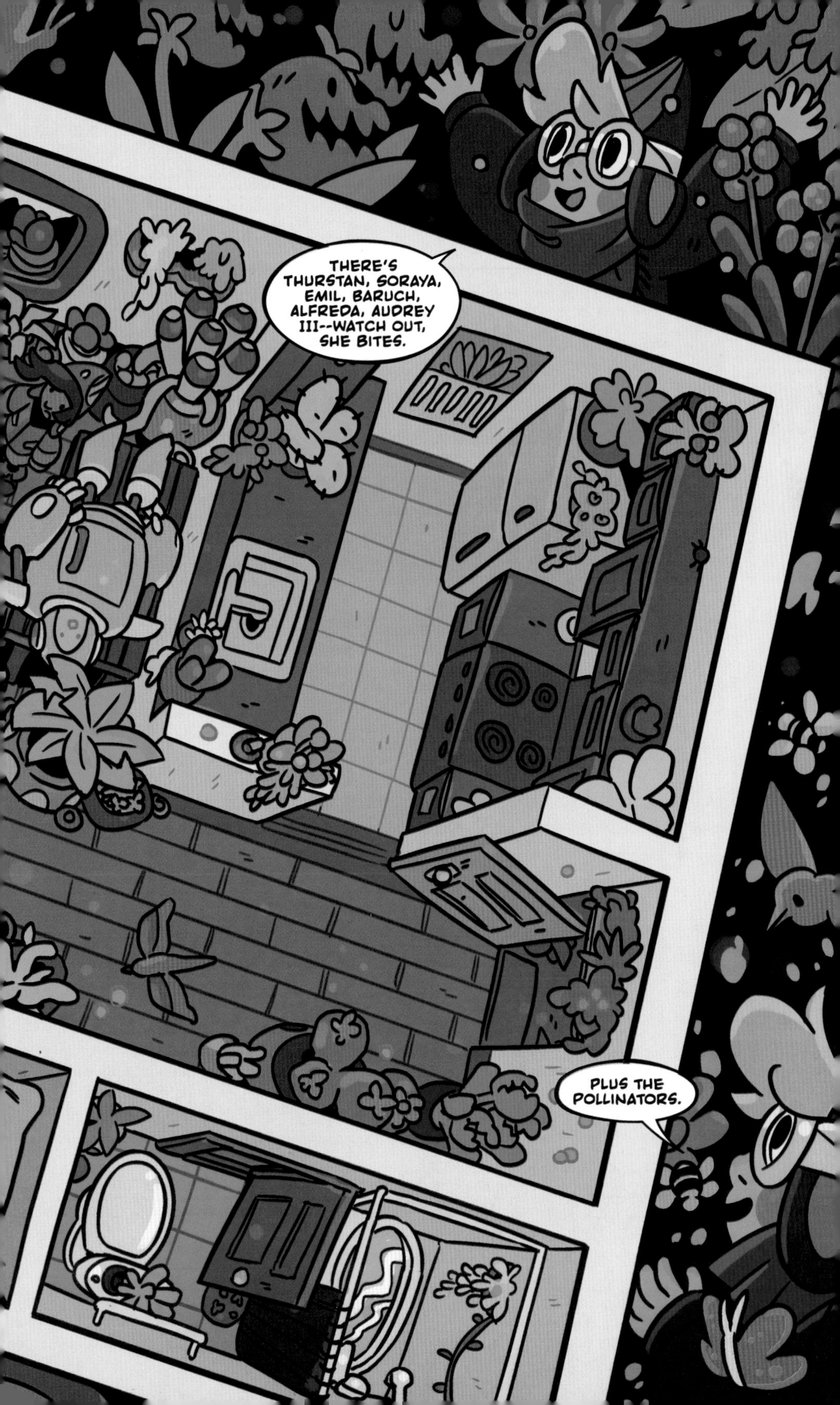
THERE'S THURSTAN, SORAYA, EMIL, BARUCH, ALFREDA, AUDREY III--WATCH OUT, SHE BITES.
PLUS THE POLLINATORS.

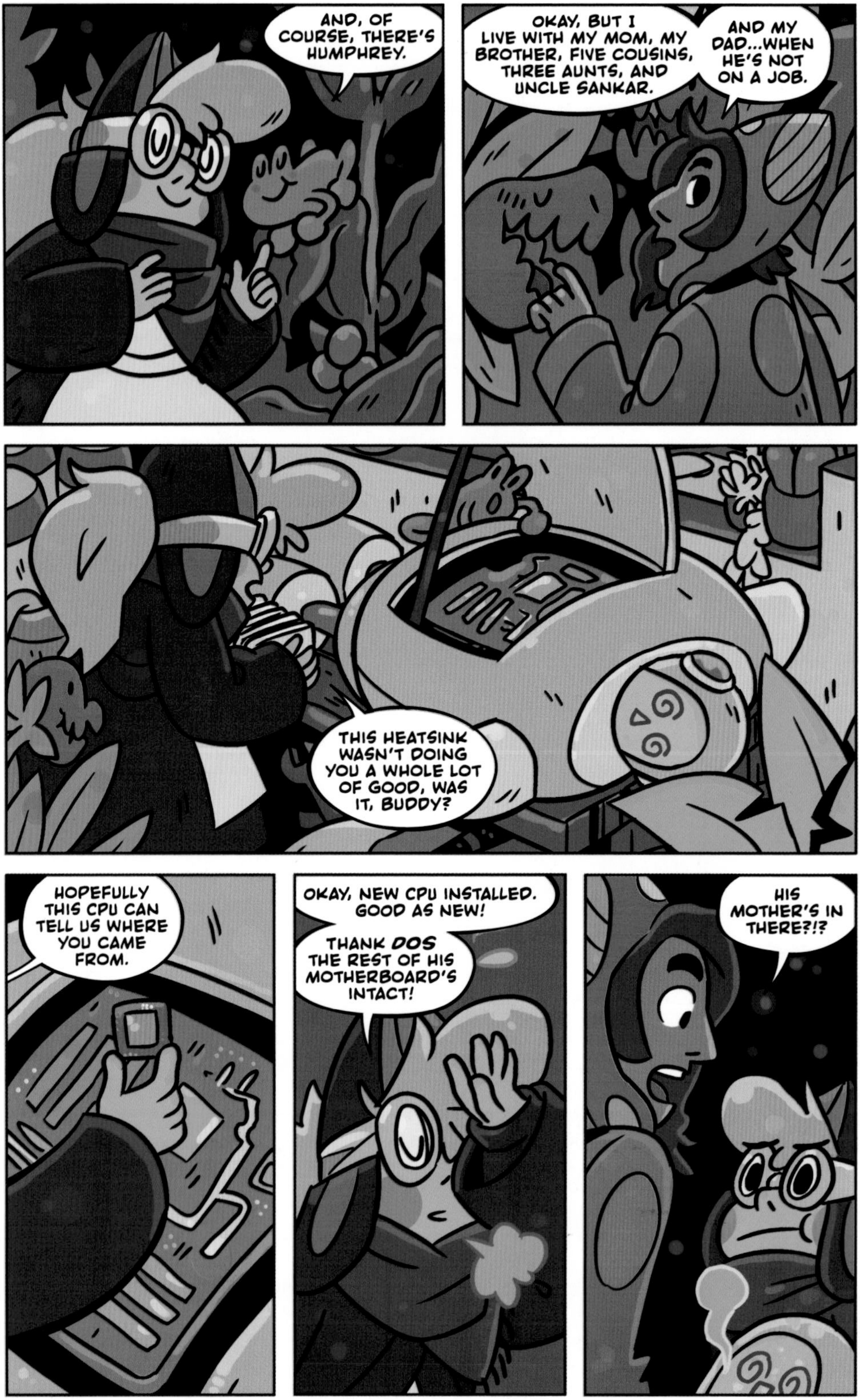
AND, OF COURSE, THERE'S HUMPHREY.
OKAY, BUT I LIVE WITH MY MOM, MY BROTHER, FIVE COUSINS, THREE AUNTS, AND UNCLE SANKAR.
AND MY DAD...WHEN HE'S NOT ON A JOB.
THIS HEATSINK WASN'T DOING YOU A WHOLE LOT OF GOOD, WAS IT, BUDDY?
HOPEFULLY THIS CPU CAN TELL US WHERE YOU CAME FROM.
OKAY, NEW CPU INSTALLED. GOOD AS NEW!
THANK *DOS* THE REST OF HIS MOTHERBOARD'S INTACT!
HIS MOTHER'S IN THERE?!?

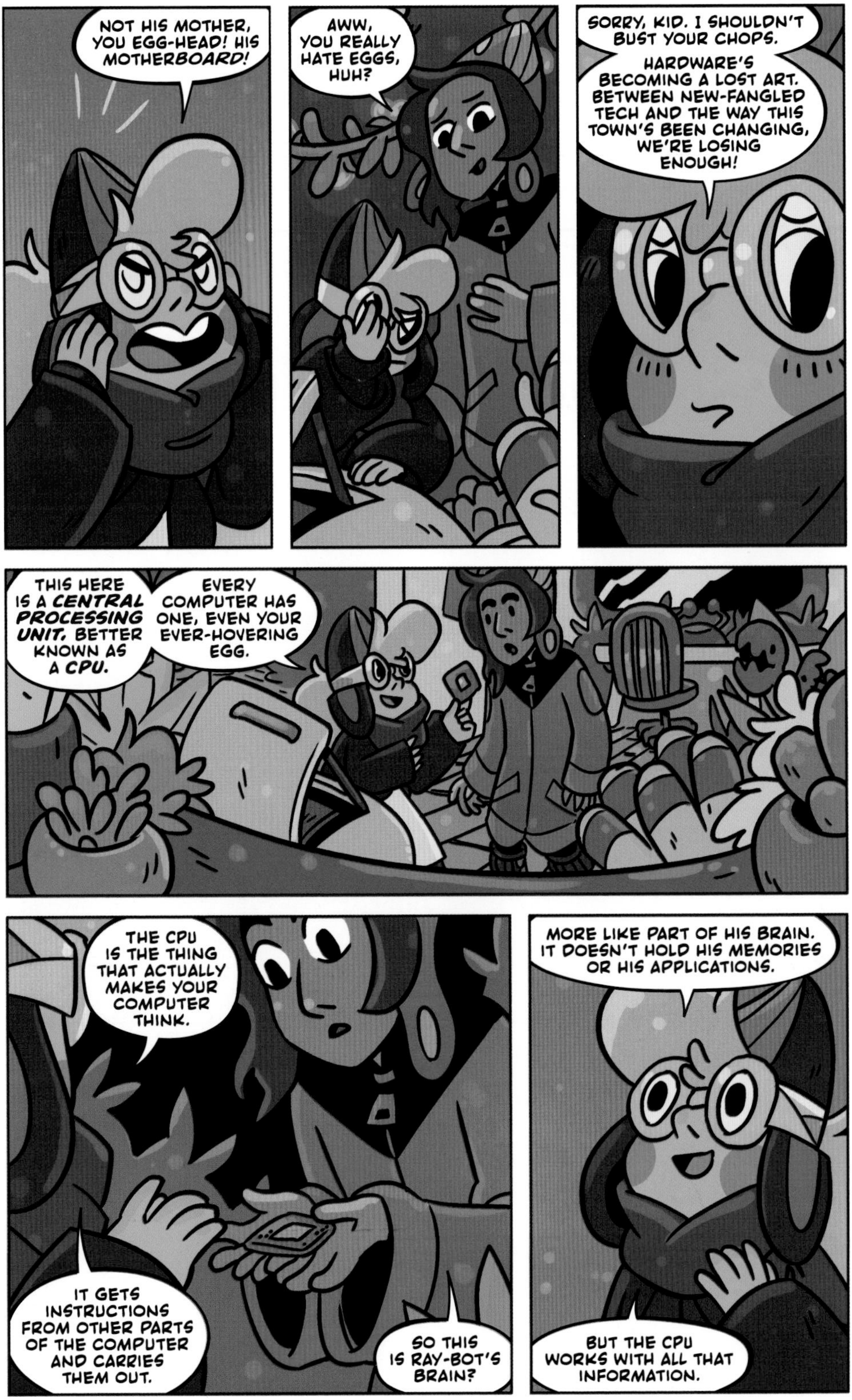
NOT HIS MOTHER, YOU EGG-HEAD! HIS MOTHERBOARD!
AWW, YOU REALLY HATE EGGS, HUH?
SORRY, KID. I SHOULDN'T BUST YOUR CHOPS.
HARDWARE'S BECOMING A LOST ART. BETWEEN NEW-FANGLED TECH AND THE WAY THIS TOWN'S BEEN CHANGING, WE'RE LOSING ENOUGH!
THIS HERE IS A CENTRAL PROCESSING UNIT. BETTER KNOWN AS A CPU.
EVERY COMPUTER HAS ONE, EVEN YOUR EVER-HOVERING EGG.
THE CPU IS THE THING THAT ACTUALLY MAKES YOUR COMPUTER THINK.
IT GETS INSTRUCTIONS FROM OTHER PARTS OF THE COMPUTER AND CARRIES THEM OUT.
SO THIS IS RAY-BOT'S BRAIN?
MORE LIKE PART OF HIS BRAIN. IT DOESN'T HOLD HIS MEMORIES OR HIS APPLICATIONS.
BUT THE CPU WORKS WITH ALL THAT INFORMATION.

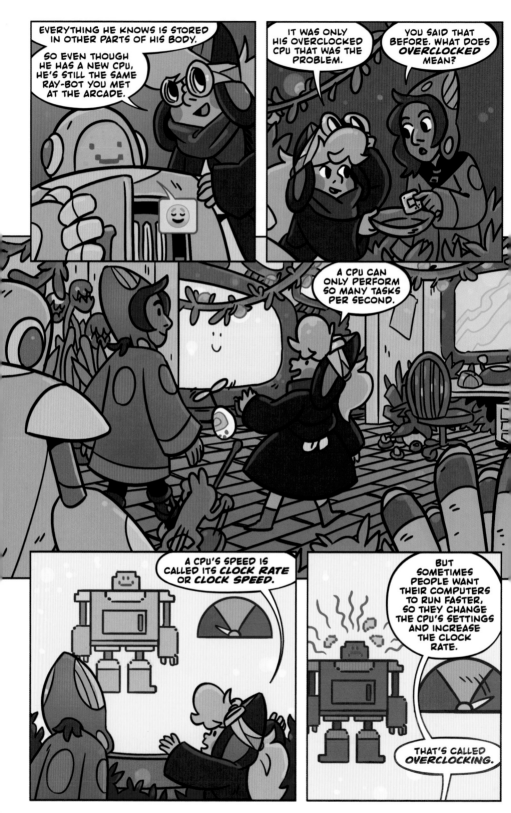

EVERYTHING HE KNOWS IS STORED IN OTHER PARTS OF HIS BODY.

SO EVEN THOUGH HE HAS A NEW CPU, HE'S STILL THE SAME RAY-BOT YOU MET AT THE ARCADE.

IT WAS ONLY HIS OVERCLOCKED CPU THAT WAS THE PROBLEM.

YOU SAID THAT BEFORE. WHAT DOES *OVERCLOCKED* MEAN?

A CPU CAN ONLY PERFORM SO MANY TASKS PER SECOND.

A CPU'S SPEED IS CALLED ITS *CLOCK RATE* OR *CLOCK SPEED*.

BUT SOMETIMES PEOPLE WANT THEIR COMPUTERS TO RUN FASTER, SO THEY CHANGE THE CPU'S SETTINGS AND INCREASE THE CLOCK RATE.

THAT'S CALLED *OVERCLOCKING*.

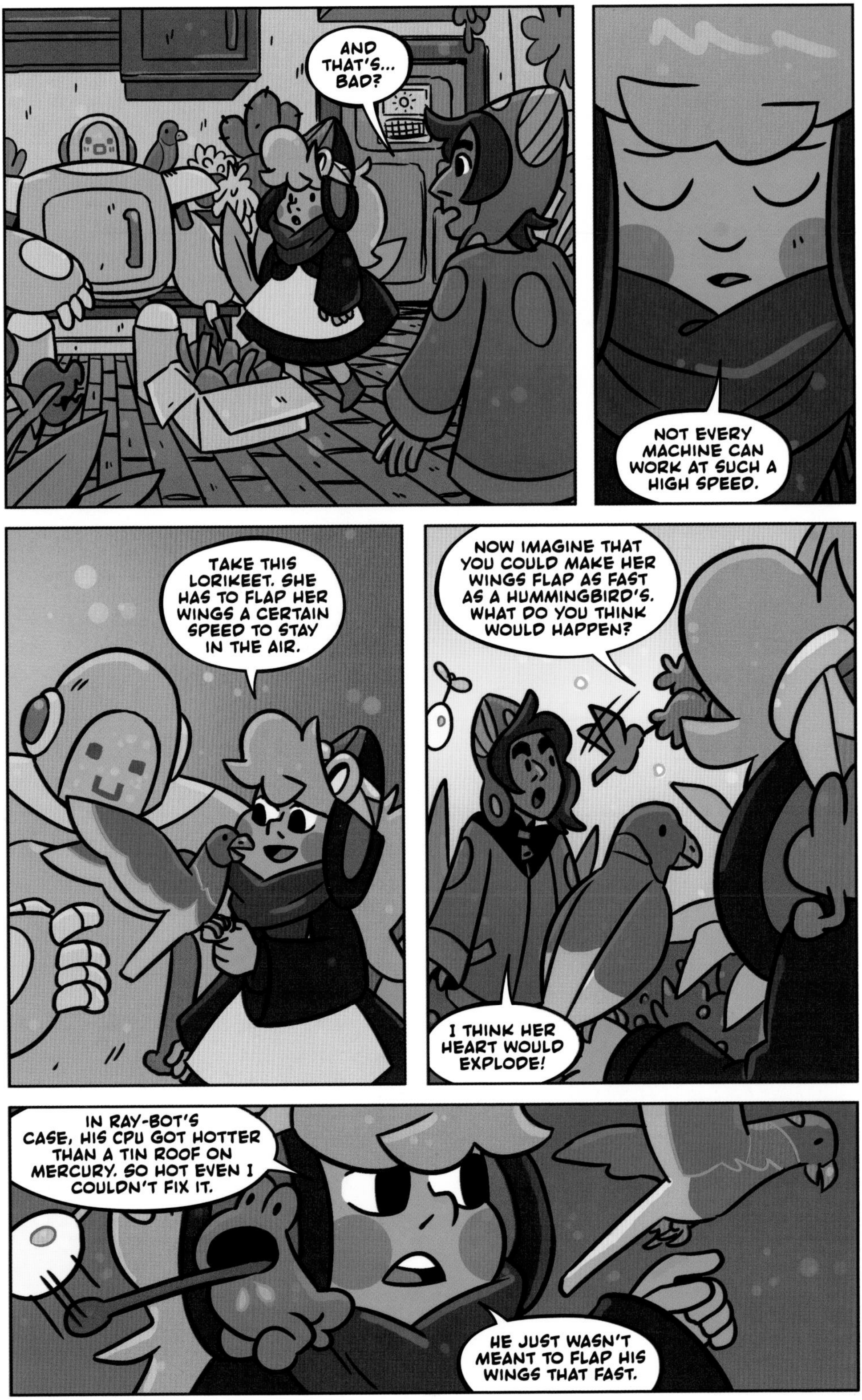

AND THAT'S... BAD?
NOT EVERY MACHINE CAN WORK AT SUCH A HIGH SPEED.
TAKE THIS LORIKEET. SHE HAS TO FLAP HER WINGS A CERTAIN SPEED TO STAY IN THE AIR.
NOW IMAGINE THAT YOU COULD MAKE HER WINGS FLAP AS FAST AS A HUMMINGBIRD'S. WHAT DO YOU THINK WOULD HAPPEN?
I THINK HER HEART WOULD EXPLODE!
IN RAY-BOT'S CASE, HIS CPU GOT HOTTER THAN A TIN ROOF ON MERCURY. SO HOT EVEN I COULDN'T FIX IT.
HE JUST WASN'T MEANT TO FLAP HIS WINGS THAT FAST.

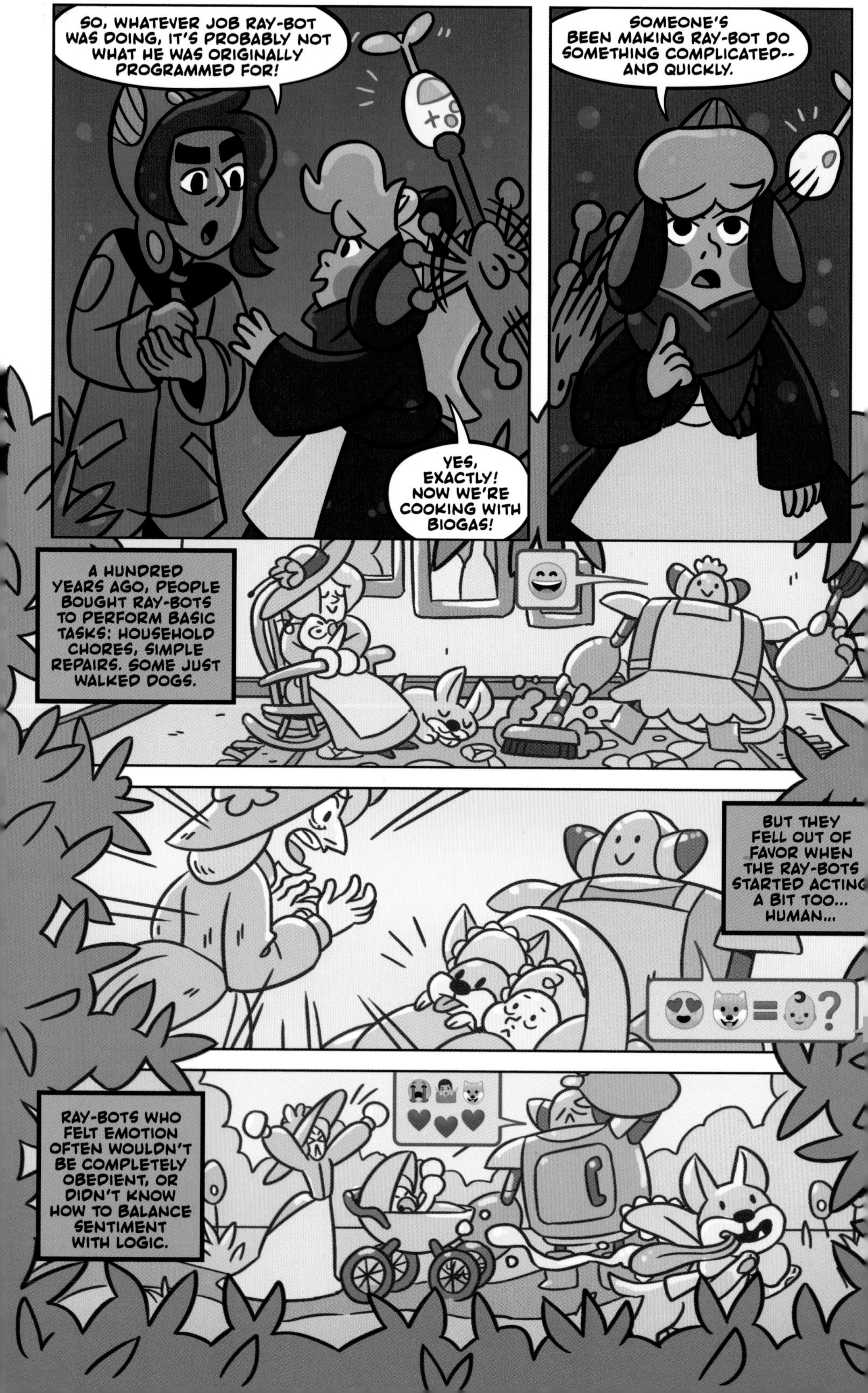
SO, WHATEVER JOB RAY-BOT WAS DOING, IT'S PROBABLY NOT WHAT HE WAS ORIGINALLY PROGRAMMED FOR!
YES, EXACTLY! NOW WE'RE COOKING WITH BIOGAS!
SOMEONE'S BEEN MAKING RAY-BOT DO SOMETHING COMPLICATED-- AND QUICKLY.
A HUNDRED YEARS AGO, PEOPLE BOUGHT RAY-BOTS TO PERFORM BASIC TASKS: HOUSEHOLD CHORES, SIMPLE REPAIRS. SOME JUST WALKED DOGS.
BUT THEY FELL OUT OF FAVOR WHEN THE RAY-BOTS STARTED ACTING A BIT TOO... HUMAN...
=?
RAY-BOTS WHO FELT EMOTION OFTEN WOULDN'T BE COMPLETELY OBEDIENT, OR DIDN'T KNOW HOW TO BALANCE SENTIMENT WITH LOGIC.

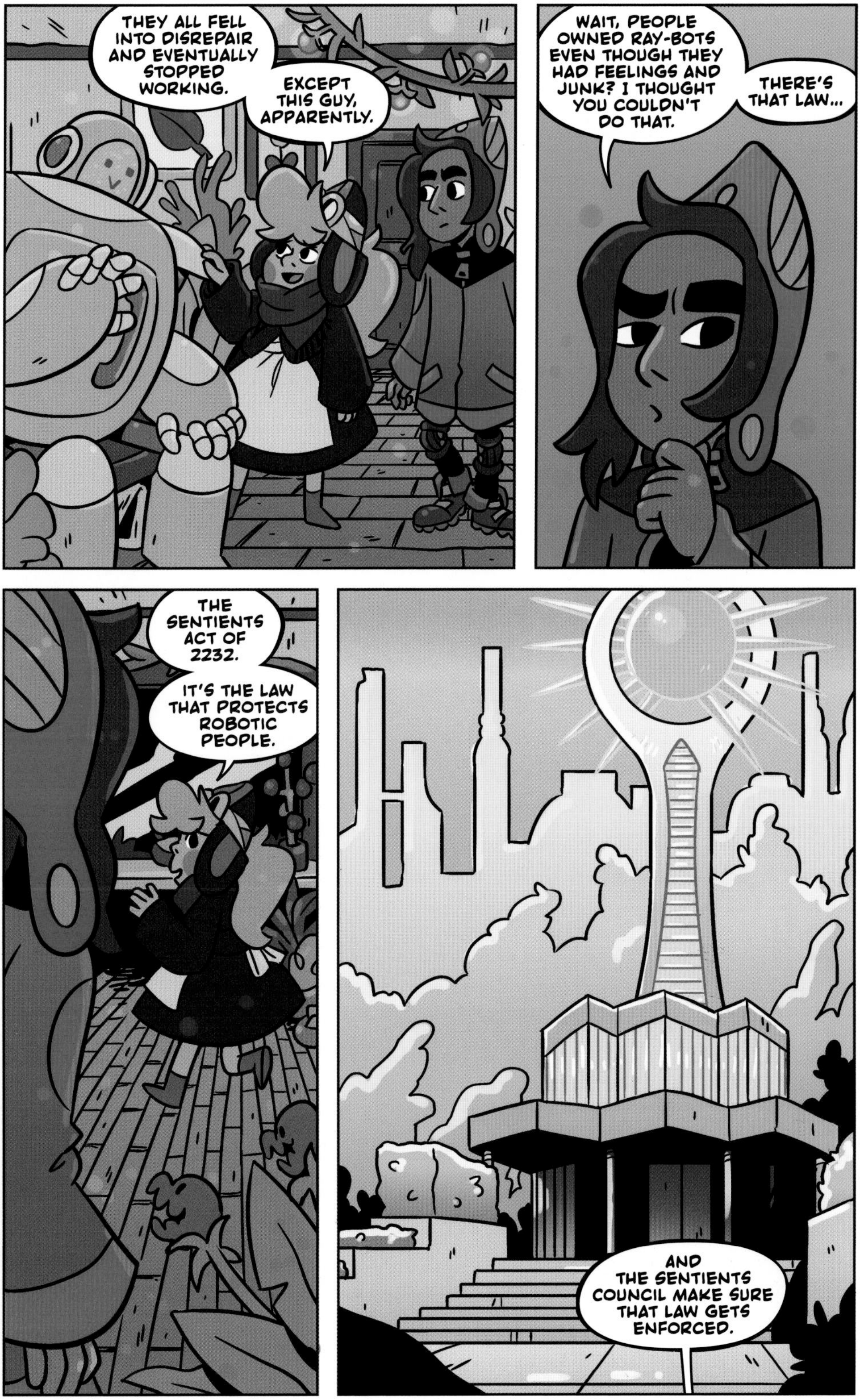
THEY ALL FELL INTO DISREPAIR AND EVENTUALLY STOPPED WORKING.
EXCEPT THIS GUY, APPARENTLY.
WAIT, PEOPLE OWNED RAY-BOTS EVEN THOUGH THEY HAD FEELINGS AND JUNK? I THOUGHT YOU COULDN'T DO THAT.
THERE'S THAT LAW...
THE SENTIENTS ACT OF 2232.
IT'S THE LAW THAT PROTECTS ROBOTIC PEOPLE.
AND THE SENTIENTS COUNCIL MAKE SURE THAT LAW GETS ENFORCED.

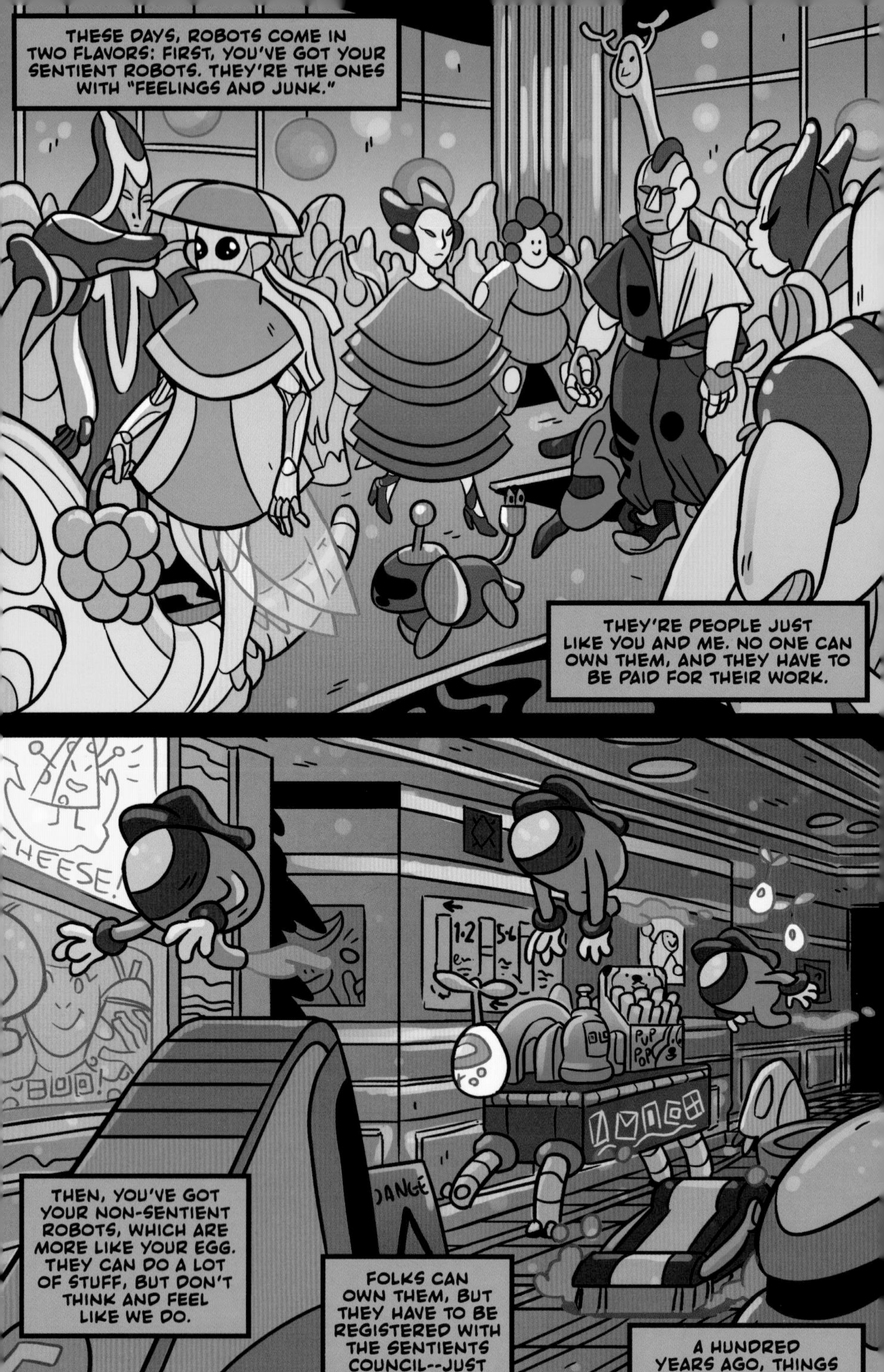
THESE DAYS, ROBOTS COME IN TWO FLAVORS: FIRST, YOU'VE GOT YOUR SENTIENT ROBOTS. THEY'RE THE ONES WITH "FEELINGS AND JUNK."
THEY'RE PEOPLE JUST LIKE YOU AND ME. NO ONE CAN OWN THEM, AND THEY HAVE TO BE PAID FOR THEIR WORK.
HEESE!
BOO!
1·2
5·6
PUP POP
DANGE
THEN, YOU'VE GOT YOUR NON-SENTIENT ROBOTS, WHICH ARE MORE LIKE YOUR EGG. THEY CAN DO A LOT OF STUFF, BUT DON'T THINK AND FEEL LIKE WE DO.
FOLKS CAN OWN THEM, BUT THEY HAVE TO BE REGISTERED WITH THE SENTIENTS COUNCIL--JUST IN CASE.
A HUNDRED YEARS AGO, THINGS WERE MURKIER. AND ROBOTS LIKE RAY-BOT PAID THE PRICE.

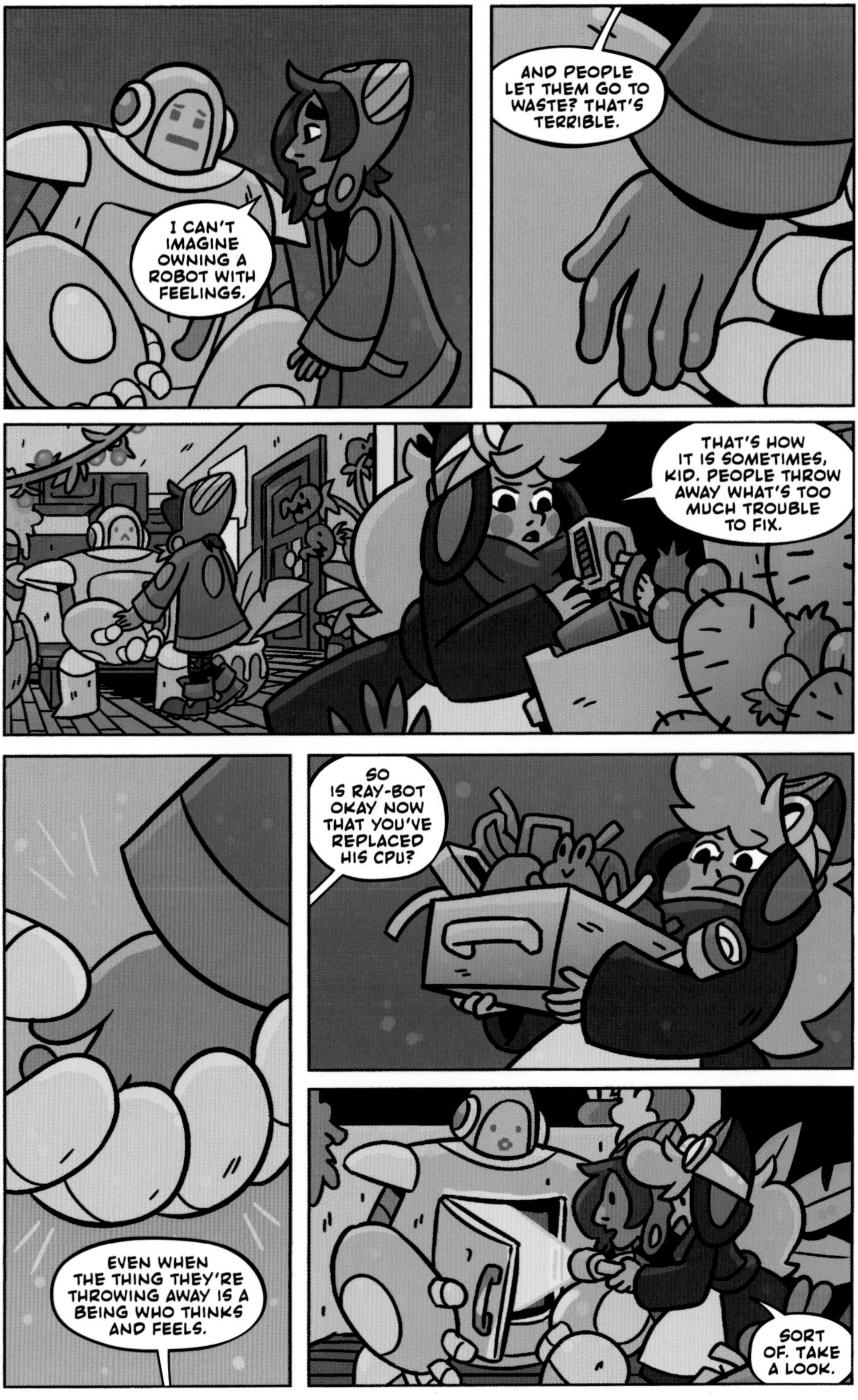

I CAN'T IMAGINE OWNING A ROBOT WITH FEELINGS.
AND PEOPLE LET THEM GO TO WASTE? THAT'S TERRIBLE.
THAT'S HOW IT IS SOMETIMES, KID. PEOPLE THROW AWAY WHAT'S TOO MUCH TROUBLE TO FIX.
EVEN WHEN THE THING THEY'RE THROWING AWAY IS A BEING WHO THINKS AND FEELS.
SO IS RAY-BOT OKAY NOW THAT YOU'VE REPLACED HIS CPU?
SORT OF. TAKE A LOOK.

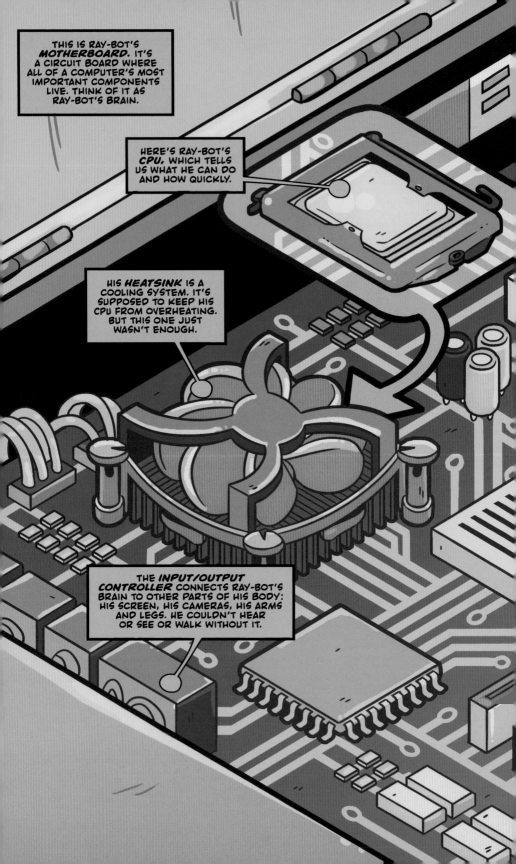

THIS IS RAY-BOT'S *MOTHERBOARD.* IT'S A CIRCUIT BOARD WHERE ALL OF A COMPUTER'S MOST IMPORTANT COMPONENTS LIVE. THINK OF IT AS RAY-BOT'S BRAIN.

HERE'S RAY-BOT'S *CPU,* WHICH TELLS US WHAT HE CAN DO AND HOW QUICKLY.

HIS *HEATSINK* IS A COOLING SYSTEM. IT'S SUPPOSED TO KEEP HIS CPU FROM OVERHEATING. BUT THIS ONE JUST WASN'T ENOUGH.

THE *INPUT/OUTPUT CONTROLLER* CONNECTS RAY-BOT'S BRAIN TO OTHER PARTS OF HIS BODY: HIS SCREEN, HIS CAMERAS, HIS ARMS AND LEGS. HE COULDN'T HEAR OR SEE OR WALK WITHOUT IT.

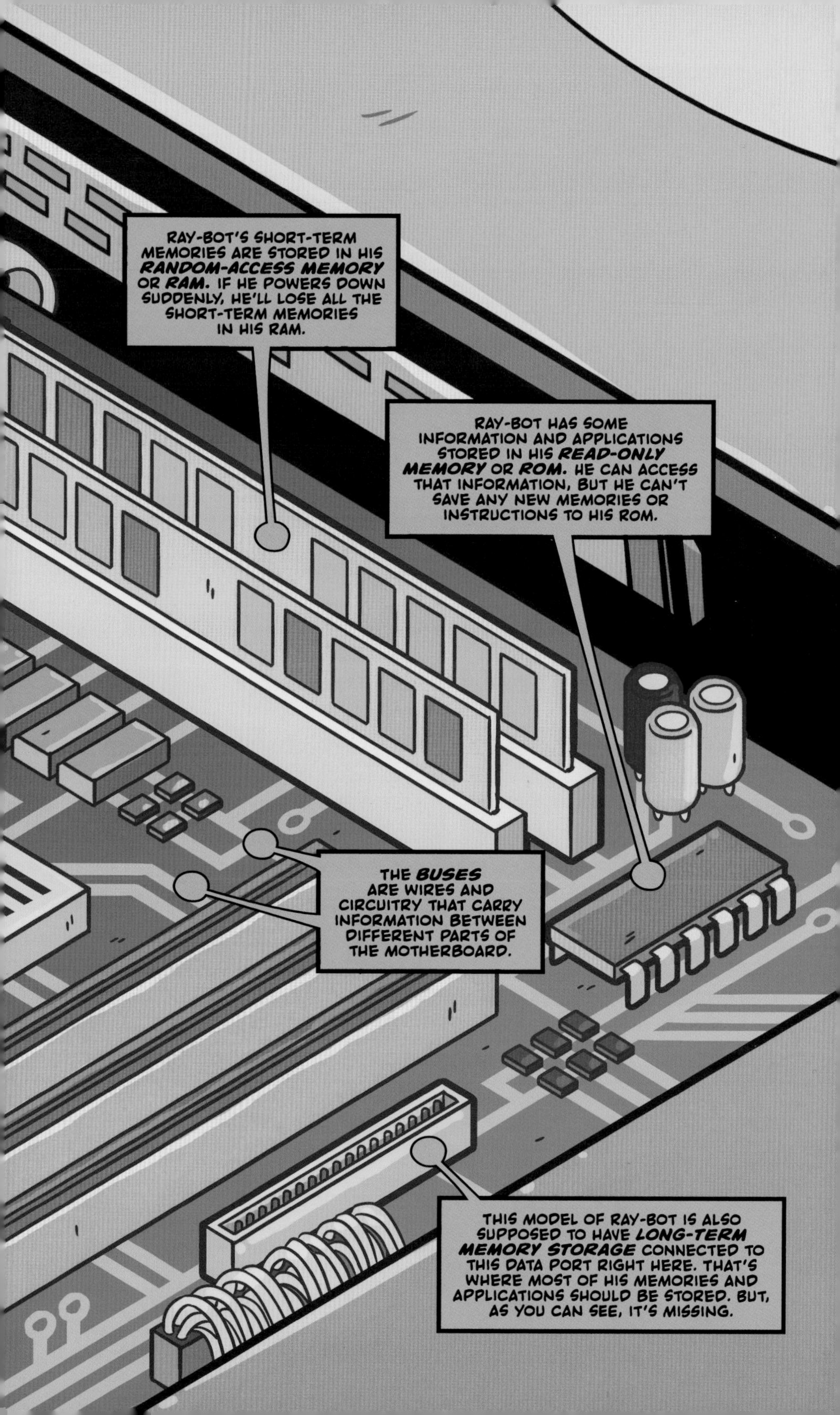
RAY-BOT'S SHORT-TERM MEMORIES ARE STORED IN HIS ***RANDOM-ACCESS MEMORY*** OR ***RAM.*** IF HE POWERS DOWN SUDDENLY, HE'LL LOSE ALL THE SHORT-TERM MEMORIES IN HIS RAM.
RAY-BOT HAS SOME INFORMATION AND APPLICATIONS STORED IN HIS ***READ-ONLY MEMORY*** OR ***ROM.*** HE CAN ACCESS THAT INFORMATION, BUT HE CAN'T SAVE ANY NEW MEMORIES OR INSTRUCTIONS TO HIS ROM.
THE ***BUSES*** ARE WIRES AND CIRCUITRY THAT CARRY INFORMATION BETWEEN DIFFERENT PARTS OF THE MOTHERBOARD.
THIS MODEL OF RAY-BOT IS ALSO SUPPOSED TO HAVE ***LONG-TERM MEMORY STORAGE*** CONNECTED TO THIS DATA PORT RIGHT HERE. THAT'S WHERE MOST OF HIS MEMORIES AND APPLICATIONS SHOULD BE STORED. BUT, AS YOU CAN SEE, IT'S MISSING.

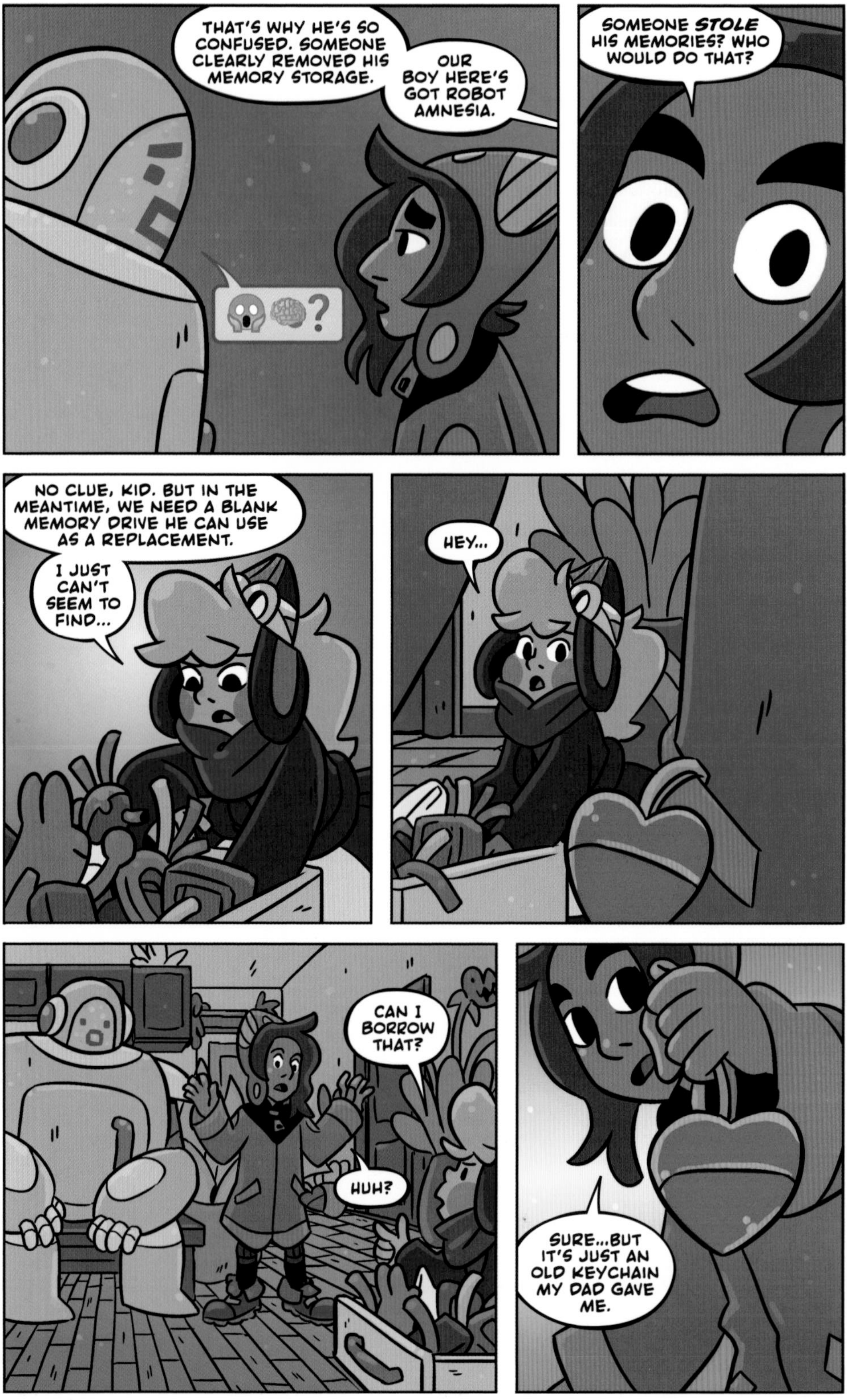
THAT'S WHY HE'S SO CONFUSED. SOMEONE CLEARLY REMOVED HIS MEMORY STORAGE.
OUR BOY HERE'S GOT ROBOT AMNESIA.
?
SOMEONE STOLE HIS MEMORIES? WHO WOULD DO THAT?
NO CLUE, KID. BUT IN THE MEANTIME, WE NEED A BLANK MEMORY DRIVE HE CAN USE AS A REPLACEMENT.
I JUST CAN'T SEEM TO FIND...
HEY...
CAN I BORROW THAT?
HUH?
SURE...BUT IT'S JUST AN OLD KEYCHAIN MY DAD GAVE ME.

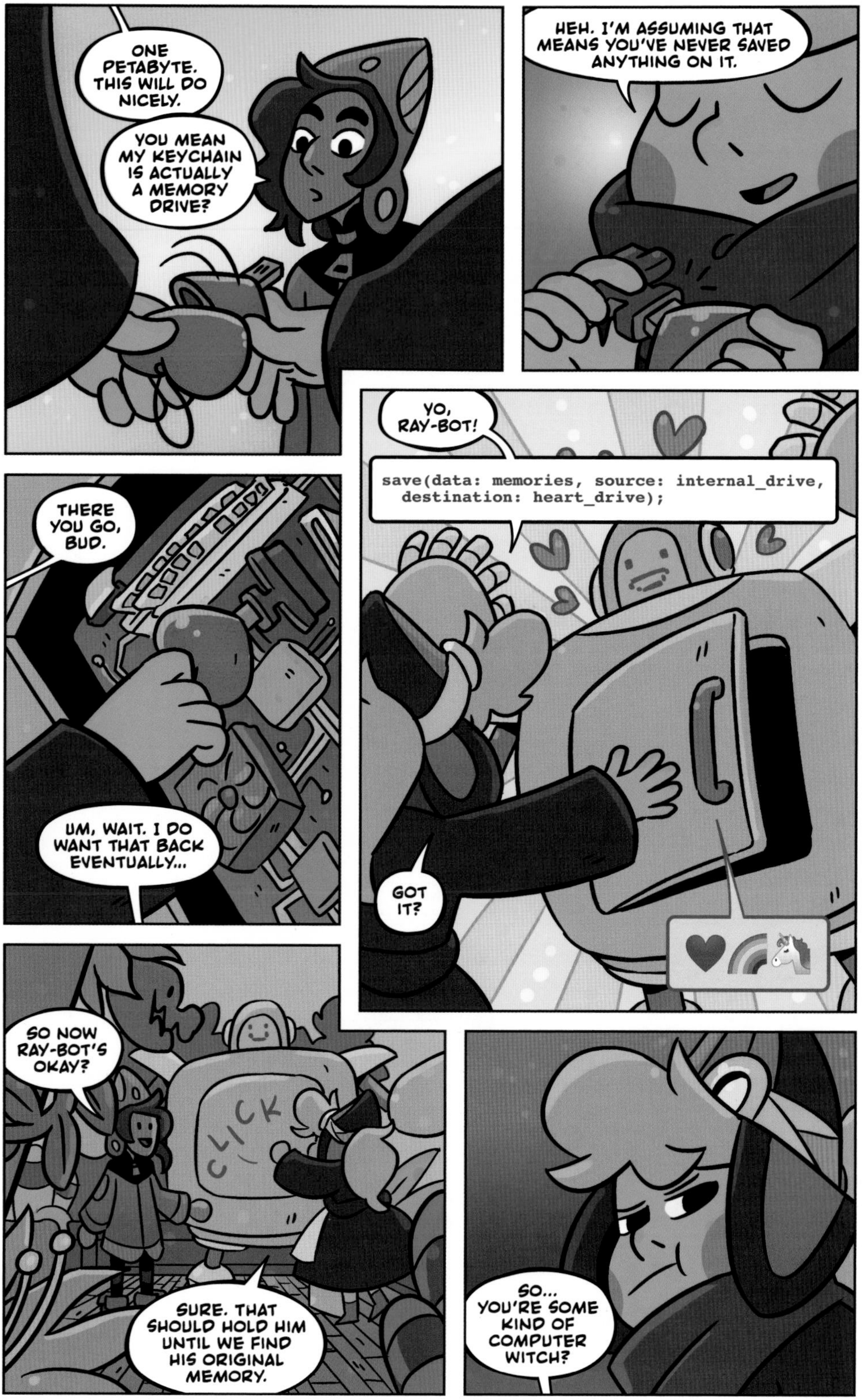
ONE PETABYTE. THIS WILL DO NICELY.
YOU MEAN MY KEYCHAIN IS ACTUALLY A MEMORY DRIVE?
HEH. I'M ASSUMING THAT MEANS YOU'VE NEVER SAVED ANYTHING ON IT.
THERE YOU GO, BUD.
UM, WAIT. I DO WANT THAT BACK EVENTUALLY...
YO, RAY-BOT!
save(data: memories, source: internal_drive, destination: heart_drive);
GOT IT?
SO NOW RAY-BOT'S OKAY?
CLICK
SURE. THAT SHOULD HOLD HIM UNTIL WE FIND HIS ORIGINAL MEMORY.
SO... YOU'RE SOME KIND OF COMPUTER WITCH?

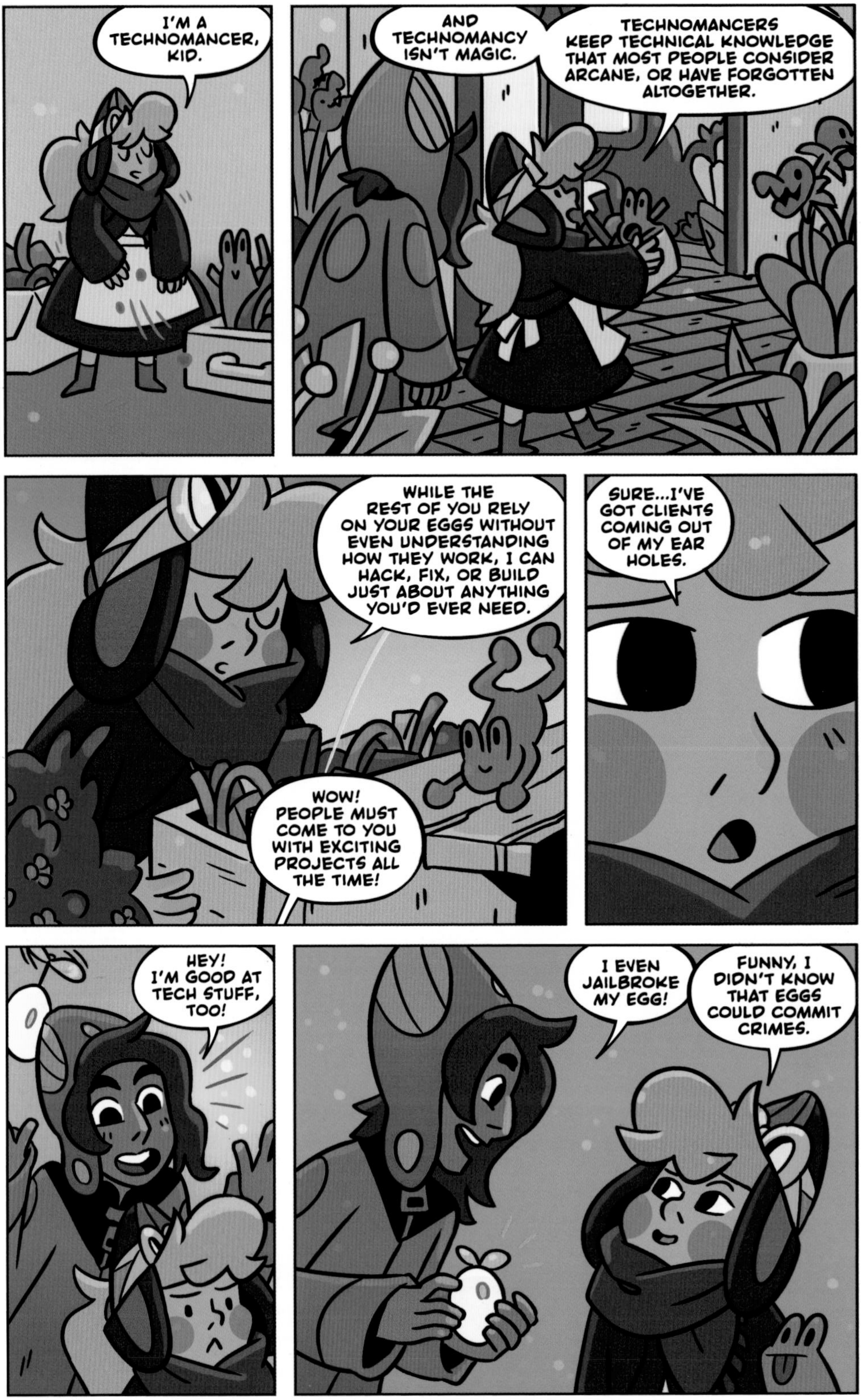

I'M A TECHNOMANCER, KID.
AND TECHNOMANCY ISN'T MAGIC.
TECHNOMANCERS KEEP TECHNICAL KNOWLEDGE THAT MOST PEOPLE CONSIDER ARCANE, OR HAVE FORGOTTEN ALTOGETHER.
WHILE THE REST OF YOU RELY ON YOUR EGGS WITHOUT EVEN UNDERSTANDING HOW THEY WORK, I CAN HACK, FIX, OR BUILD JUST ABOUT ANYTHING YOU'D EVER NEED.
WOW! PEOPLE MUST COME TO YOU WITH EXCITING PROJECTS ALL THE TIME!
SURE...I'VE GOT CLIENTS COMING OUT OF MY EAR HOLES.
HEY! I'M GOOD AT TECH STUFF, TOO!
I EVEN JAILBROKE MY EGG!
FUNNY, I DIDN'T KNOW THAT EGGS COULD COMMIT CRIMES.

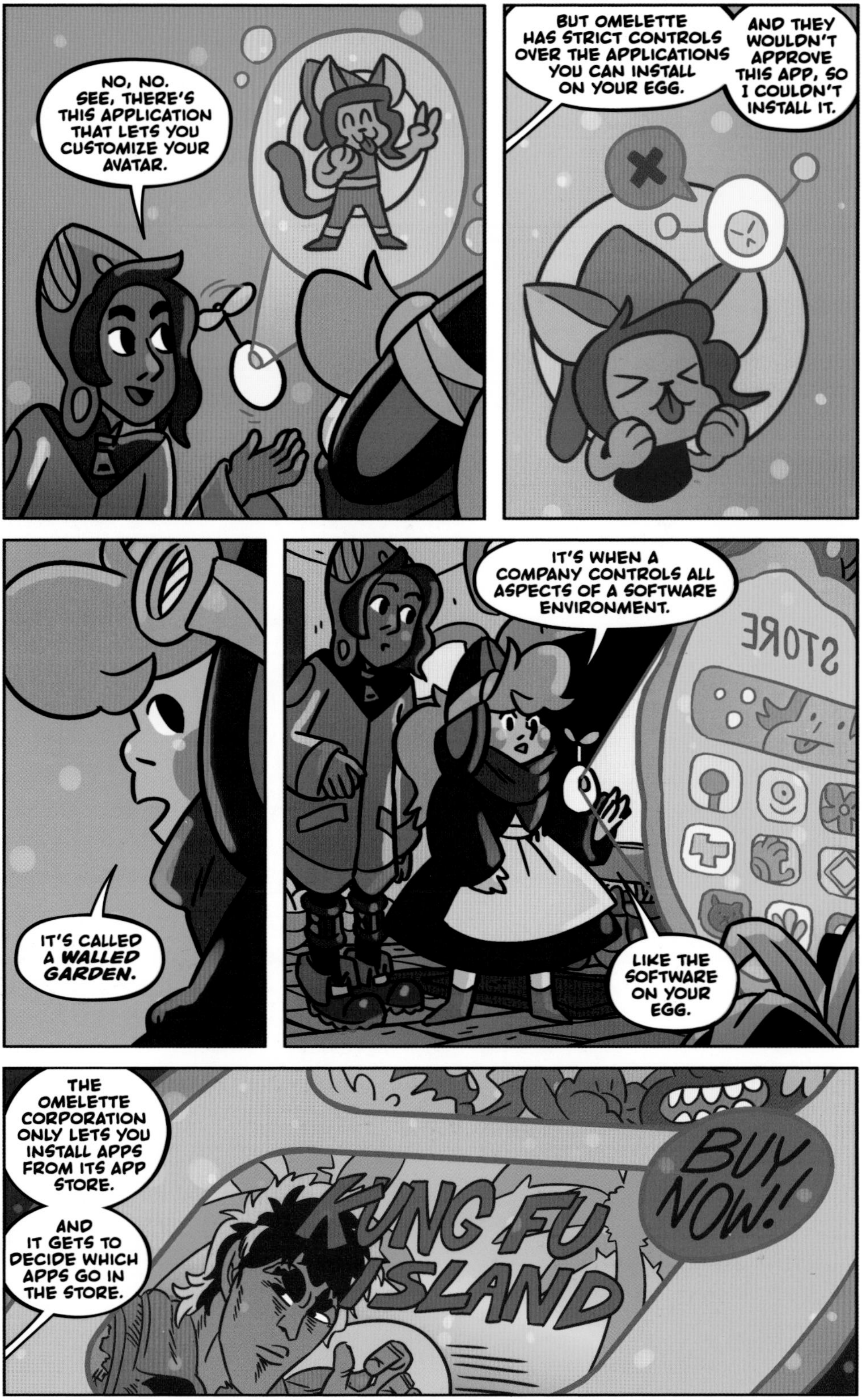
NO, NO. SEE, THERE'S THIS APPLICATION THAT LETS YOU CUSTOMIZE YOUR AVATAR.
BUT OMELETTE HAS STRICT CONTROLS OVER THE APPLICATIONS YOU CAN INSTALL ON YOUR EGG.
AND THEY WOULDN'T APPROVE THIS APP, SO I COULDN'T INSTALL IT.
IT'S CALLED A *WALLED GARDEN*.
IT'S WHEN A COMPANY CONTROLS ALL ASPECTS OF A SOFTWARE ENVIRONMENT.
STORE
LIKE THE SOFTWARE ON YOUR EGG.
THE OMELETTE CORPORATION ONLY LETS YOU INSTALL APPS FROM ITS APP STORE.
AND IT GETS TO DECIDE WHICH APPS GO IN THE STORE.
KUNG FU ISLAND
BUY NOW!

THERE ARE DEFINITE ADVANTAGES TO DOING THINGS THIS WAY!

THIS WAY

GO THIS WAY!

HERE

IT CAN MAKE USING EGGS A LOT EASIER, ESPECIALLY FOR PEOPLE WHO AREN'T PARTICULARLY TECH-SAVVY.

AND IT PREVENTS SOFTWARE THAT COULD HURT YOUR EGG FROM GETTING IN.

THWAP!

BUT IT ALSO MEANS THAT OMELETTE CONTROLS WHAT YOU SEE.

EGG

BUY BUY BUY

EGGS ARE COOL

STOP SLOWING DOWN OLD EGGS!

WHO WATCHES THE EG

PLANNED OBSOLESCENCE BITES

AND WHAT YOU DON'T.

44

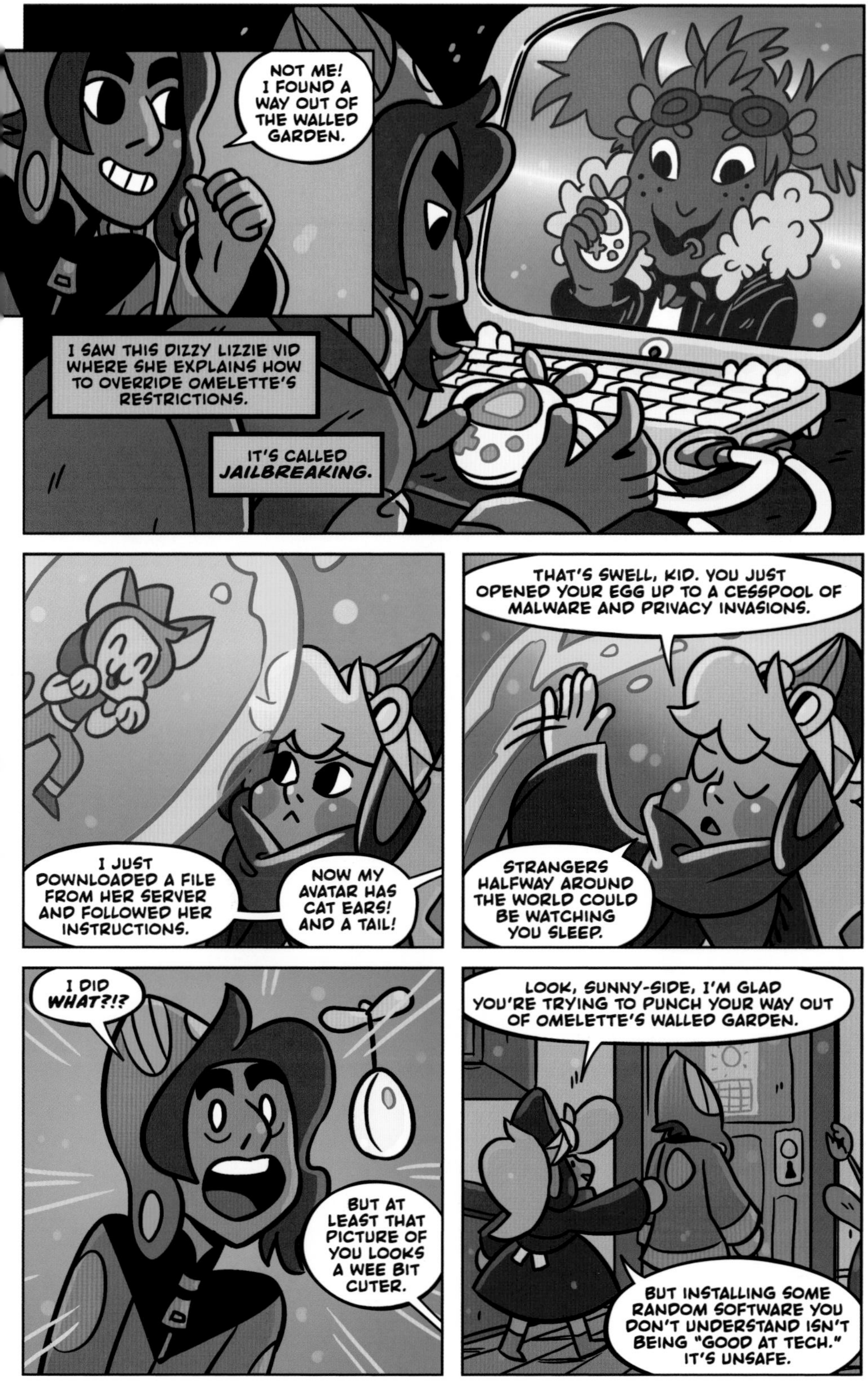
NOT ME! I FOUND A WAY OUT OF THE WALLED GARDEN.
I SAW THIS DIZZY LIZZIE VID WHERE SHE EXPLAINS HOW TO OVERRIDE OMELETTE'S RESTRICTIONS.
IT'S CALLED *JAILBREAKING.*
I JUST DOWNLOADED A FILE FROM HER SERVER AND FOLLOWED HER INSTRUCTIONS.
NOW MY AVATAR HAS CAT EARS! AND A TAIL!
THAT'S SWELL, KID. YOU JUST OPENED YOUR EGG UP TO A CESSPOOL OF MALWARE AND PRIVACY INVASIONS.
STRANGERS HALFWAY AROUND THE WORLD COULD BE WATCHING YOU SLEEP.
I DID *WHAT?!?*
BUT AT LEAST THAT PICTURE OF YOU LOOKS A WEE BIT CUTER.
LOOK, SUNNY-SIDE, I'M GLAD YOU'RE TRYING TO PUNCH YOUR WAY OUT OF OMELETTE'S WALLED GARDEN.
BUT INSTALLING SOME RANDOM SOFTWARE YOU DON'T UNDERSTAND ISN'T BEING "GOOD AT TECH." IT'S UNSAFE.

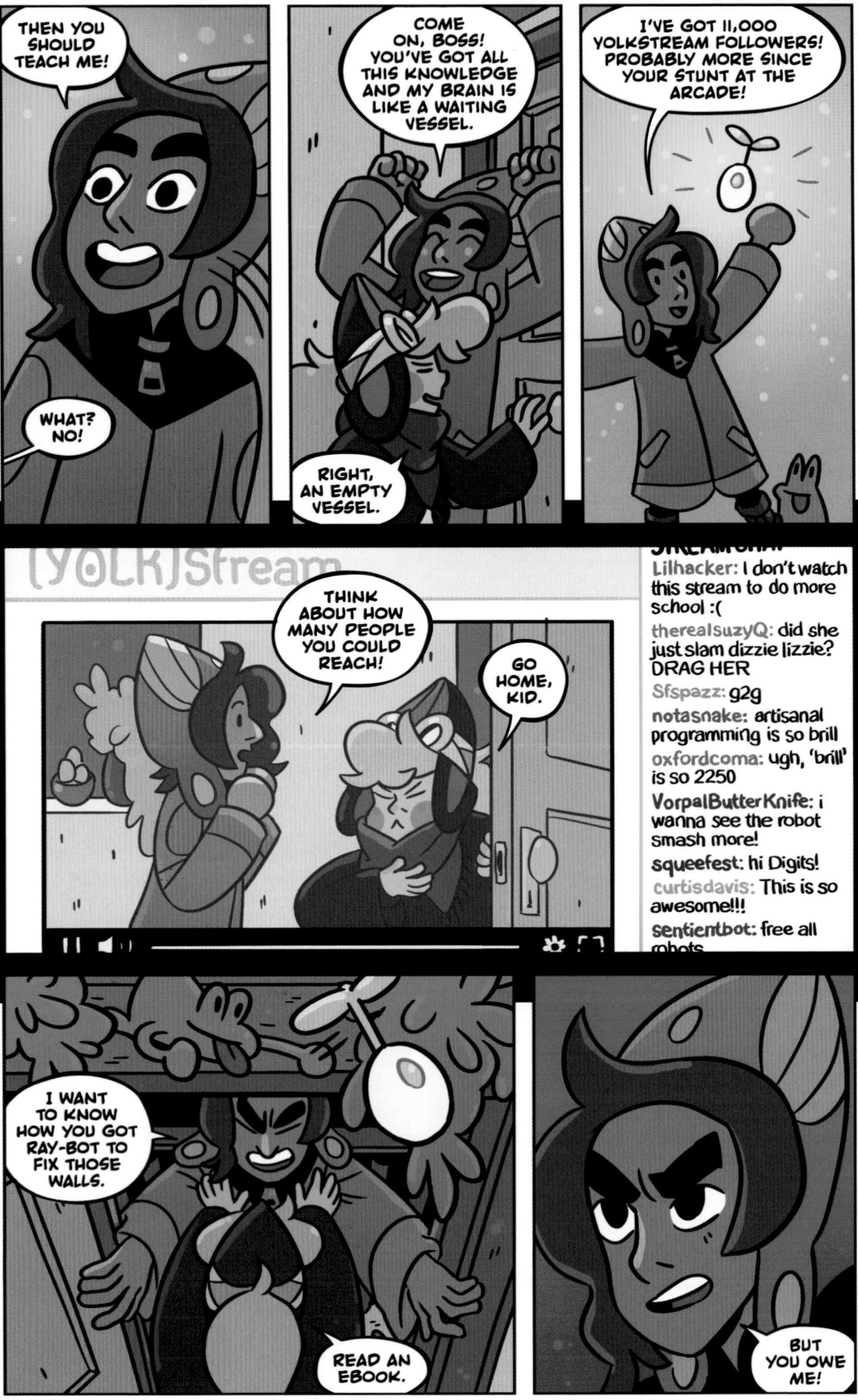
THEN YOU SHOULD TEACH ME!
WHAT? NO!
COME ON, BOSS! YOU'VE GOT ALL THIS KNOWLEDGE AND MY BRAIN IS LIKE A WAITING VESSEL.
RIGHT, AN EMPTY VESSEL.
I'VE GOT 11,000 YOLKSTREAM FOLLOWERS! PROBABLY MORE SINCE YOUR STUNT AT THE ARCADE!
[YOLK]Stream
THINK ABOUT HOW MANY PEOPLE YOU COULD REACH!
GO HOME, KID.
Lilhacker: I don't watch this stream to do more school :(
therealsuzyQ: did she just slam dizzie lizzie? DRAG HER
Sfspazz: g2g
notasnake: artisanal programming is so brill
oxfordcoma: ugh, 'brill' is so 2250
VorpalButterKnife: i wanna see the robot smash more!
squeefest: hi Digits!
curtisdavis: This is so awesome!!!
sentientbot: free all
I WANT TO KNOW HOW YOU GOT RAY-BOT TO FIX THOSE WALLS.
READ AN EBOOK.
BUT YOU OWE ME!

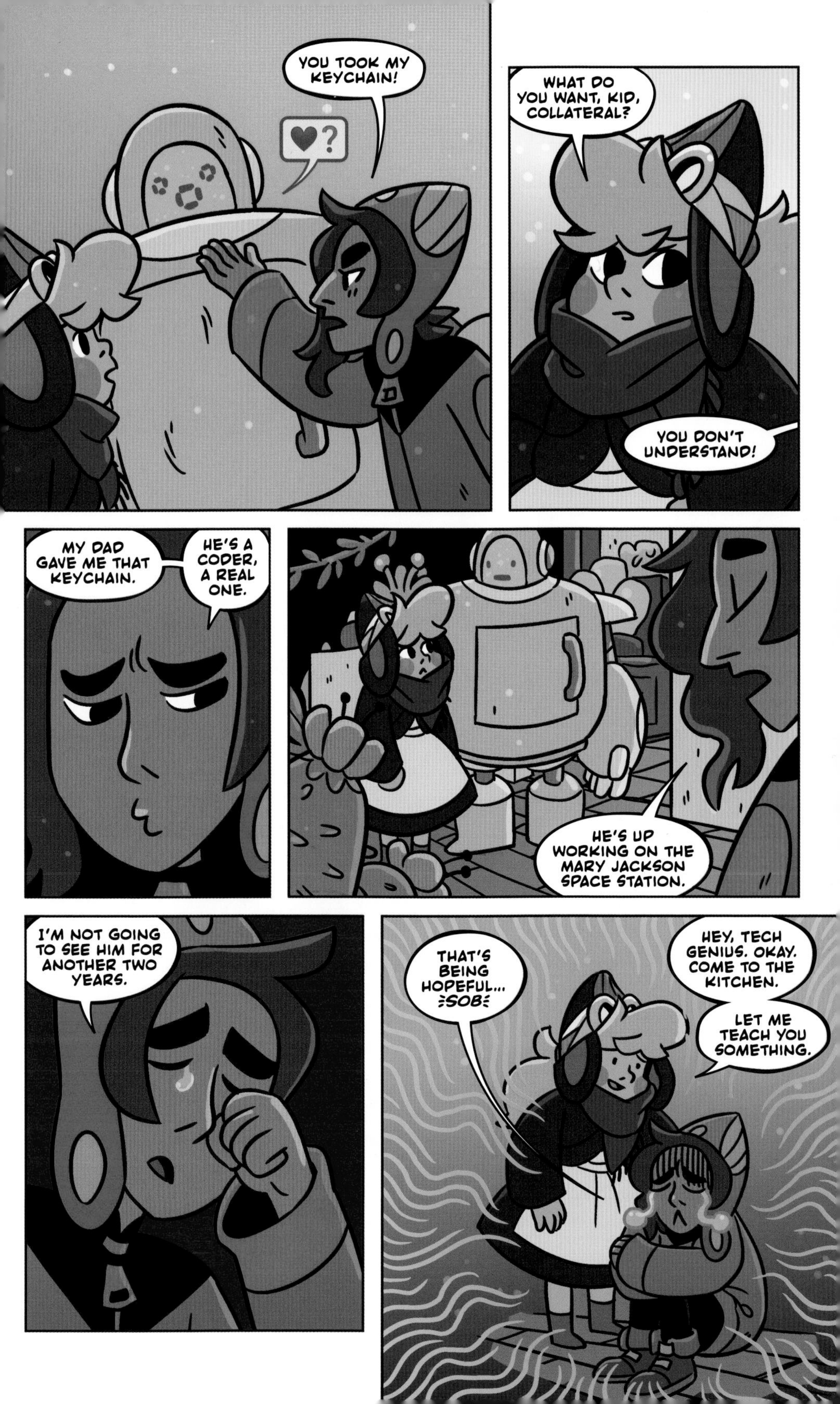
YOU TOOK MY KEYCHAIN!
♥?
WHAT DO YOU WANT, KID, COLLATERAL?
YOU DON'T UNDERSTAND!
MY DAD GAVE ME THAT KEYCHAIN.
HE'S A CODER, A REAL ONE.
HE'S UP WORKING ON THE MARY JACKSON SPACE STATION.
I'M NOT GOING TO SEE HIM FOR ANOTHER TWO YEARS.
THAT'S BEING HOPEFUL... SOB
HEY, TECH GENIUS. OKAY. COME TO THE KITCHEN.
LET ME TEACH YOU SOMETHING.

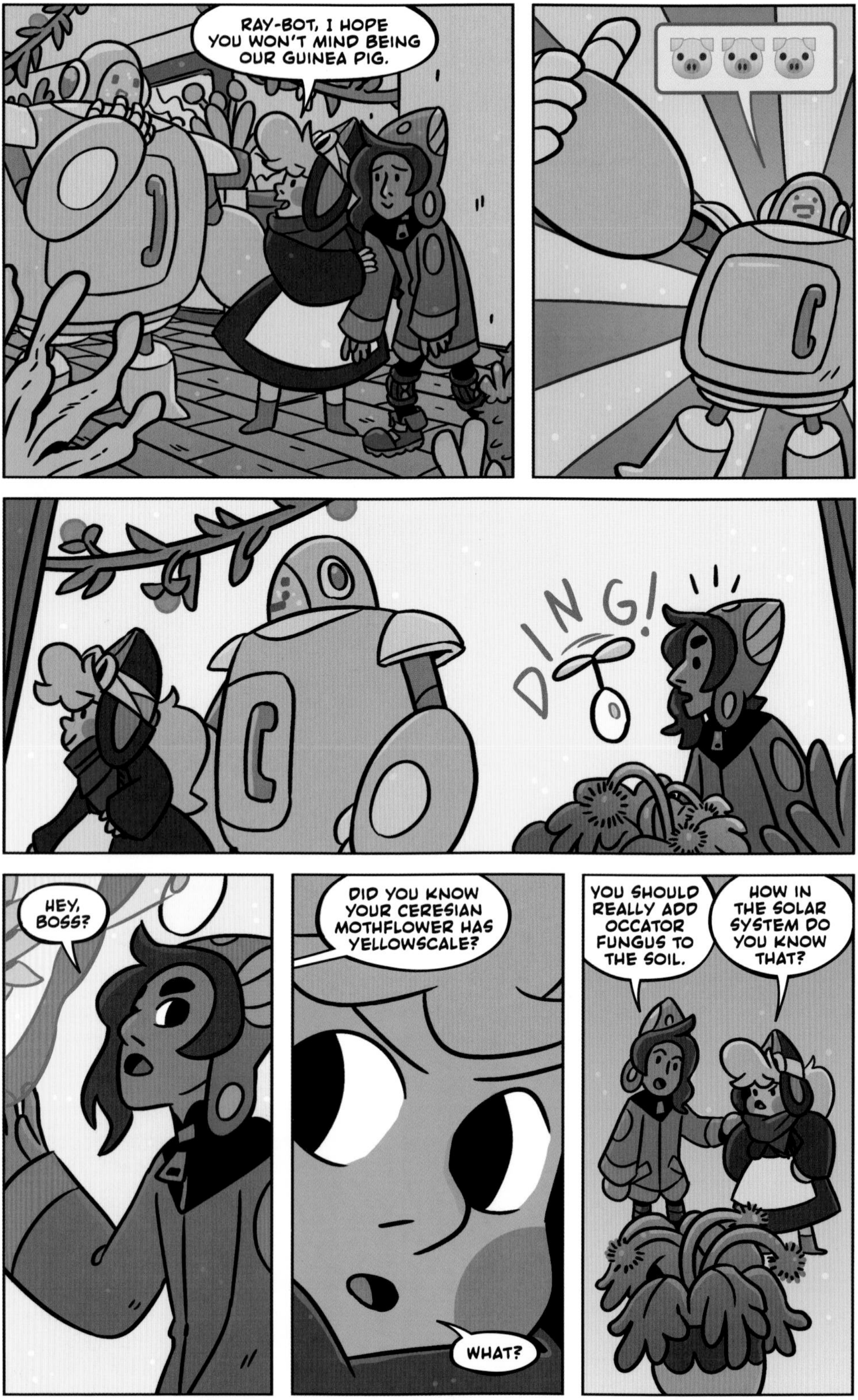
RAY-BOT, I HOPE YOU WON'T MIND BEING OUR GUINEA PIG.
DING!
HEY, BOSS?
DID YOU KNOW YOUR CERESIAN MOTHFLOWER HAS YELLOWSCALE?
WHAT?
YOU SHOULD REALLY ADD OCCATOR FUNGUS TO THE SOIL.
HOW IN THE SOLAR SYSTEM DO YOU KNOW THAT?

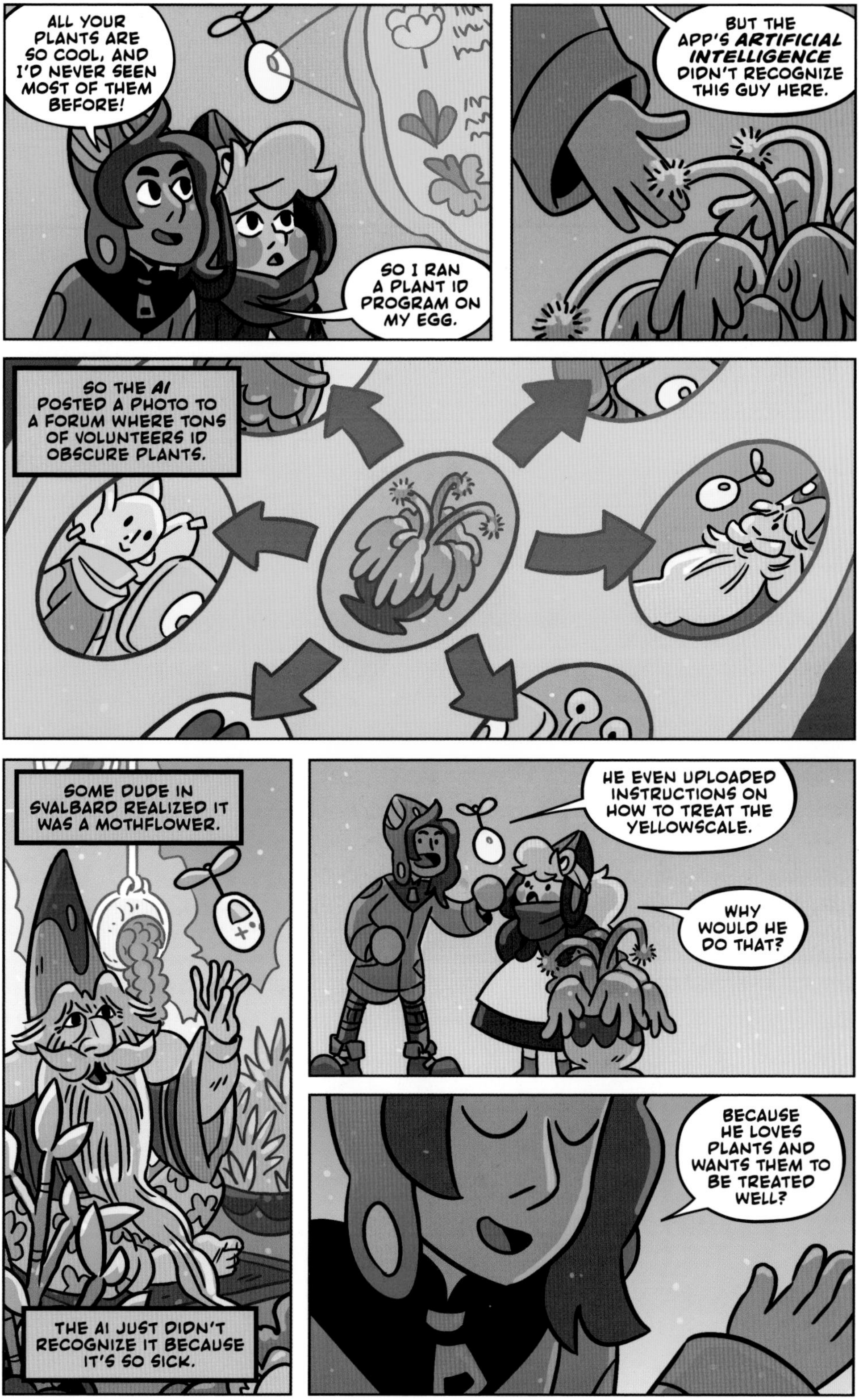

ALL YOUR PLANTS ARE SO COOL, AND I'D NEVER SEEN MOST OF THEM BEFORE!
SO I RAN A PLANT ID PROGRAM ON MY EGG.
BUT THE APP'S ***ARTIFICIAL INTELLIGENCE*** DIDN'T RECOGNIZE THIS GUY HERE.
SO THE *AI* POSTED A PHOTO TO A FORUM WHERE TONS OF VOLUNTEERS ID OBSCURE PLANTS.
SOME DUDE IN SVALBARD REALIZED IT WAS A MOTHFLOWER.
THE AI JUST DIDN'T RECOGNIZE IT BECAUSE IT'S SO SICK.
HE EVEN UPLOADED INSTRUCTIONS ON HOW TO TREAT THE YELLOWSCALE.
WHY WOULD HE DO THAT?
BECAUSE HE LOVES PLANTS AND WANTS THEM TO BE TREATED WELL?

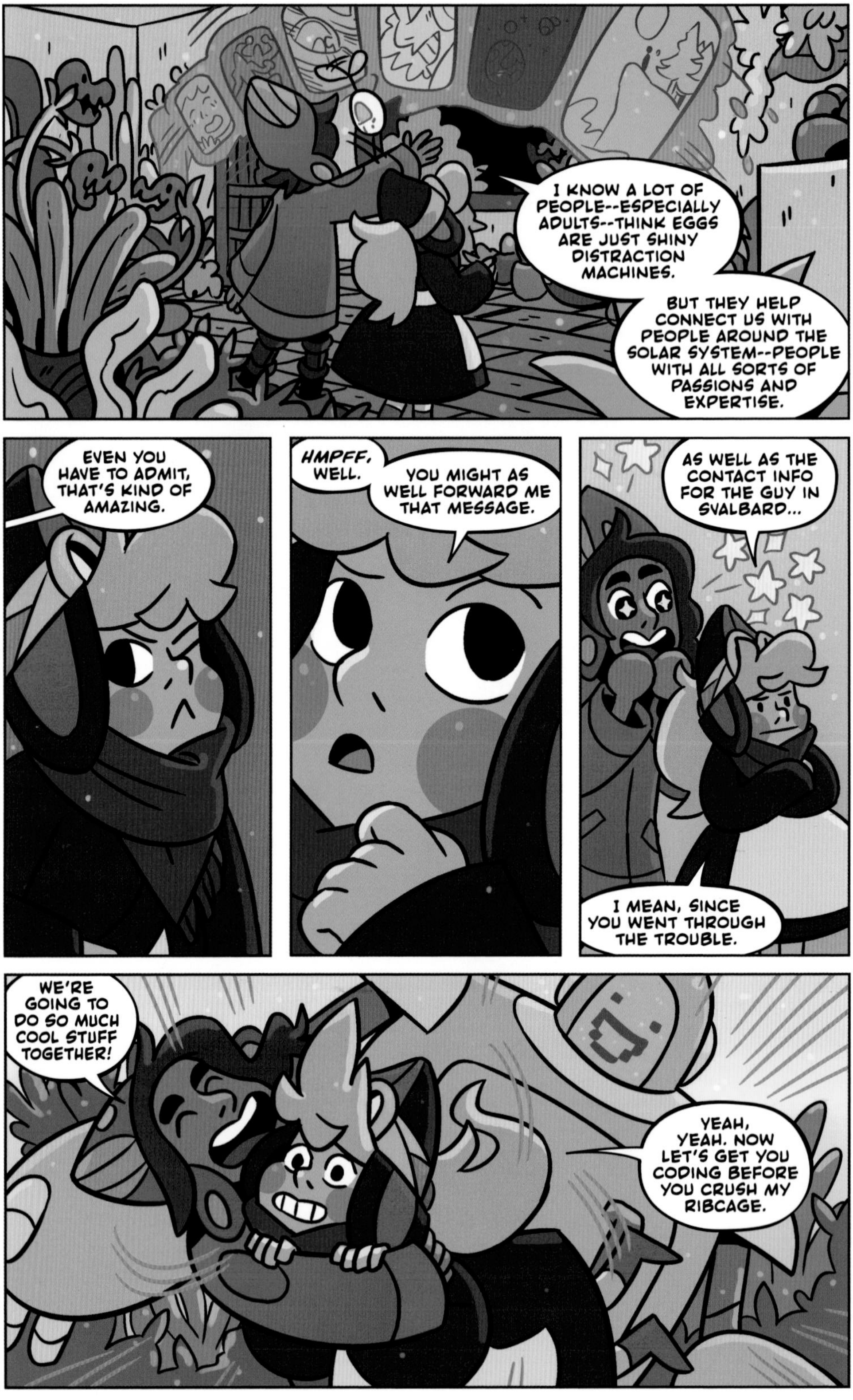
I KNOW A LOT OF PEOPLE--ESPECIALLY ADULTS--THINK EGGS ARE JUST SHINY DISTRACTION MACHINES.
BUT THEY HELP CONNECT US WITH PEOPLE AROUND THE SOLAR SYSTEM--PEOPLE WITH ALL SORTS OF PASSIONS AND EXPERTISE.
EVEN YOU HAVE TO ADMIT, THAT'S KIND OF AMAZING.
HMPFF. WELL.
YOU MIGHT AS WELL FORWARD ME THAT MESSAGE.
AS WELL AS THE CONTACT INFO FOR THE GUY IN SVALBARD...
I MEAN, SINCE YOU WENT THROUGH THE TROUBLE.
WE'RE GOING TO DO SO MUCH COOL STUFF TOGETHER!
YEAH, YEAH. NOW LET'S GET YOU CODING BEFORE YOU CRUSH MY RIBCAGE.

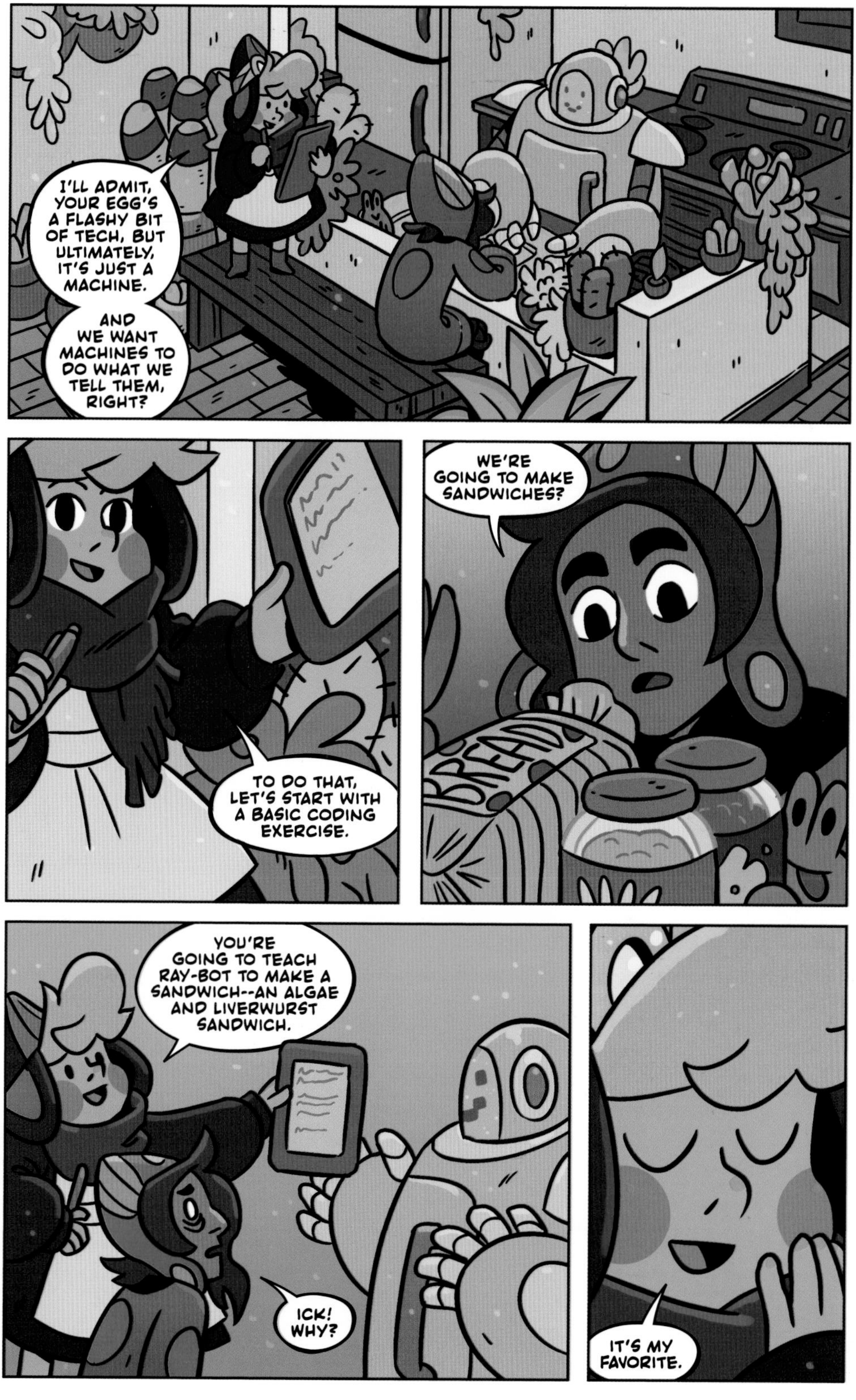
I'LL ADMIT, YOUR EGG'S A FLASHY BIT OF TECH, BUT ULTIMATELY, IT'S JUST A MACHINE.
AND WE WANT MACHINES TO DO WHAT WE TELL THEM, RIGHT?
TO DO THAT, LET'S START WITH A BASIC CODING EXERCISE.
WE'RE GOING TO MAKE SANDWICHES?
BREAD
YOU'RE GOING TO TEACH RAY-BOT TO MAKE A SANDWICH--AN ALGAE AND LIVERWURST SANDWICH.
ICK! WHY?
IT'S MY FAVORITE.

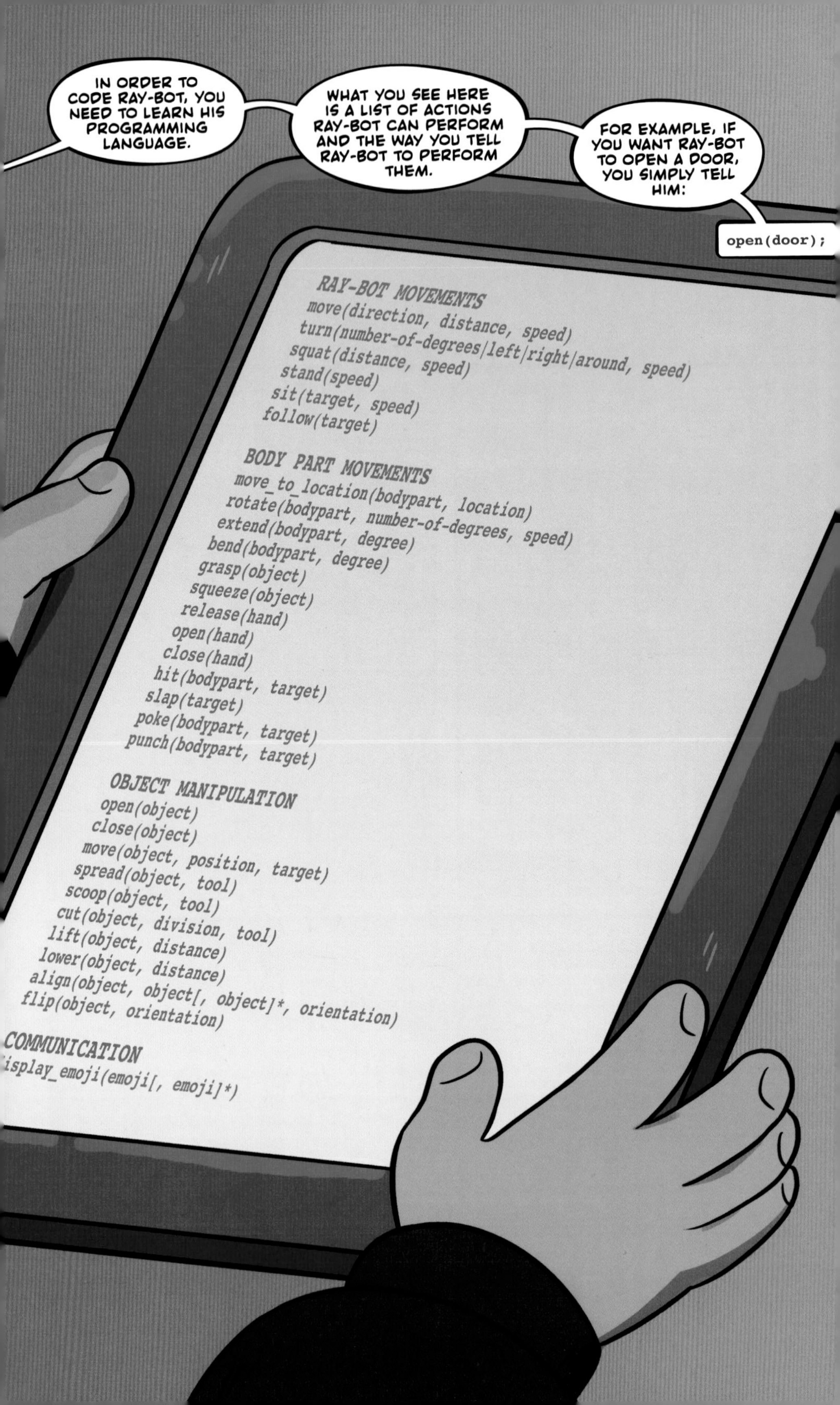
IN ORDER TO CODE RAY-BOT, YOU NEED TO LEARN HIS PROGRAMMING LANGUAGE.
WHAT YOU SEE HERE IS A LIST OF ACTIONS RAY-BOT CAN PERFORM AND THE WAY YOU TELL RAY-BOT TO PERFORM THEM.
FOR EXAMPLE, IF YOU WANT RAY-BOT TO OPEN A DOOR, YOU SIMPLY TELL HIM:
open(door);
RAY-BOT MOVEMENTS
move(direction, distance, speed)
turn(number-of-degrees|left|right|around, speed)
squat(distance, speed)
stand(speed)
sit(target, speed)
follow(target)
BODY PART MOVEMENTS
move_to_location(bodypart, location)
rotate(bodypart, number-of-degrees, speed)
extend(bodypart, degree)
bend(bodypart, degree)
grasp(object)
squeeze(object)
release(hand)
open(hand)
close(hand)
hit(bodypart, target)
slap(target)
poke(bodypart, target)
punch(bodypart, target)
OBJECT MANIPULATION
open(object)
close(object)
move(object, position, target)
spread(object, tool)
scoop(object, tool)
cut(object, division, tool)
lift(object, distance)
lower(object, distance)
align(object, object[, object]*, orientation)
flip(object, orientation)
COMMUNICATION
isplay_emoji(emoji[, emoji]*)

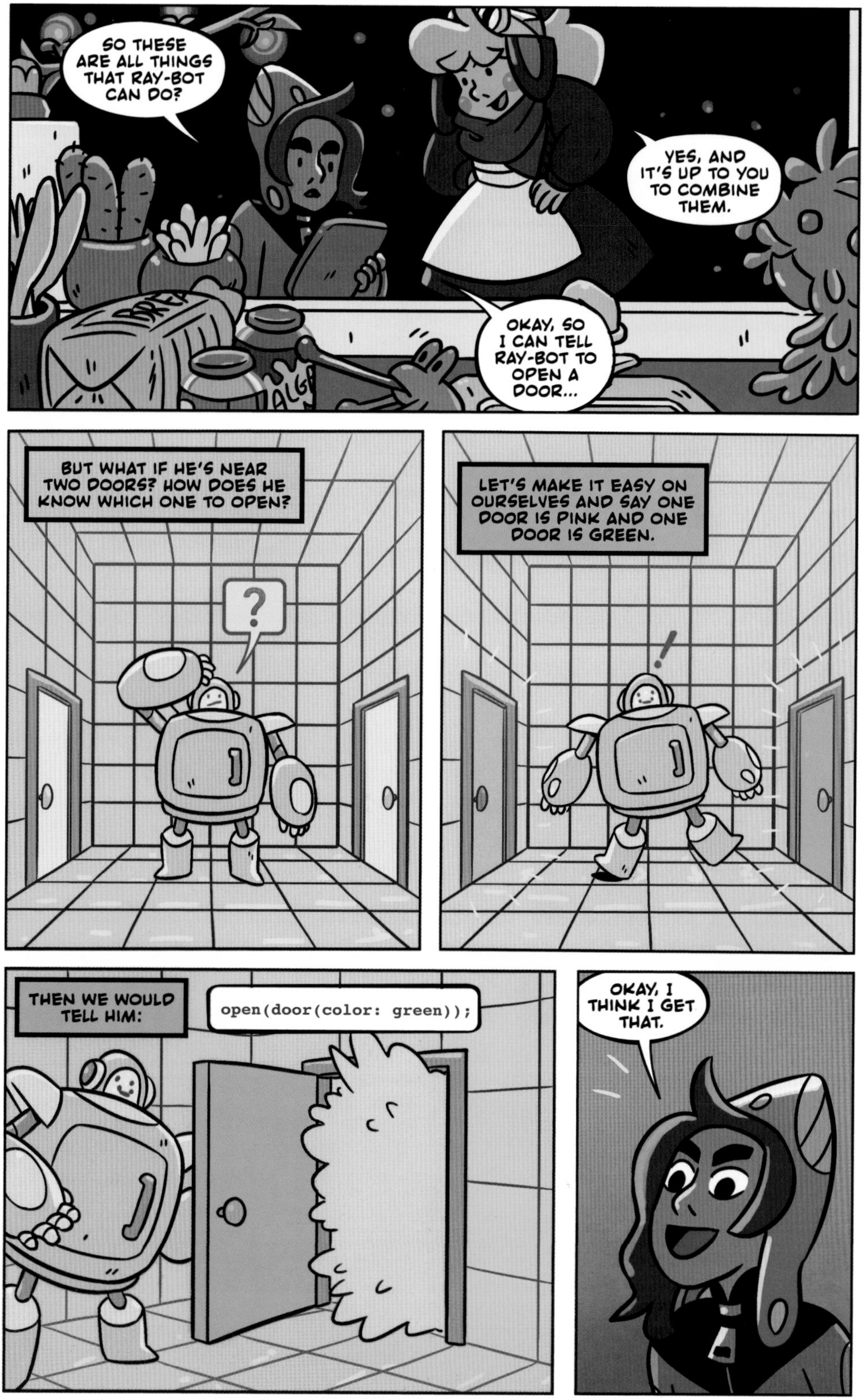

SO THESE ARE ALL THINGS THAT RAY-BOT CAN DO?
YES, AND IT'S UP TO YOU TO COMBINE THEM.
OKAY, SO I CAN TELL RAY-BOT TO OPEN A DOOR...
BREA
ALG
BUT WHAT IF HE'S NEAR TWO DOORS? HOW DOES HE KNOW WHICH ONE TO OPEN?
?
LET'S MAKE IT EASY ON OURSELVES AND SAY ONE DOOR IS PINK AND ONE DOOR IS GREEN.
!
THEN WE WOULD TELL HIM:
open(door(color: green));
OKAY, I THINK I GET THAT.

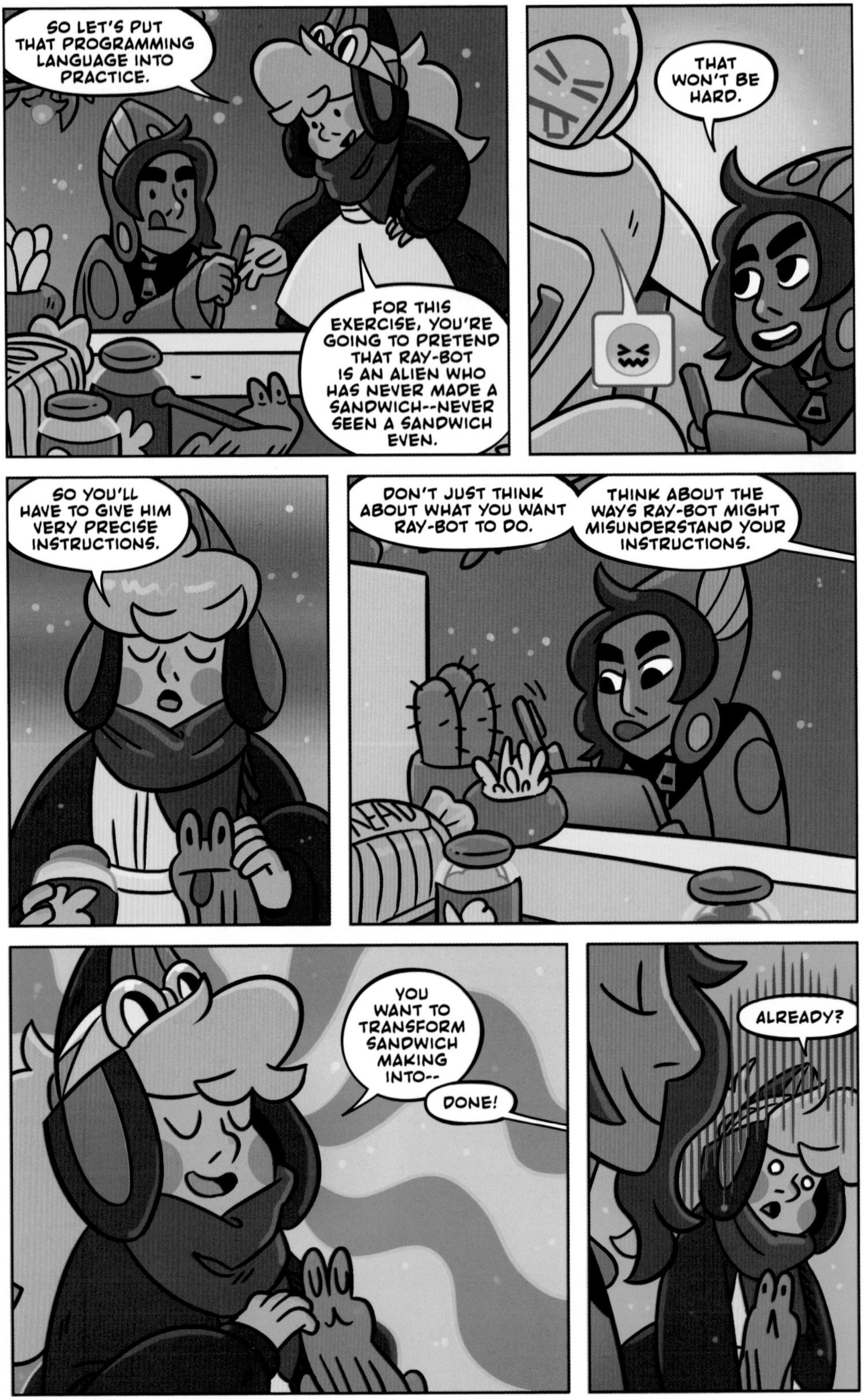

SO LET'S PUT THAT PROGRAMMING LANGUAGE INTO PRACTICE.
FOR THIS EXERCISE, YOU'RE GOING TO PRETEND THAT RAY-BOT IS AN ALIEN WHO HAS NEVER MADE A SANDWICH--NEVER SEEN A SANDWICH EVEN.
THAT WON'T BE HARD.
SO YOU'LL HAVE TO GIVE HIM VERY PRECISE INSTRUCTIONS.
DON'T JUST THINK ABOUT WHAT YOU WANT RAY-BOT TO DO.
THINK ABOUT THE WAYS RAY-BOT MIGHT MISUNDERSTAND YOUR INSTRUCTIONS.
YOU WANT TO TRANSFORM SANDWICH MAKING INTO--
DONE!
ALREADY?

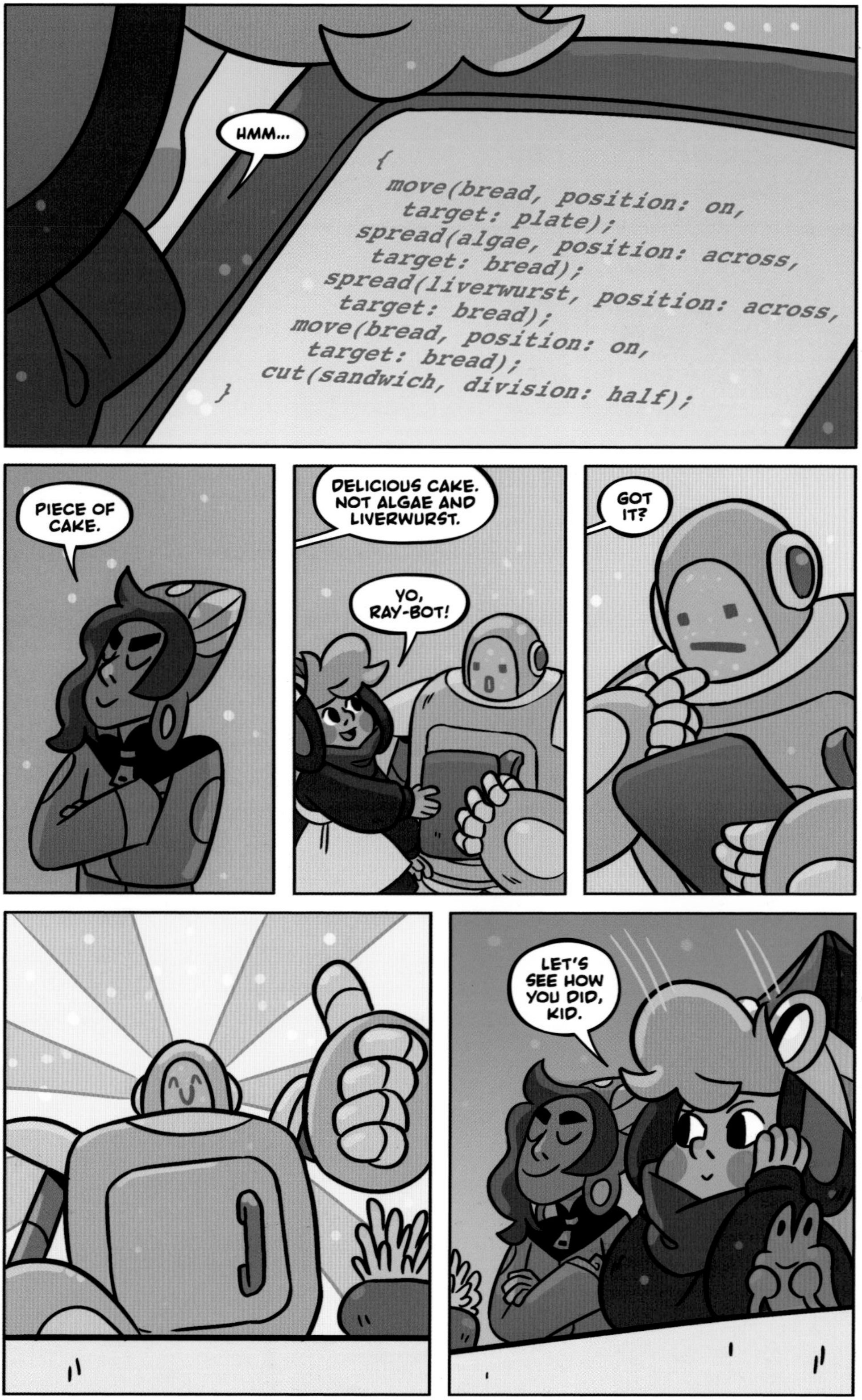
HMM...
{
move(bread, position: on,
target: plate);
spread(algae, position: across,
target: bread);
spread(liverwurst, position: across,
target: bread);
move(bread, position: on,
target: bread);
cut(sandwich, division: half);
}
PIECE OF CAKE.
DELICIOUS CAKE. NOT ALGAE AND LIVERWURST.
YO, RAY-BOT!
GOT IT?
LET'S SEE HOW YOU DID, KID.

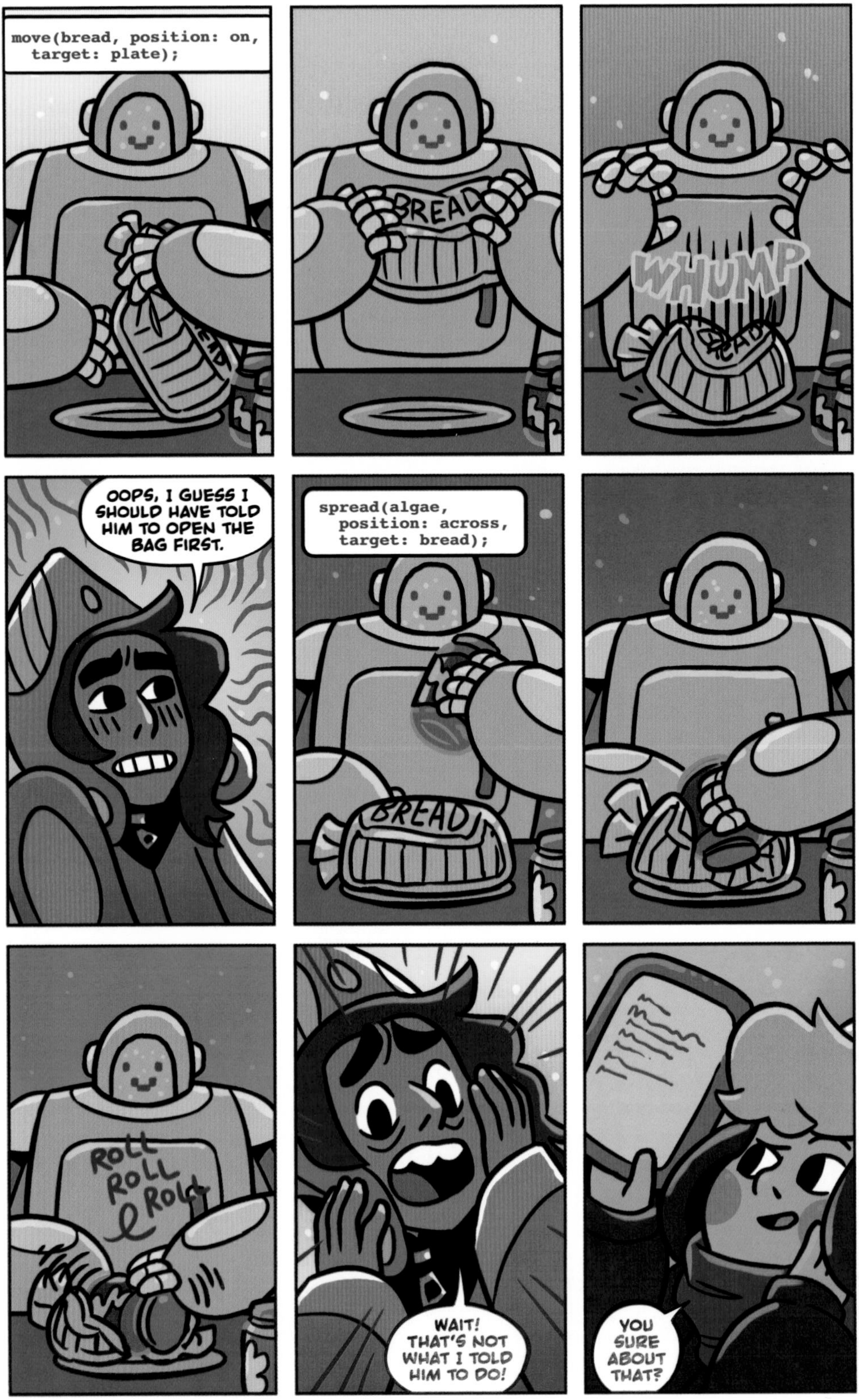
move(bread, position: on,
target: plate);
BREAD
WHUMP
BREAD
OOPS, I GUESS I SHOULD HAVE TOLD HIM TO OPEN THE BAG FIRST.
spread(algae,
position: across,
target: bread);
BREAD
ROLL
ROLL
ROLL
WAIT! THAT'S NOT WHAT I TOLD HIM TO DO!
YOU SURE ABOUT THAT?

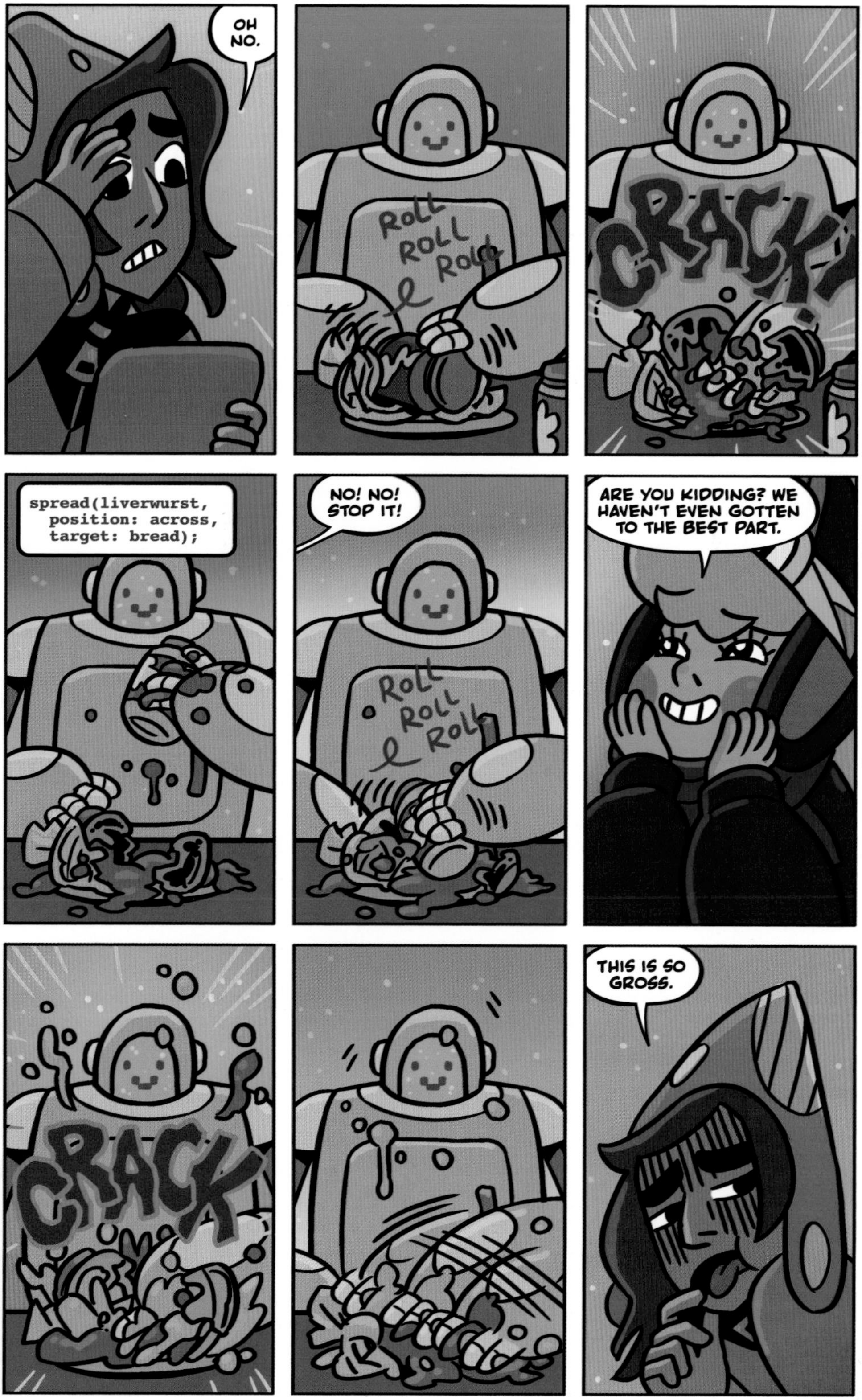
OH NO.
ROLL ROLL ROLL
CRACK
spread(liverwurst,
  position: across,
  target: bread);
NO! NO! STOP IT!
ROLL ROLL ROLL
ARE YOU KIDDING? WE HAVEN'T EVEN GOTTEN TO THE BEST PART.
CRACK
THIS IS SO GROSS.

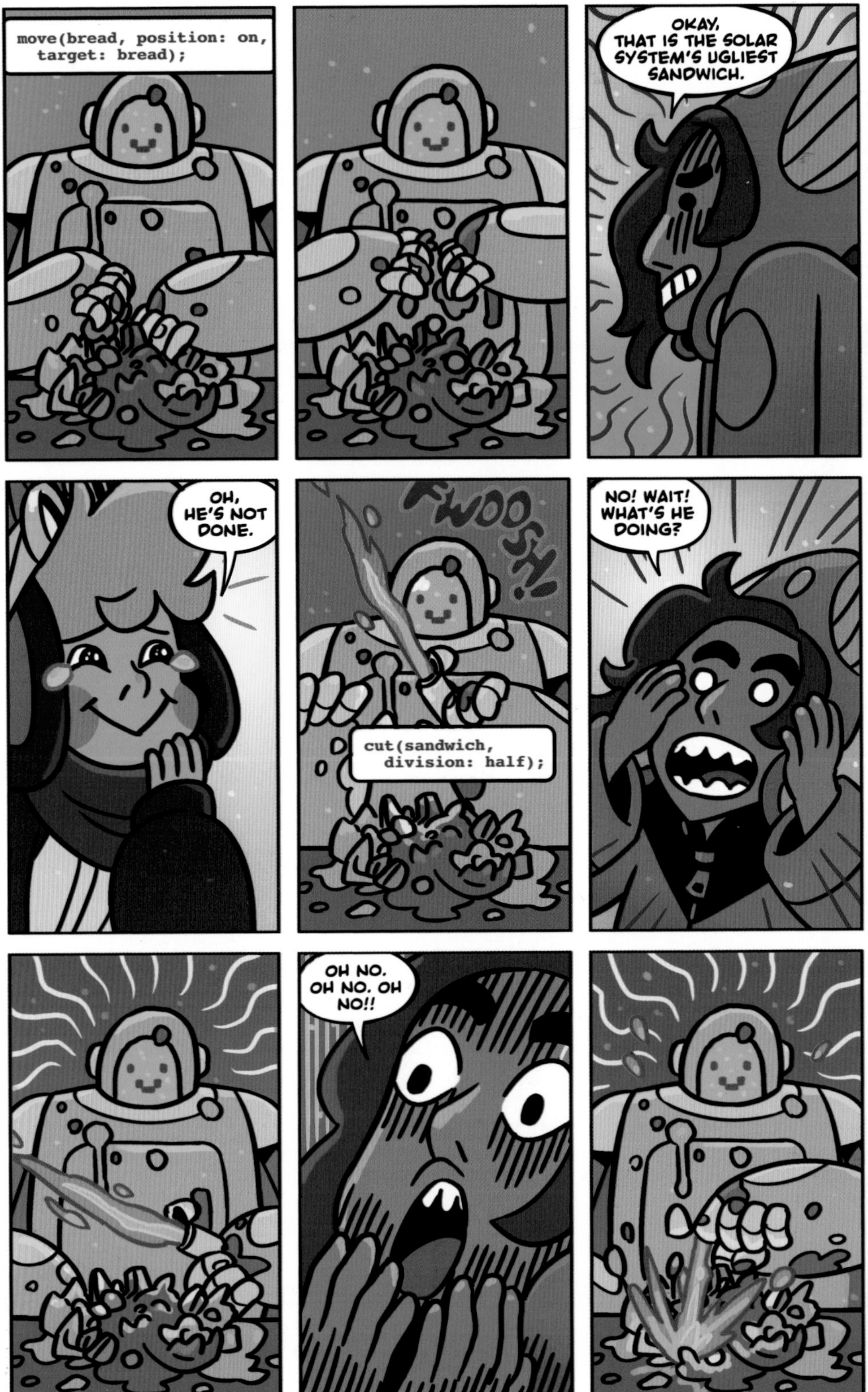

move(bread, position: on, target: bread);
OKAY, THAT IS THE SOLAR SYSTEM'S UGLIEST SANDWICH.
OH, HE'S NOT DONE.
FWOOSH!
cut(sandwich, division: half);
NO! WAIT! WHAT'S HE DOING?
OH NO. OH NO. OH NO!!

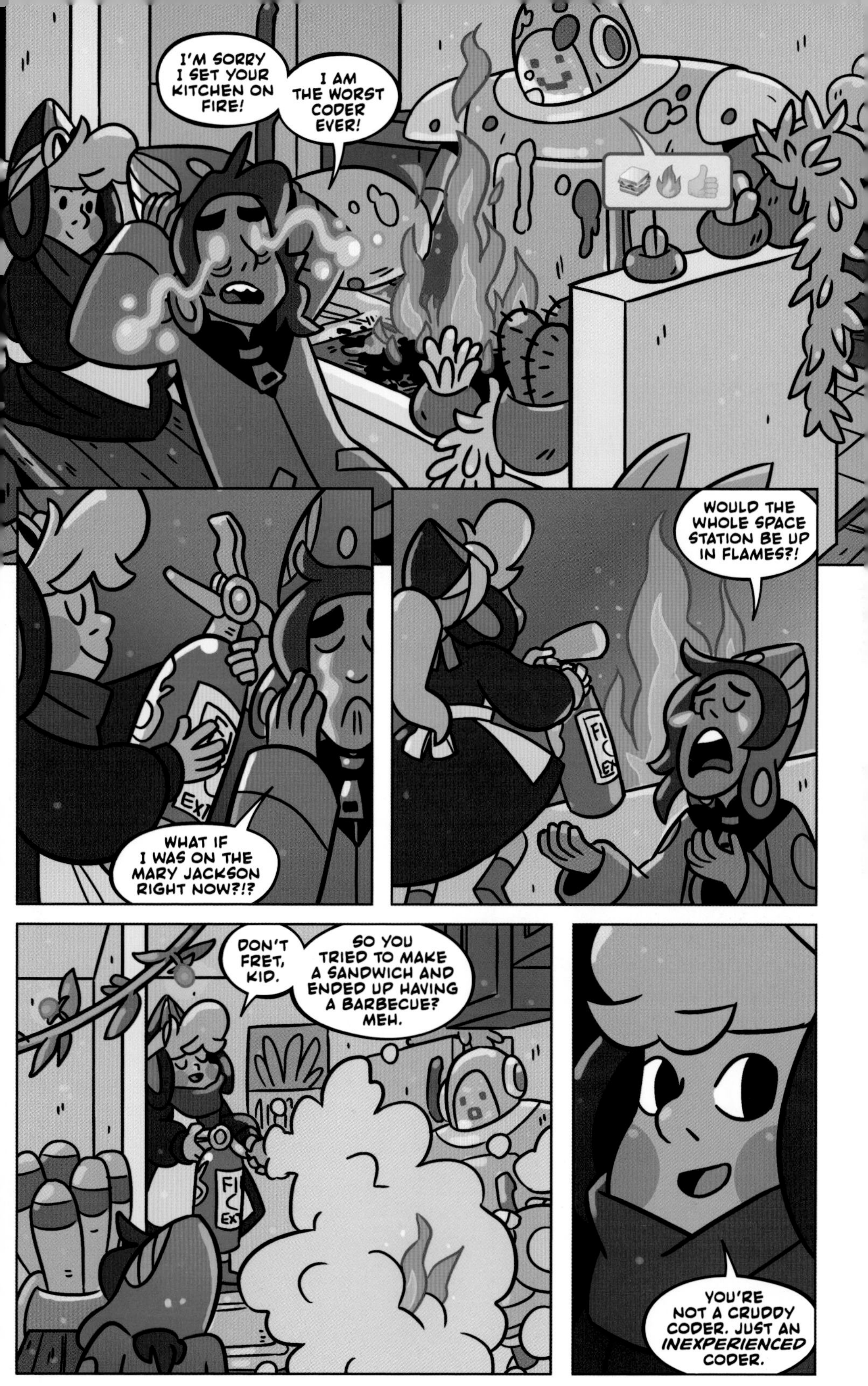

I'M SORRY I SET YOUR KITCHEN ON FIRE!
I AM THE WORST CODER EVER!
WHAT IF I WAS ON THE MARY JACKSON RIGHT NOW?!?
WOULD THE WHOLE SPACE STATION BE UP IN FLAMES?!
DON'T FRET, KID.
SO YOU TRIED TO MAKE A SANDWICH AND ENDED UP HAVING A BARBECUE? MEH.
YOU'RE NOT A CRUDDY CODER. JUST AN *INEXPERIENCED* CODER.

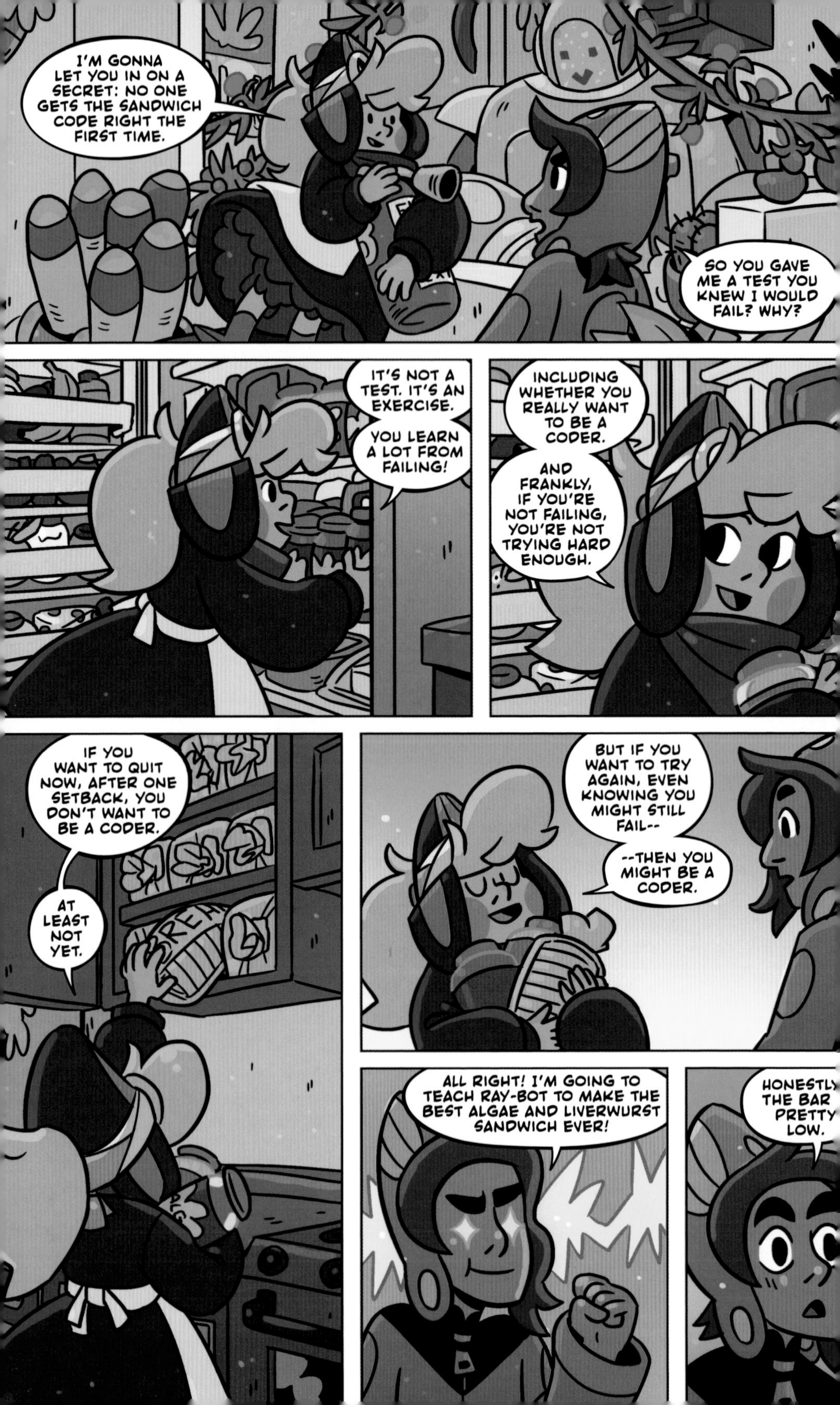
I'M GONNA LET YOU IN ON A SECRET: NO ONE GETS THE SANDWICH CODE RIGHT THE FIRST TIME.
SO YOU GAVE ME A TEST YOU KNEW I WOULD FAIL? WHY?
IT'S NOT A TEST. IT'S AN EXERCISE.
YOU LEARN A LOT FROM FAILING!
INCLUDING WHETHER YOU REALLY WANT TO BE A CODER.
AND FRANKLY, IF YOU'RE NOT FAILING, YOU'RE NOT TRYING HARD ENOUGH.
IF YOU WANT TO QUIT NOW, AFTER ONE SETBACK, YOU DON'T WANT TO BE A CODER.
AT LEAST NOT YET.
BUT IF YOU WANT TO TRY AGAIN, EVEN KNOWING YOU MIGHT STILL FAIL--
--THEN YOU MIGHT BE A CODER.
ALL RIGHT! I'M GOING TO TEACH RAY-BOT TO MAKE THE BEST ALGAE AND LIVERWURST SANDWICH EVER!
HONESTLY THE BAR PRETTY LOW.

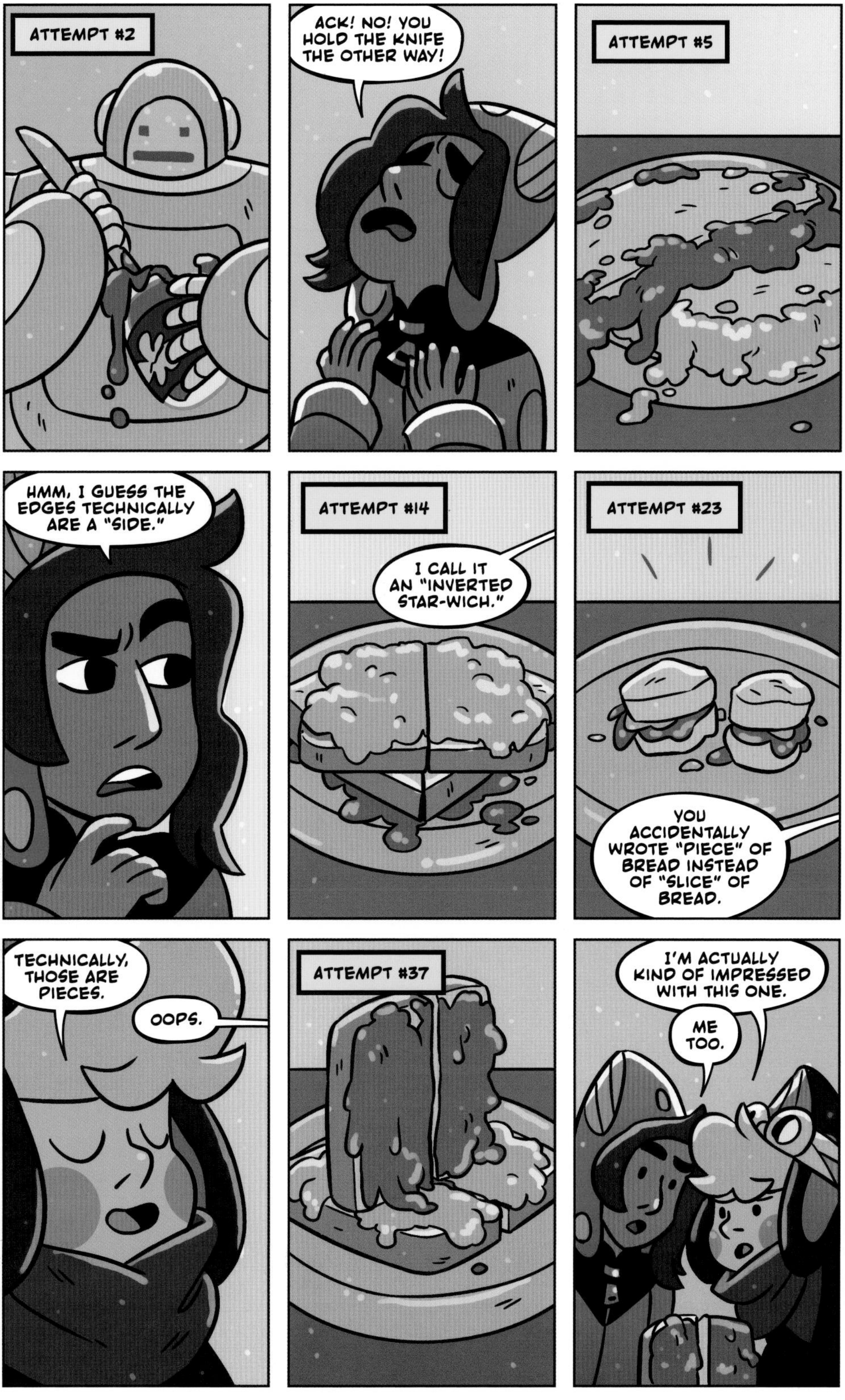
ATTEMPT #2
ACK! NO! YOU HOLD THE KNIFE THE OTHER WAY!
ATTEMPT #5
HMM, I GUESS THE EDGES TECHNICALLY ARE A "SIDE."
ATTEMPT #14
I CALL IT AN "INVERTED STAR-WICH."
ATTEMPT #23
YOU ACCIDENTALLY WROTE "PIECE" OF BREAD INSTEAD OF "SLICE" OF BREAD.
TECHNICALLY, THOSE ARE PIECES.
OOPS.
ATTEMPT #37
I'M ACTUALLY KIND OF IMPRESSED WITH THIS ONE.
ME TOO.

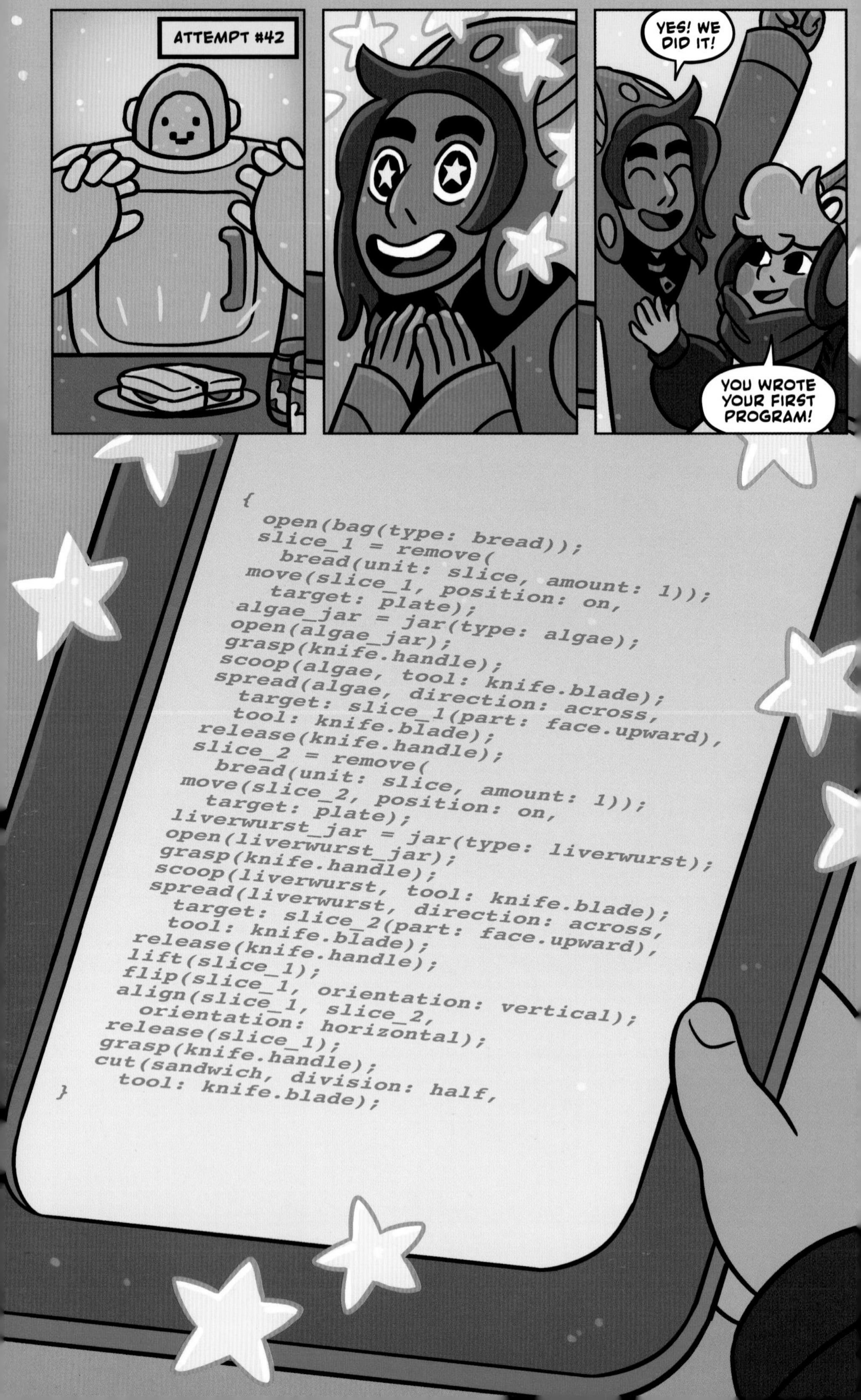
ATTEMPT #42
YES! WE DID IT!
YOU WROTE YOUR FIRST PROGRAM!
{
open(bag(type: bread));
slice_1 = remove(
bread(unit: slice, amount: 1));
move(slice_1, position: on,
target: plate);
algae_jar = jar(type: algae);
open(algae_jar);
grasp(knife.handle);
scoop(algae, tool: knife.blade);
spread(algae, direction: across,
target: slice_1(part: face.upward),
tool: knife.blade);
release(knife.handle);
slice_2 = remove(
bread(unit: slice, amount: 1));
move(slice_2, position: on,
target: plate);
liverwurst_jar = jar(type: liverwurst);
open(liverwurst_jar);
grasp(knife.handle);
scoop(liverwurst, tool: knife.blade);
spread(liverwurst, direction: across,
target: slice_2(part: face.upward),
tool: knife.blade);
release(knife.handle);
lift(slice_1);
flip(slice_1, orientation: vertical);
align(slice_1, slice_2,
orientation: horizontal);
release(slice_1);
grasp(knife.handle);
cut(sandwich, division: half,
tool: knife.blade);
}

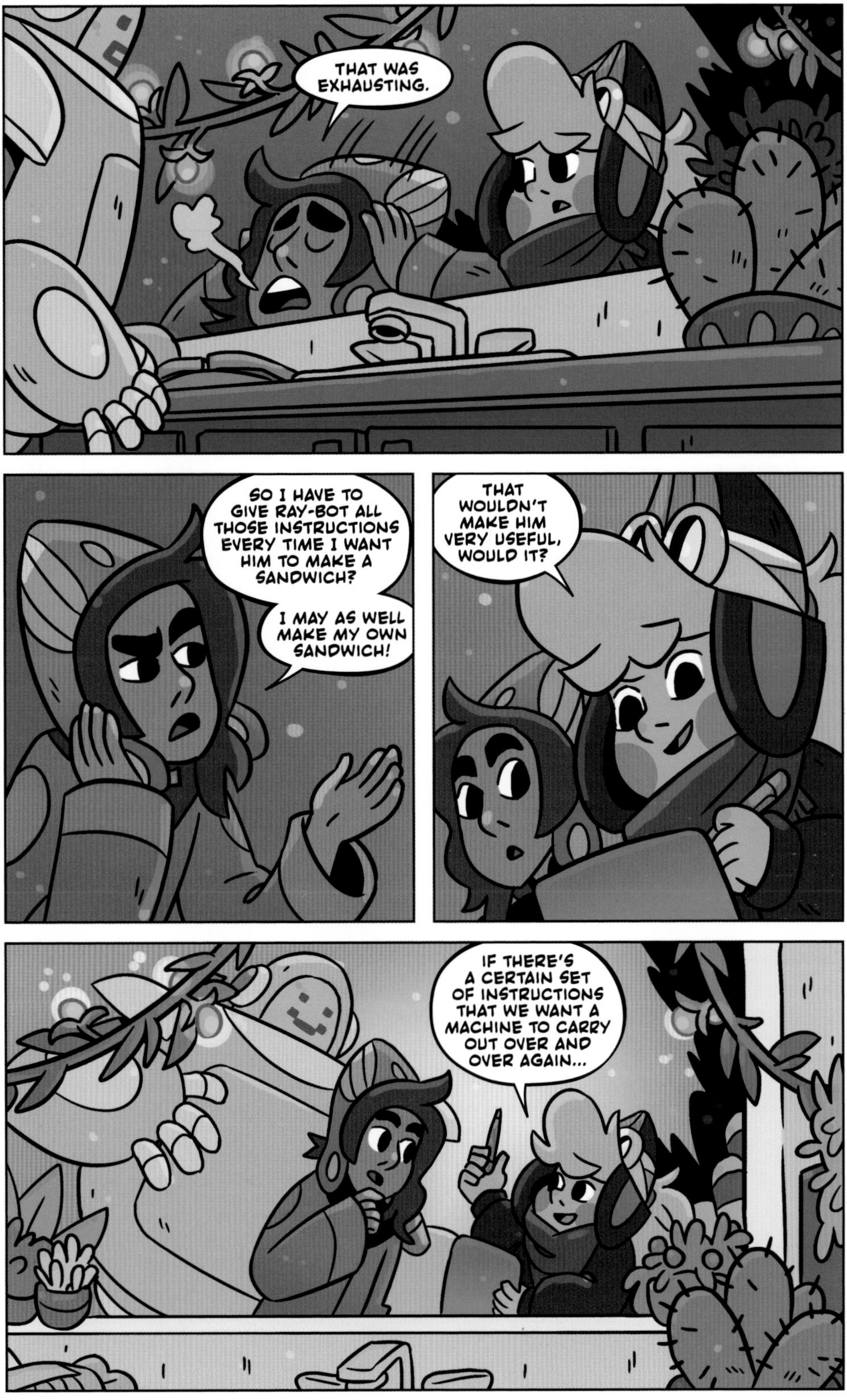
THAT WAS EXHAUSTING.
SO I HAVE TO GIVE RAY-BOT ALL THOSE INSTRUCTIONS EVERY TIME I WANT HIM TO MAKE A SANDWICH?
I MAY AS WELL MAKE MY OWN SANDWICH!
THAT WOULDN'T MAKE HIM VERY USEFUL, WOULD IT?
IF THERE'S A CERTAIN SET OF INSTRUCTIONS THAT WE WANT A MACHINE TO CARRY OUT OVER AND OVER AGAIN...

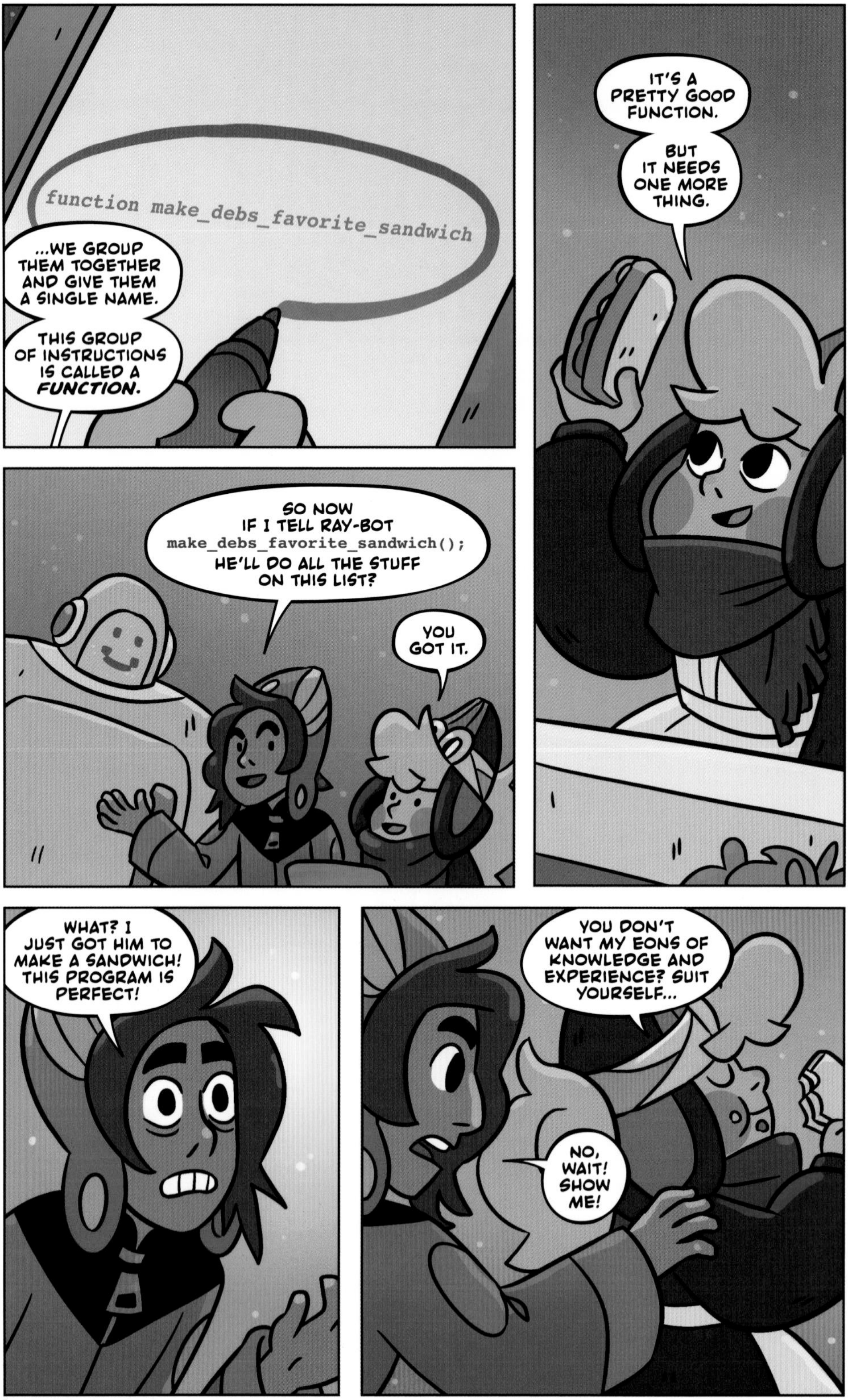
function make_debs_favorite_sandwich
...WE GROUP THEM TOGETHER AND GIVE THEM A SINGLE NAME.
THIS GROUP OF INSTRUCTIONS IS CALLED A *FUNCTION.*
IT'S A PRETTY GOOD FUNCTION.
BUT IT NEEDS ONE MORE THING.
SO NOW IF I TELL RAY-BOT make_debs_favorite_sandwich(); HE'LL DO ALL THE STUFF ON THIS LIST?
YOU GOT IT.
WHAT? I JUST GOT HIM TO MAKE A SANDWICH! THIS PROGRAM IS PERFECT!
YOU DON'T WANT MY EONS OF KNOWLEDGE AND EXPERIENCE? SUIT YOURSELF...
NO, WAIT! SHOW ME!

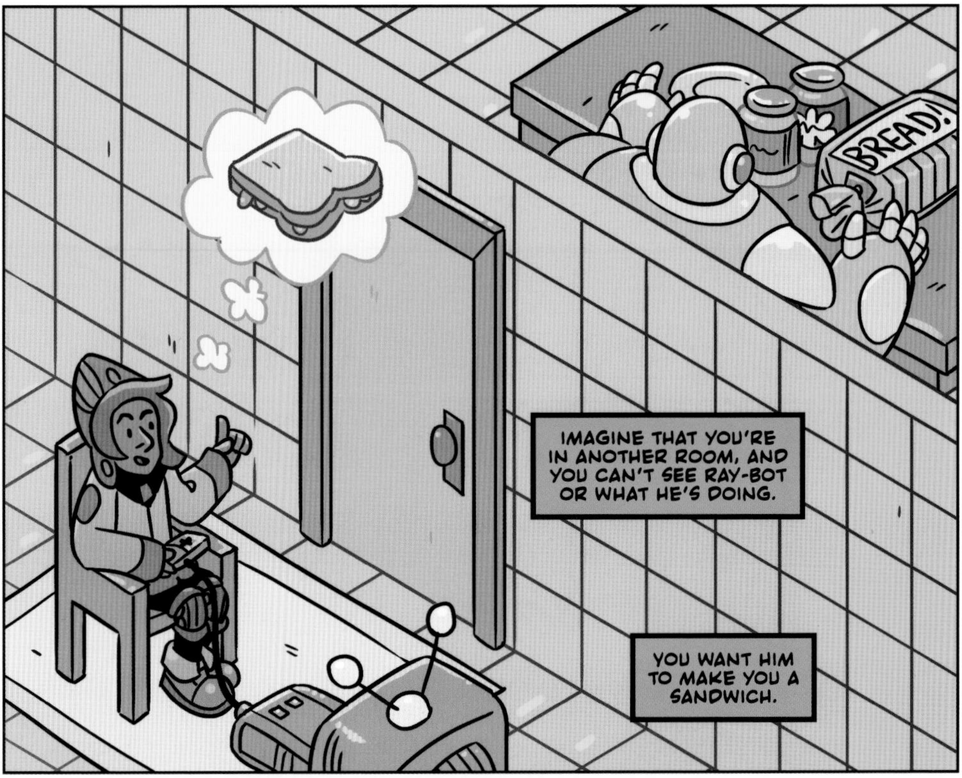
BREAD!
IMAGINE THAT YOU'RE IN ANOTHER ROOM, AND YOU CAN'T SEE RAY-BOT OR WHAT HE'S DOING.
YOU WANT HIM TO MAKE YOU A SANDWICH.

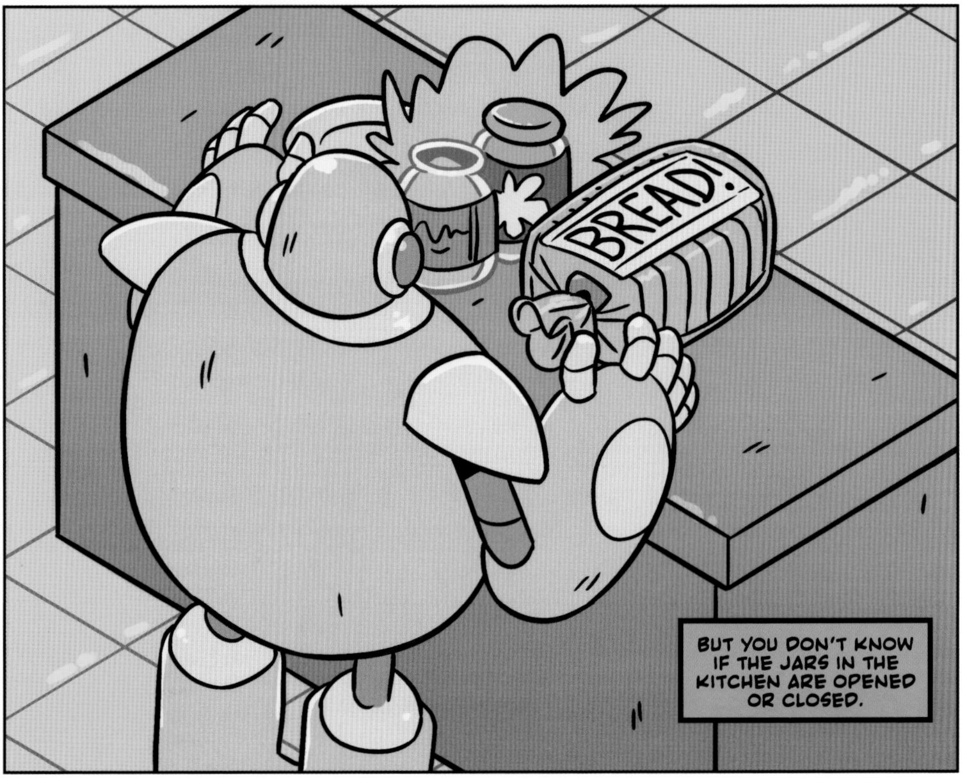
BREAD!
BUT YOU DON'T KNOW IF THE JARS IN THE KITCHEN ARE OPENED OR CLOSED.

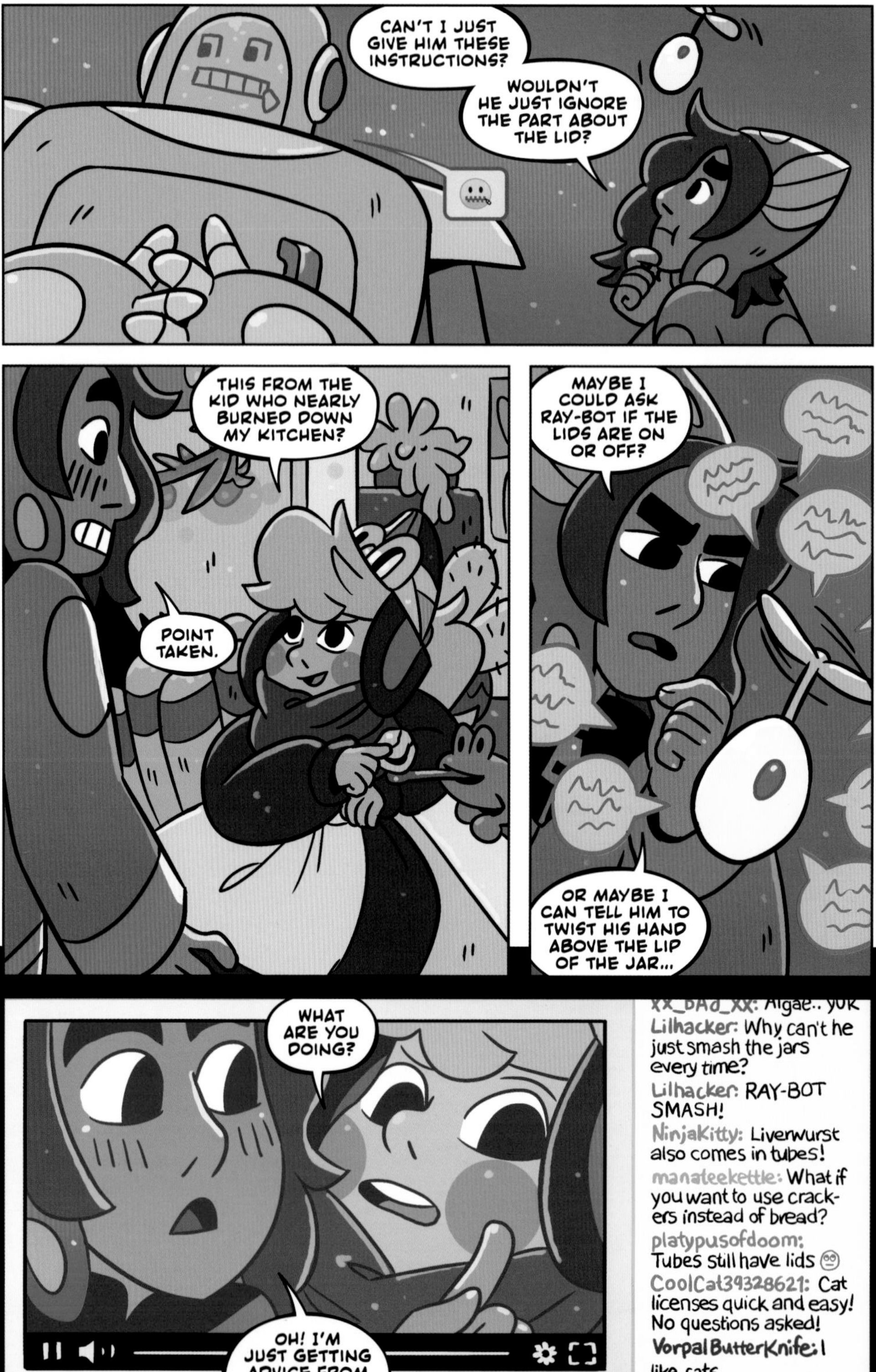

CAN'T I JUST GIVE HIM THESE INSTRUCTIONS?
WOULDN'T HE JUST IGNORE THE PART ABOUT THE LID?
THIS FROM THE KID WHO NEARLY BURNED DOWN MY KITCHEN?
POINT TAKEN.
MAYBE I COULD ASK RAY-BOT IF THE LIDS ARE ON OR OFF?
OR MAYBE I CAN TELL HIM TO TWIST HIS HAND ABOVE THE LIP OF THE JAR...
WHAT ARE YOU DOING?
OH! I'M JUST GETTING ADVICE FROM SOME OF MY FOLLOWERS.
Lilhacker: Why can't he just smash the jars every time?
Lilhacker: RAY-BOT SMASH!
NinjaKitty: Liverwurst also comes in tubes!
manateekettle: What if you want to use crackers instead of bread?
platypusofdoom: Tubes still have lids
CoolCat39328621: Cat licenses quick and easy! No questions asked!
VorpalButterKnife: I like cats
NinjaKitty: not again

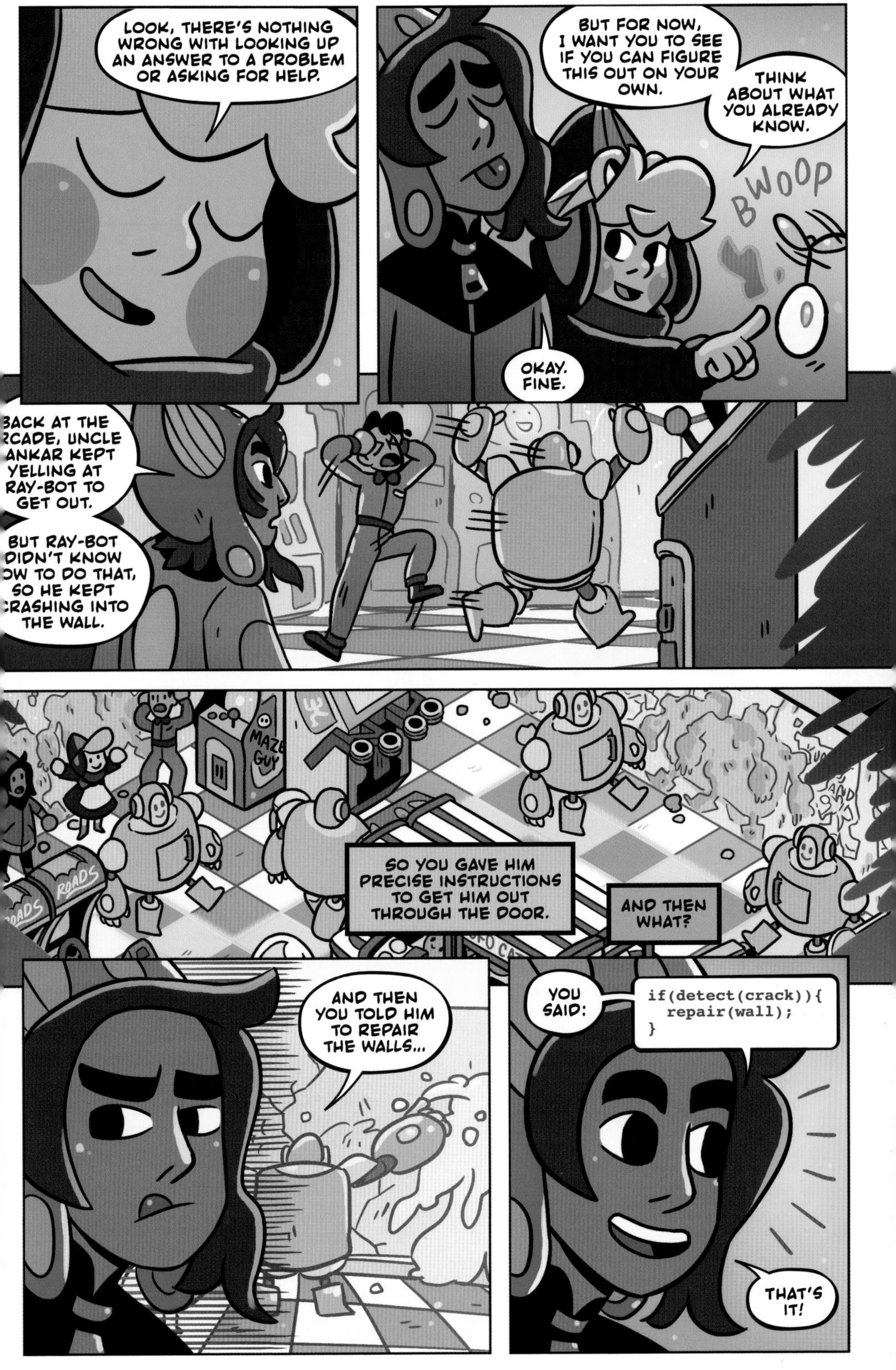
LOOK, THERE'S NOTHING WRONG WITH LOOKING UP AN ANSWER TO A PROBLEM OR ASKING FOR HELP.
BUT FOR NOW, I WANT YOU TO SEE IF YOU CAN FIGURE THIS OUT ON YOUR OWN.
THINK ABOUT WHAT YOU ALREADY KNOW.
BWOOP
OKAY. FINE.
BACK AT THE ARCADE, UNCLE ANKAR KEPT YELLING AT RAY-BOT TO GET OUT.
BUT RAY-BOT DIDN'T KNOW HOW TO DO THAT, SO HE KEPT CRASHING INTO THE WALL.
MAZE GUY
ROADS
SO YOU GAVE HIM PRECISE INSTRUCTIONS TO GET HIM OUT THROUGH THE DOOR.
AND THEN WHAT?
AND THEN YOU TOLD HIM TO REPAIR THE WALLS...
YOU SAID:
if(detect(crack)){
repair(wall);
}
THAT'S IT!

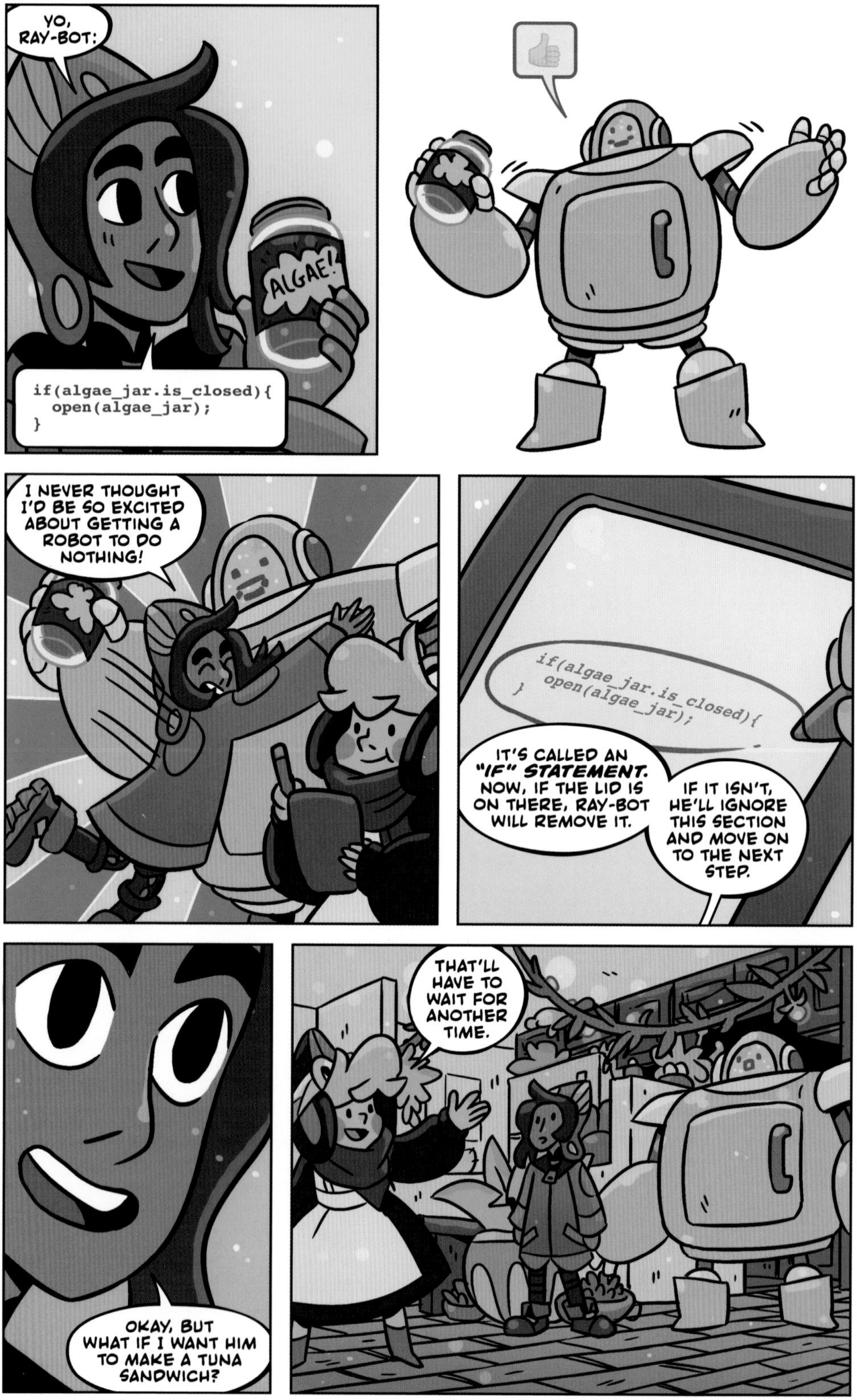

YO, RAY-BOT:
if(algae_jar.is_closed){
open(algae_jar);
}
ALGAE!
I NEVER THOUGHT I'D BE SO EXCITED ABOUT GETTING A ROBOT TO DO NOTHING!
if(algae_jar.is_closed){
open(algae_jar);
}
IT'S CALLED AN "IF" STATEMENT. NOW, IF THE LID IS ON THERE, RAY-BOT WILL REMOVE IT.
IF IT ISN'T, HE'LL IGNORE THIS SECTION AND MOVE ON TO THE NEXT STEP.
OKAY, BUT WHAT IF I WANT HIM TO MAKE A TUNA SANDWICH?
THAT'LL HAVE TO WAIT FOR ANOTHER TIME.

WE'VE STILL GOT TO FIGURE OUT WHERE RAY-BOT CAME FROM.

IT'S THE ONLY WAY TO GET HIS MEMORIES BACK.

HOW ARE YOU GOING TO DO THAT?

I'M GOING TO COMPARE HIS OLD CPU WITH THE ONE I JUST INSTALLED.

IS IT OKAY IF I PLUG THIS IN?

THAT WAY WE CAN SEE IF THE MICROCODE ON HIS OLD CPU WAS CHANGED.

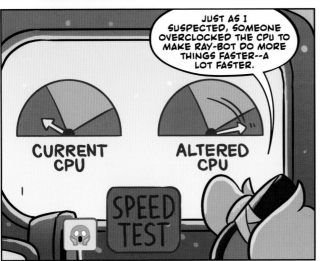

JUST AS I SUSPECTED, SOMEONE OVERCLOCKED THE CPU TO MAKE RAY-BOT DO MORE THINGS FASTER--A LOT FASTER.

CURRENT CPU

ALTERED CPU

SPEED TEST

RAY-BOT'S ORIGINAL MICROCODE HAD SOME SAFETY CHECKS THAT WOULD TURN DOWN THE CLOCK RATE IF HIS CPU WAS OVERHEATING. IN THIS NEW CODE, THOSE CHECKS HAVE BEEN DISABLED.

THE NEW CODE IS PECULIAR...AND FAMILIAR...

69

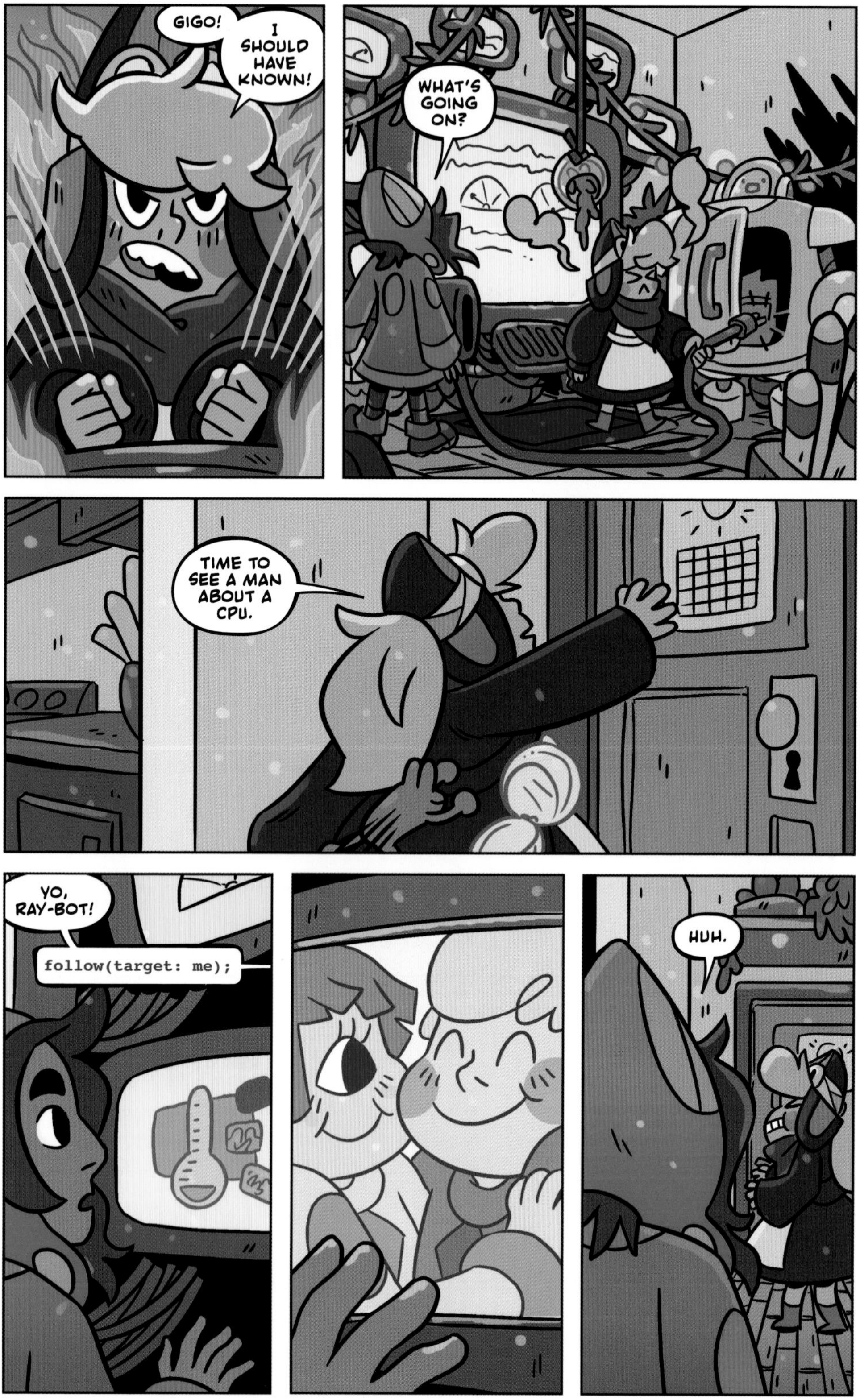

GIGO!
I SHOULD HAVE KNOWN!
WHAT'S GOING ON?
TIME TO SEE A MAN ABOUT A CPU.
YO, RAY-BOT!
follow(target: me);
HUH.

SO WHAT'S THIS "GUY-GO" PLACE WE'RE HEADED TO?

AUTOPIL [ON] GIGO'S WORKSH

GIGO'S NOT A PLACE. HE'S A--

WAIT. ARE YOU STILL FILMING?

TIME TO CUT THE CORD, KID. THIS IS PRIVATE TECHNOMANCER STUFF.

BUT MY FOLLOWERS WILL DEMAND TO KNOW WHAT HAPPENS NEXT!

Oshkesand43: nice

majinsquee: I want to be a technomancer too! #crimesolvers

Idle_hands: I wanna see the robot set something on fire again!

VorpalButterKnife: Who puts flowers on a hovercraft?

LordPancake: Must be fake. Real flowers wouldn't survive.

gothiclol33ta: Where are they going again? #crimesolvers

Nyura: g2g

Drag0nM3ch: hi digits

NinjaKitty: I, for one, welcome our clunker overlords

I CAN'T CUT THEM OFF NOW.

YO, RAY-BOT.

```
grasp(
    digits.
    bodypart.
    shoulders);
```

HEY!

71

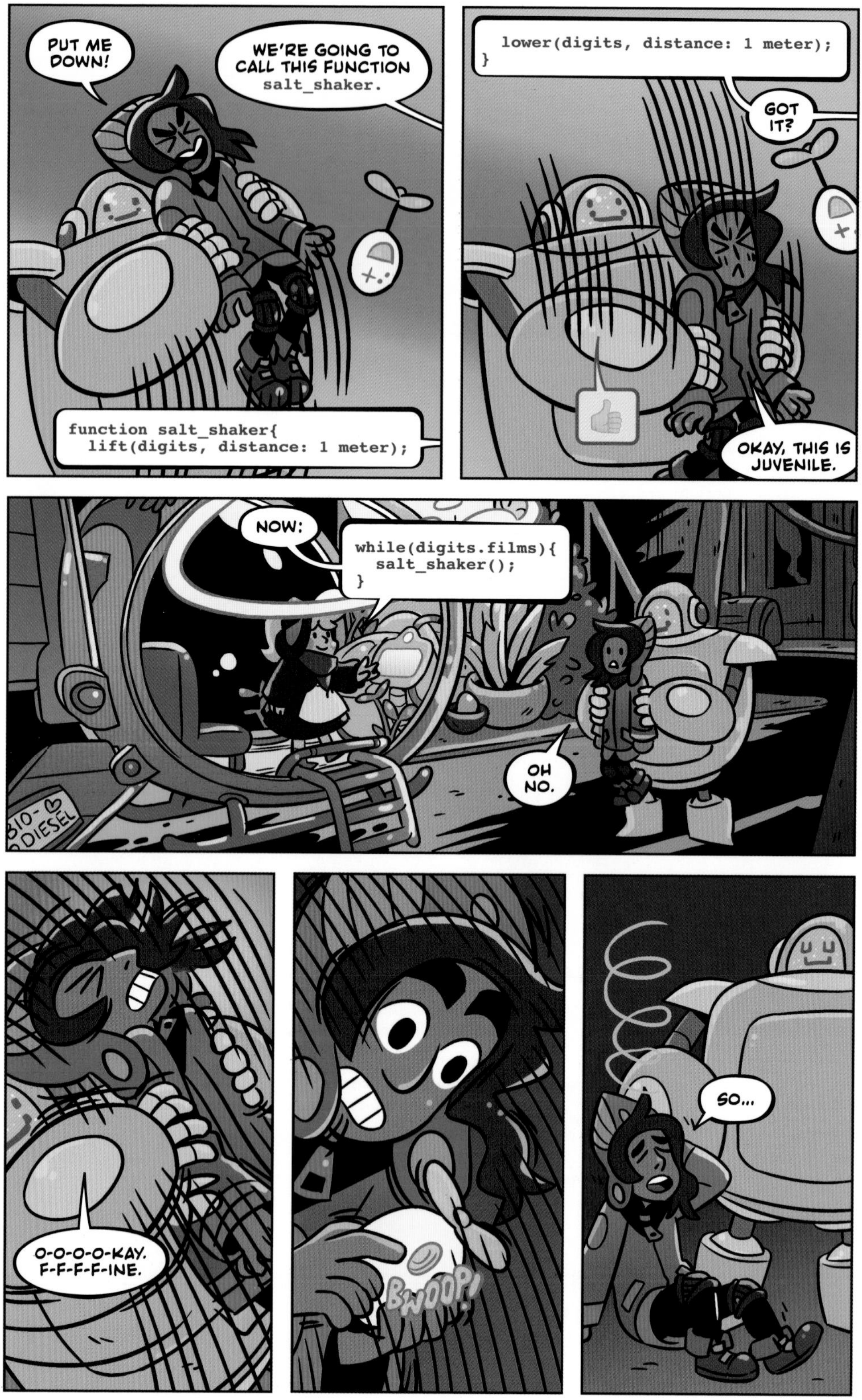
PUT ME DOWN!
WE'RE GOING TO CALL THIS FUNCTION salt_shaker.
function salt_shaker{
lift(digits, distance: 1 meter);
lower(digits, distance: 1 meter);
}
GOT IT?
OKAY, THIS IS JUVENILE.
NOW:
while(digits.films){
salt_shaker();
}
BIO-DIESEL
OH NO.
O-O-O-O-KAY. F-F-F-F-INE.
BWOOP!
SO...

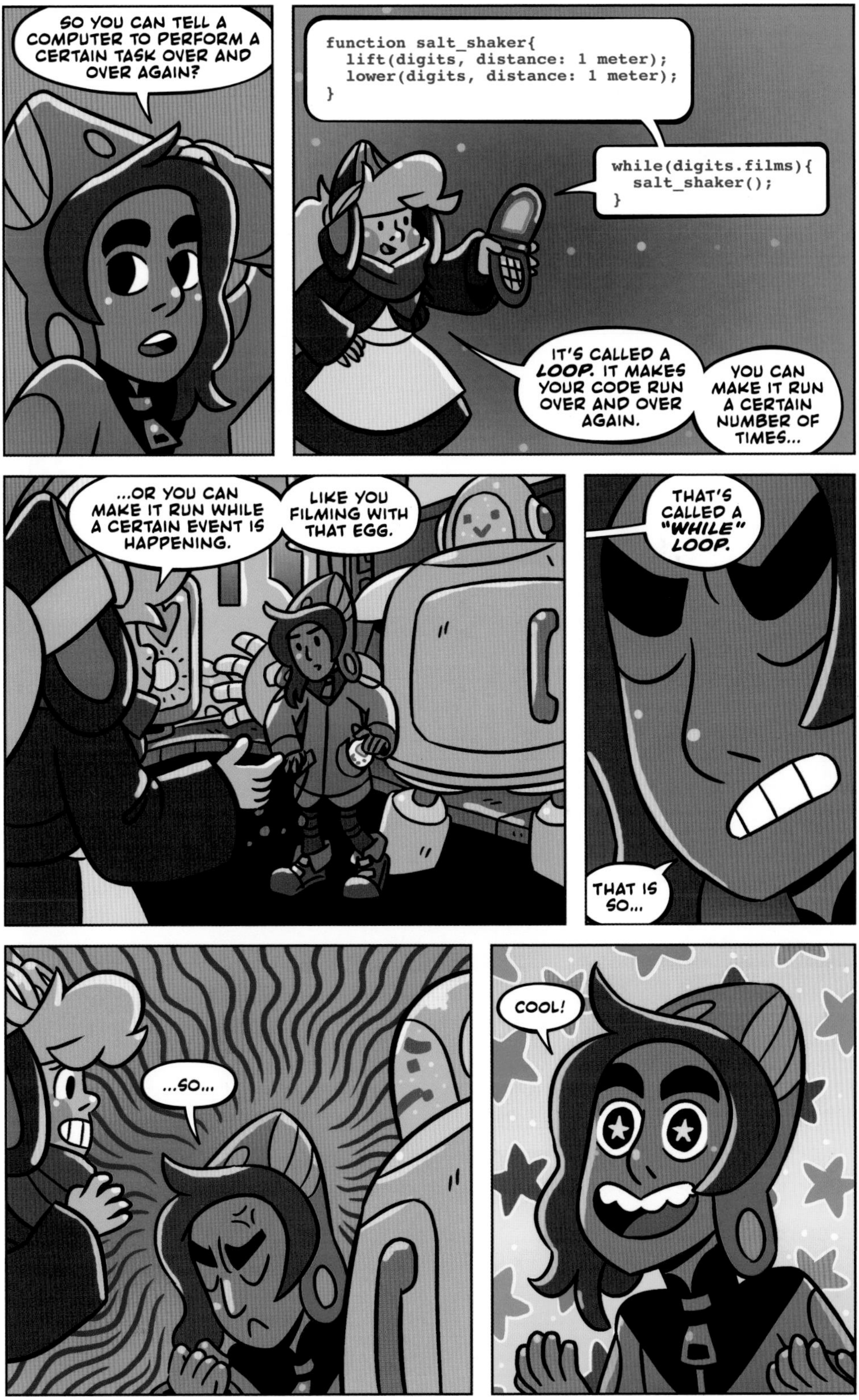
SO YOU CAN TELL A COMPUTER TO PERFORM A CERTAIN TASK OVER AND OVER AGAIN?
function salt_shaker{
lift(digits, distance: 1 meter);
lower(digits, distance: 1 meter);
}
while(digits.films){
salt_shaker();
}
IT'S CALLED A LOOP. IT MAKES YOUR CODE RUN OVER AND OVER AGAIN.
YOU CAN MAKE IT RUN A CERTAIN NUMBER OF TIMES...
...OR YOU CAN MAKE IT RUN WHILE A CERTAIN EVENT IS HAPPENING.
LIKE YOU FILMING WITH THAT EGG.
THAT'S CALLED A "WHILE" LOOP.
THAT IS SO...
...SO...
COOL!

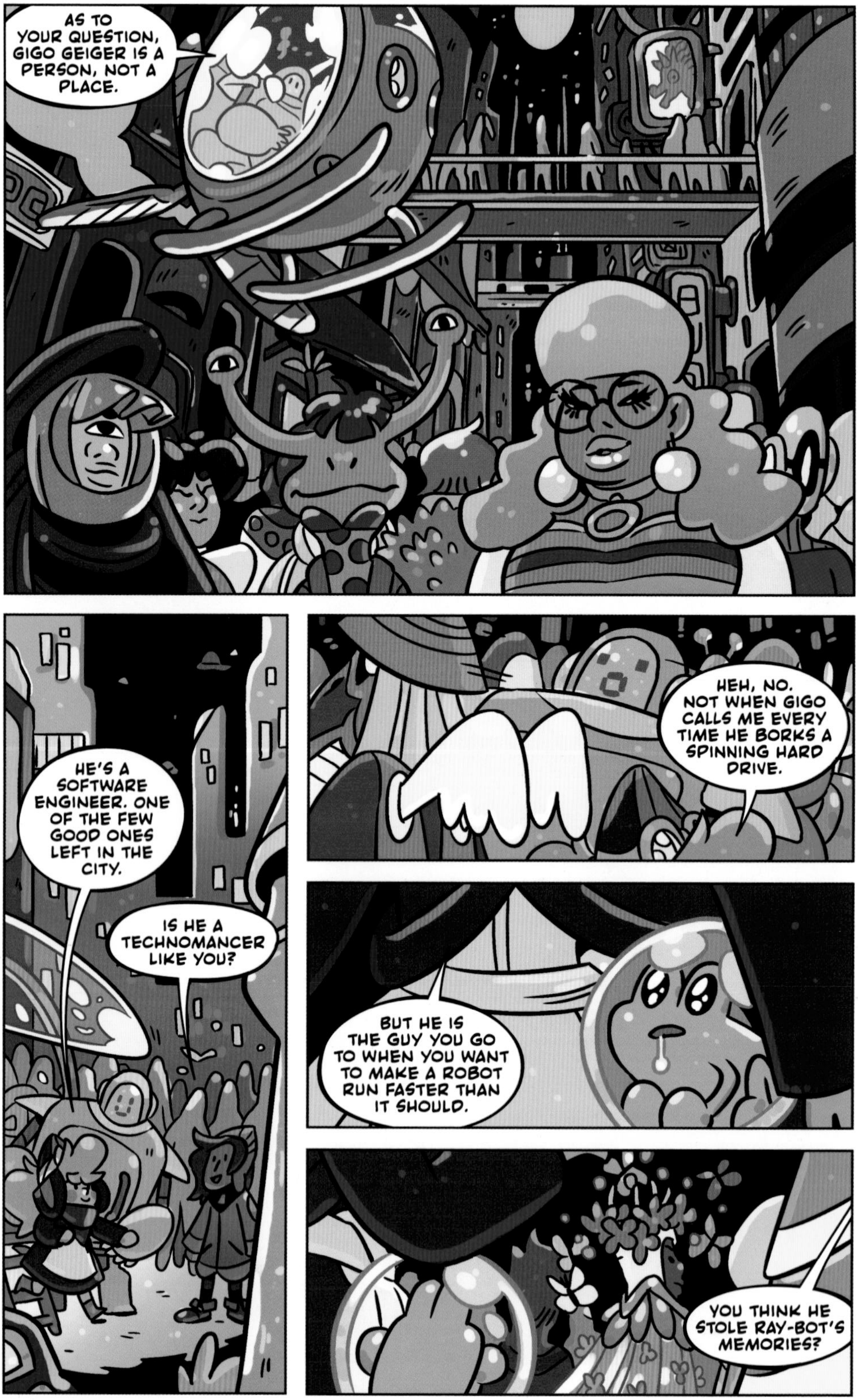
AS TO YOUR QUESTION, GIGO GEIGER IS A PERSON, NOT A PLACE.
HE'S A SOFTWARE ENGINEER. ONE OF THE FEW GOOD ONES LEFT IN THE CITY.
IS HE A TECHNOMANCER LIKE YOU?
HEH, NO. NOT WHEN GIGO CALLS ME EVERY TIME HE BORKS A SPINNING HARD DRIVE.
BUT HE IS THE GUY YOU GO TO WHEN YOU WANT TO MAKE A ROBOT RUN FASTER THAN IT SHOULD.
YOU THINK HE STOLE RAY-BOT'S MEMORIES?

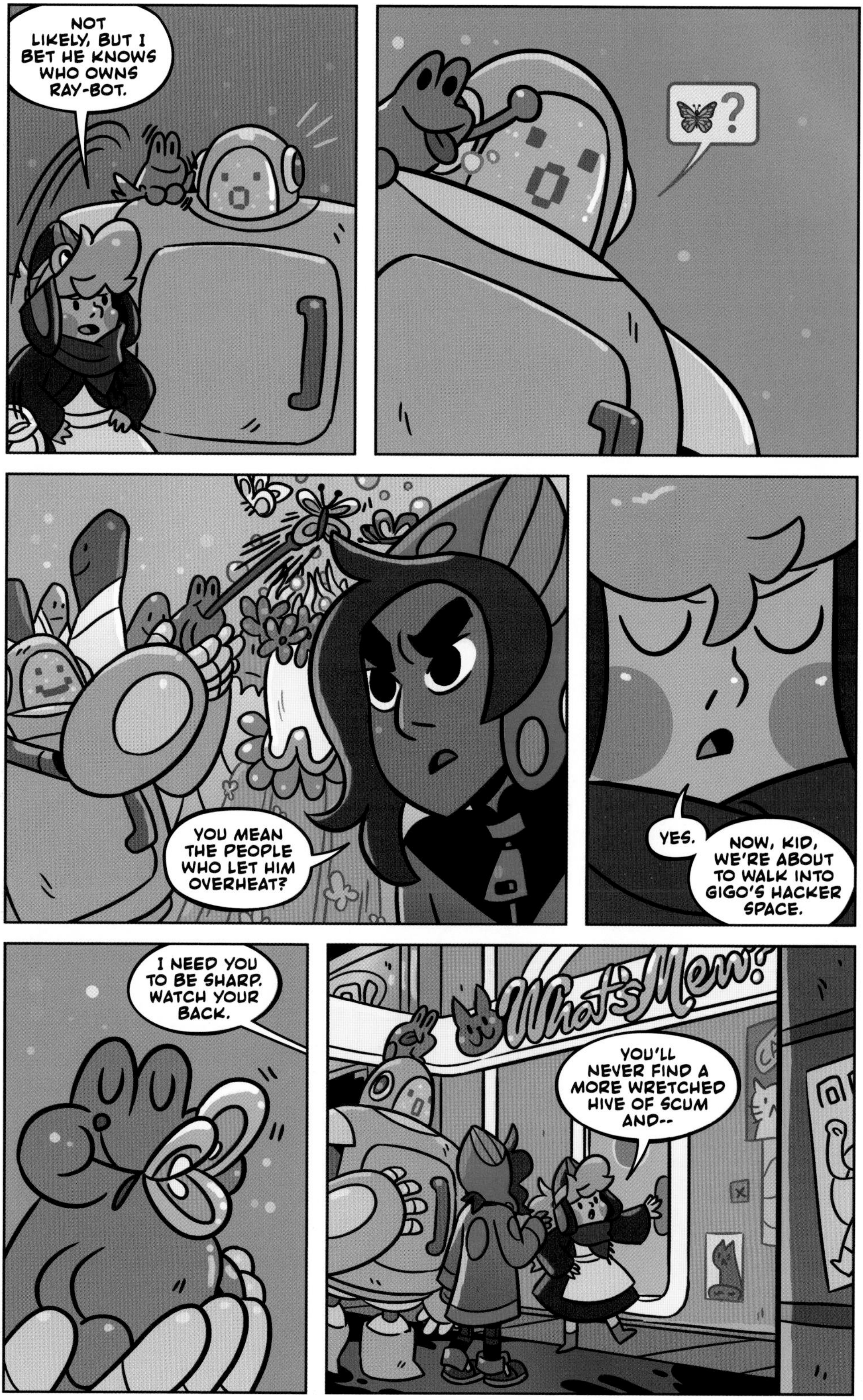
NOT LIKELY, BUT I BET HE KNOWS WHO OWNS RAY-BOT.
?
YOU MEAN THE PEOPLE WHO LET HIM OVERHEAT?
YES.
NOW, KID, WE'RE ABOUT TO WALK INTO GIGO'S HACKER SPACE.
I NEED YOU TO BE SHARP. WATCH YOUR BACK.
What's Mew?
YOU'LL NEVER FIND A MORE WRETCHED HIVE OF SCUM AND--

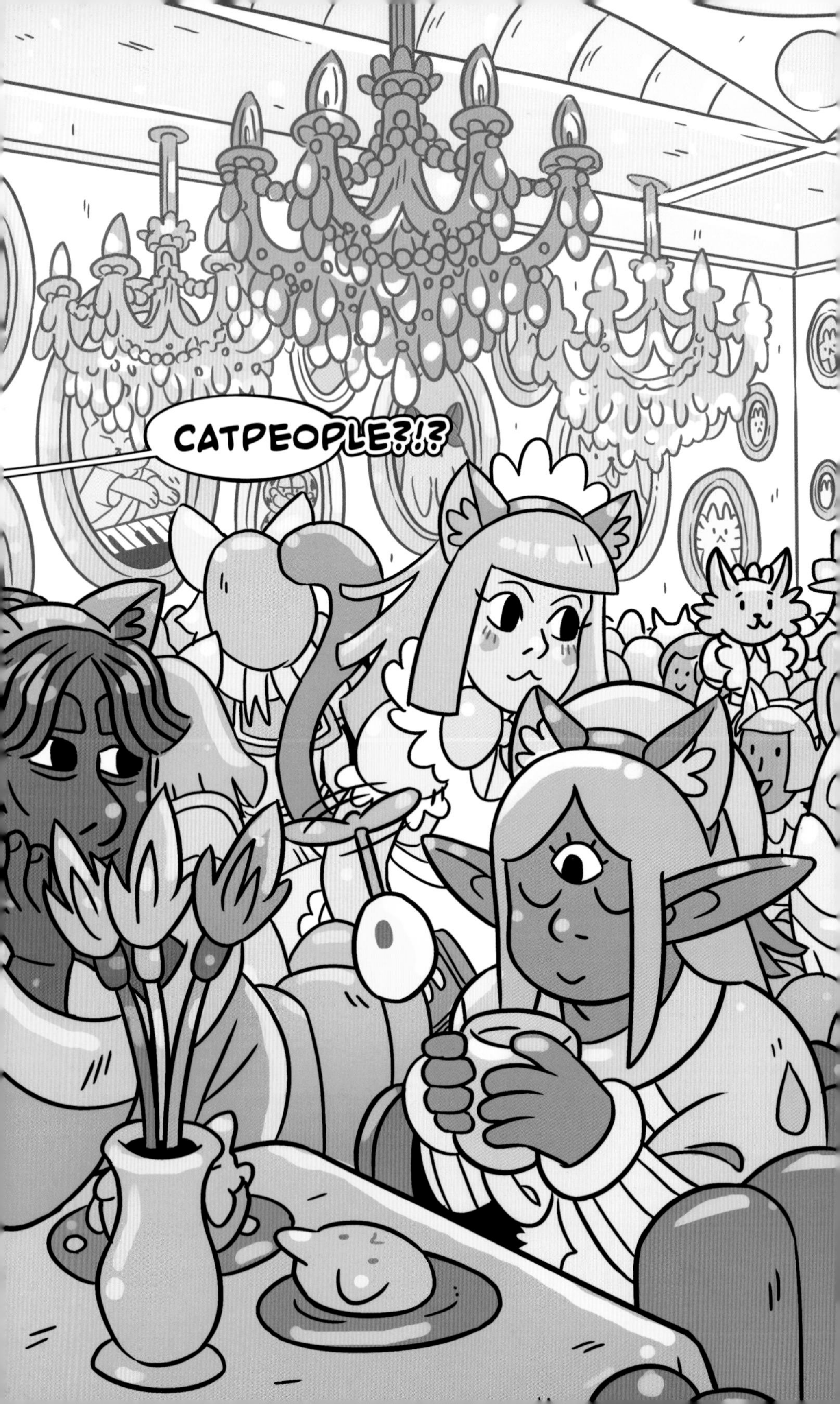
CATPEOPLE?!?

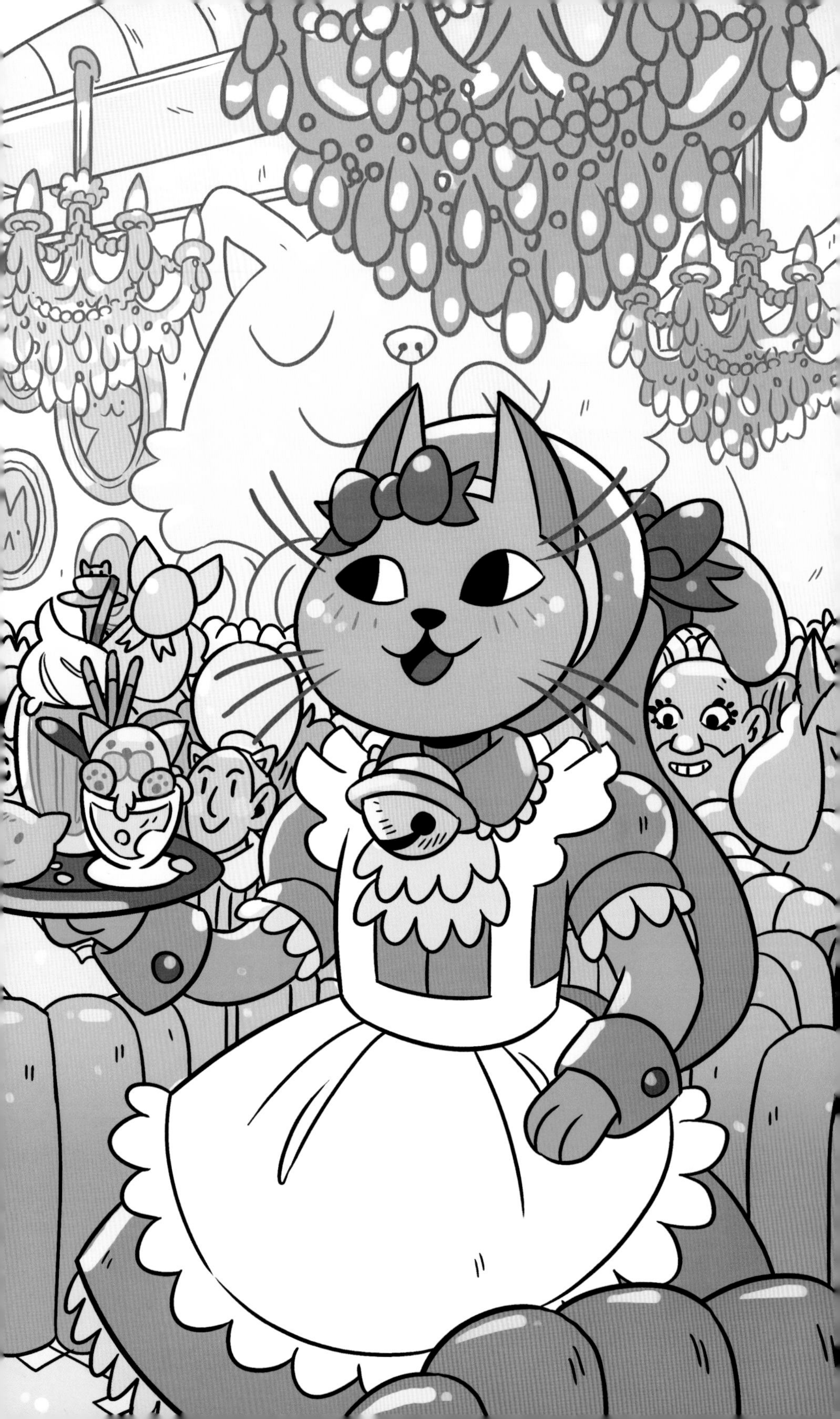

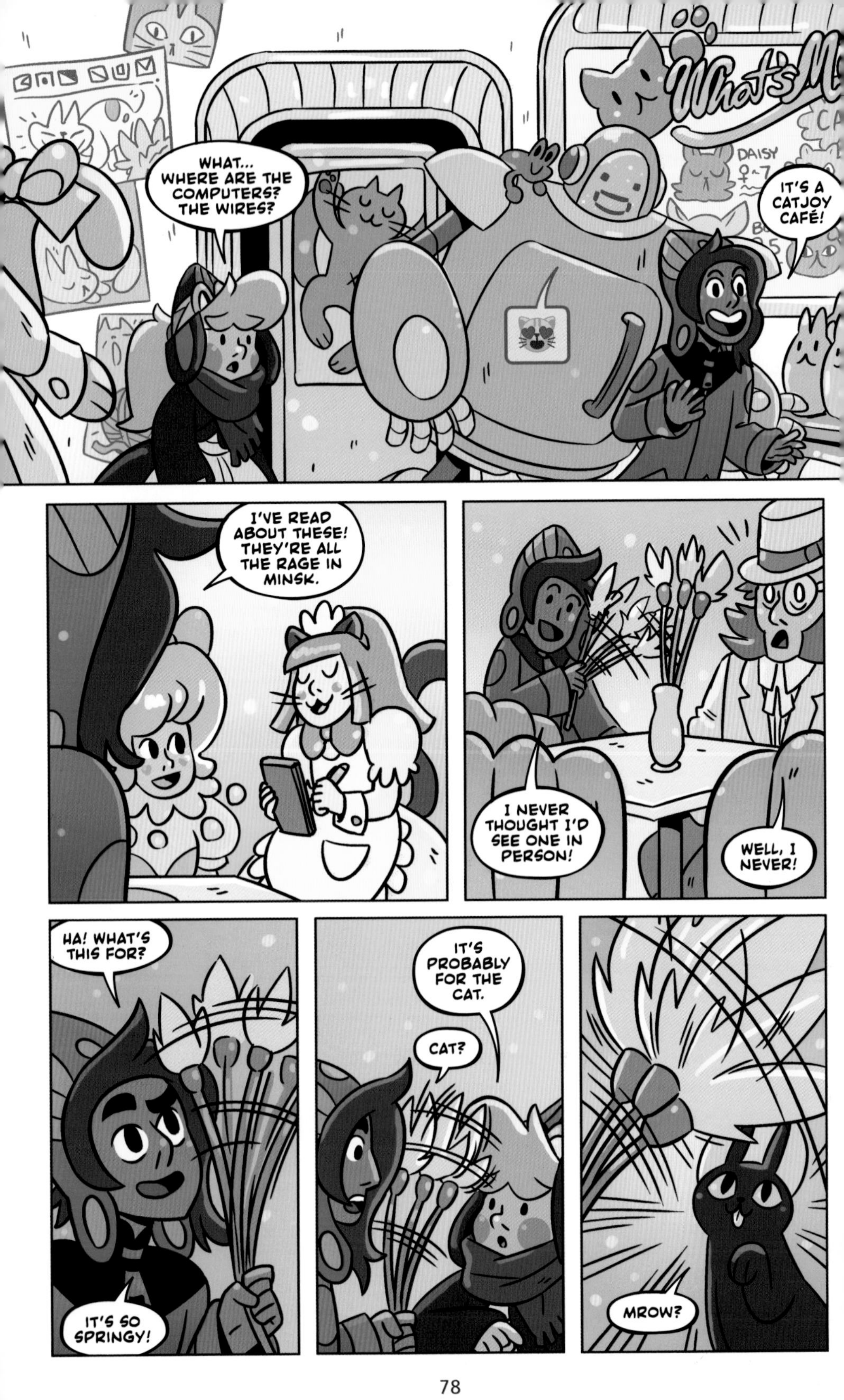
WHAT... WHERE ARE THE COMPUTERS? THE WIRES?
IT'S A CATJOY CAFÉ!
DAISY
I'VE READ ABOUT THESE! THEY'RE ALL THE RAGE IN MINSK.
I NEVER THOUGHT I'D SEE ONE IN PERSON!
WELL, I NEVER!
HA! WHAT'S THIS FOR?
IT'S SO SPRINGY!
IT'S PROBABLY FOR THE CAT.
CAT?
MROW?

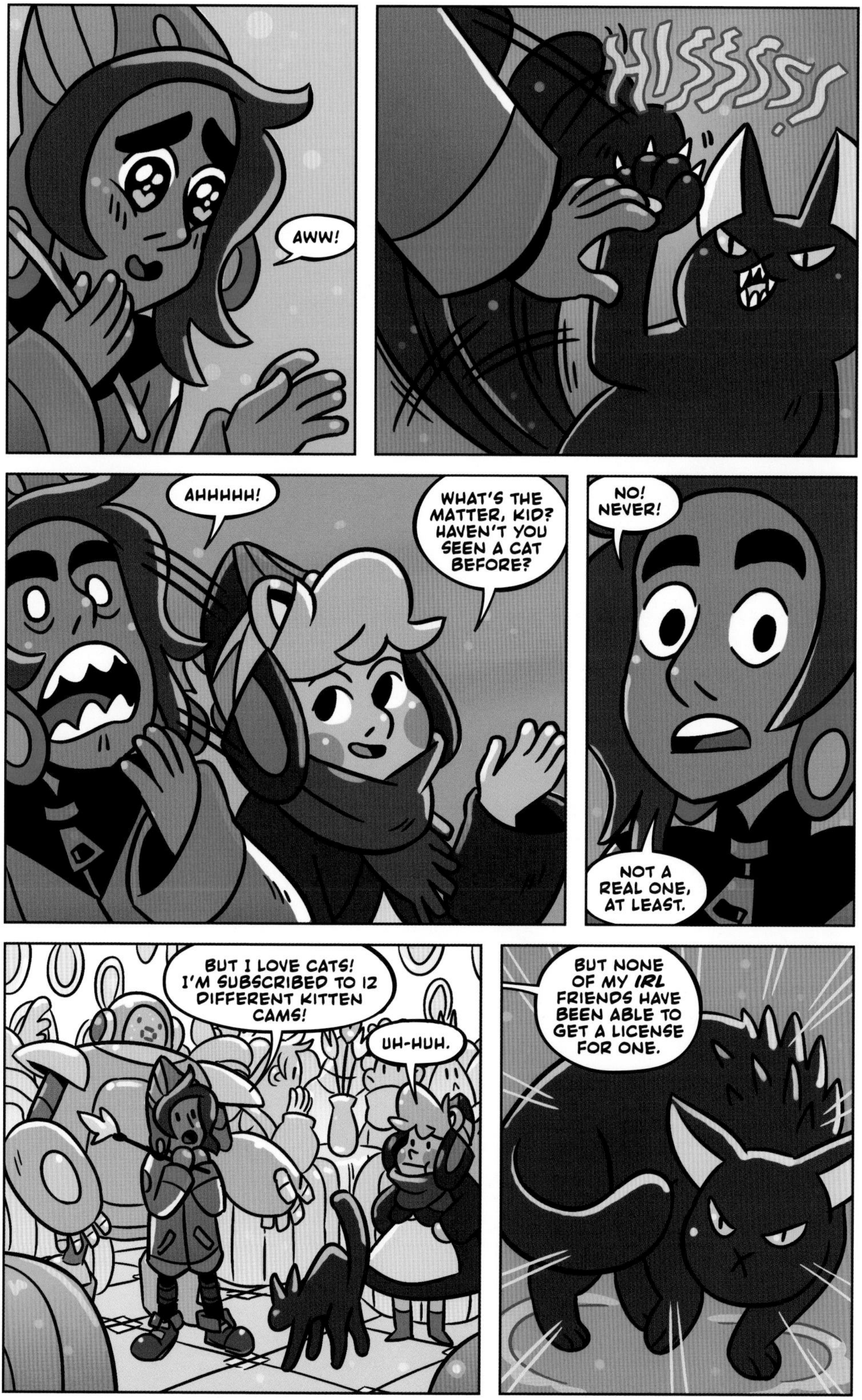
AWW!
HISSSSS
AHHHHHH!
WHAT'S THE MATTER, KID? HAVEN'T YOU SEEN A CAT BEFORE?
NO! NEVER!
NOT A REAL ONE, AT LEAST.
BUT I LOVE CATS! I'M SUBSCRIBED TO 12 DIFFERENT KITTEN CAMS!
UH-HUH.
BUT NONE OF MY *IRL* FRIENDS HAVE BEEN ABLE TO GET A LICENSE FOR ONE.

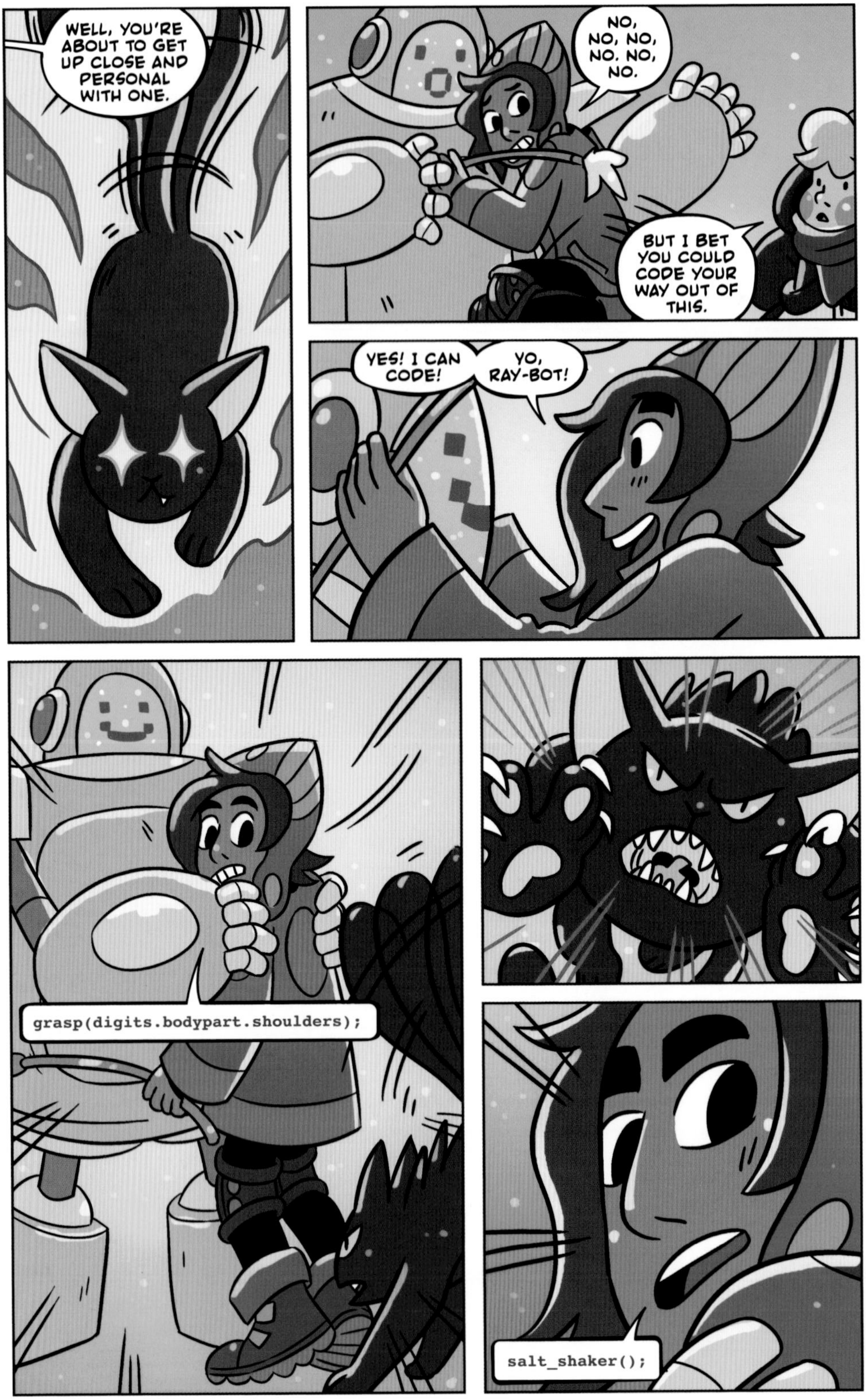
WELL, YOU'RE ABOUT TO GET UP CLOSE AND PERSONAL WITH ONE.
NO, NO, NO, NO. NO, NO.
BUT I BET YOU COULD CODE YOUR WAY OUT OF THIS.
YES! I CAN CODE!
YO, RAY-BOT!
grasp(digits.bodypart.shoulders);
salt_shaker();

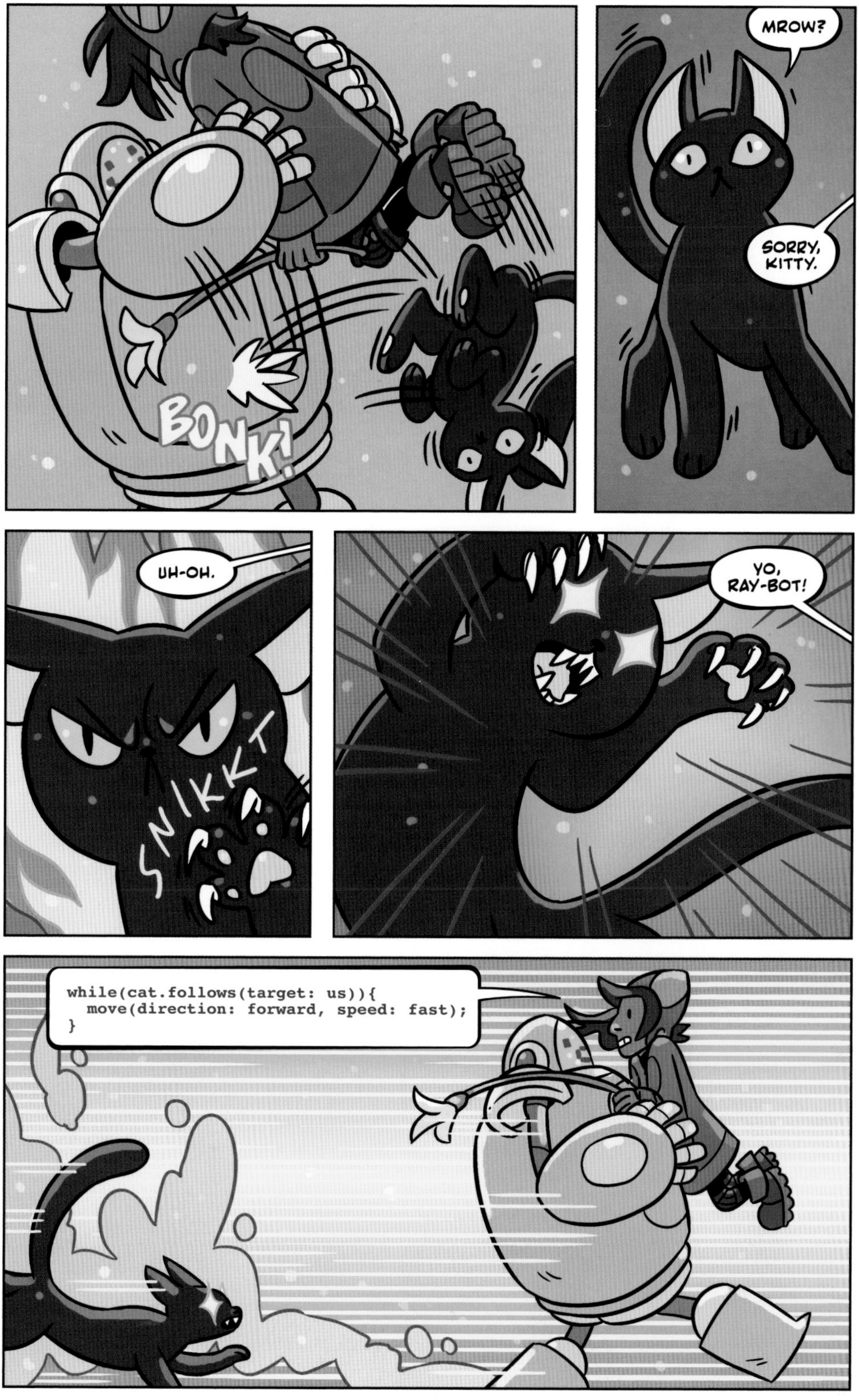
BONK!
MROW?
SORRY, KITTY.
UH-OH.
SNIKKT
YO, RAY-BOT!
while(cat.follows(target: us)){
  move(direction: forward, speed: fast);
}

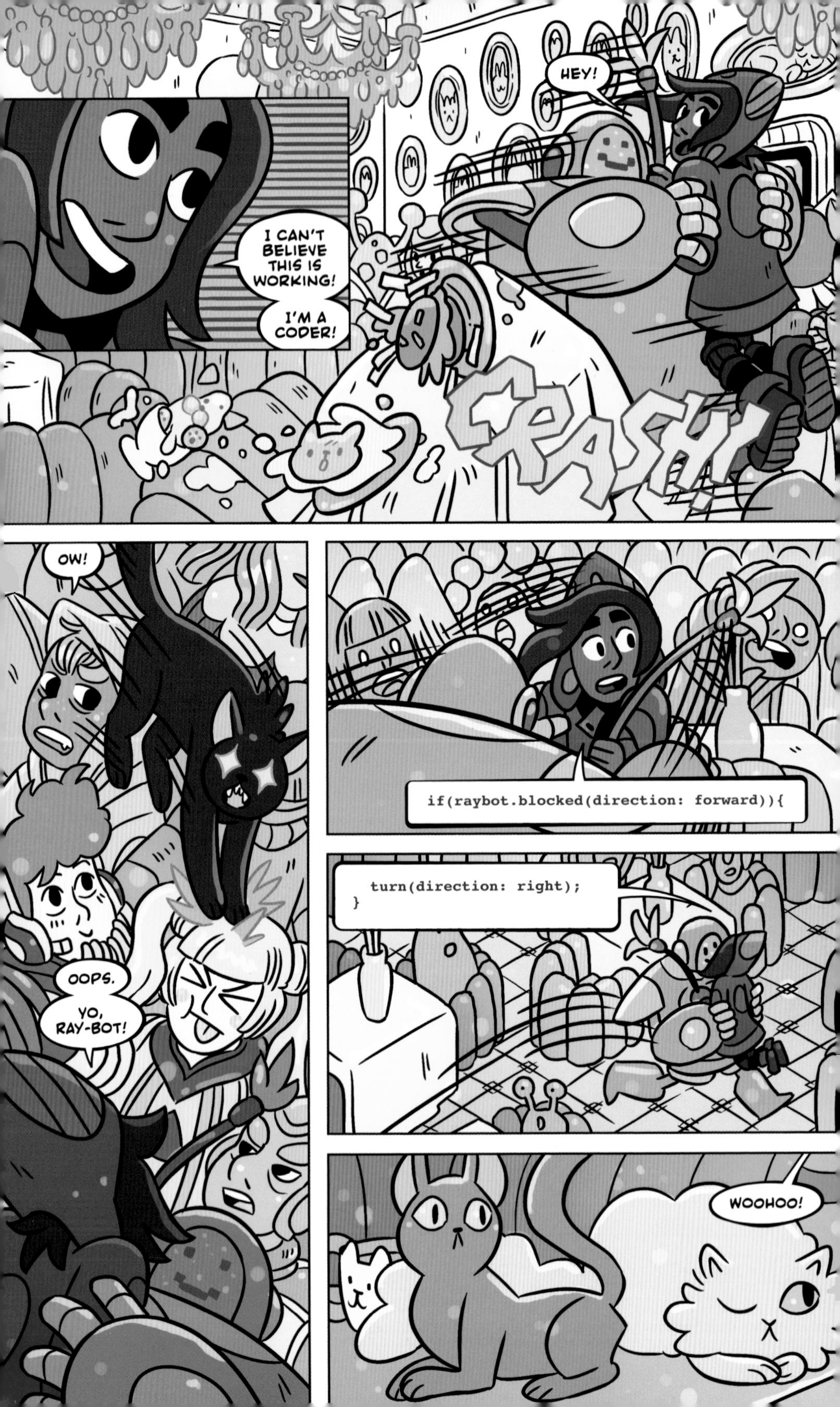
HEY!
I CAN'T BELIEVE THIS IS WORKING!
I'M A CODER!
CRASH!
OW!
OOPS.
YO, RAY-BOT!
if(raybot.blocked(direction: forward)){
turn(direction: right);
}
WOOHOO!

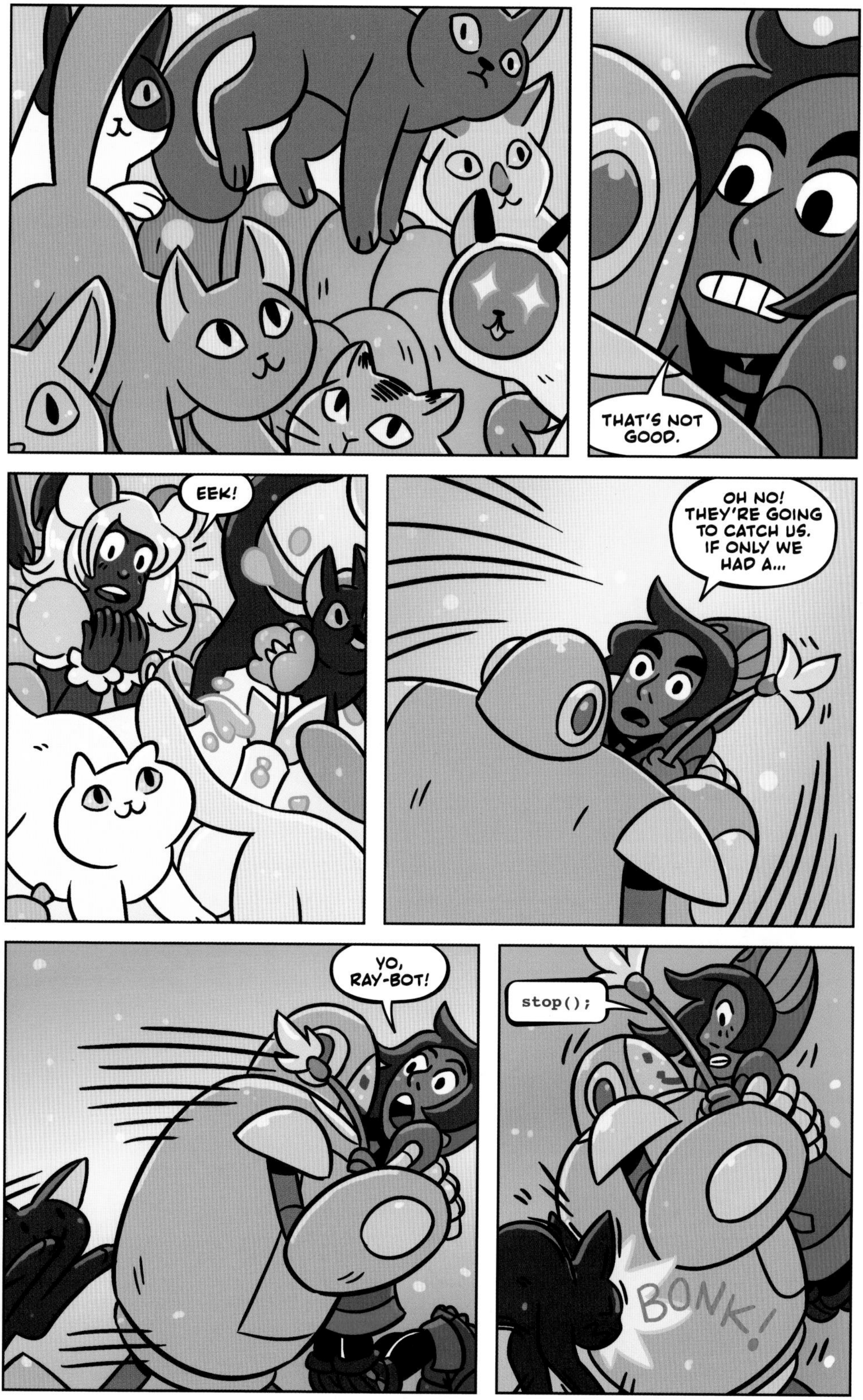
THAT'S NOT GOOD.
EEK!
OH NO! THEY'RE GOING TO CATCH US. IF ONLY WE HAD A...
YO, RAY-BOT!
stop();
BONK!

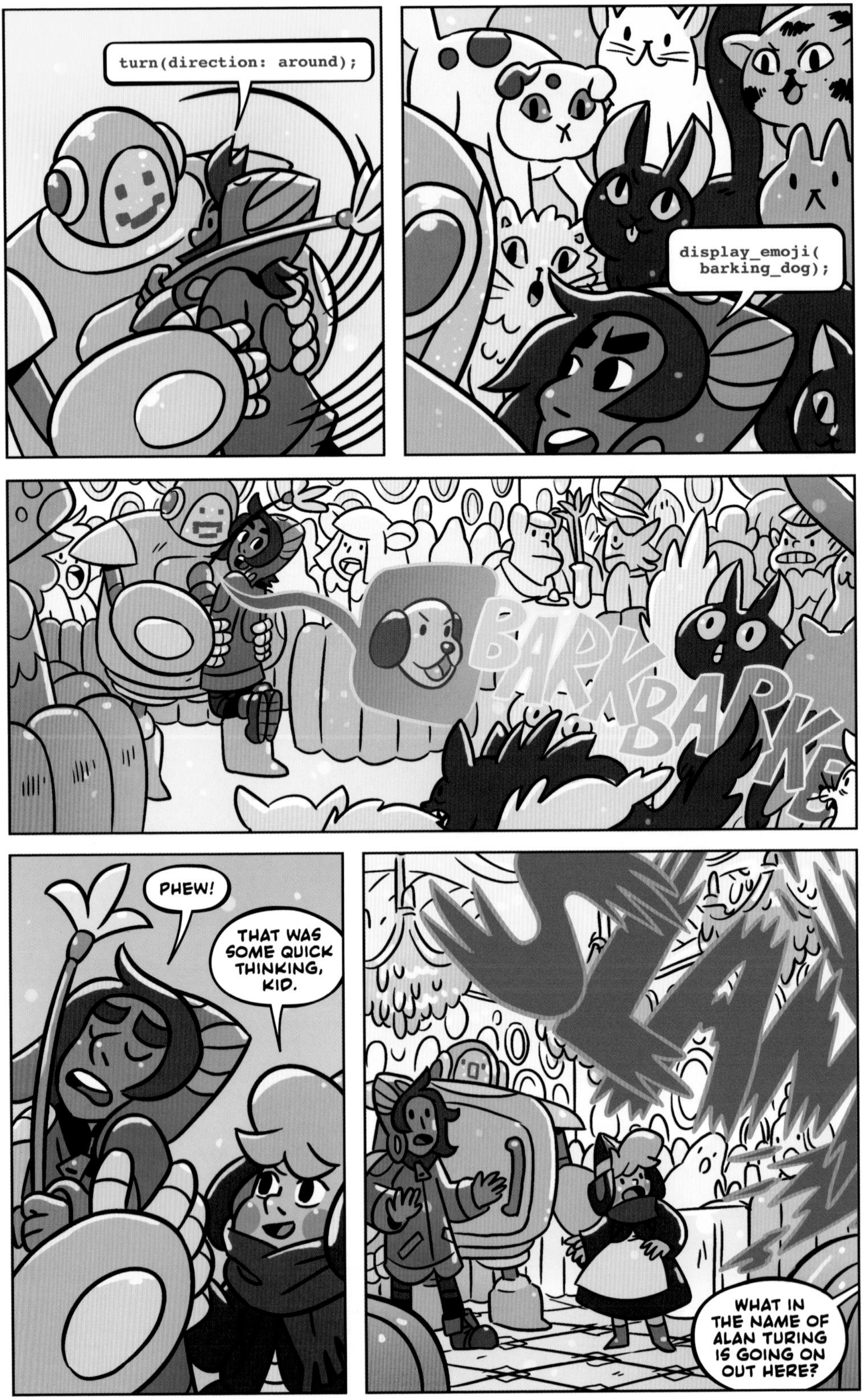
turn(direction: around);
display_emoji(barking_dog);
BARK BARK BARK
PHEW!
THAT WAS SOME QUICK THINKING, KID.
SLAM
WHAT IN THE NAME OF ALAN TURING IS GOING ON OUT HERE?

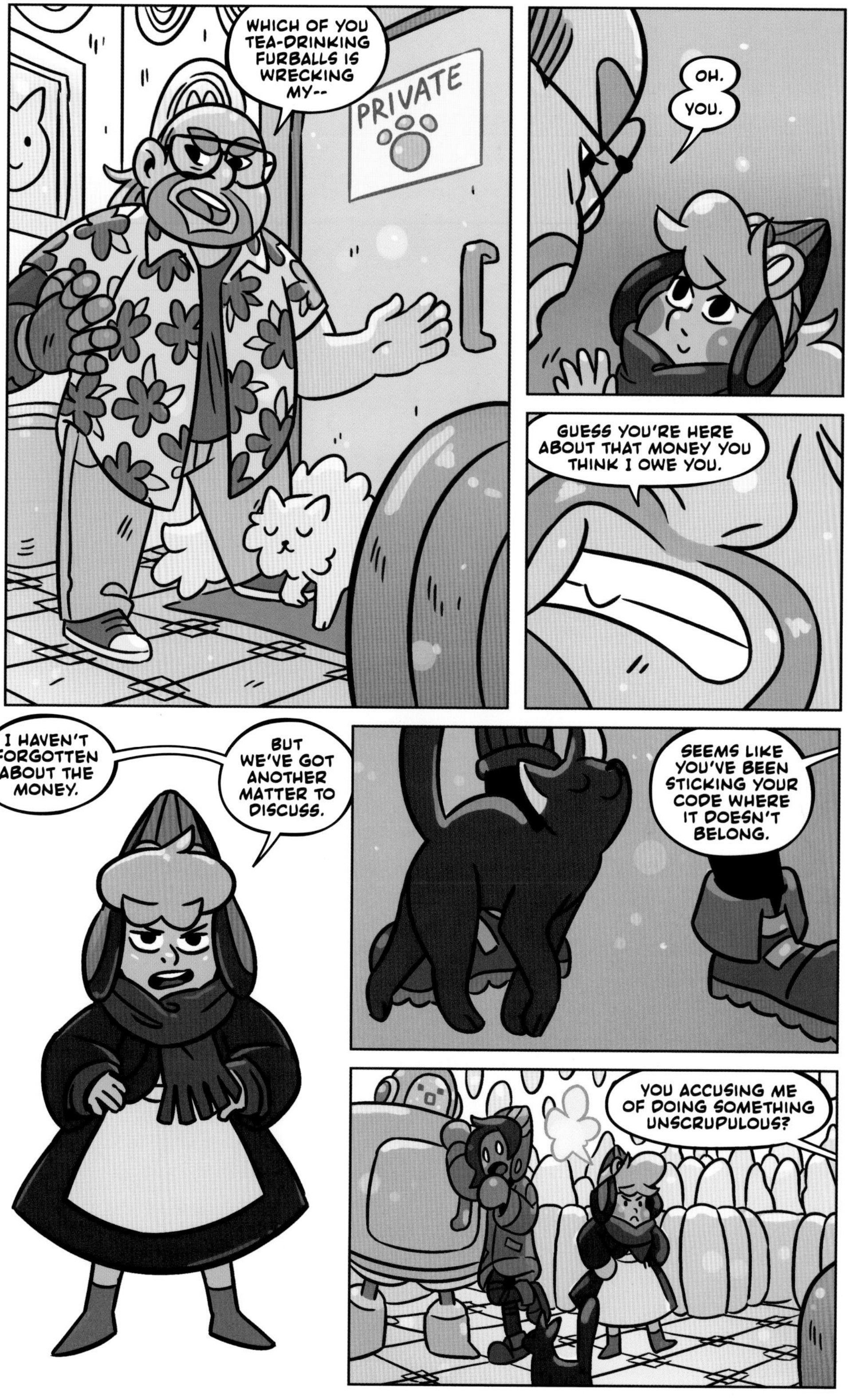
WHICH OF YOU TEA-DRINKING FURBALLS IS WRECKING MY--
PRIVATE
OH.
YOU.
GUESS YOU'RE HERE ABOUT THAT MONEY YOU THINK I OWE YOU.
I HAVEN'T FORGOTTEN ABOUT THE MONEY.
BUT WE'VE GOT ANOTHER MATTER TO DISCUSS.
SEEMS LIKE YOU'VE BEEN STICKING YOUR CODE WHERE IT DOESN'T BELONG.
YOU ACCUSING ME OF DOING SOMETHING UNSCRUPULOUS?

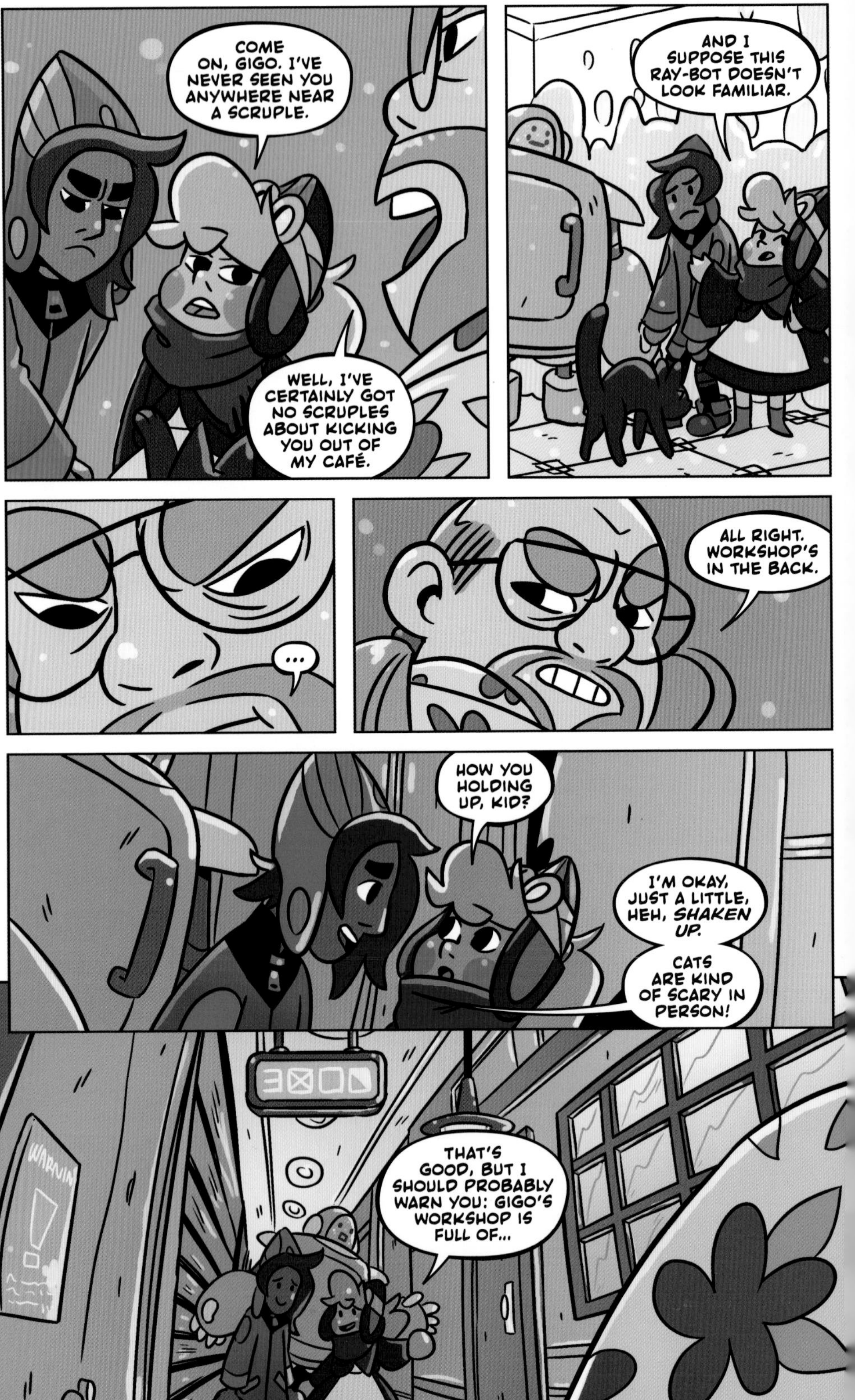
COME ON, GIGO. I'VE NEVER SEEN YOU ANYWHERE NEAR A SCRUPLE.
WELL, I'VE CERTAINLY GOT NO SCRUPLES ABOUT KICKING YOU OUT OF MY CAFÉ.
AND I SUPPOSE THIS RAY-BOT DOESN'T LOOK FAMILIAR.
...
ALL RIGHT. WORKSHOP'S IN THE BACK.
HOW YOU HOLDING UP, KID?
I'M OKAY, JUST A LITTLE, HEH, *SHAKEN UP.*
CATS ARE KIND OF SCARY IN PERSON!
THAT'S GOOD, BUT I SHOULD PROBABLY WARN YOU: GIGO'S WORKSHOP IS FULL OF...
WARNIN

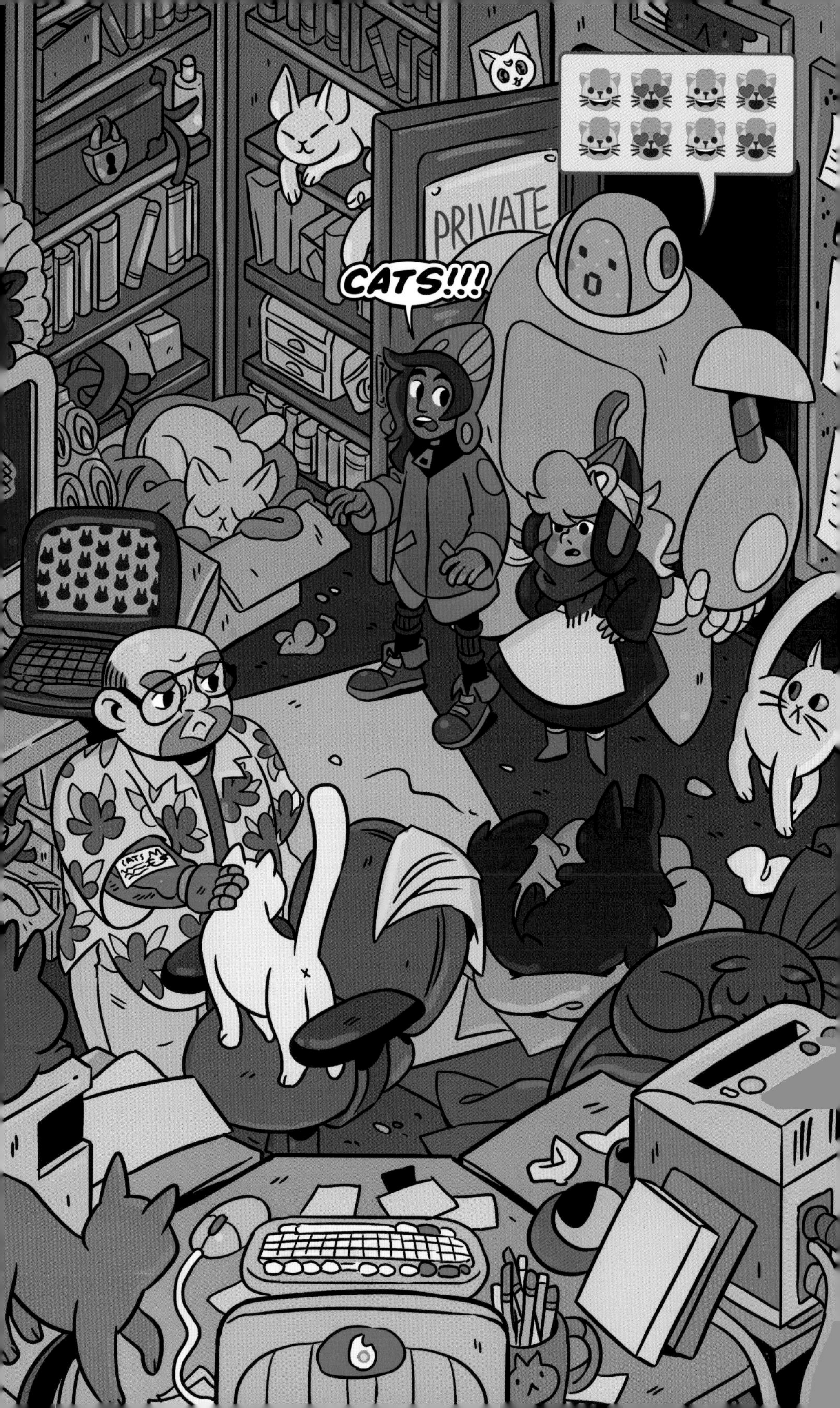
PRIVATE
CATS!!!
CATS

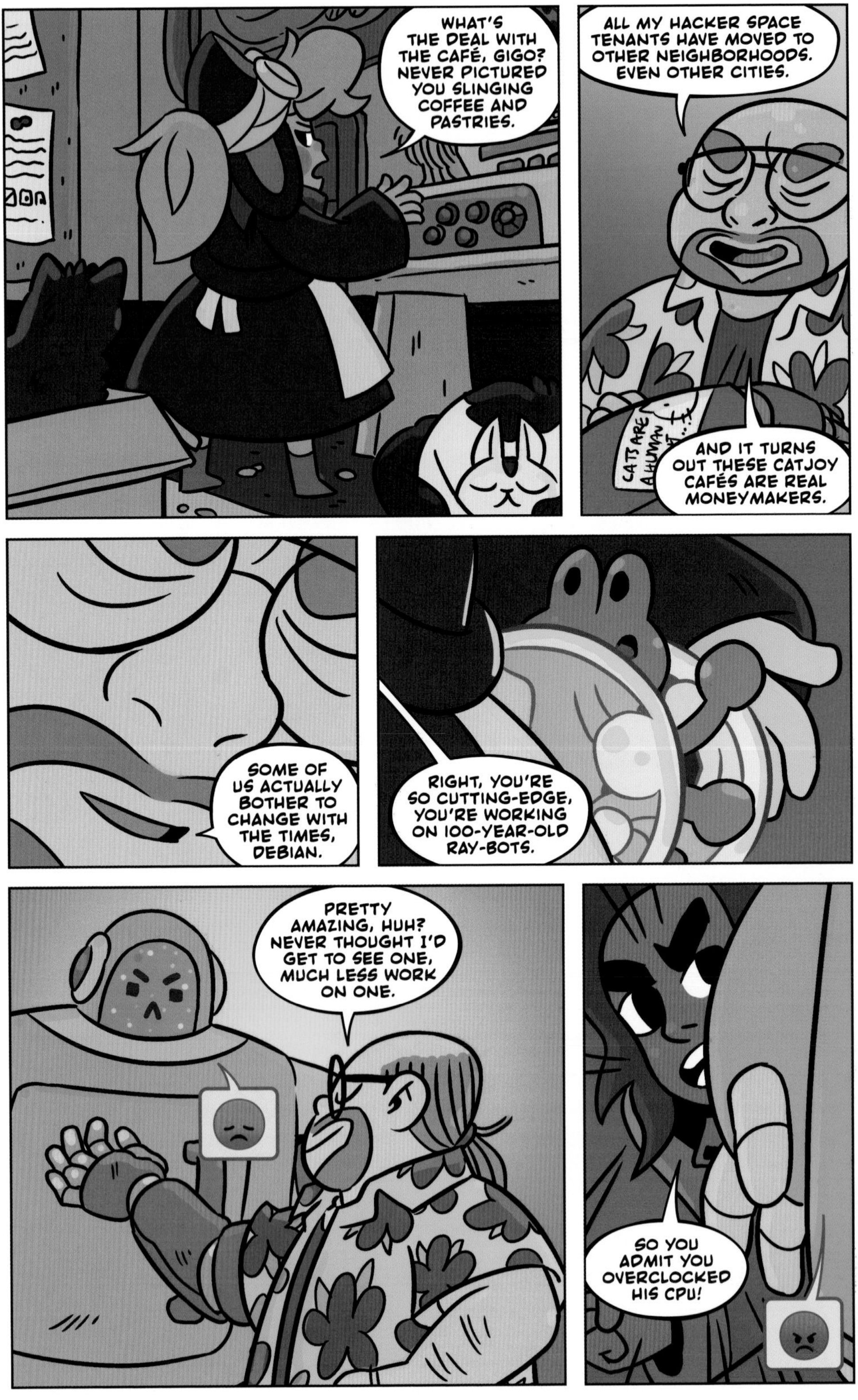
WHAT'S THE DEAL WITH THE CAFÉ, GIGO? NEVER PICTURED YOU SLINGING COFFEE AND PASTRIES.
ALL MY HACKER SPACE TENANTS HAVE MOVED TO OTHER NEIGHBORHOODS. EVEN OTHER CITIES.
AND IT TURNS OUT THESE CATJOY CAFÉS ARE REAL MONEYMAKERS.
SOME OF US ACTUALLY BOTHER TO CHANGE WITH THE TIMES, DEBIAN.
RIGHT, YOU'RE SO CUTTING-EDGE, YOU'RE WORKING ON 100-YEAR-OLD RAY-BOTS.
PRETTY AMAZING, HUH? NEVER THOUGHT I'D GET TO SEE ONE, MUCH LESS WORK ON ONE.
SO YOU ADMIT YOU OVERCLOCKED HIS CPU!

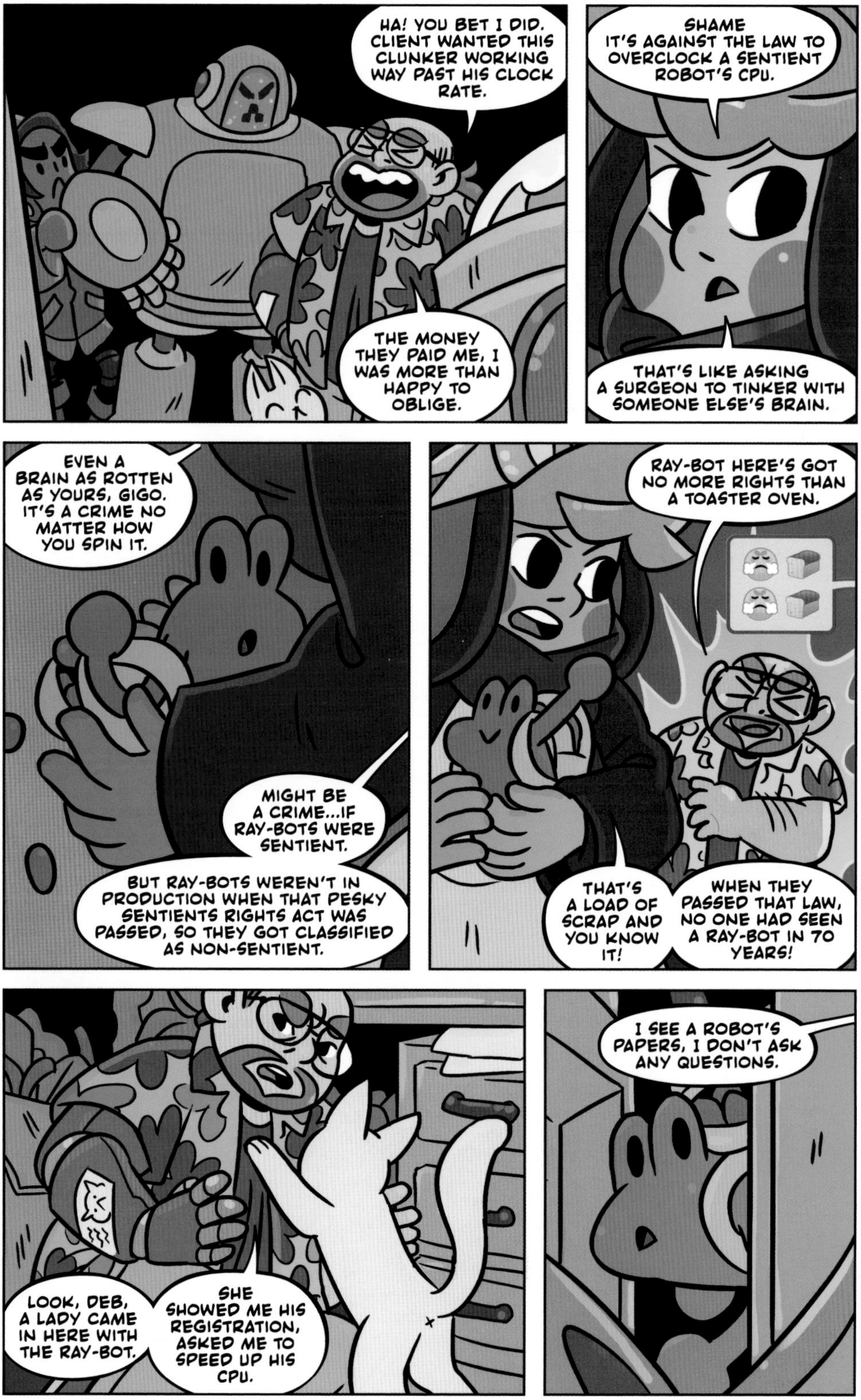
HA! YOU BET I DID. CLIENT WANTED THIS CLUNKER WORKING WAY PAST HIS CLOCK RATE.
THE MONEY THEY PAID ME, I WAS MORE THAN HAPPY TO OBLIGE.
SHAME IT'S AGAINST THE LAW TO OVERCLOCK A SENTIENT ROBOT'S CPU.
THAT'S LIKE ASKING A SURGEON TO TINKER WITH SOMEONE ELSE'S BRAIN.
EVEN A BRAIN AS ROTTEN AS YOURS, GIGO. IT'S A CRIME NO MATTER HOW YOU SPIN IT.
MIGHT BE A CRIME...IF RAY-BOTS WERE SENTIENT.
BUT RAY-BOTS WEREN'T IN PRODUCTION WHEN THAT PESKY SENTIENTS RIGHTS ACT WAS PASSED, SO THEY GOT CLASSIFIED AS NON-SENTIENT.
RAY-BOT HERE'S GOT NO MORE RIGHTS THAN A TOASTER OVEN.
THAT'S A LOAD OF SCRAP AND YOU KNOW IT!
WHEN THEY PASSED THAT LAW, NO ONE HAD SEEN A RAY-BOT IN 70 YEARS!
LOOK, DEB, A LADY CAME IN HERE WITH THE RAY-BOT.
SHE SHOWED ME HIS REGISTRATION, ASKED ME TO SPEED UP HIS CPU.
I SEE A ROBOT'S PAPERS, I DON'T ASK ANY QUESTIONS.

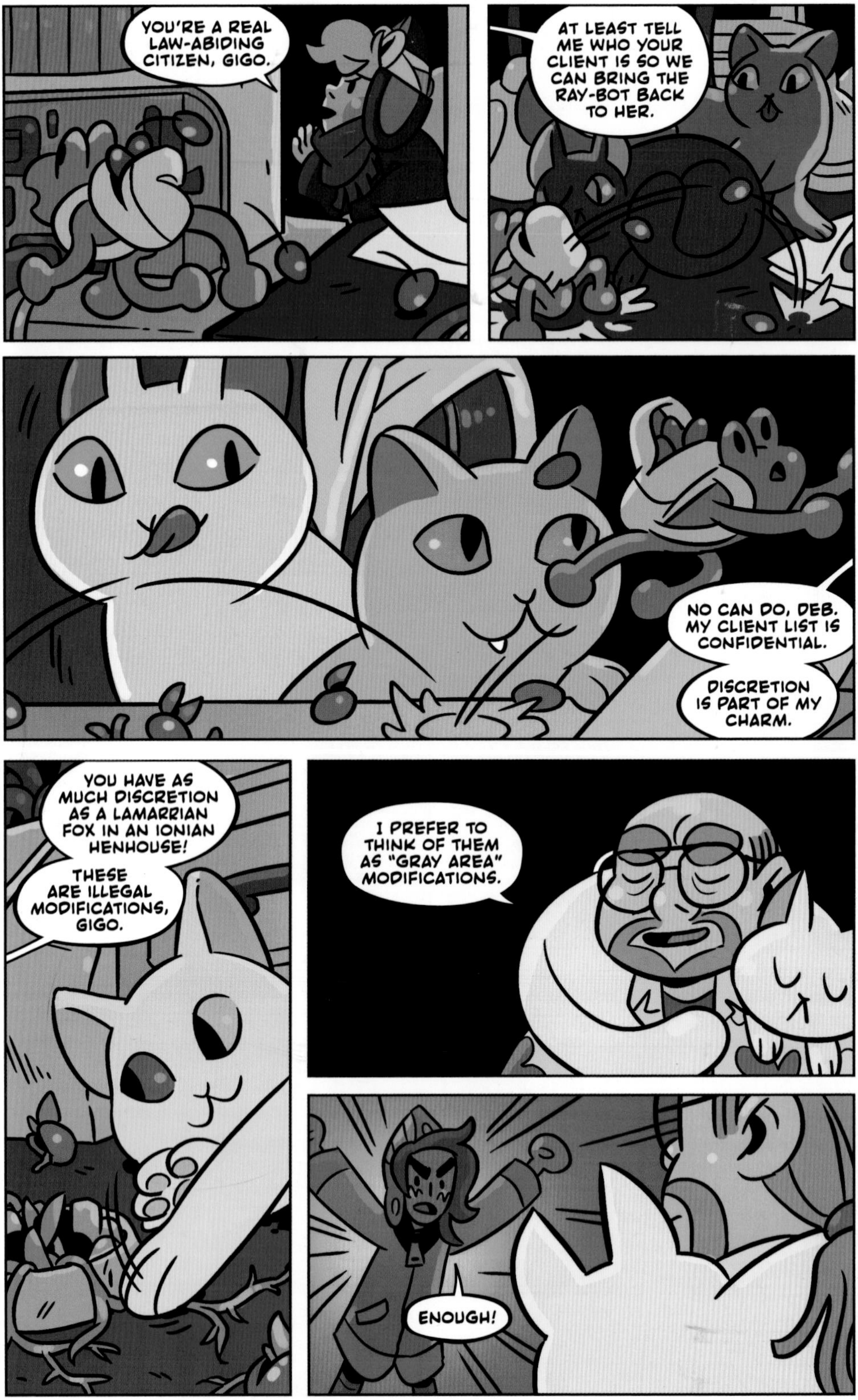
YOU'RE A REAL LAW-ABIDING CITIZEN, GIGO.
AT LEAST TELL ME WHO YOUR CLIENT IS SO WE CAN BRING THE RAY-BOT BACK TO HER.
NO CAN DO, DEB. MY CLIENT LIST IS CONFIDENTIAL.
DISCRETION IS PART OF MY CHARM.
YOU HAVE AS MUCH DISCRETION AS A LAMARRIAN FOX IN AN IONIAN HENHOUSE!
THESE ARE ILLEGAL MODIFICATIONS, GIGO.
I PREFER TO THINK OF THEM AS "GRAY AREA" MODIFICATIONS.
ENOUGH!

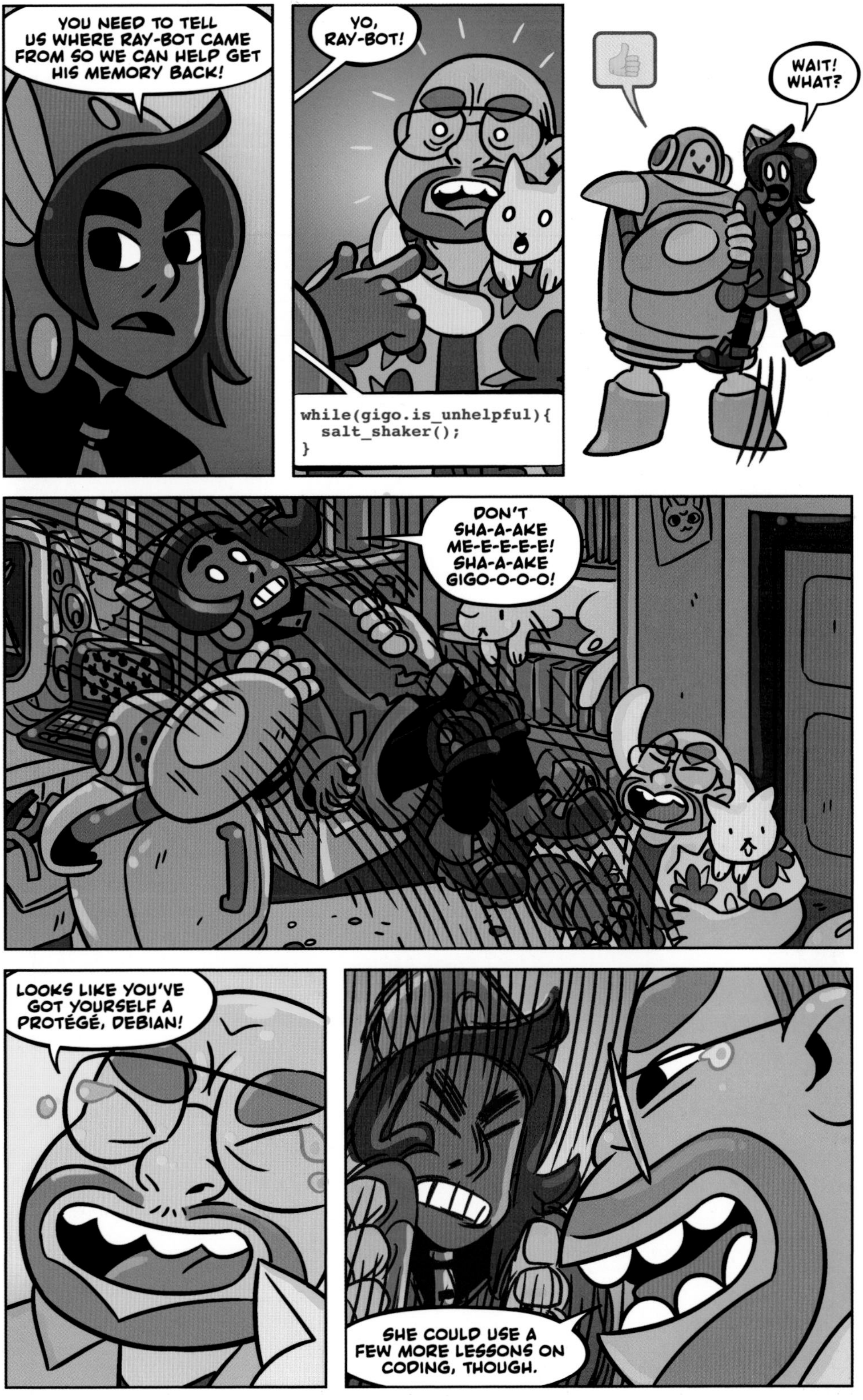
YOU NEED TO TELL US WHERE RAY-BOT CAME FROM SO WE CAN HELP GET HIS MEMORY BACK!
YO, RAY-BOT!
while(gigo.is_unhelpful){
salt_shaker();
}
WAIT! WHAT?
DON'T SHA-A-AKE ME-E-E-E-E! SHA-A-AKE GIGO-O-O-O!
LOOKS LIKE YOU'VE GOT YOURSELF A PROTÉGÉ, DEBIAN!
SHE COULD USE A FEW MORE LESSONS ON CODING, THOUGH.

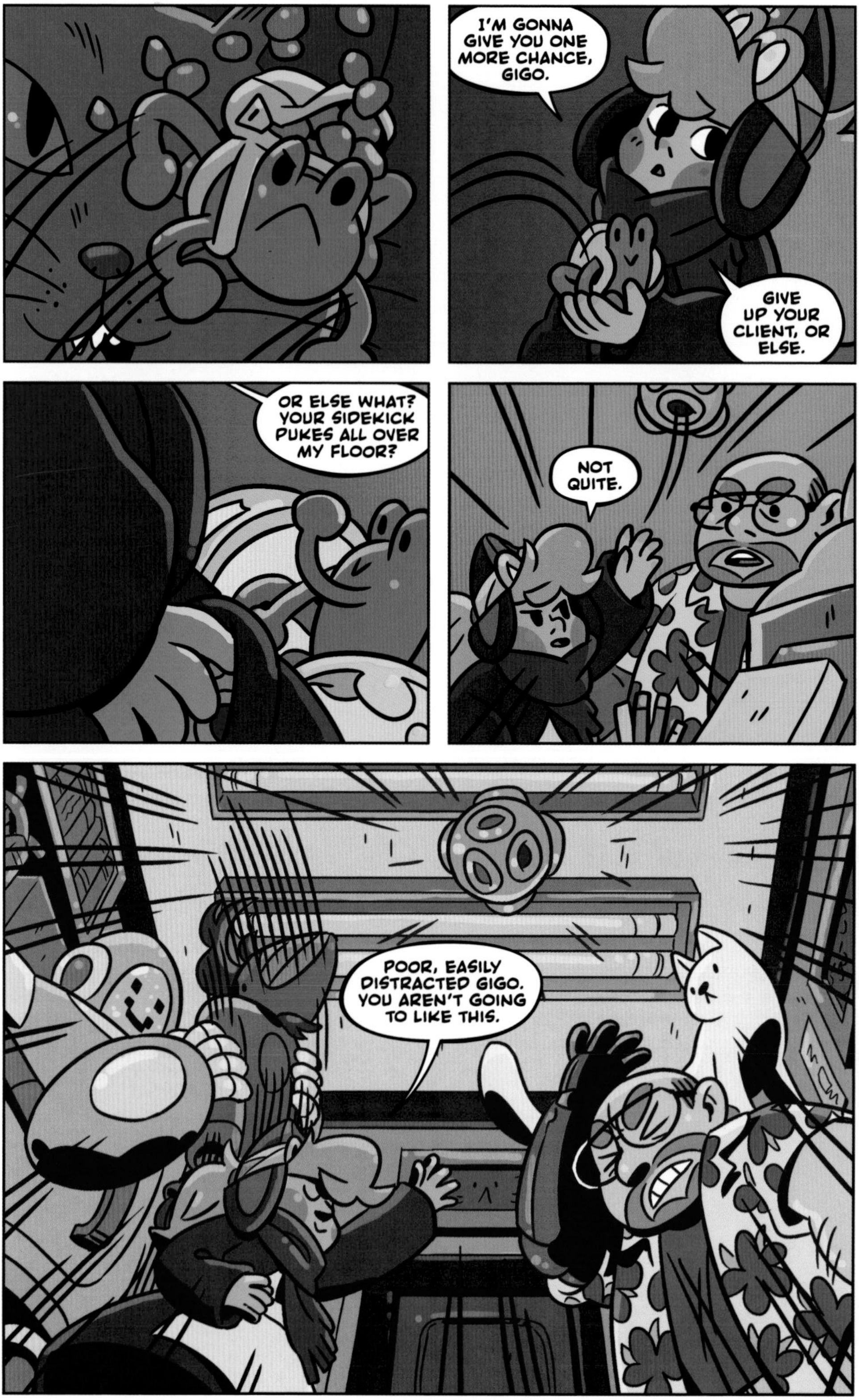
I'M GONNA GIVE YOU ONE MORE CHANCE, GIGO.
GIVE UP YOUR CLIENT, OR ELSE.
OR ELSE WHAT? YOUR SIDEKICK PUKES ALL OVER MY FLOOR?
NOT QUITE.
POOR, EASILY DISTRACTED GIGO. YOU AREN'T GOING TO LIKE THIS.

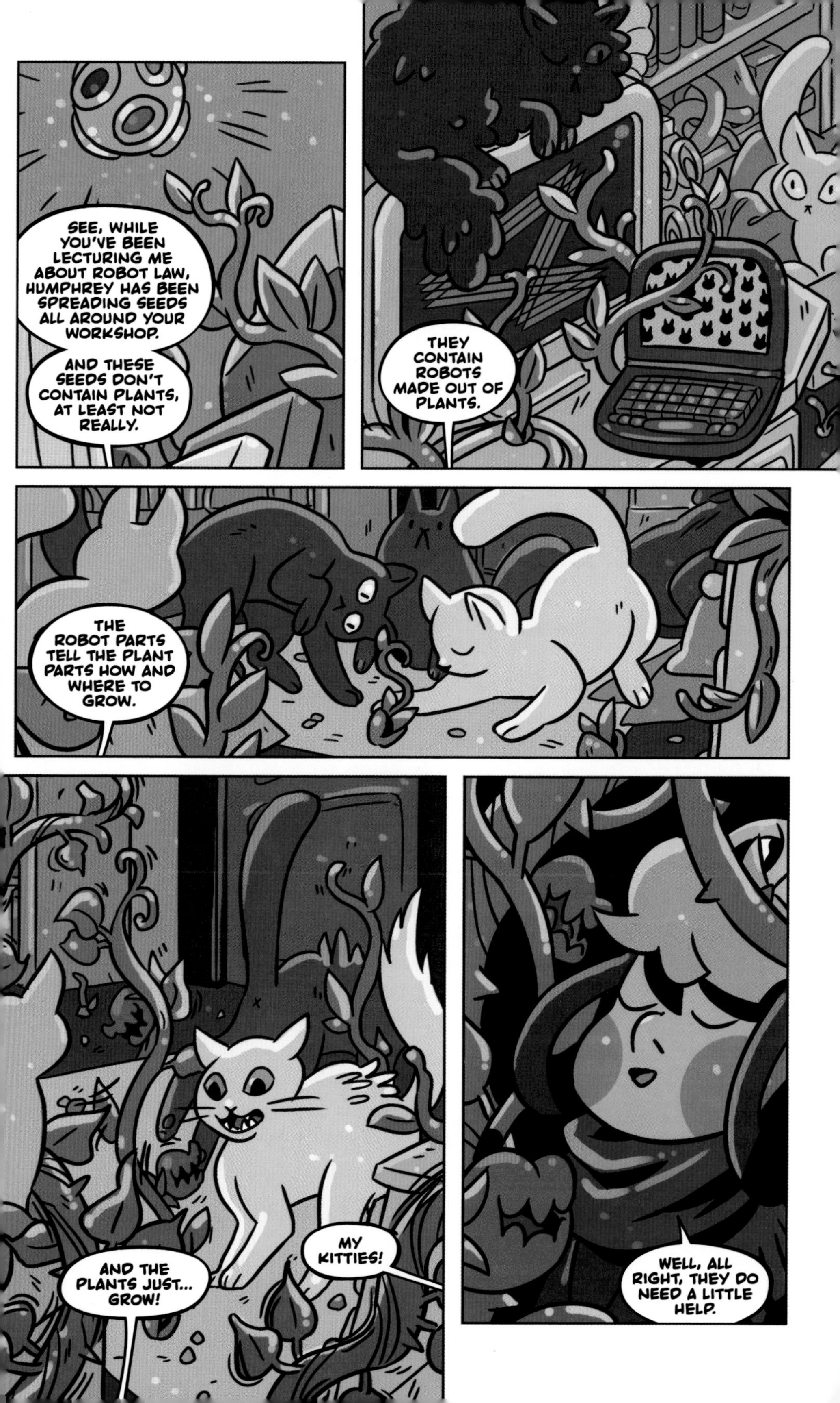
SEE, WHILE YOU'VE BEEN LECTURING ME ABOUT ROBOT LAW, HUMPHREY HAS BEEN SPREADING SEEDS ALL AROUND YOUR WORKSHOP.
AND THESE SEEDS DON'T CONTAIN PLANTS, AT LEAST NOT REALLY.
THEY CONTAIN ROBOTS MADE OUT OF PLANTS.
THE ROBOT PARTS TELL THE PLANT PARTS HOW AND WHERE TO GROW.
AND THE PLANTS JUST... GROW!
MY KITTIES!
WELL, ALL RIGHT, THEY DO NEED A LITTLE HELP.

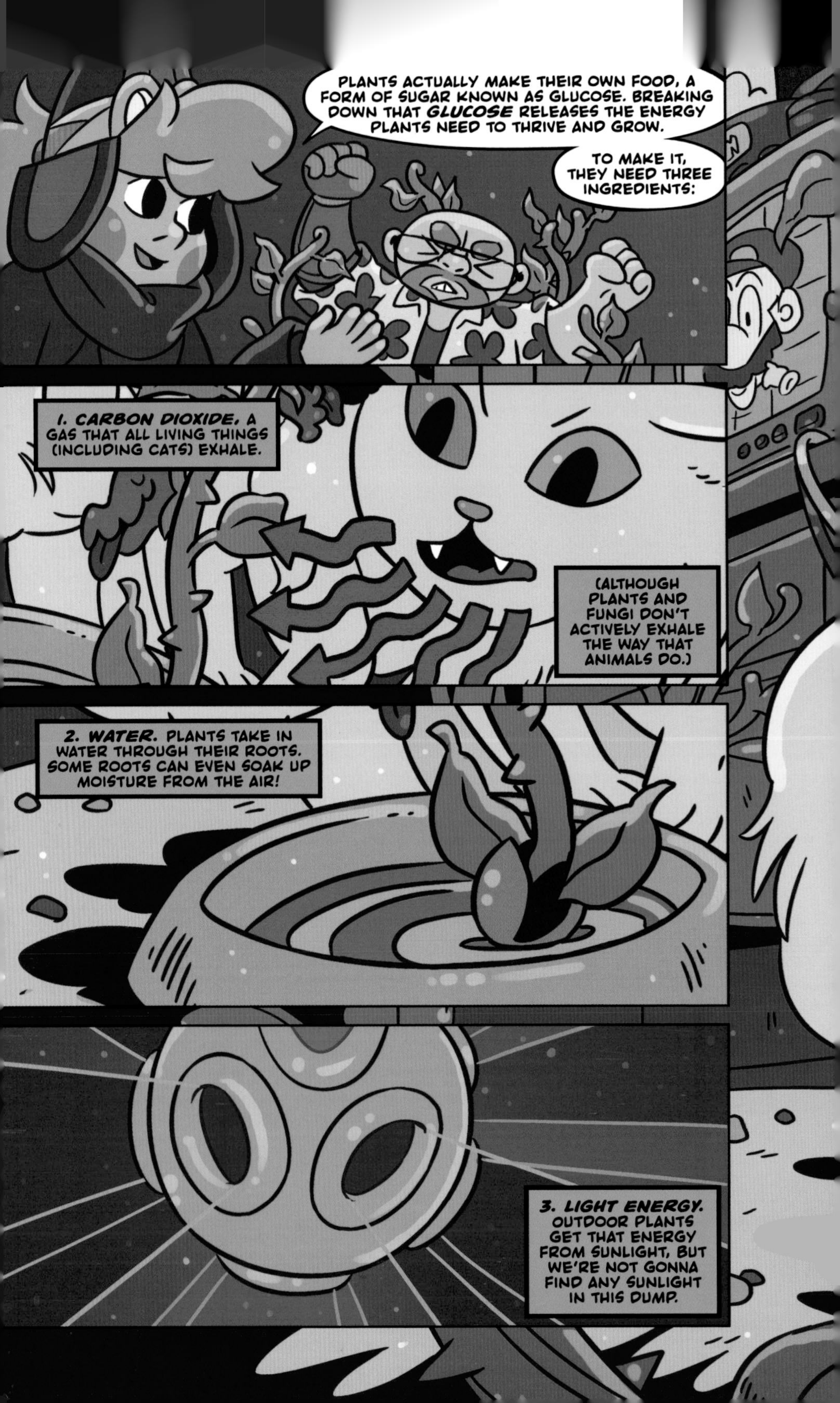

PLANTS ACTUALLY MAKE THEIR OWN FOOD, A FORM OF SUGAR KNOWN AS GLUCOSE. BREAKING DOWN THAT *GLUCOSE* RELEASES THE ENERGY PLANTS NEED TO THRIVE AND GROW.
TO MAKE IT, THEY NEED THREE INGREDIENTS:
1. CARBON DIOXIDE, A GAS THAT ALL LIVING THINGS (INCLUDING CATS) EXHALE.
(ALTHOUGH PLANTS AND FUNGI DON'T ACTIVELY EXHALE THE WAY THAT ANIMALS DO.)
2. WATER. PLANTS TAKE IN WATER THROUGH THEIR ROOTS. SOME ROOTS CAN EVEN SOAK UP MOISTURE FROM THE AIR!
3. LIGHT ENERGY. OUTDOOR PLANTS GET THAT ENERGY FROM SUNLIGHT, BUT WE'RE NOT GONNA FIND ANY SUNLIGHT IN THIS DUMP.

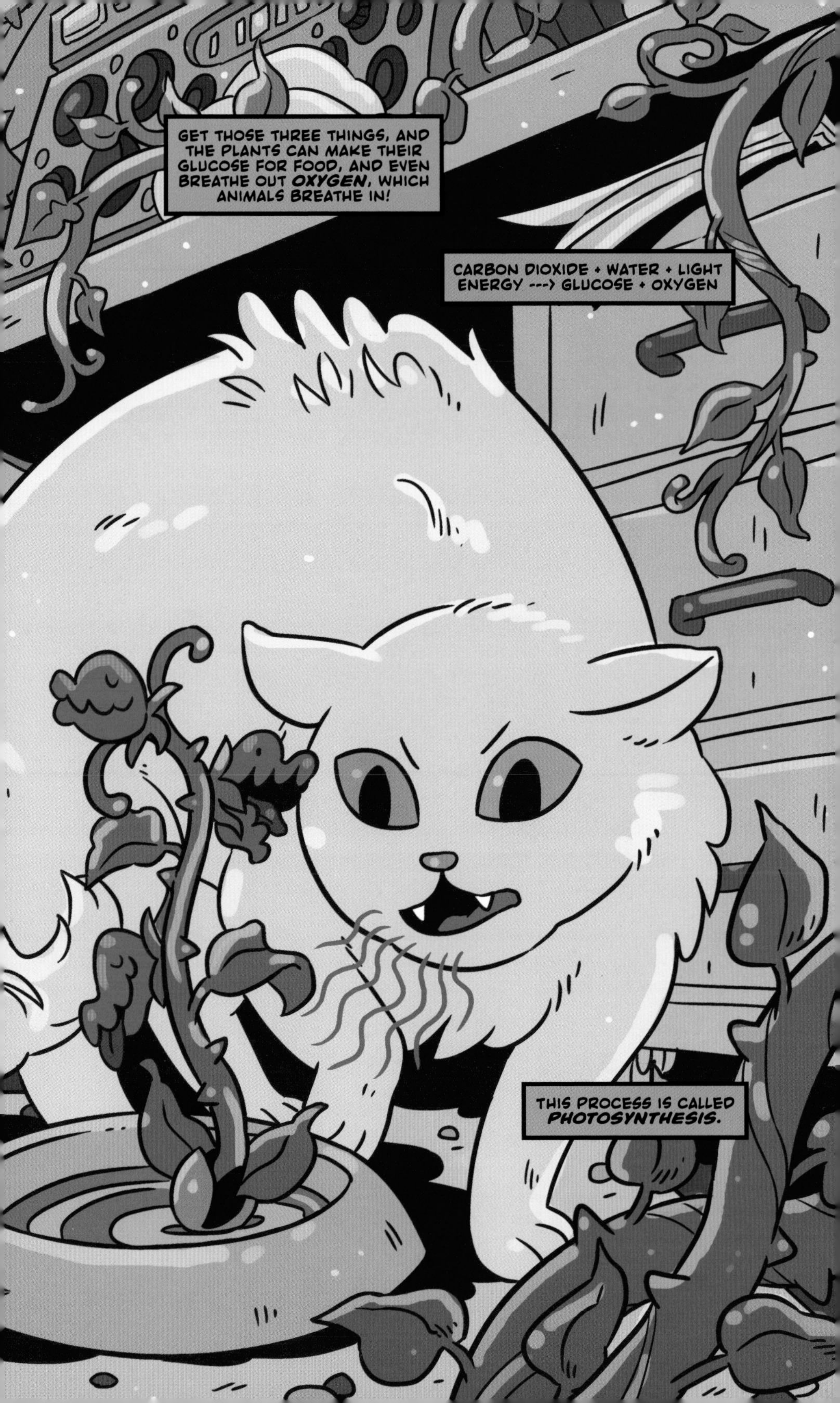
GET THOSE THREE THINGS, AND THE PLANTS CAN MAKE THEIR GLUCOSE FOR FOOD, AND EVEN BREATHE OUT *OXYGEN*, WHICH ANIMALS BREATHE IN!
CARBON DIOXIDE + WATER + LIGHT ENERGY ---> GLUCOSE + OXYGEN
THIS PROCESS IS CALLED *PHOTOSYNTHESIS*.

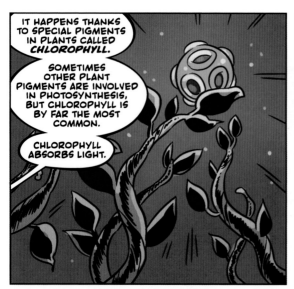

IT HAPPENS THANKS TO SPECIAL PIGMENTS IN PLANTS CALLED *CHLOROPHYLL*.

SOMETIMES OTHER PLANT PIGMENTS ARE INVOLVED IN PHOTOSYNTHESIS, BUT CHLOROPHYLL IS BY FAR THE MOST COMMON.

CHLOROPHYLL ABSORBS LIGHT.

I DON'T NEED A BOTANY LESSON! JUST TURN THAT LIGHT OFF!

OH, BUT THIS PART'S IMPORTANT.

IT ACTUALLY ABSORBS RED AND BLUE LIGHT BEST--AND LOOKS GREEN BECAUSE IT REFLECTS GREEN LIGHT.

THAT'S WHY PLANTS--AND PLANT PEOPLE--TEND TO BE GREEN.

RIGHT NOW, I'M FEEDING MY PLANT ROBOTS THEIR FAVORITE KINDS OF LIGHT...

...AND ENABLING PHOTOSYNTHESIS...

...SO THEY CAN GROW BIG AND STRONG!

96

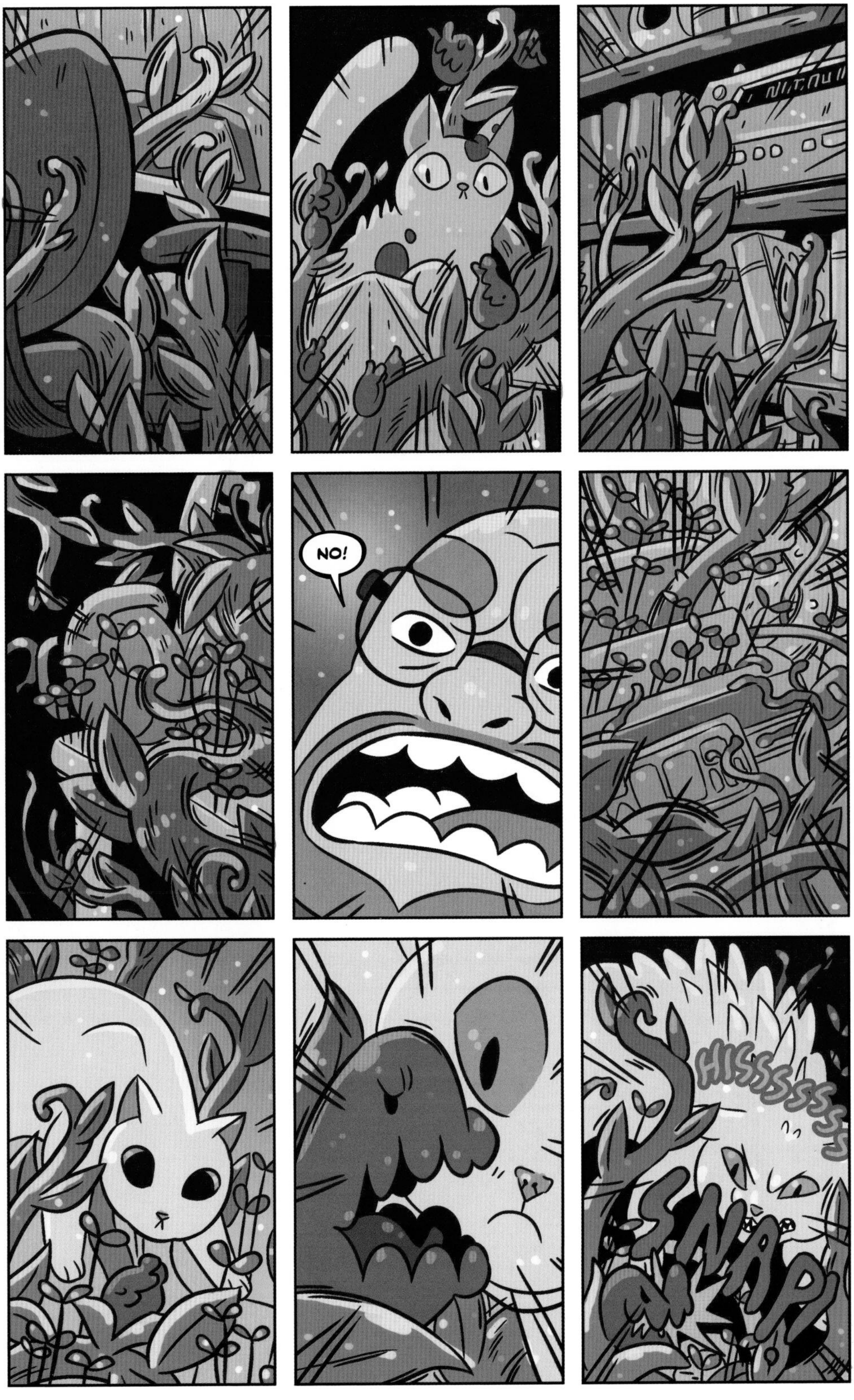
NO!
HISSSSSSS
SNAP!

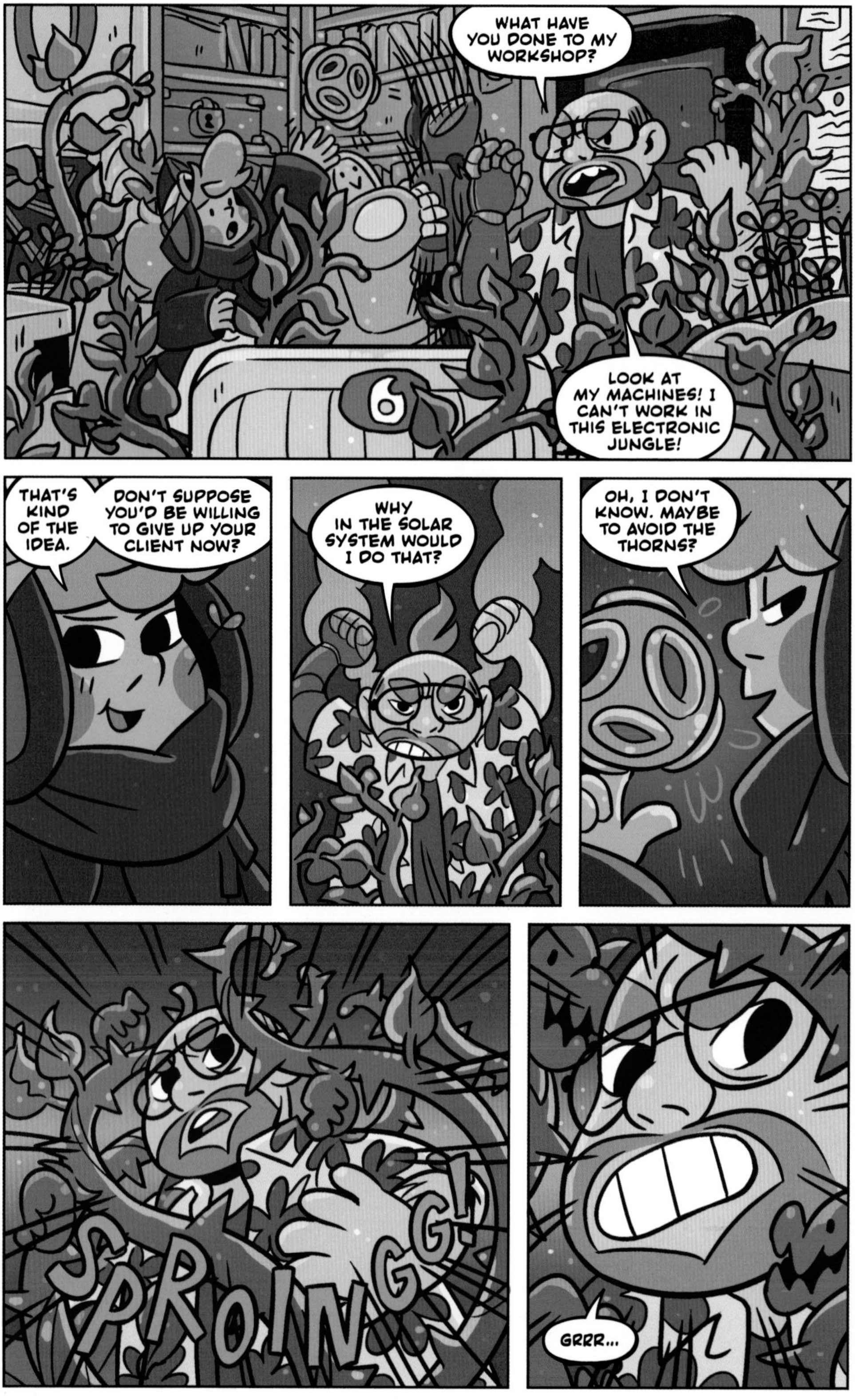
WHAT HAVE YOU DONE TO MY WORKSHOP?
LOOK AT MY MACHINES! I CAN'T WORK IN THIS ELECTRONIC JUNGLE!
THAT'S KIND OF THE IDEA.
DON'T SUPPOSE YOU'D BE WILLING TO GIVE UP YOUR CLIENT NOW?
WHY IN THE SOLAR SYSTEM WOULD I DO THAT?
OH, I DON'T KNOW. MAYBE TO AVOID THE THORNS?
SPROINGG!
GRRR...

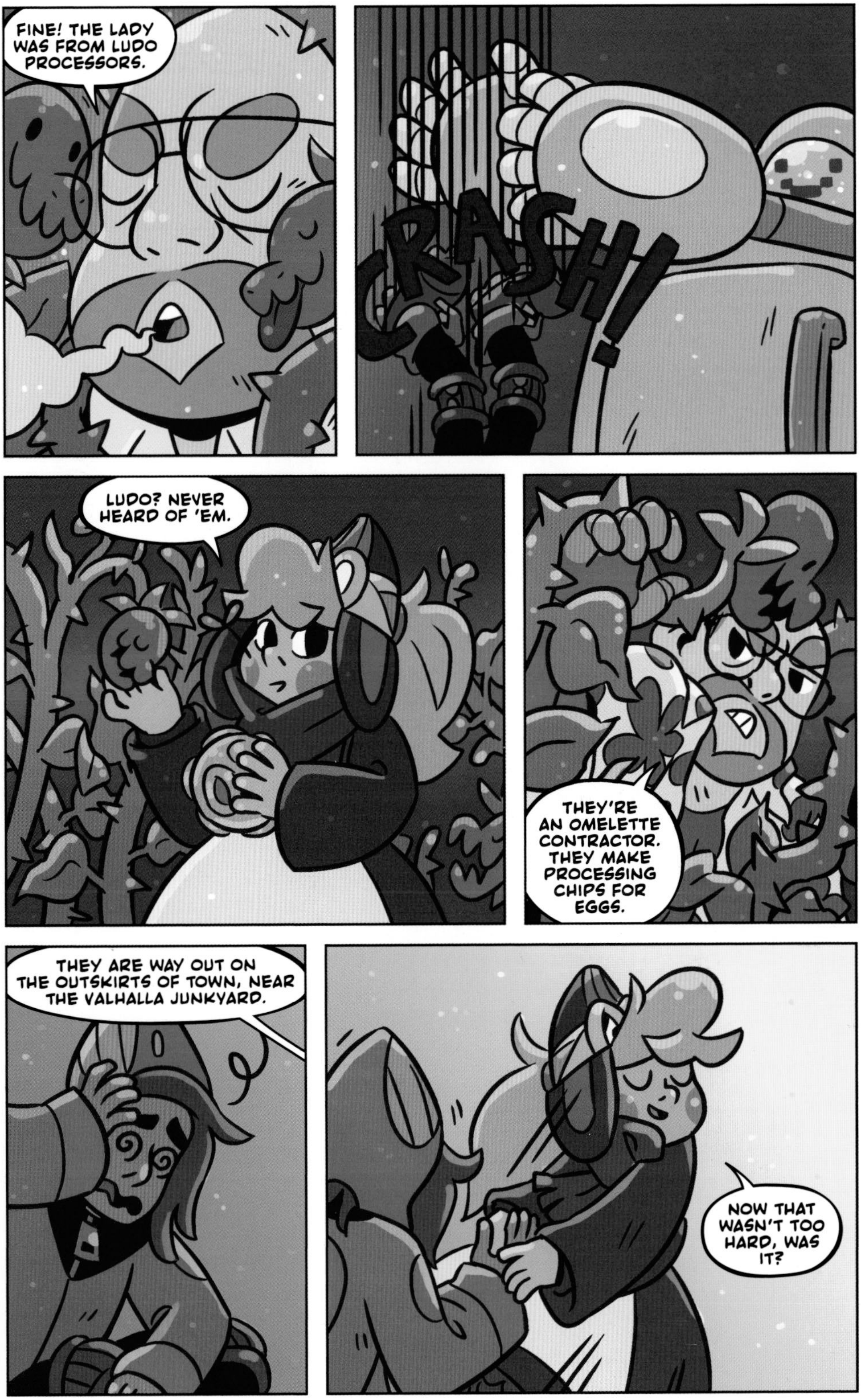
FINE! THE LADY WAS FROM LUDO PROCESSORS.
CRASH!
LUDO? NEVER HEARD OF 'EM.
THEY'RE AN OMELETTE CONTRACTOR. THEY MAKE PROCESSING CHIPS FOR EGGS.
THEY ARE WAY OUT ON THE OUTSKIRTS OF TOWN, NEAR THE VALHALLA JUNKYARD.
NOW THAT WASN'T TOO HARD, WAS IT?

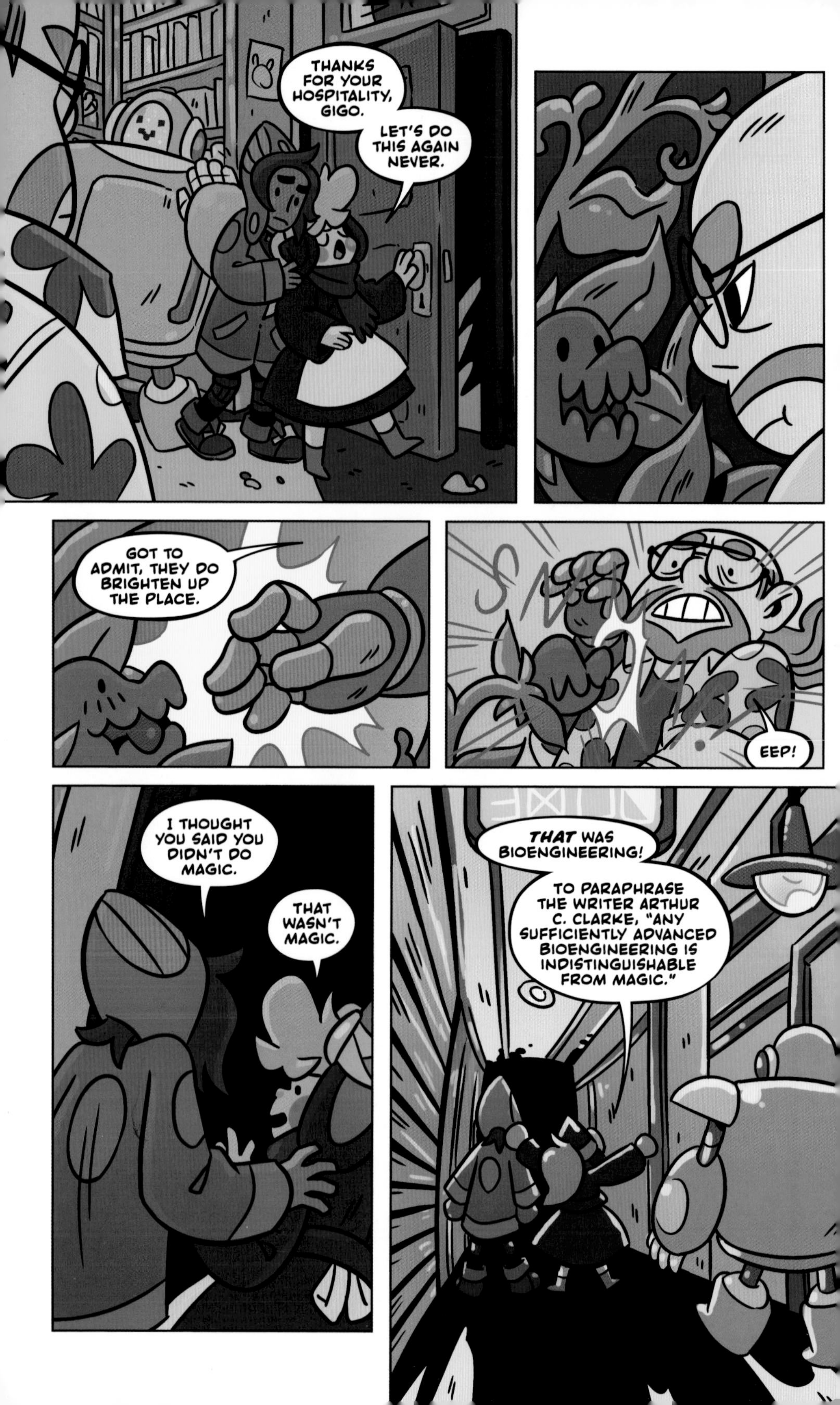
THANKS FOR YOUR HOSPITALITY, GIGO.
LET'S DO THIS AGAIN NEVER.
GOT TO ADMIT, THEY DO BRIGHTEN UP THE PLACE.
EEP!
I THOUGHT YOU SAID YOU DIDN'T DO MAGIC.
THAT WASN'T MAGIC.
THAT WAS BIOENGINEERING!
TO PARAPHRASE THE WRITER ARTHUR C. CLARKE, "ANY SUFFICIENTLY ADVANCED BIOENGINEERING IS INDISTINGUISHABLE FROM MAGIC."

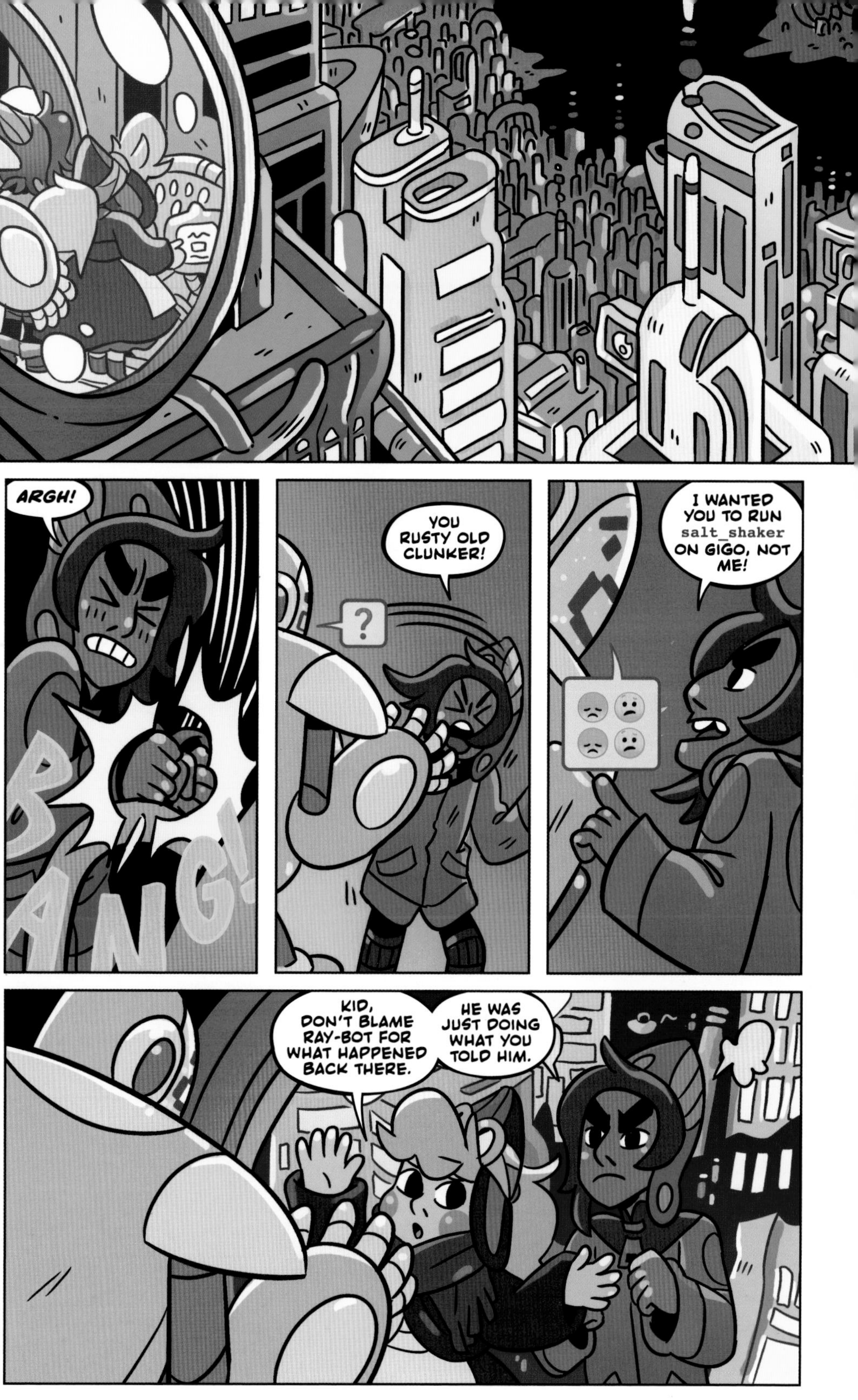
ARGH!
BANG!
YOU RUSTY OLD CLUNKER!
?
I WANTED YOU TO RUN salt_shaker ON GIGO, NOT ME!
KID, DON'T BLAME RAY-BOT FOR WHAT HAPPENED BACK THERE.
HE WAS JUST DOING WHAT YOU TOLD HIM.

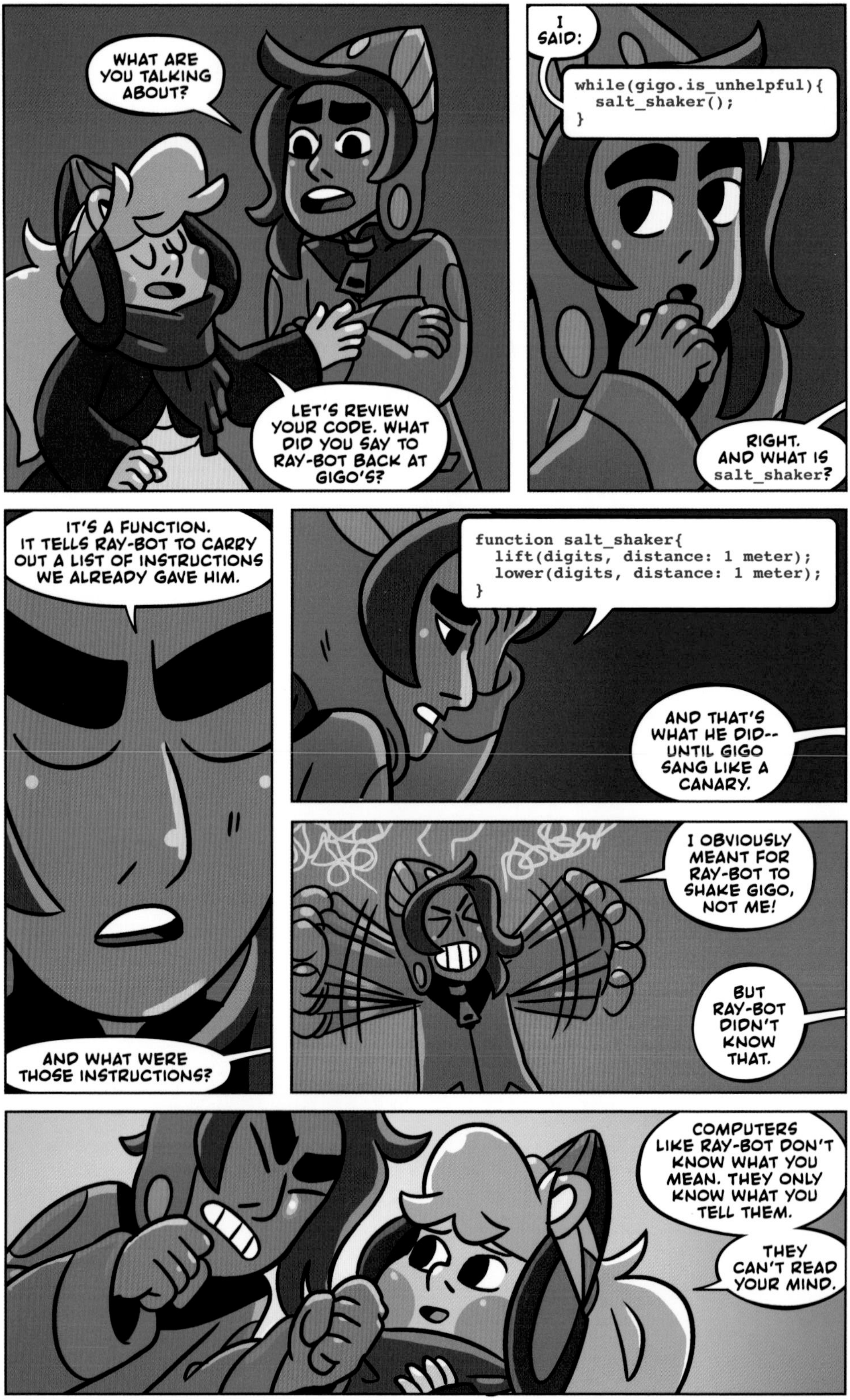
WHAT ARE YOU TALKING ABOUT?
LET'S REVIEW YOUR CODE. WHAT DID YOU SAY TO RAY-BOT BACK AT GIGO'S?
I SAID:
while(gigo.is_unhelpful){
  salt_shaker();
}
RIGHT. AND WHAT IS salt_shaker?
IT'S A FUNCTION. IT TELLS RAY-BOT TO CARRY OUT A LIST OF INSTRUCTIONS WE ALREADY GAVE HIM.
AND WHAT WERE THOSE INSTRUCTIONS?
function salt_shaker{
  lift(digits, distance: 1 meter);
  lower(digits, distance: 1 meter);
}
AND THAT'S WHAT HE DID-- UNTIL GIGO SANG LIKE A CANARY.
I OBVIOUSLY MEANT FOR RAY-BOT TO SHAKE GIGO, NOT ME!
BUT RAY-BOT DIDN'T KNOW THAT.
COMPUTERS LIKE RAY-BOT DON'T KNOW WHAT YOU MEAN. THEY ONLY KNOW WHAT YOU TELL THEM.
THEY CAN'T READ YOUR MIND.

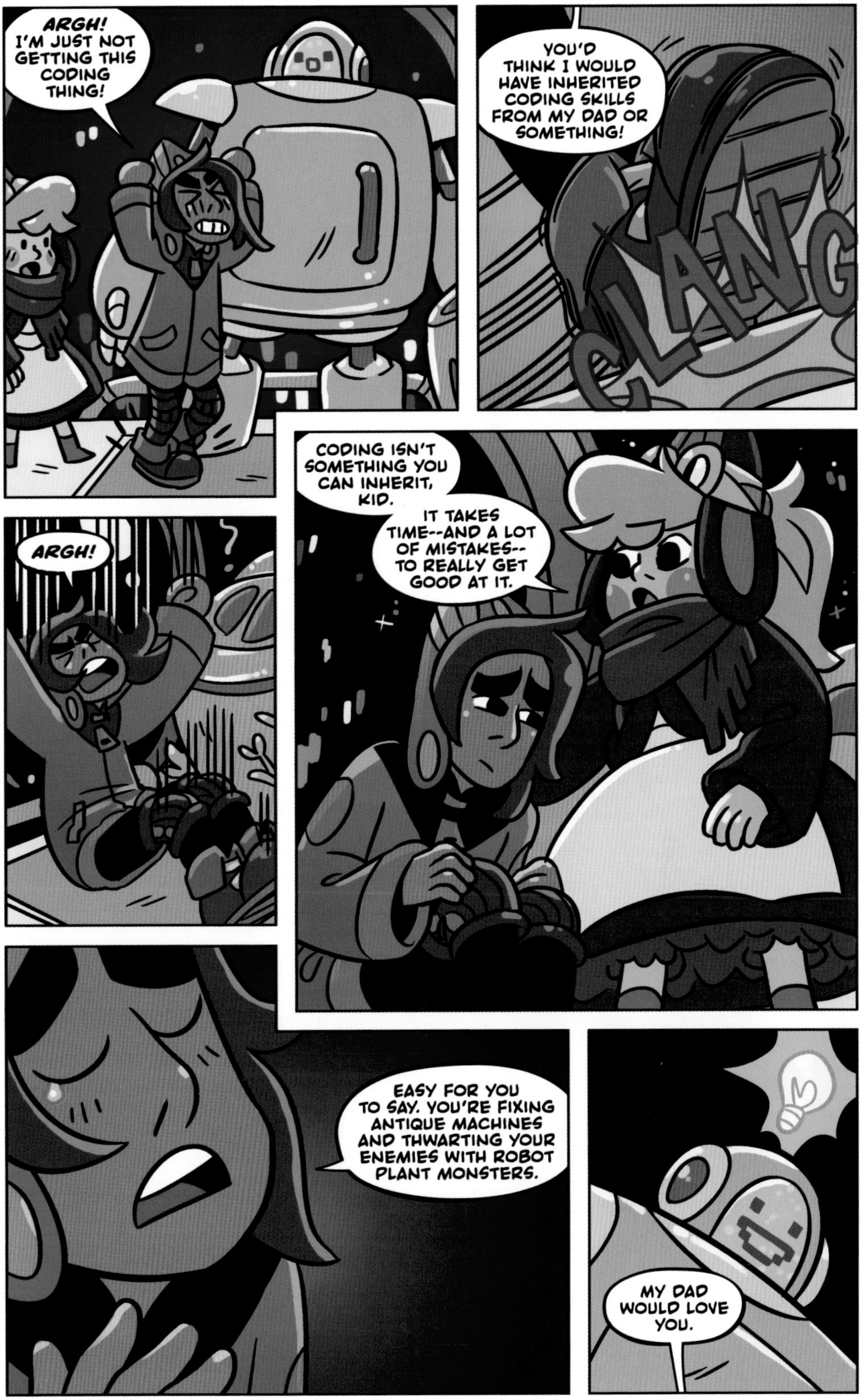
ARGH! I'M JUST NOT GETTING THIS CODING THING!
YOU'D THINK I WOULD HAVE INHERITED CODING SKILLS FROM MY DAD OR SOMETHING!
CLANG
ARGH!
CODING ISN'T SOMETHING YOU CAN INHERIT, KID.
IT TAKES TIME--AND A LOT OF MISTAKES--TO REALLY GET GOOD AT IT.
EASY FOR YOU TO SAY. YOU'RE FIXING ANTIQUE MACHINES AND THWARTING YOUR ENEMIES WITH ROBOT PLANT MONSTERS.
MY DAD WOULD LOVE YOU.

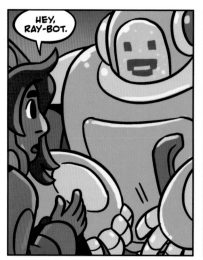

HEY, RAY-BOT.

WHAT'S THIS?

OH!

IS THAT...MY DAD?

HUH. GUESS THAT MEMORY DRIVE YOUR DAD GAVE YOU WASN'T EMPTY AFTER ALL.

HEY, DIGITS. IT'S ME, DAD.

I GUESS YOU ALREADY KNEW THAT.

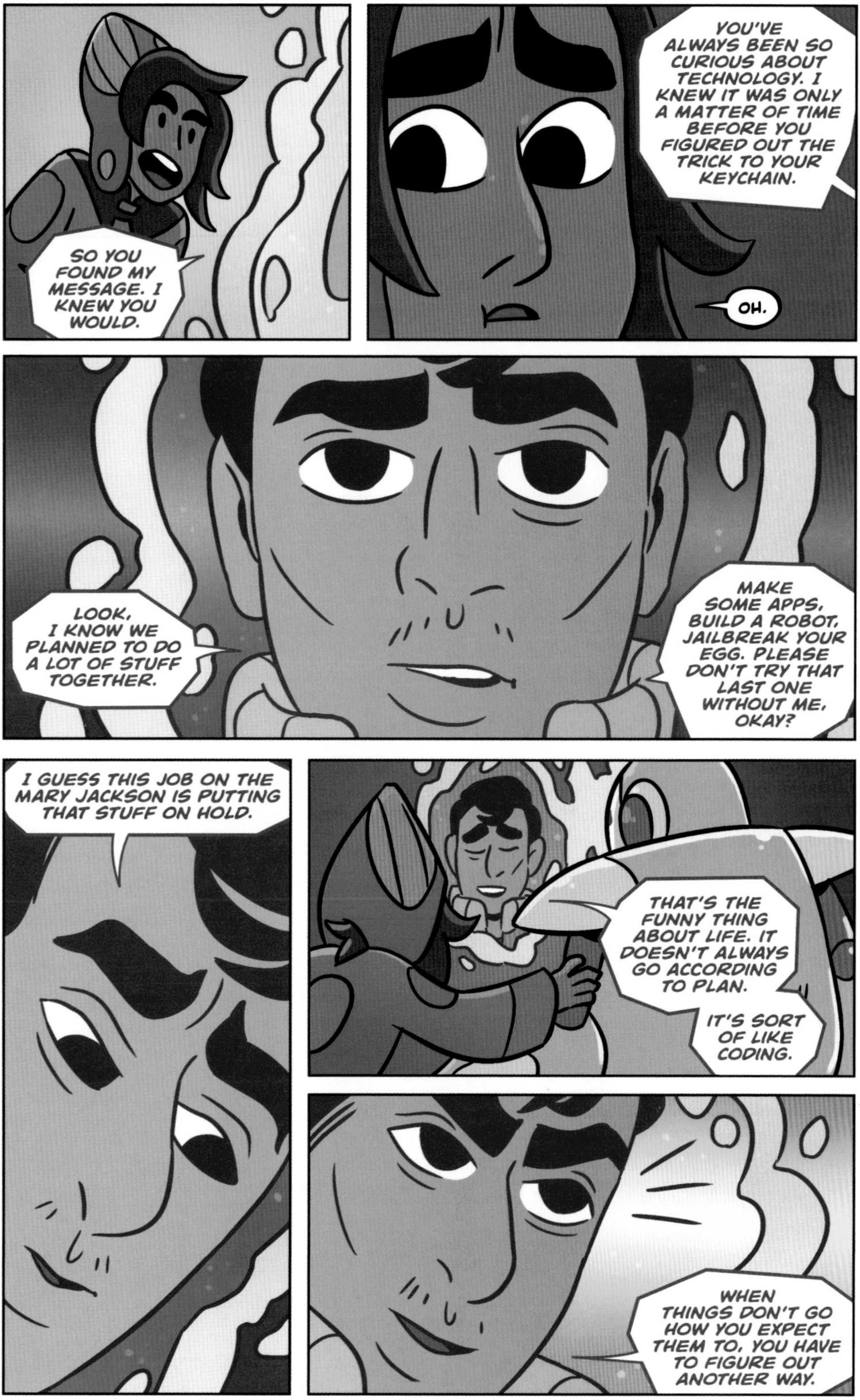
SO YOU FOUND MY MESSAGE. I KNEW YOU WOULD.
YOU'VE ALWAYS BEEN SO CURIOUS ABOUT TECHNOLOGY. I KNEW IT WAS ONLY A MATTER OF TIME BEFORE YOU FIGURED OUT THE TRICK TO YOUR KEYCHAIN.
OH.
LOOK, I KNOW WE PLANNED TO DO A LOT OF STUFF TOGETHER.
MAKE SOME APPS, BUILD A ROBOT, JAILBREAK YOUR EGG. PLEASE DON'T TRY THAT LAST ONE WITHOUT ME, OKAY?
I GUESS THIS JOB ON THE MARY JACKSON IS PUTTING THAT STUFF ON HOLD.
THAT'S THE FUNNY THING ABOUT LIFE. IT DOESN'T ALWAYS GO ACCORDING TO PLAN.
IT'S SORT OF LIKE CODING.
WHEN THINGS DON'T GO HOW YOU EXPECT THEM TO, YOU HAVE TO FIGURE OUT ANOTHER WAY.

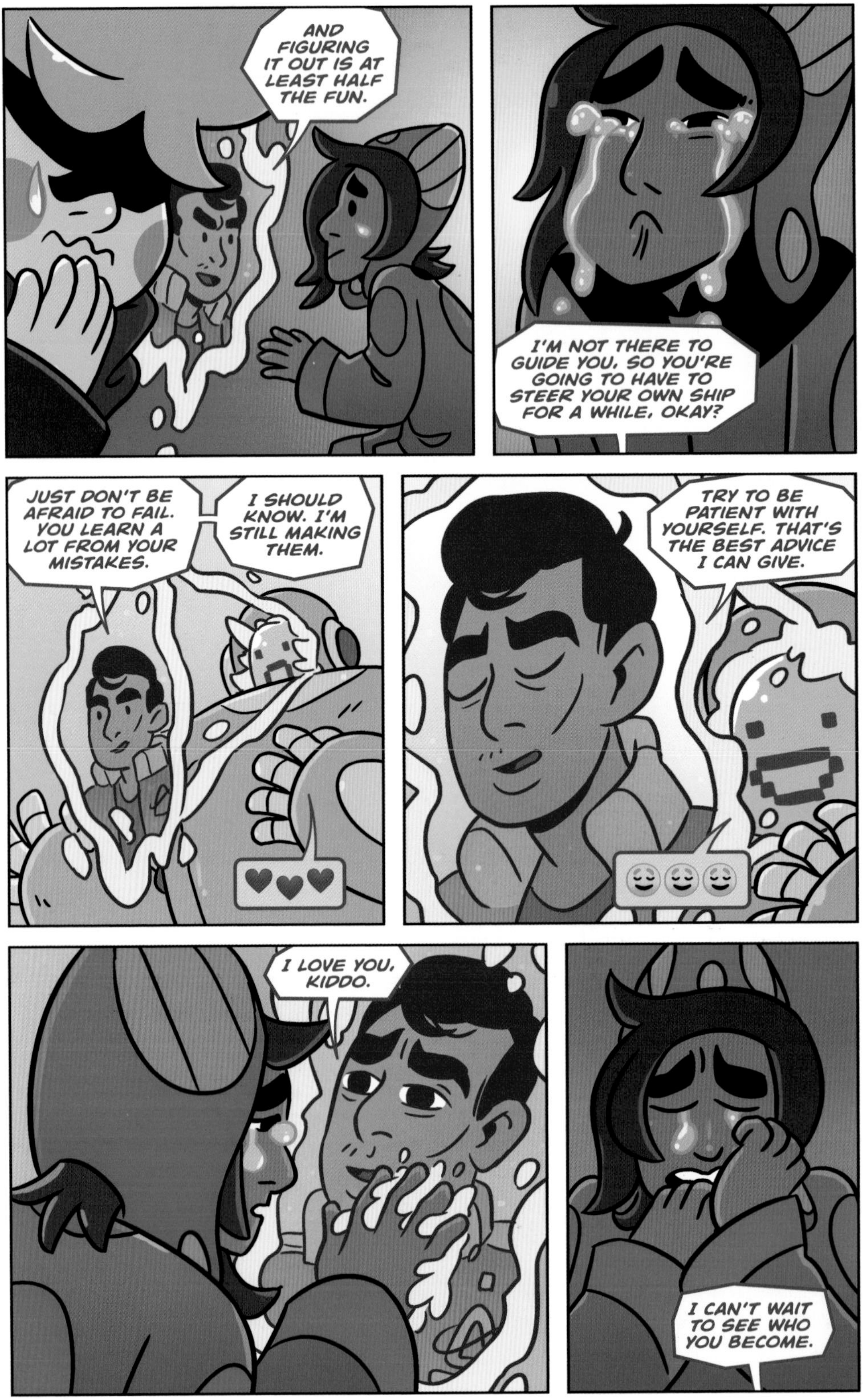
AND FIGURING IT OUT IS AT LEAST HALF THE FUN.
I'M NOT THERE TO GUIDE YOU, SO YOU'RE GOING TO HAVE TO STEER YOUR OWN SHIP FOR A WHILE, OKAY?
JUST DON'T BE AFRAID TO FAIL. YOU LEARN A LOT FROM YOUR MISTAKES.
I SHOULD KNOW. I'M STILL MAKING THEM.
TRY TO BE PATIENT WITH YOURSELF. THAT'S THE BEST ADVICE I CAN GIVE.
I LOVE YOU, KIDDO.
I CAN'T WAIT TO SEE WHO YOU BECOME.

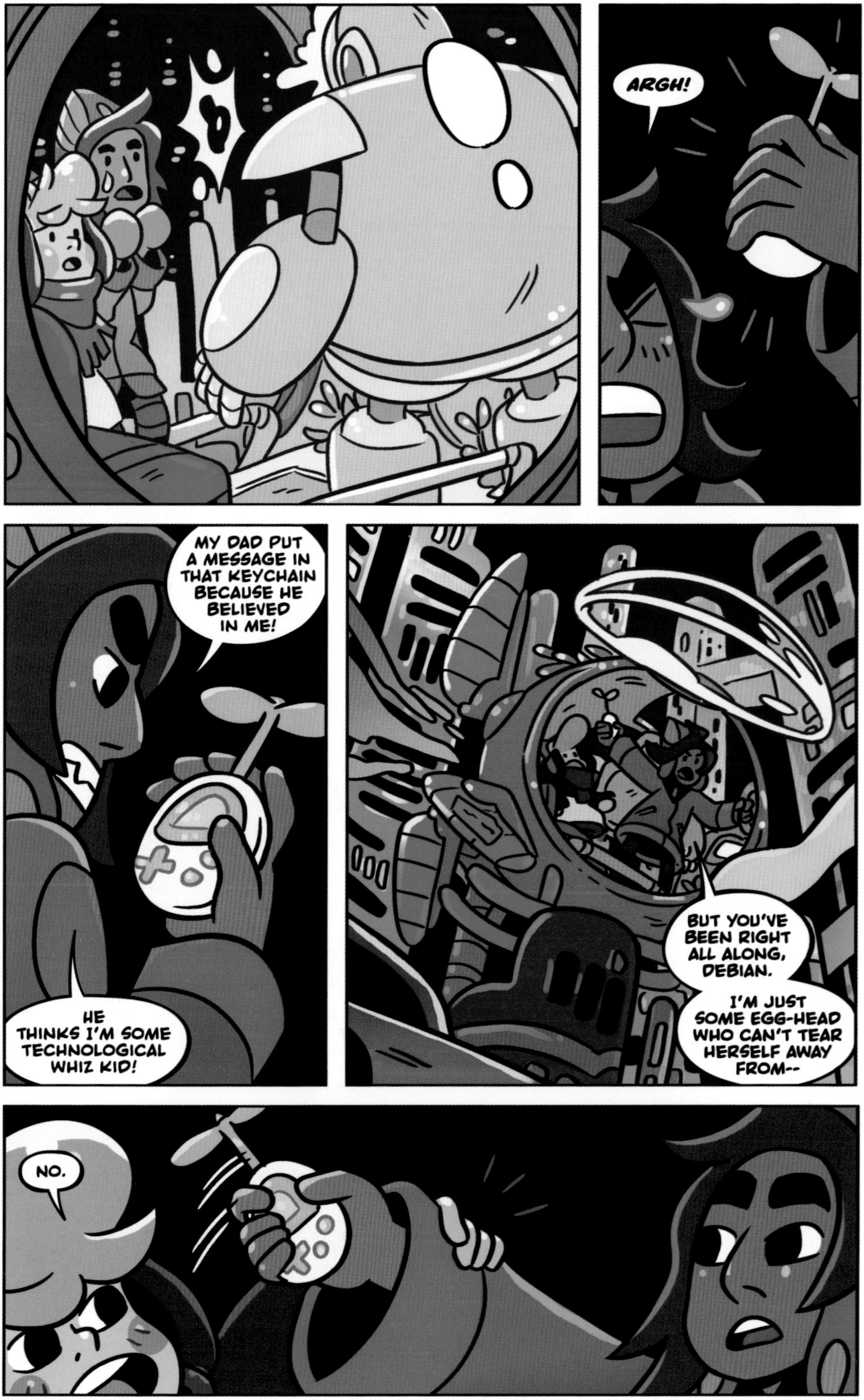
ARGH!
MY DAD PUT A MESSAGE IN THAT KEYCHAIN BECAUSE HE BELIEVED IN ME!
HE THINKS I'M SOME TECHNOLOGICAL WHIZ KID!
BUT YOU'VE BEEN RIGHT ALL ALONG, DEBIAN.
I'M JUST SOME EGG-HEAD WHO CAN'T TEAR HERSELF AWAY FROM--
NO.

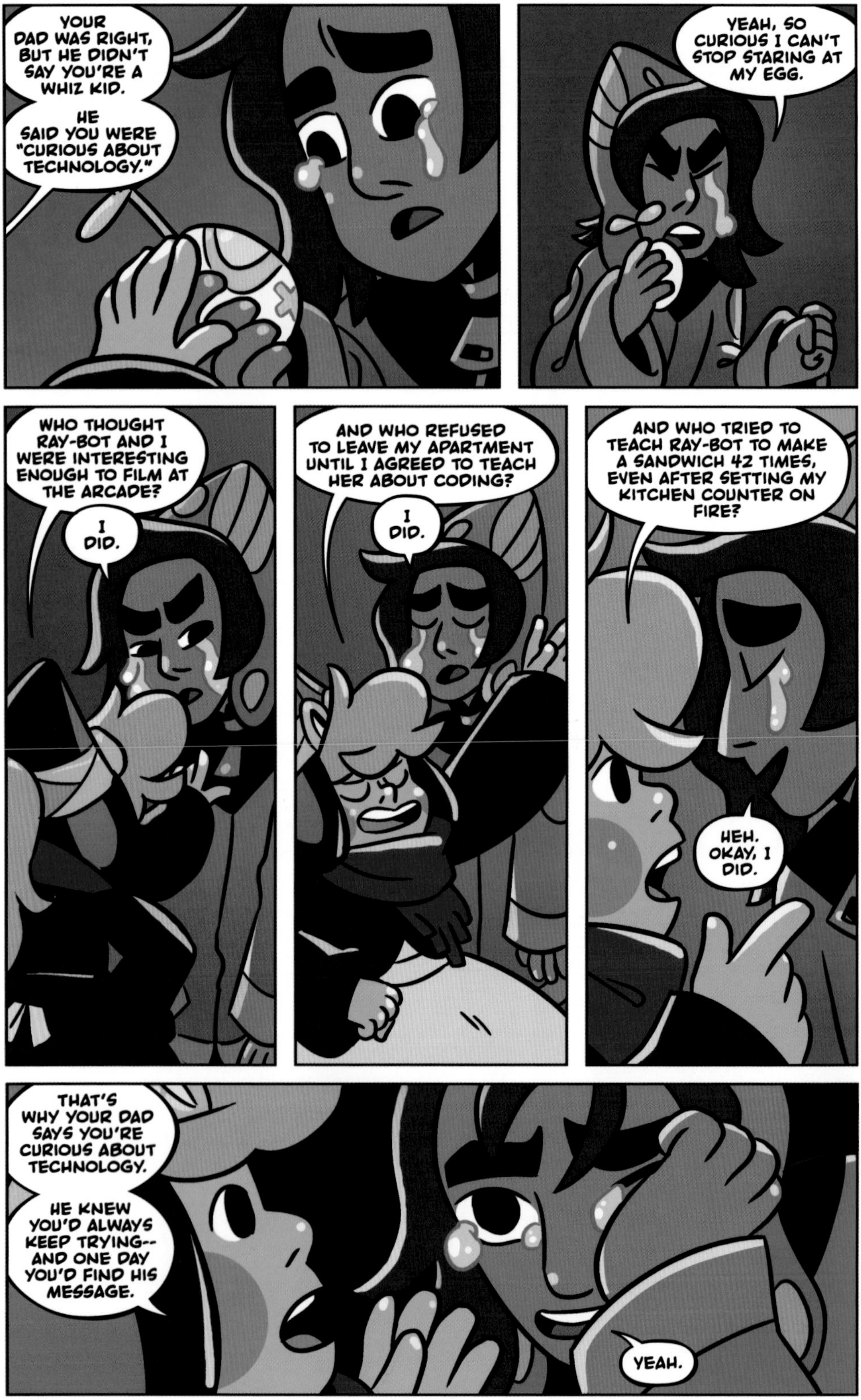
YOUR DAD WAS RIGHT, BUT HE DIDN'T SAY YOU'RE A WHIZ KID.
HE SAID YOU WERE "CURIOUS ABOUT TECHNOLOGY."
YEAH, SO CURIOUS I CAN'T STOP STARING AT MY EGG.
WHO THOUGHT RAY-BOT AND I WERE INTERESTING ENOUGH TO FILM AT THE ARCADE?
I DID.
AND WHO REFUSED TO LEAVE MY APARTMENT UNTIL I AGREED TO TEACH HER ABOUT CODING?
I DID.
AND WHO TRIED TO TEACH RAY-BOT TO MAKE A SANDWICH 42 TIMES, EVEN AFTER SETTING MY KITCHEN COUNTER ON FIRE?
HEH. OKAY, I DID.
THAT'S WHY YOUR DAD SAYS YOU'RE CURIOUS ABOUT TECHNOLOGY.
HE KNEW YOU'D ALWAYS KEEP TRYING-- AND ONE DAY YOU'D FIND HIS MESSAGE.
YEAH.

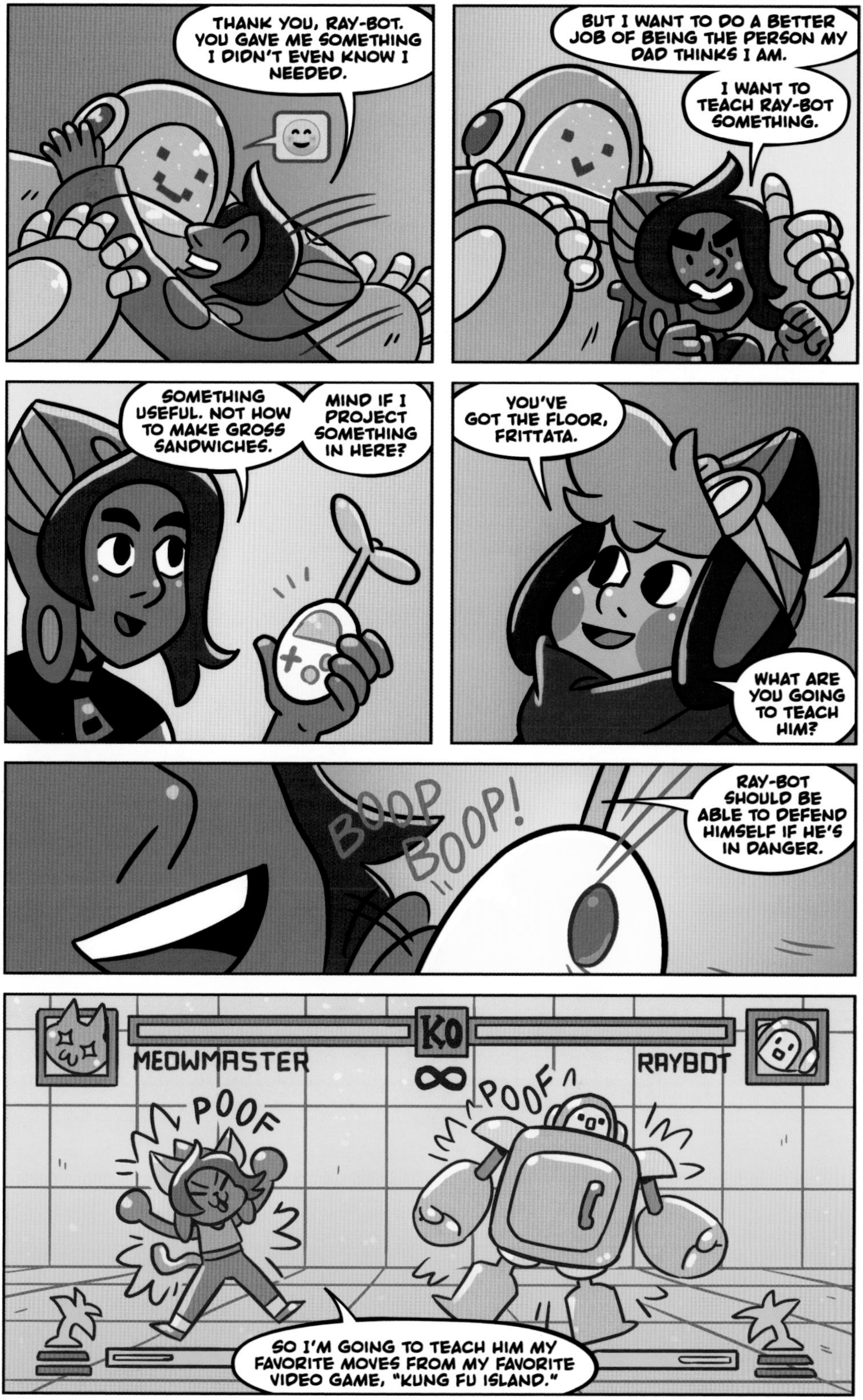
THANK YOU, RAY-BOT. YOU GAVE ME SOMETHING I DIDN'T EVEN KNOW I NEEDED.
BUT I WANT TO DO A BETTER JOB OF BEING THE PERSON MY DAD THINKS I AM.
I WANT TO TEACH RAY-BOT SOMETHING.
SOMETHING USEFUL. NOT HOW TO MAKE GROSS SANDWICHES.
MIND IF I PROJECT SOMETHING IN HERE?
YOU'VE GOT THE FLOOR, FRITTATA.
WHAT ARE YOU GOING TO TEACH HIM?
BOOP BOOP!
RAY-BOT SHOULD BE ABLE TO DEFEND HIMSELF IF HE'S IN DANGER.
MEOWMASTER
KO
∞
RAYBOT
POOF
POOF
SO I'M GOING TO TEACH HIM MY FAVORITE MOVES FROM MY FAVORITE VIDEO GAME, "KUNG FU ISLAND."

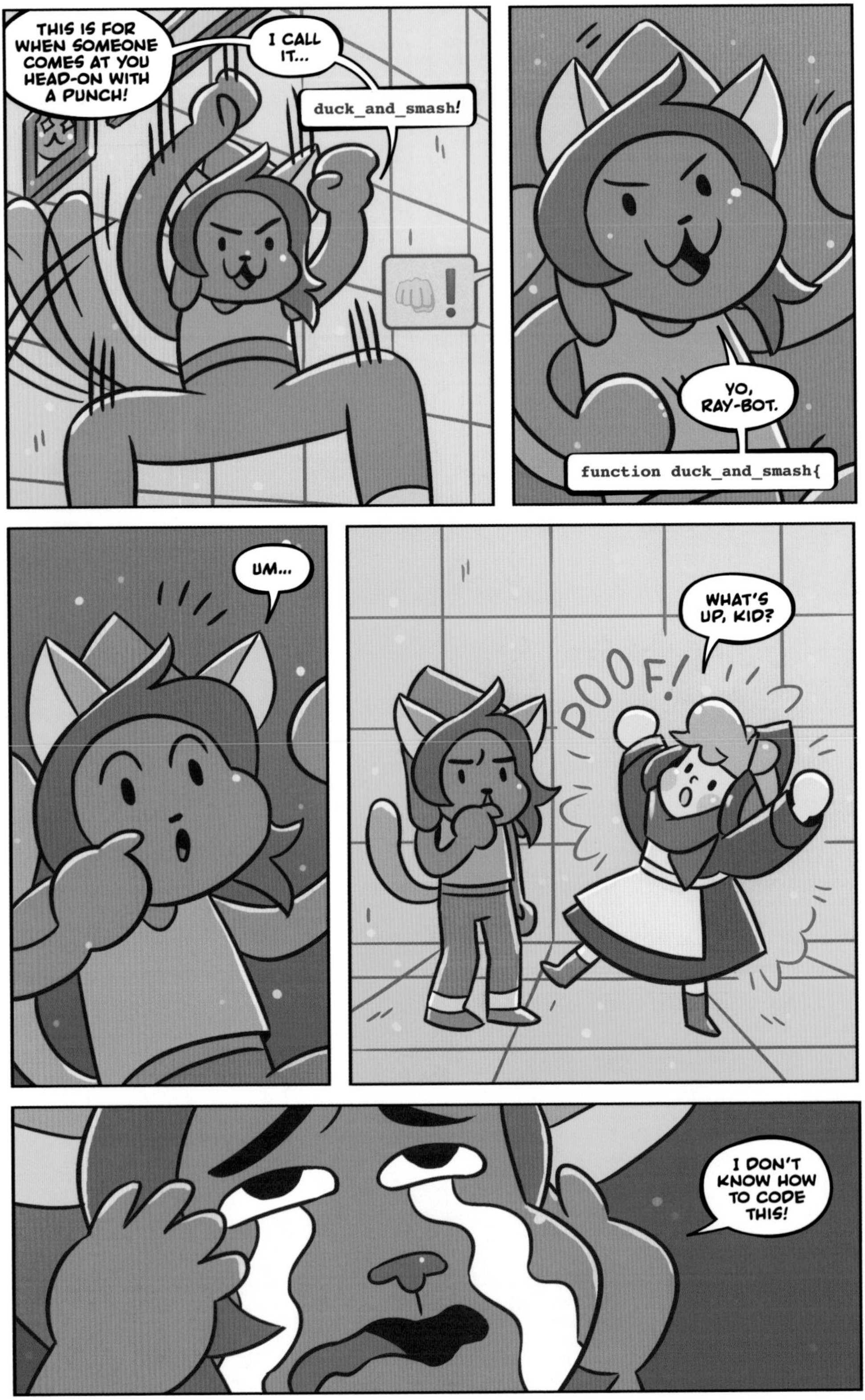
THIS IS FOR WHEN SOMEONE COMES AT YOU HEAD-ON WITH A PUNCH!
I CALL IT...
duck_and_smash!
!
YO, RAY-BOT.
function duck_and_smash{
UM...
WHAT'S UP, KID?
POOF!
I DON'T KNOW HOW TO CODE THIS!

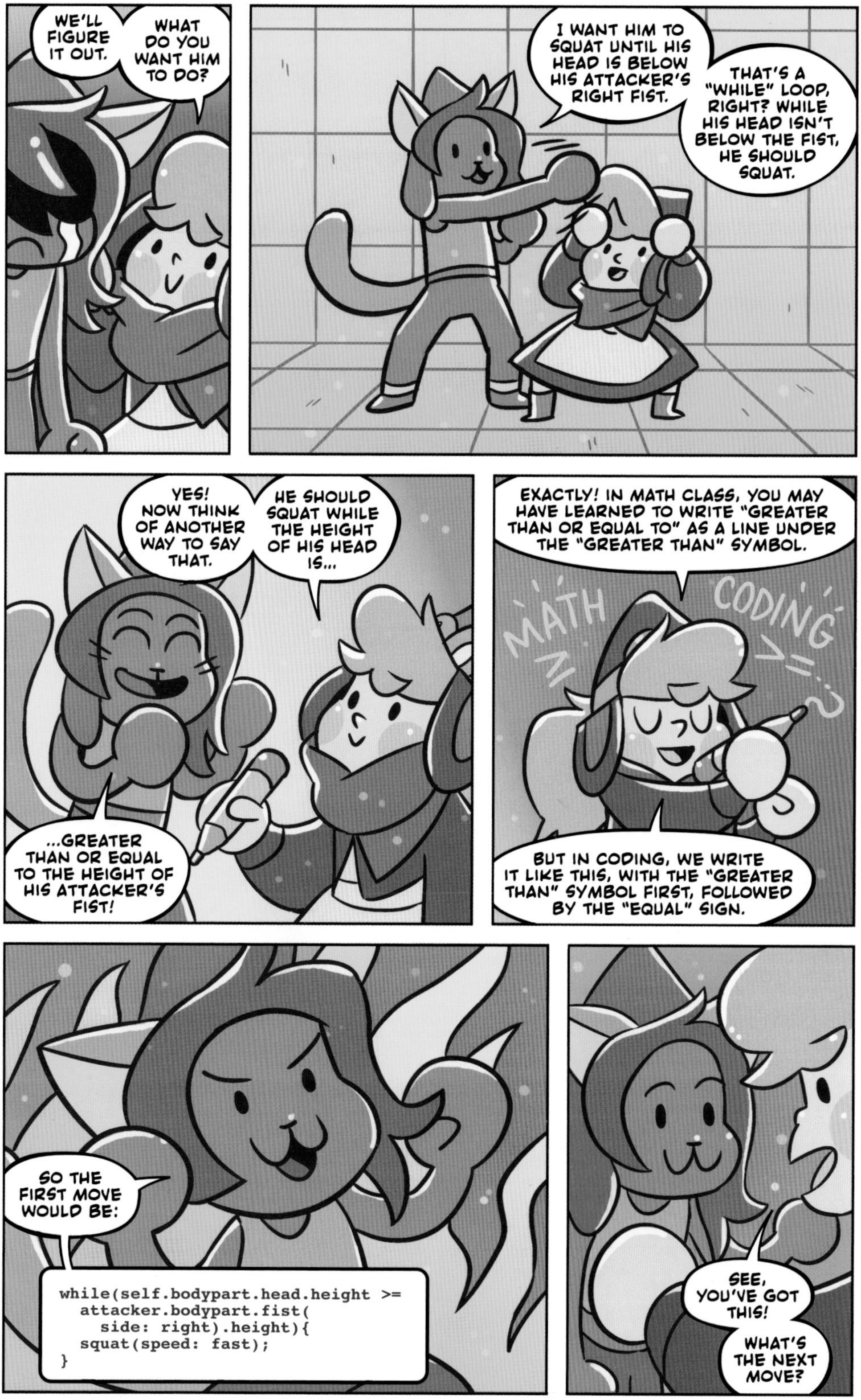
WE'LL FIGURE IT OUT.
WHAT DO YOU WANT HIM TO DO?
I WANT HIM TO SQUAT UNTIL HIS HEAD IS BELOW HIS ATTACKER'S RIGHT FIST.
THAT'S A "WHILE" LOOP, RIGHT? WHILE HIS HEAD ISN'T BELOW THE FIST, HE SHOULD SQUAT.
YES! NOW THINK OF ANOTHER WAY TO SAY THAT.
HE SHOULD SQUAT WHILE THE HEIGHT OF HIS HEAD IS...
...GREATER THAN OR EQUAL TO THE HEIGHT OF HIS ATTACKER'S FIST!
EXACTLY! IN MATH CLASS, YOU MAY HAVE LEARNED TO WRITE "GREATER THAN OR EQUAL TO" AS A LINE UNDER THE "GREATER THAN" SYMBOL.
MATH
≥
CODING
>=...?
BUT IN CODING, WE WRITE IT LIKE THIS, WITH THE "GREATER THAN" SYMBOL FIRST, FOLLOWED BY THE "EQUAL" SIGN.
SO THE FIRST MOVE WOULD BE:
while(self.bodypart.head.height >=
attacker.bodypart.fist(
side: right).height){
squat(speed: fast);
}
SEE, YOU'VE GOT THIS!
WHAT'S THE NEXT MOVE?

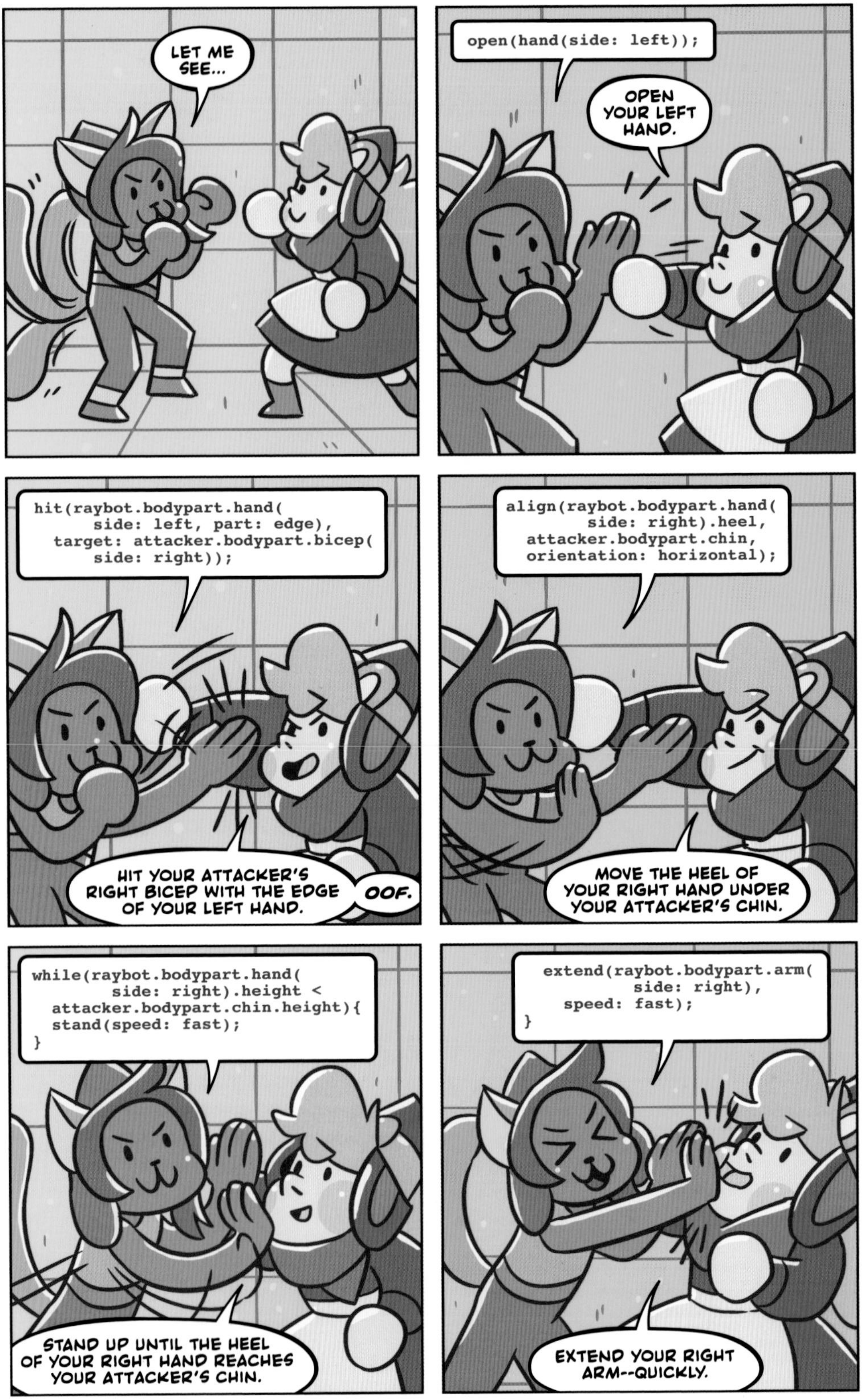

LET ME SEE...
open(hand(side: left));
OPEN YOUR LEFT HAND.
hit(raybot.bodypart.hand(
side: left, part: edge),
target: attacker.bodypart.bicep(
side: right));
HIT YOUR ATTACKER'S RIGHT BICEP WITH THE EDGE OF YOUR LEFT HAND.
OOF.
align(raybot.bodypart.hand(
side: right).heel,
attacker.bodypart.chin,
orientation: horizontal);
MOVE THE HEEL OF YOUR RIGHT HAND UNDER YOUR ATTACKER'S CHIN.
while(raybot.bodypart.hand(
side: right).height <
attacker.bodypart.chin.height){
stand(speed: fast);
}
STAND UP UNTIL THE HEEL OF YOUR RIGHT HAND REACHES YOUR ATTACKER'S CHIN.
extend(raybot.bodypart.arm(
side: right),
speed: fast);
}
EXTEND YOUR RIGHT ARM--QUICKLY.

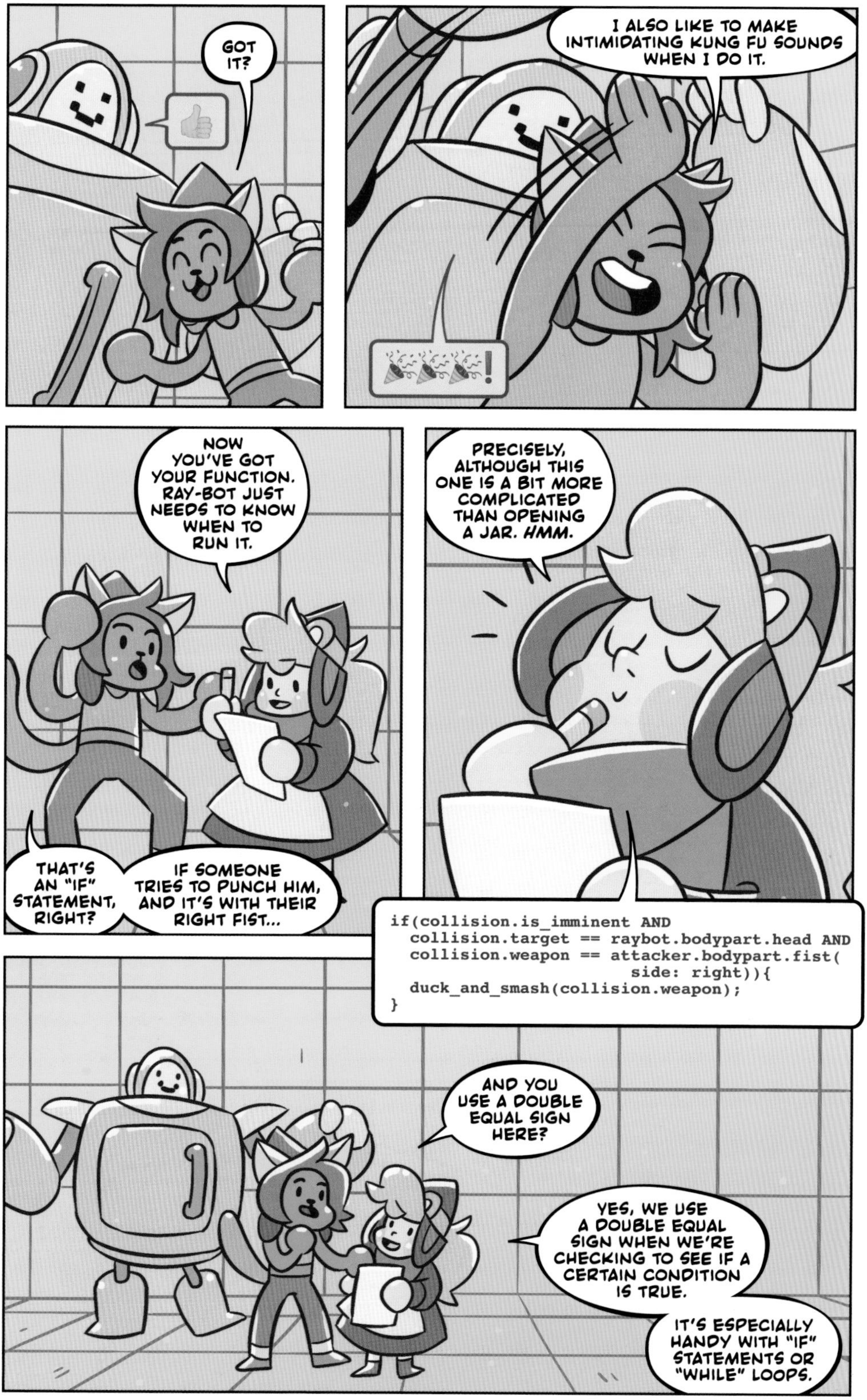
GOT IT?
I ALSO LIKE TO MAKE INTIMIDATING KUNG FU SOUNDS WHEN I DO IT.
NOW YOU'VE GOT YOUR FUNCTION. RAY-BOT JUST NEEDS TO KNOW WHEN TO RUN IT.
THAT'S AN "IF" STATEMENT, RIGHT?
IF SOMEONE TRIES TO PUNCH HIM, AND IT'S WITH THEIR RIGHT FIST...
PRECISELY, ALTHOUGH THIS ONE IS A BIT MORE COMPLICATED THAN OPENING A JAR. *HMM.*
if(collision.is_imminent AND
  collision.target == raybot.bodypart.head AND
  collision.weapon == attacker.bodypart.fist(
      side: right)){
  duck_and_smash(collision.weapon);
}
AND YOU USE A DOUBLE EQUAL SIGN HERE?
YES, WE USE A DOUBLE EQUAL SIGN WHEN WE'RE CHECKING TO SEE IF A CERTAIN CONDITION IS TRUE.
IT'S ESPECIALLY HANDY WITH "IF" STATEMENTS OR "WHILE" LOOPS.

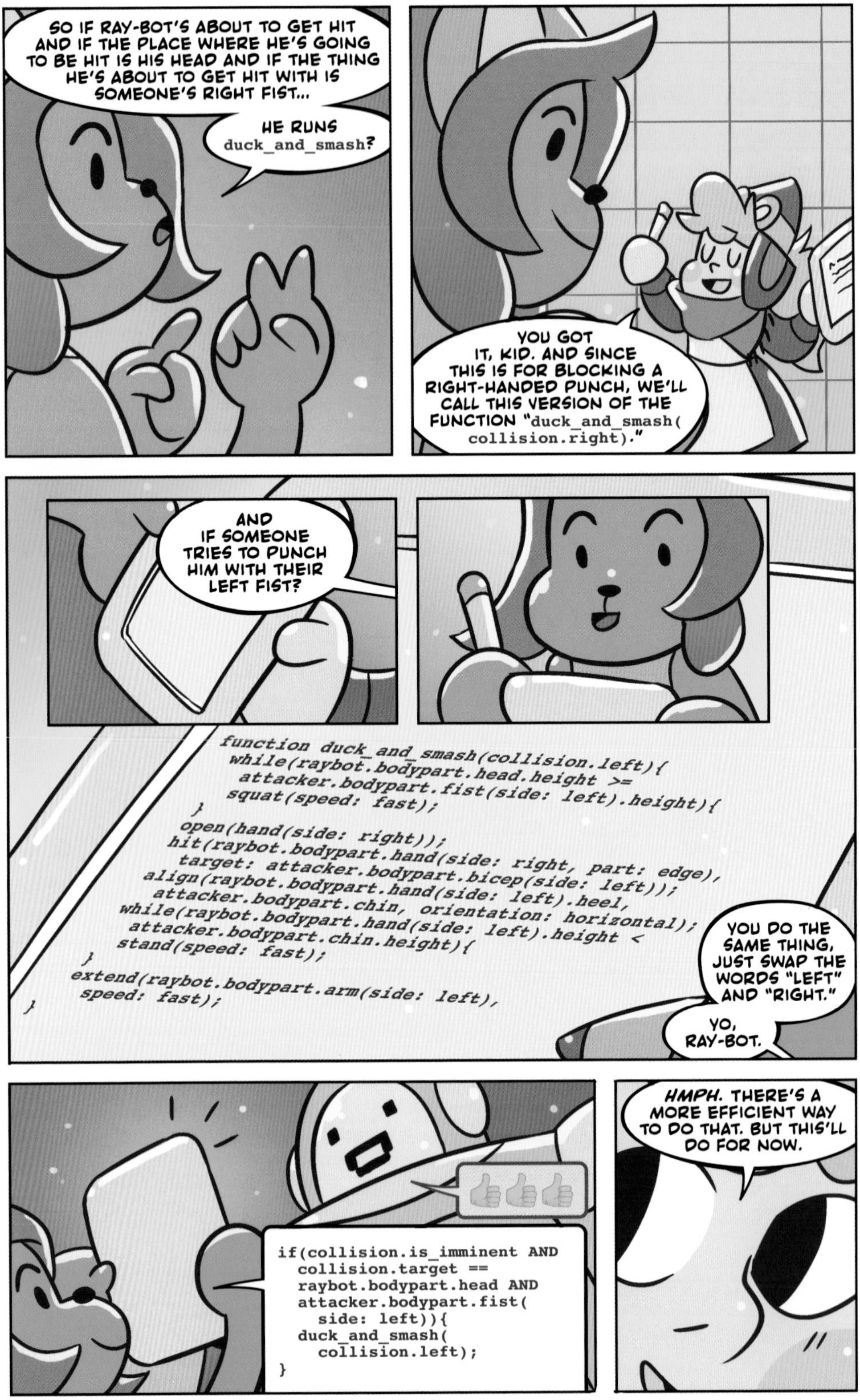
SO IF RAY-BOT'S ABOUT TO GET HIT AND IF THE PLACE WHERE HE'S GOING TO BE HIT IS HIS HEAD AND IF THE THING HE'S ABOUT TO GET HIT WITH IS SOMEONE'S RIGHT FIST...
HE RUNS duck_and_smash?
YOU GOT IT, KID. AND SINCE THIS IS FOR BLOCKING A RIGHT-HANDED PUNCH, WE'LL CALL THIS VERSION OF THE FUNCTION "duck_and_smash(collision.right)."
AND IF SOMEONE TRIES TO PUNCH HIM WITH THEIR LEFT FIST?
function duck_and_smash(collision.left){
while(raybot.bodypart.head.height >=
attacker.bodypart.fist(side: left).height){
squat(speed: fast);
}
open(hand(side: right));
hit(raybot.bodypart.hand(side: right, part: edge),
target: attacker.bodypart.bicep(side: left));
align(raybot.bodypart.hand(side: left).heel,
attacker.bodypart.chin, orientation: horizontal);
while(raybot.bodypart.hand(side: left).height <
attacker.bodypart.chin.height){
stand(speed: fast);
}
extend(raybot.bodypart.arm(side: left),
speed: fast);
}
YOU DO THE SAME THING, JUST SWAP THE WORDS "LEFT" AND "RIGHT."
YO, RAY-BOT.
if(collision.is_imminent AND
collision.target ==
raybot.bodypart.head AND
attacker.bodypart.fist(
side: left)){
duck_and_smash(
collision.left);
}
HMPH. THERE'S A MORE EFFICIENT WAY TO DO THAT. BUT THIS'LL DO FOR NOW.

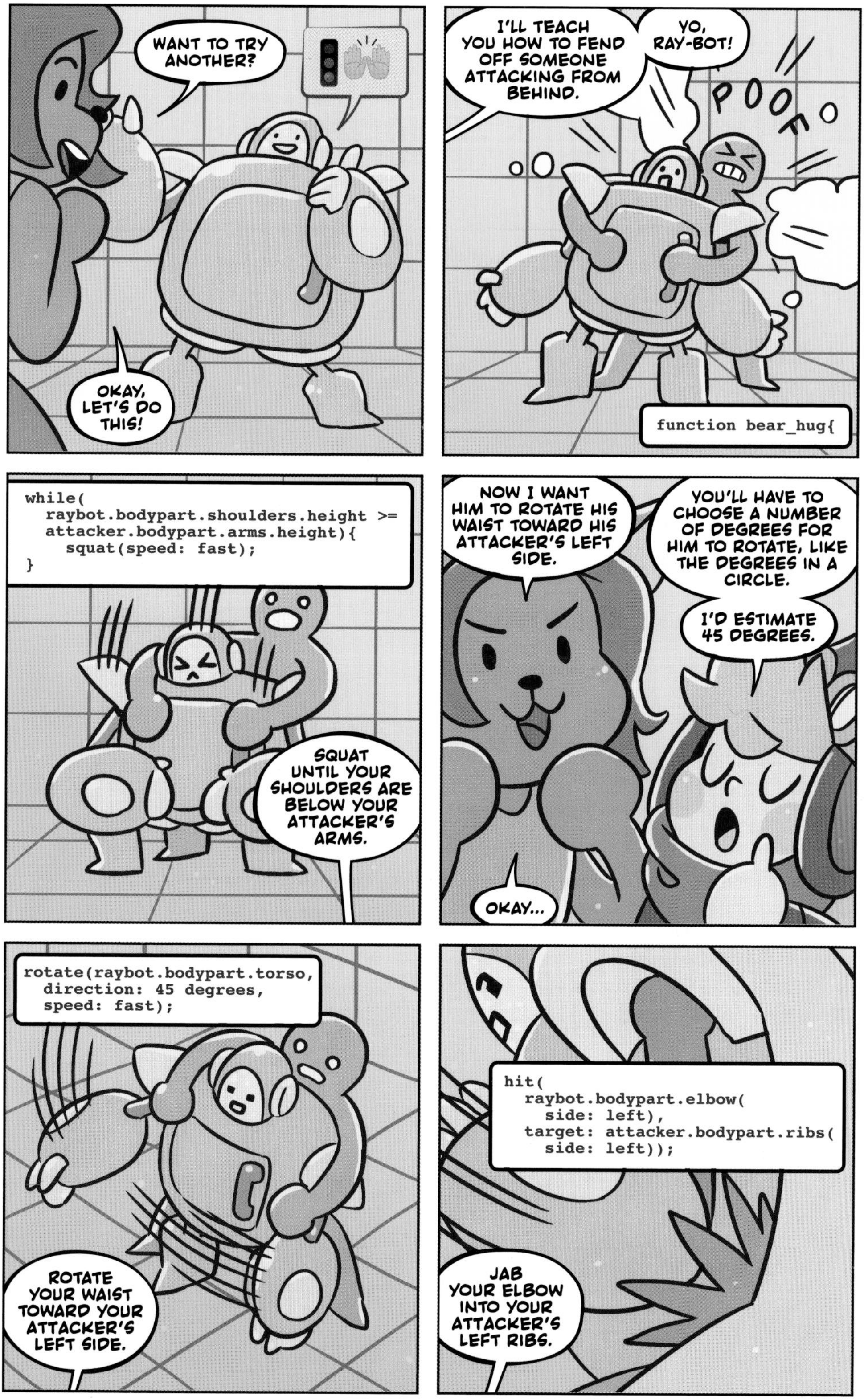

WANT TO TRY ANOTHER?
OKAY, LET'S DO THIS!
I'LL TEACH YOU HOW TO FEND OFF SOMEONE ATTACKING FROM BEHIND.
YO, RAY-BOT!
POOF
function bear_hug{
while(
raybot.bodypart.shoulders.height >=
attacker.bodypart.arms.height){
squat(speed: fast);
}
SQUAT UNTIL YOUR SHOULDERS ARE BELOW YOUR ATTACKER'S ARMS.
NOW I WANT HIM TO ROTATE HIS WAIST TOWARD HIS ATTACKER'S LEFT SIDE.
YOU'LL HAVE TO CHOOSE A NUMBER OF DEGREES FOR HIM TO ROTATE, LIKE THE DEGREES IN A CIRCLE.
I'D ESTIMATE 45 DEGREES.
OKAY...
rotate(raybot.bodypart.torso,
direction: 45 degrees,
speed: fast);
ROTATE YOUR WAIST TOWARD YOUR ATTACKER'S LEFT SIDE.
hit(
raybot.bodypart.elbow(
side: left),
target: attacker.bodypart.ribs(
side: left));
JAB YOUR ELBOW INTO YOUR ATTACKER'S LEFT RIBS.

NOW I WANT HIM TO ROTATE HIS WAIST TOWARD HIS ATTACKER'S RIGHT SIDE.

WELL...

FIRST WE HAVE TO SUBTRACT 45 DEGREES FROM HIS CURRENT POSITION TO GET HIM BACK TO CENTER.

THEN SUBTRACT ANOTHER 45 DEGREES TO TURN HIM TOWARD THE RIGHT.

SO THAT'S A TOTAL OF -90 DEGREES.

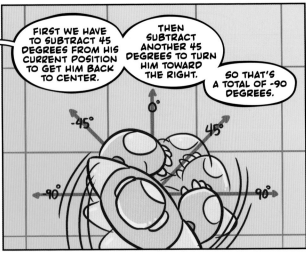

-45° 45°

-90° 90°

```
rotate(
  raybot.bodypart.torso,
  direction: -90 degrees,
  speed: fast);

hit(
  raybot.bodypart.elbow(
    side: right),
  target: attacker.bodypart.ribs(
    side: right));
```

ROTATE YOUR WAIST TOWARD YOUR ATTACKER'S LEFT SIDE. JAB YOUR ELBOW INTO YOUR ATTACKER'S RIGHT RIBS.

```
move(direction: forward,
  distance: 1 step);

  hit(raybot.bodypart.foot(
    side: right),
    target: attacker.bodypart.knee(
      side: right));
}
```

MOVE ONE STEP FORWARD. KICK YOUR ATTACKER'S RIGHT KNEE WITH YOUR RIGHT FOOT.

CLAP!

THAT WAS AMAZING!

YO, RAY-BOT!

```
if(collision.is_immenent AND
  collision.target == self.body_part.waist AND
  collision.weapon == attacker.bodypart.arms){
  bear_hug();
}
```

NICE WORK.

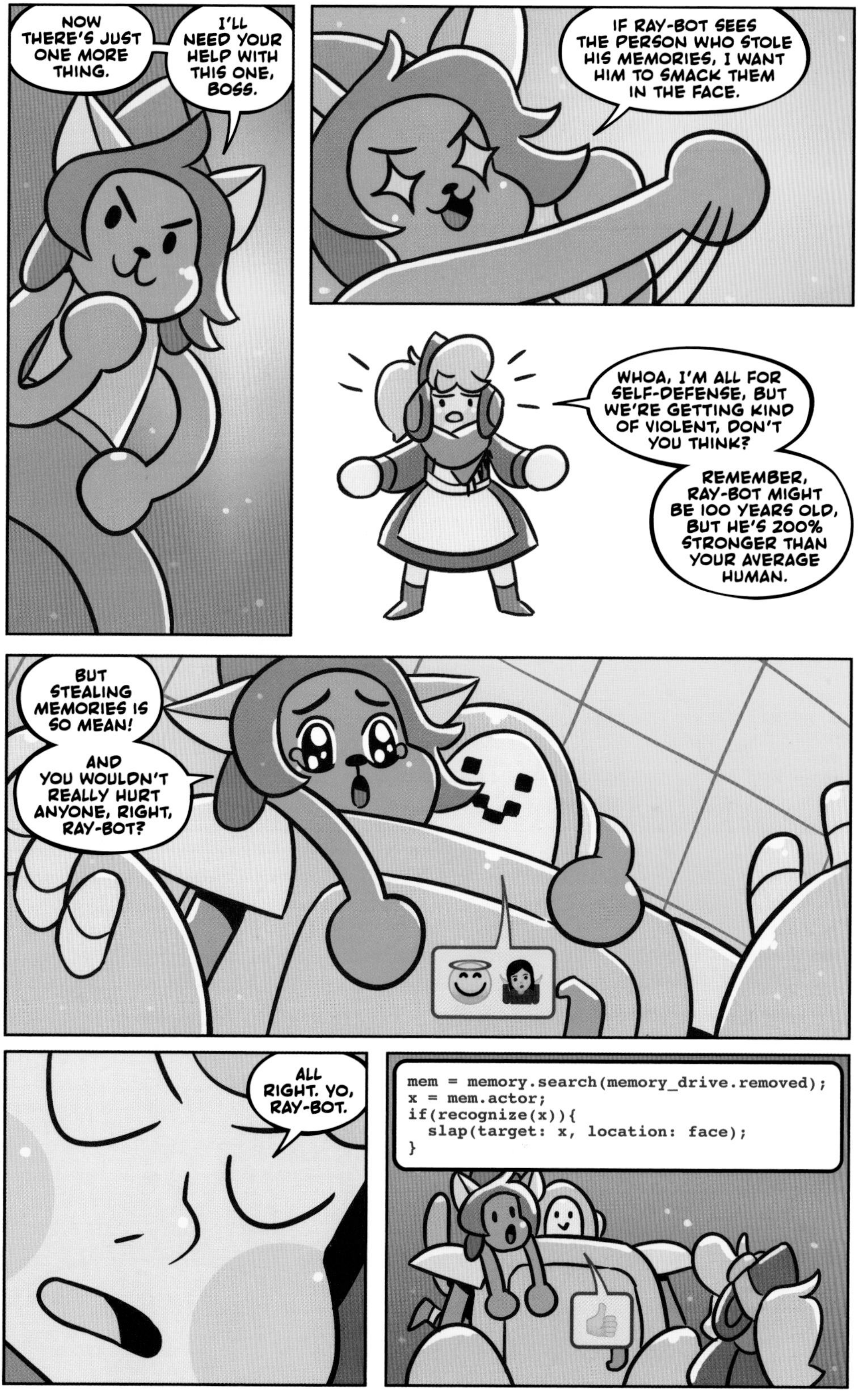
NOW THERE'S JUST ONE MORE THING.
I'LL NEED YOUR HELP WITH THIS ONE, BOSS.
IF RAY-BOT SEES THE PERSON WHO STOLE HIS MEMORIES, I WANT HIM TO SMACK THEM IN THE FACE.
WHOA, I'M ALL FOR SELF-DEFENSE, BUT WE'RE GETTING KIND OF VIOLENT, DON'T YOU THINK?
REMEMBER, RAY-BOT MIGHT BE 100 YEARS OLD, BUT HE'S 200% STRONGER THAN YOUR AVERAGE HUMAN.
BUT STEALING MEMORIES IS SO MEAN!
AND YOU WOULDN'T REALLY HURT ANYONE, RIGHT, RAY-BOT?
ALL RIGHT. YO, RAY-BOT.
mem = memory.search(memory_drive.removed);
x = mem.actor;
if(recognize(x)){
slap(target: x, location: face);
}

OKAY, YOU HAVE TO TELL ME WHAT THAT MEANS!

WELL, FIRST WE HAVE TO TELL RAY-BOT WHAT HE'S LOOKING FOR.

WE WANT HIM TO SEARCH FOR A CERTAIN MEMORY, THE ONE WHERE HIS MEMORY DRIVE WAS REMOVED.

SO THAT'S THE `memory.search(memory_drive.removed);` PART.

WHAT DOES `mem =` MEAN?

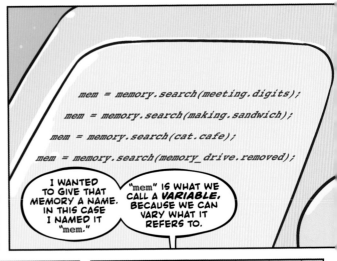

```
mem = memory.search(meeting.digits);

mem = memory.search(making.sandwich);

mem = memory.search(cat.cafe);

mem = memory.search(memory_drive.removed);
```

I WANTED TO GIVE THAT MEMORY A NAME. IN THIS CASE I NAMED IT "mem."

"mem" IS WHAT WE CALL A **VARIABLE,** BECAUSE WE CAN VARY WHAT IT REFERS TO.

SO WHEN I TELL RAY-BOT...

```
mem = memory.search(
memory_drive.removed);
```

```
mem = memory.search(
memory_drive.removed);
```

I'M SAYING, "SEARCH FOR THE MEMORY WHERE YOUR MEMORY DRIVE WAS REMOVED, AND CALL THAT MEMORY 'mem.'"

AND YOU USE JUST ONE EQUAL SIGN FOR THAT?

RIGHT, WE USE DOUBLE EQUAL SIGNS IF WE'RE ASKING RAY-BOT TO FIGURE OUT IF TWO THINGS ARE EQUAL.

BUT IF WE'RE TELLING RAY-BOT TO ASSIGN SOMETHING SPECIFIC TO A VARIABLE, WE JUST USE ONE EQUAL SIGN. IT'S CALLED **ASSIGNMENT.**

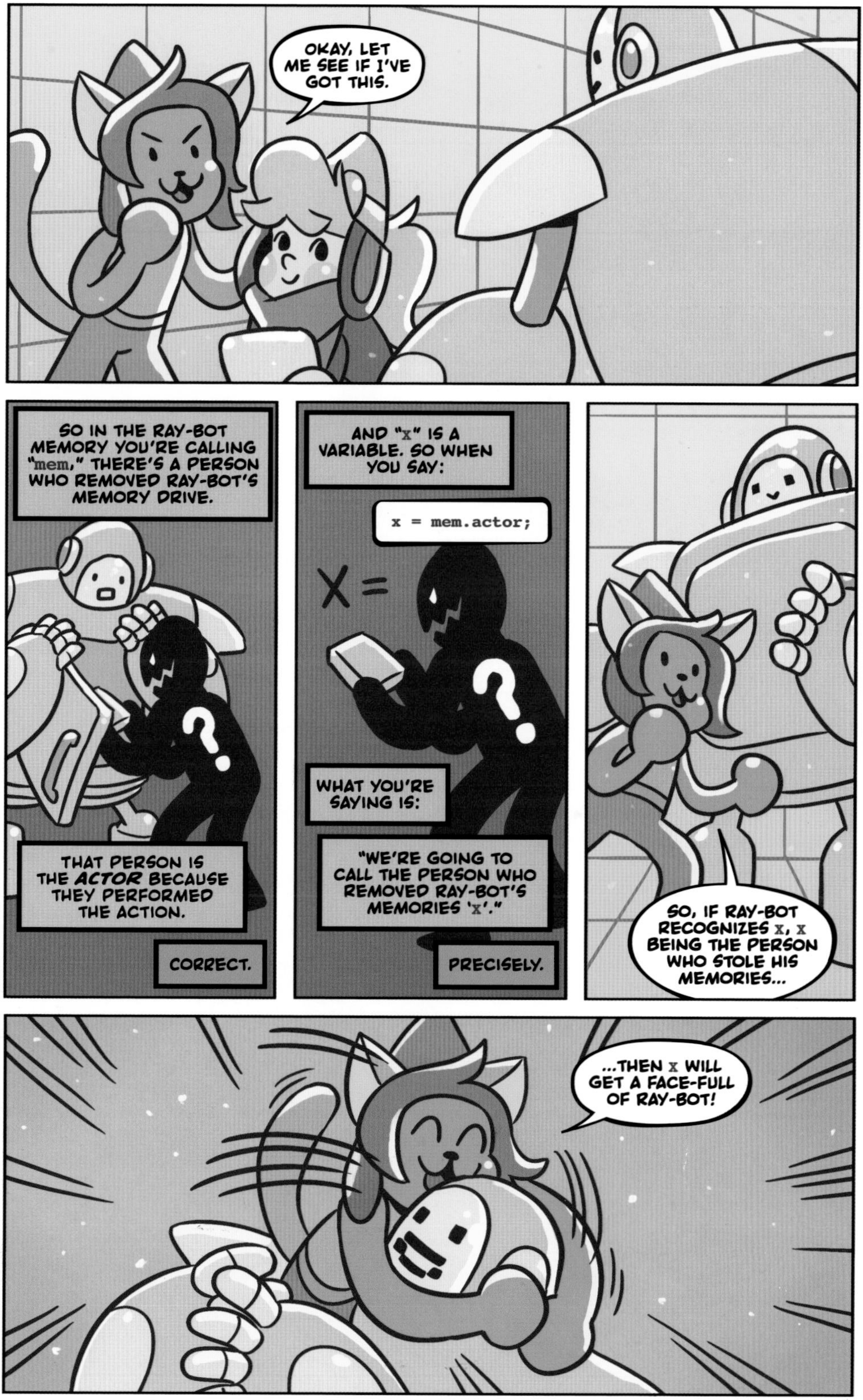
OKAY, LET ME SEE IF I'VE GOT THIS.
SO IN THE RAY-BOT MEMORY YOU'RE CALLING "mem," THERE'S A PERSON WHO REMOVED RAY-BOT'S MEMORY DRIVE.
THAT PERSON IS THE *ACTOR* BECAUSE THEY PERFORMED THE ACTION.
CORRECT.
AND "x" IS A VARIABLE. SO WHEN YOU SAY:
x = mem.actor;
X =
WHAT YOU'RE SAYING IS:
"WE'RE GOING TO CALL THE PERSON WHO REMOVED RAY-BOT'S MEMORIES 'x'."
PRECISELY.
SO, IF RAY-BOT RECOGNIZES x, x BEING THE PERSON WHO STOLE HIS MEMORIES...
...THEN x WILL GET A FACE-FULL OF RAY-BOT!

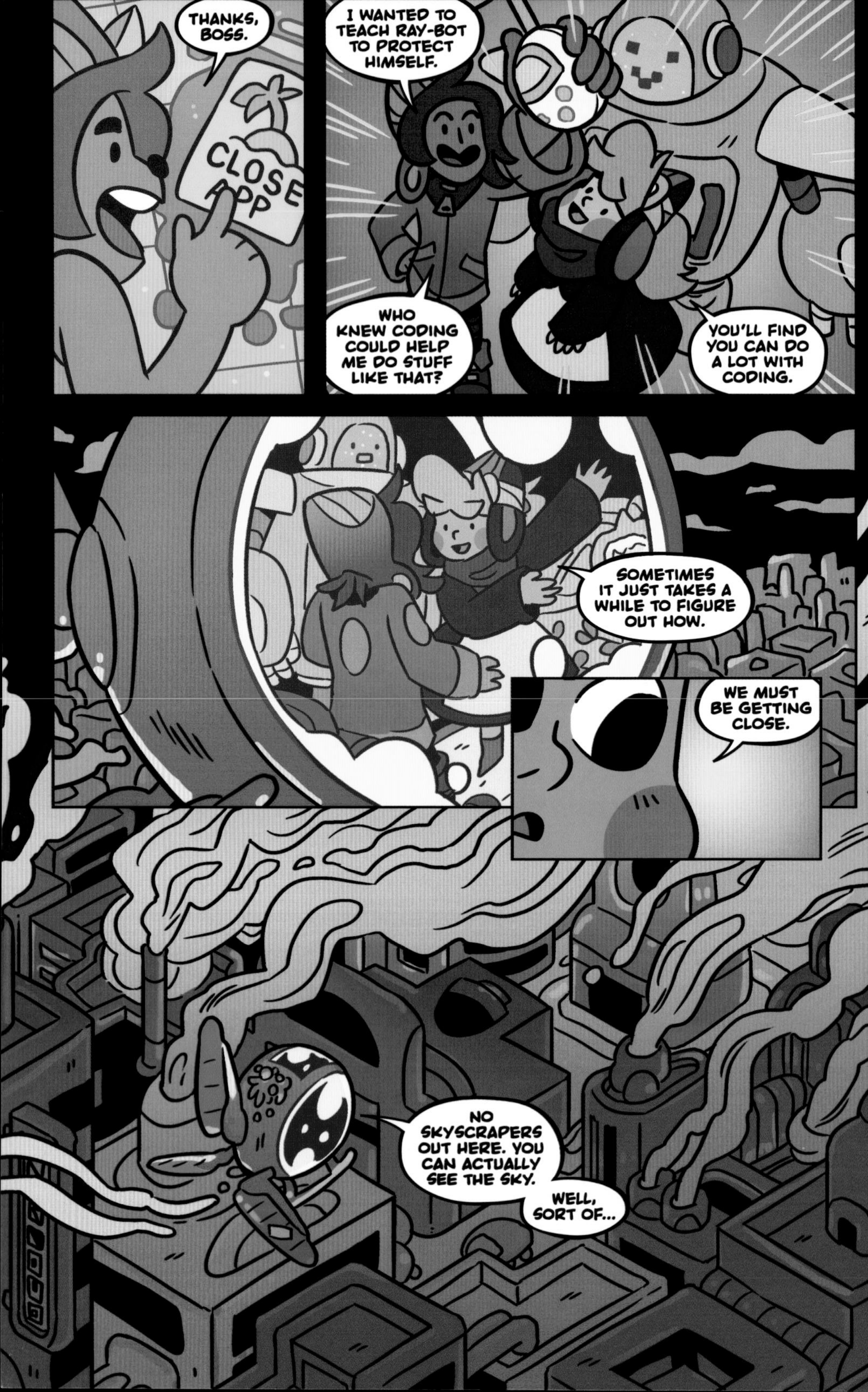
THANKS, BOSS.
CLOSE APP
I WANTED TO TEACH RAY-BOT TO PROTECT HIMSELF.
WHO KNEW CODING COULD HELP ME DO STUFF LIKE THAT?
YOU'LL FIND YOU CAN DO A LOT WITH CODING.
SOMETIMES IT JUST TAKES A WHILE TO FIGURE OUT HOW.
WE MUST BE GETTING CLOSE.
NO SKYSCRAPERS OUT HERE. YOU CAN ACTUALLY SEE THE SKY.
WELL, SORT OF...

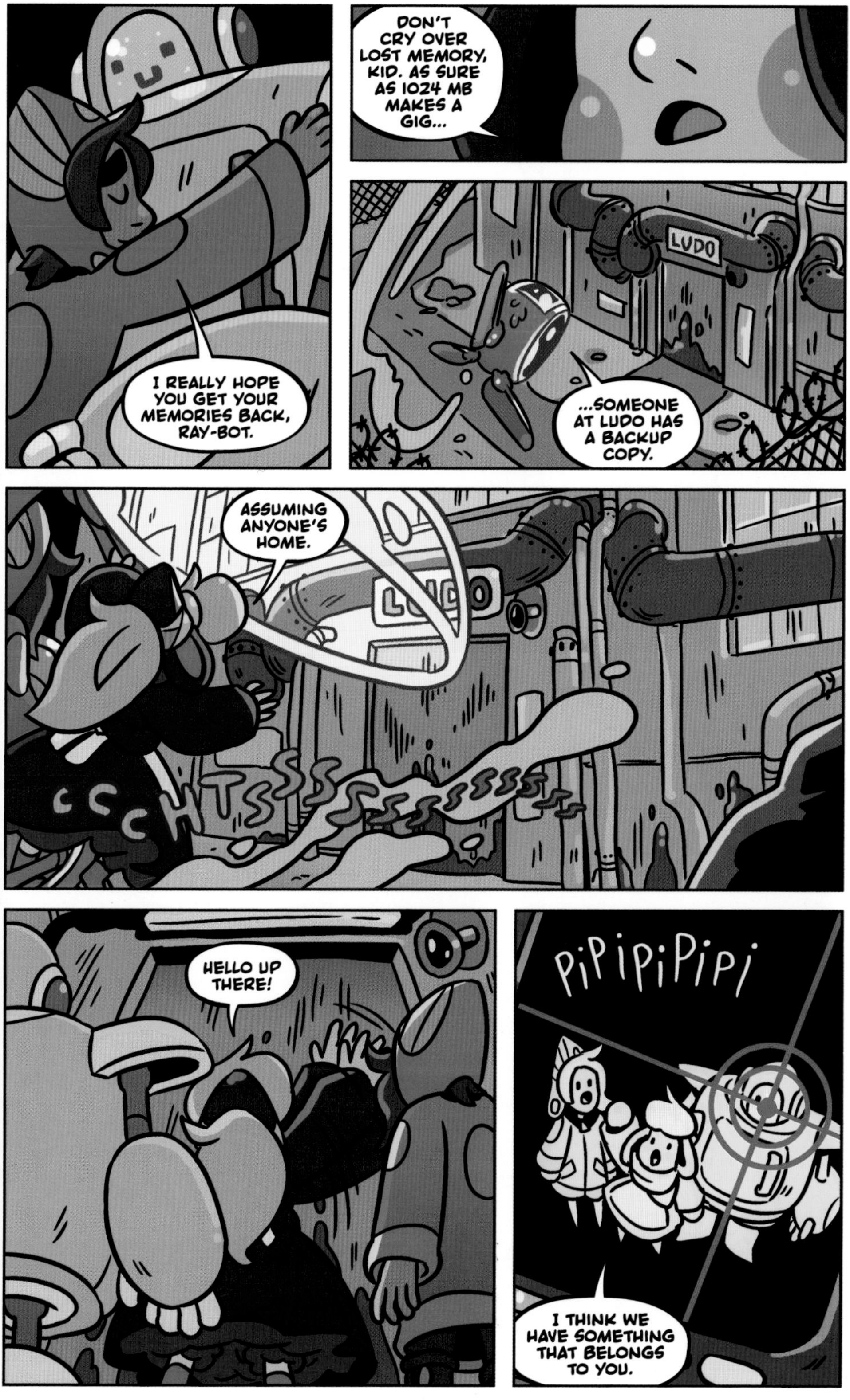
I REALLY HOPE YOU GET YOUR MEMORIES BACK, RAY-BOT.
DON'T CRY OVER LOST MEMORY, KID. AS SURE AS 1024 MB MAKES A GIG...
LUDO
...SOMEONE AT LUDO HAS A BACKUP COPY.
ASSUMING ANYONE'S HOME.
LUDO
CCCHTSSSSSSSSSSSSSS
HELLO UP THERE!
PIPIPIPIPI
I THINK WE HAVE SOMETHING THAT BELONGS TO YOU.

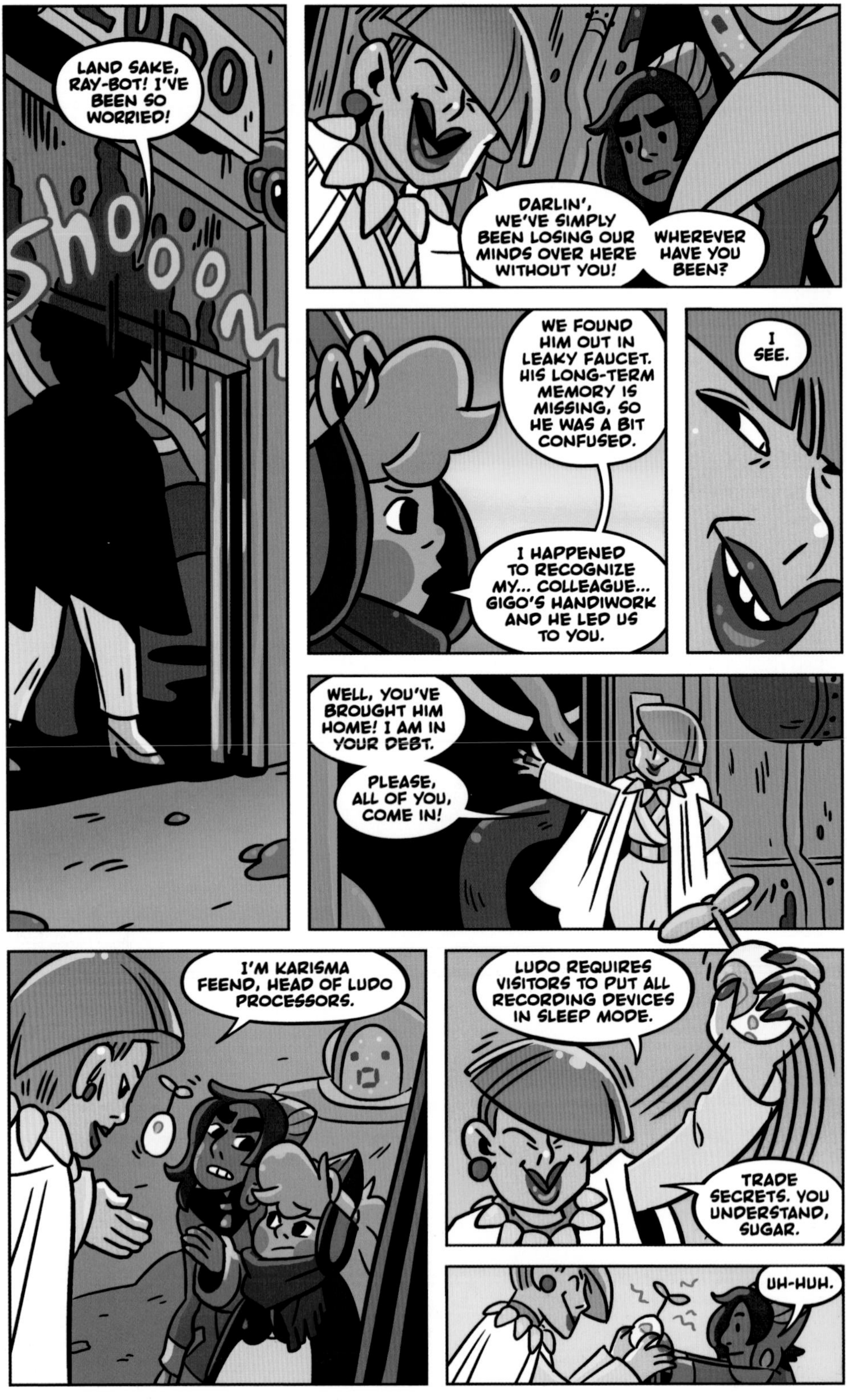
LAND SAKE, RAY-BOT! I'VE BEEN SO WORRIED!
SHOOOM
DARLIN', WE'VE SIMPLY BEEN LOSING OUR MINDS OVER HERE WITHOUT YOU!
WHEREVER HAVE YOU BEEN?
WE FOUND HIM OUT IN LEAKY FAUCET. HIS LONG-TERM MEMORY IS MISSING, SO HE WAS A BIT CONFUSED.
I HAPPENED TO RECOGNIZE MY... COLLEAGUE... GIGO'S HANDIWORK AND HE LED US TO YOU.
I SEE.
WELL, YOU'VE BROUGHT HIM HOME! I AM IN YOUR DEBT.
PLEASE, ALL OF YOU, COME IN!
I'M KARISMA FEEND, HEAD OF LUDO PROCESSORS.
LUDO REQUIRES VISITORS TO PUT ALL RECORDING DEVICES IN SLEEP MODE.
TRADE SECRETS. YOU UNDERSTAND, SUGAR.
UH-HUH.

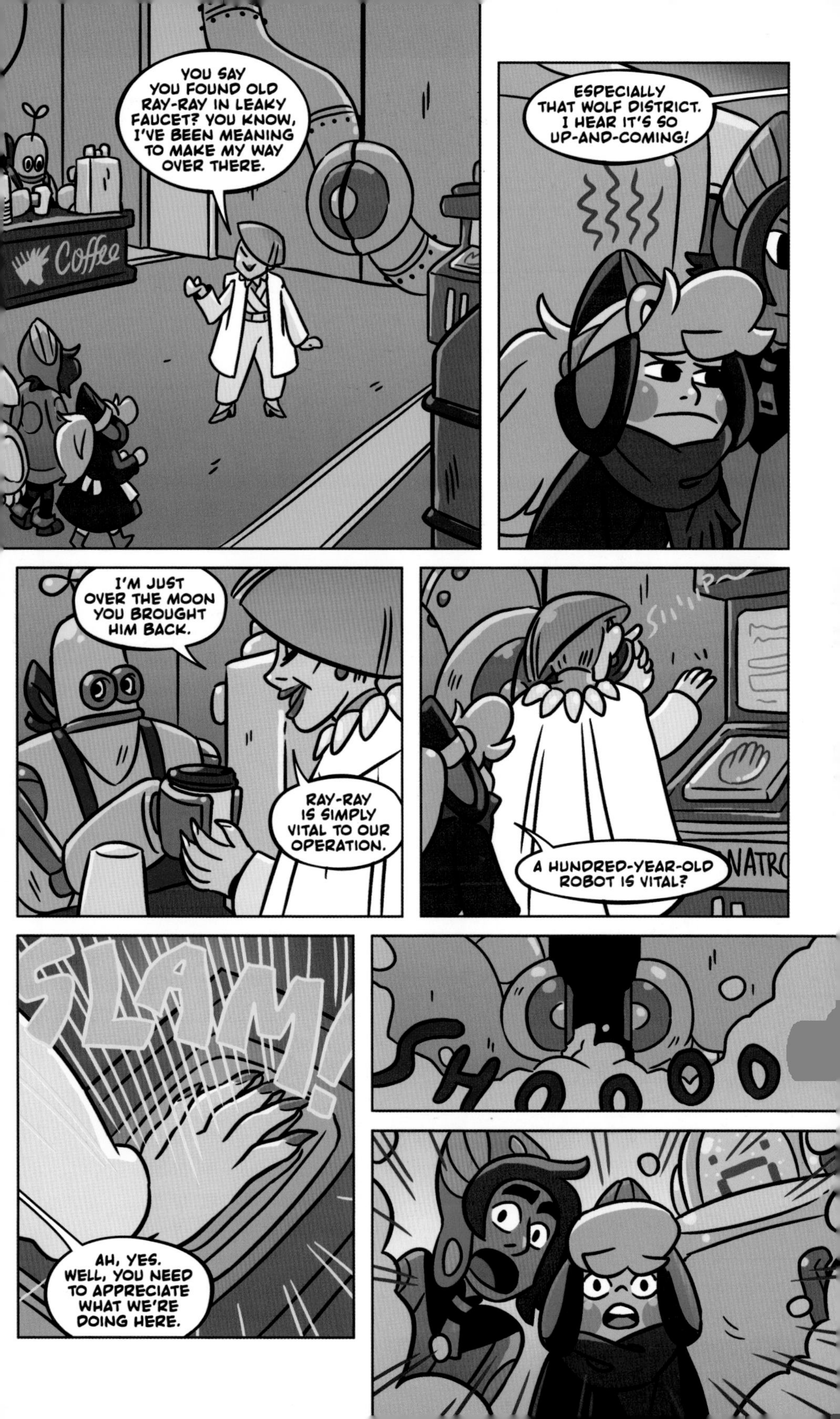
YOU SAY YOU FOUND OLD RAY-RAY IN LEAKY FAUCET? YOU KNOW, I'VE BEEN MEANING TO MAKE MY WAY OVER THERE.
Coffee
ESPECIALLY THAT WOLF DISTRICT. I HEAR IT'S SO UP-AND-COMING!
I'M JUST OVER THE MOON YOU BROUGHT HIM BACK.
RAY-RAY IS SIMPLY VITAL TO OUR OPERATION.
A HUNDRED-YEAR-OLD ROBOT IS VITAL?
SLAM!
AH, YES. WELL, YOU NEED TO APPRECIATE WHAT WE'RE DOING HERE.
SHOOOOO

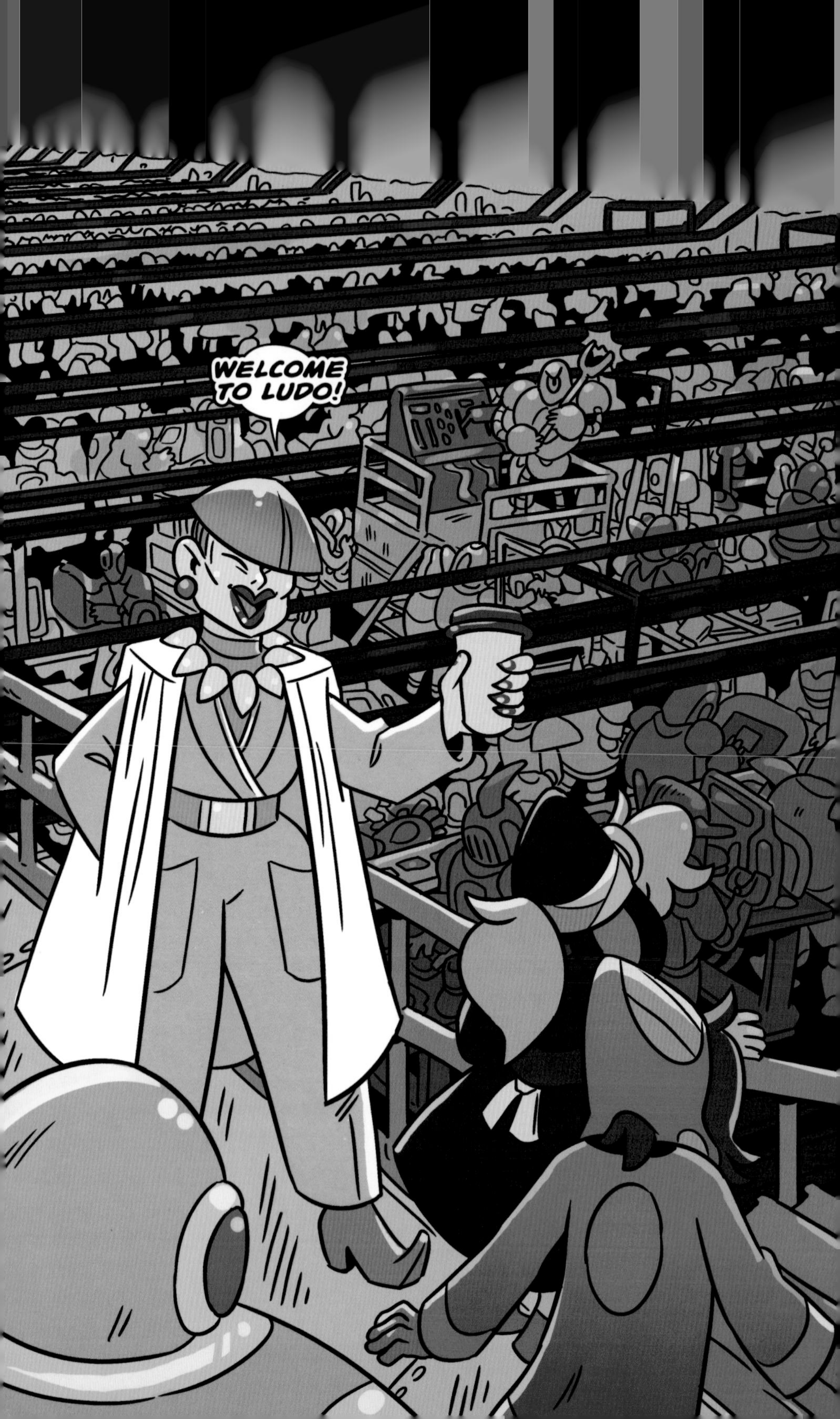
WELCOME TO LUDO!

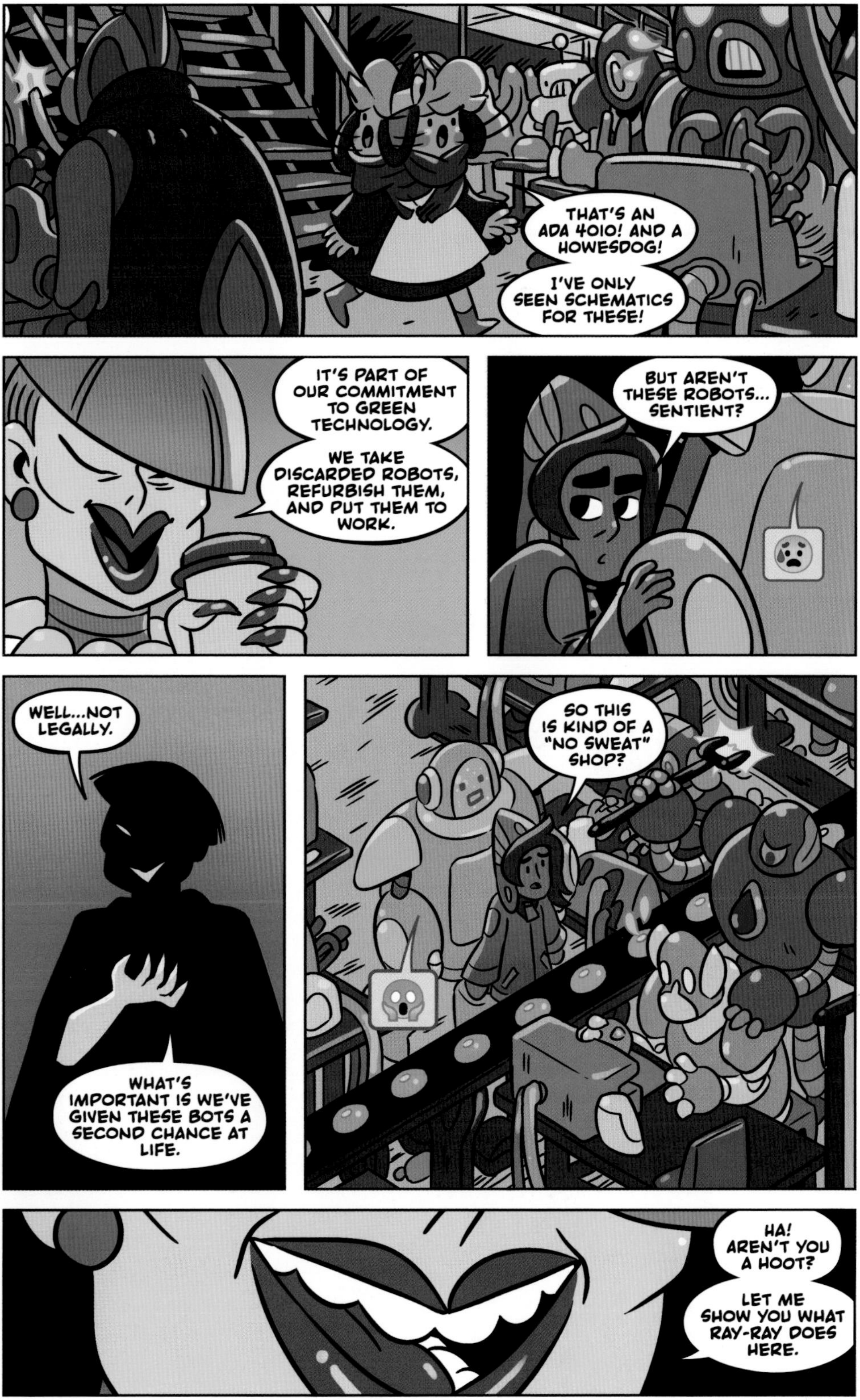
THAT'S AN ADA 4010! AND A HOWESDOG!
I'VE ONLY SEEN SCHEMATICS FOR THESE!
IT'S PART OF OUR COMMITMENT TO GREEN TECHNOLOGY.
WE TAKE DISCARDED ROBOTS, REFURBISH THEM, AND PUT THEM TO WORK.
BUT AREN'T THESE ROBOTS... SENTIENT?
WELL...NOT LEGALLY.
WHAT'S IMPORTANT IS WE'VE GIVEN THESE BOTS A SECOND CHANCE AT LIFE.
SO THIS IS KIND OF A "NO SWEAT" SHOP?
HA! AREN'T YOU A HOOT?
LET ME SHOW YOU WHAT RAY-RAY DOES HERE.

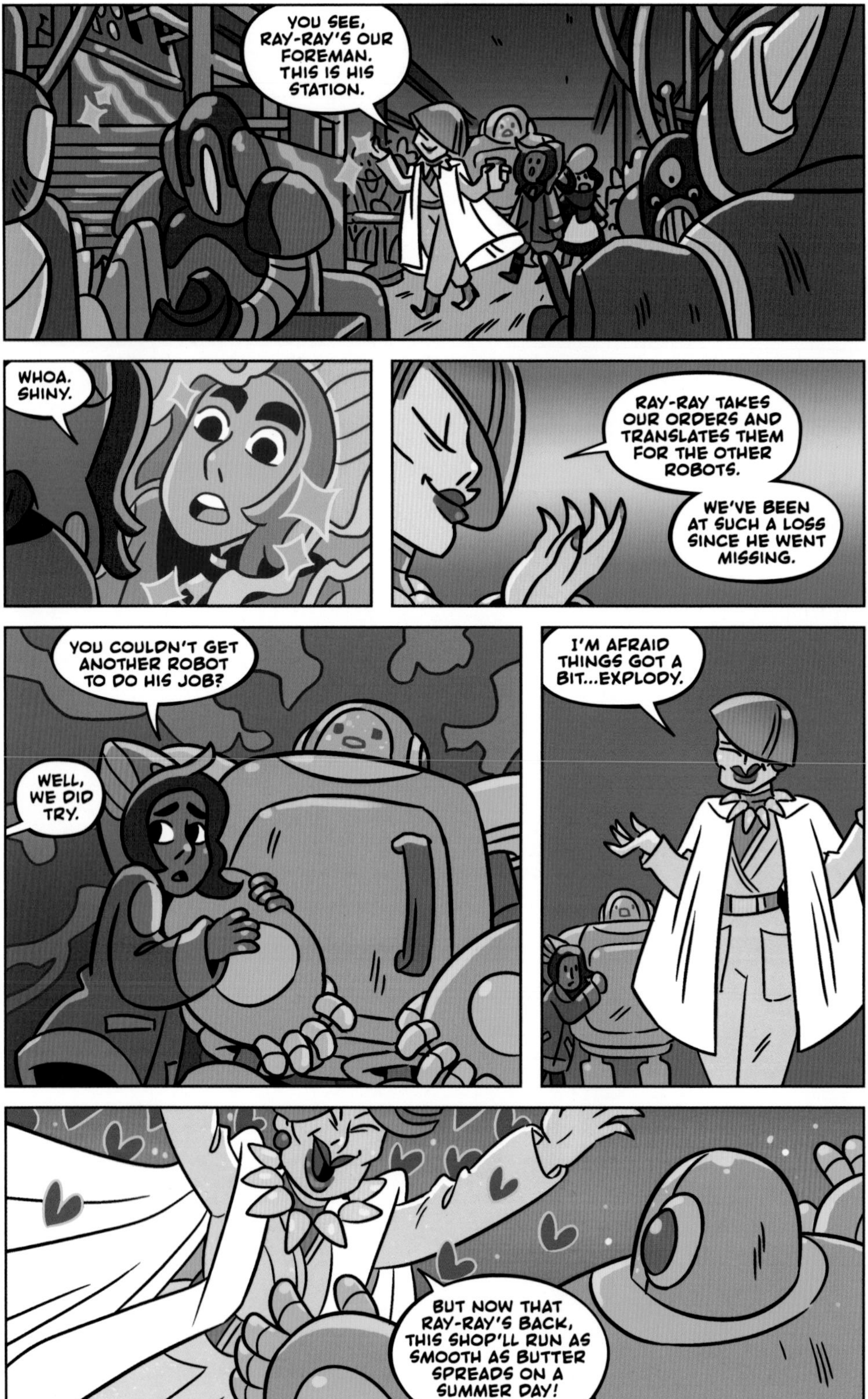
YOU SEE, RAY-RAY'S OUR FOREMAN. THIS IS HIS STATION.
WHOA. SHINY.
RAY-RAY TAKES OUR ORDERS AND TRANSLATES THEM FOR THE OTHER ROBOTS.
WE'VE BEEN AT SUCH A LOSS SINCE HE WENT MISSING.
YOU COULDN'T GET ANOTHER ROBOT TO DO HIS JOB?
WELL, WE DID TRY.
I'M AFRAID THINGS GOT A BIT...EXPLODY.
BUT NOW THAT RAY-RAY'S BACK, THIS SHOP'LL RUN AS SMOOTH AS BUTTER SPREADS ON A SUMMER DAY!

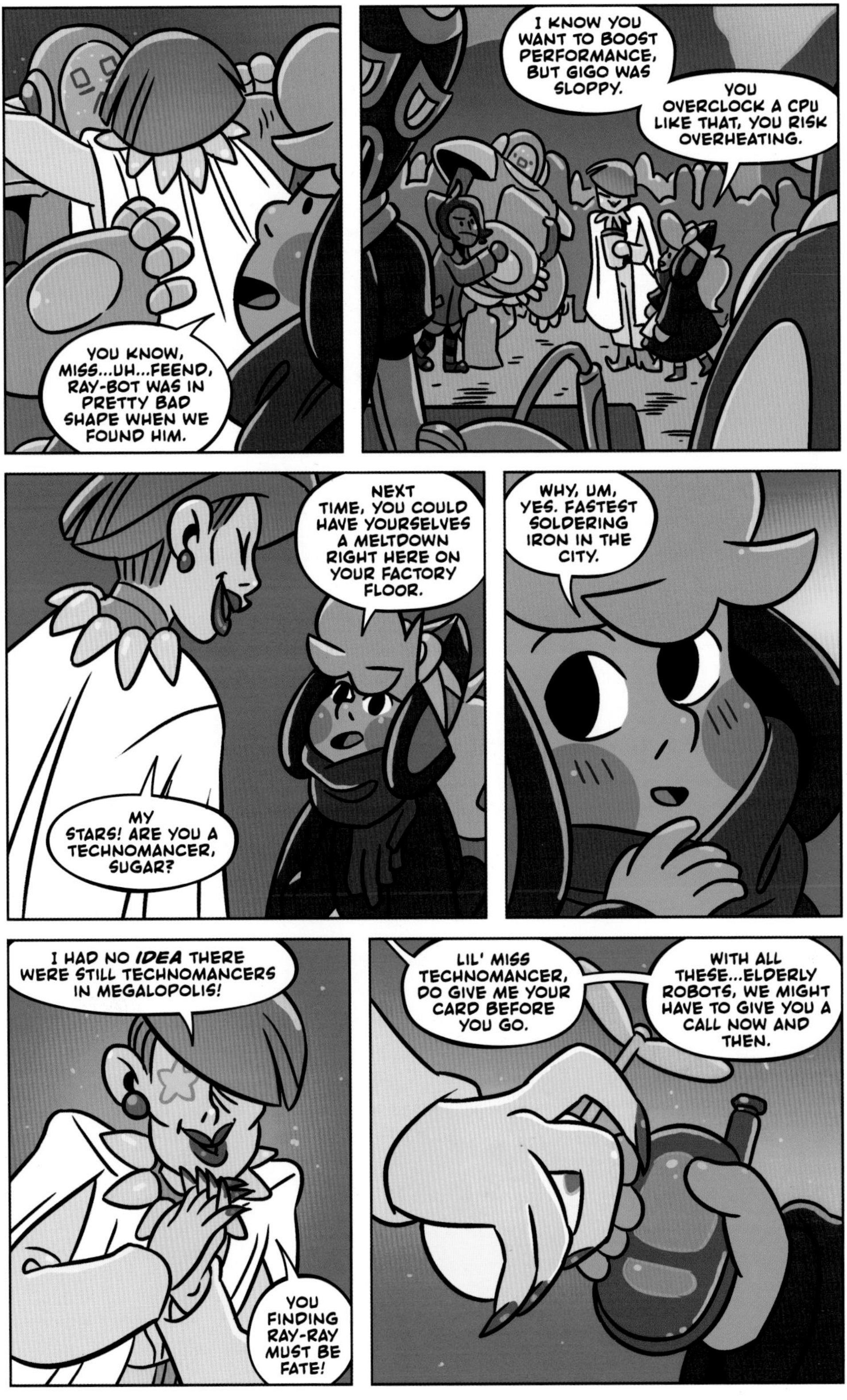
YOU KNOW, MISS...UH...FEEND, RAY-BOT WAS IN PRETTY BAD SHAPE WHEN WE FOUND HIM.
I KNOW YOU WANT TO BOOST PERFORMANCE, BUT GIGO WAS SLOPPY.
YOU OVERCLOCK A CPU LIKE THAT, YOU RISK OVERHEATING.
NEXT TIME, YOU COULD HAVE YOURSELVES A MELTDOWN RIGHT HERE ON YOUR FACTORY FLOOR.
MY STARS! ARE YOU A TECHNOMANCER, SUGAR?
WHY, UM, YES. FASTEST SOLDERING IRON IN THE CITY.
I HAD NO *IDEA* THERE WERE STILL TECHNOMANCERS IN MEGALOPOLIS!
YOU FINDING RAY-RAY MUST BE FATE!
LIL' MISS TECHNOMANCER, DO GIVE ME YOUR CARD BEFORE YOU GO.
WITH ALL THESE...ELDERLY ROBOTS, WE MIGHT HAVE TO GIVE YOU A CALL NOW AND THEN.

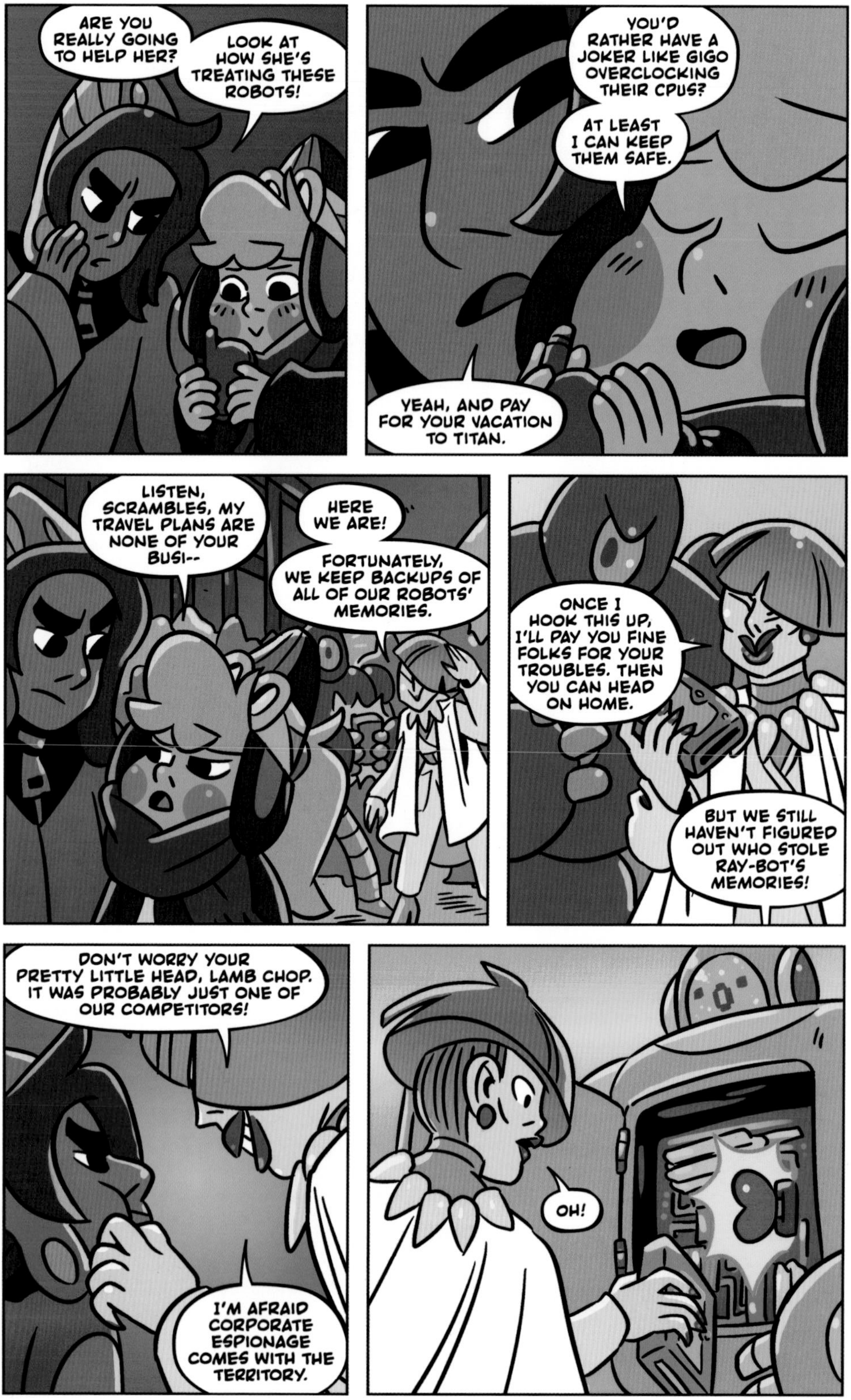
ARE YOU REALLY GOING TO HELP HER?
LOOK AT HOW SHE'S TREATING THESE ROBOTS!
YOU'D RATHER HAVE A JOKER LIKE GIGO OVERCLOCKING THEIR CPUS?
AT LEAST I CAN KEEP THEM SAFE.
YEAH, AND PAY FOR YOUR VACATION TO TITAN.
LISTEN, SCRAMBLES, MY TRAVEL PLANS ARE NONE OF YOUR BUSI--
HERE WE ARE!
FORTUNATELY, WE KEEP BACKUPS OF ALL OF OUR ROBOTS' MEMORIES.
ONCE I HOOK THIS UP, I'LL PAY YOU FINE FOLKS FOR YOUR TROUBLES. THEN YOU CAN HEAD ON HOME.
BUT WE STILL HAVEN'T FIGURED OUT WHO STOLE RAY-BOT'S MEMORIES!
DON'T WORRY YOUR PRETTY LITTLE HEAD, LAMB CHOP. IT WAS PROBABLY JUST ONE OF OUR COMPETITORS!
I'M AFRAID CORPORATE ESPIONAGE COMES WITH THE TERRITORY.
OH!

THIS LIL' OLD TRINKET BELONG TO YOU?
OH, YES, THAT'S MINE!
I DIDN'T WANT HIM TO FORGET--
POP!
--US.
SHH
OOM

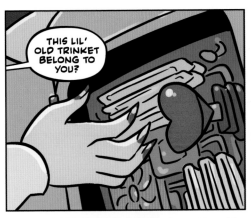

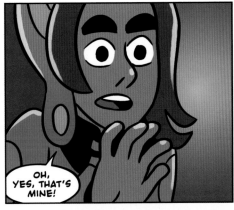

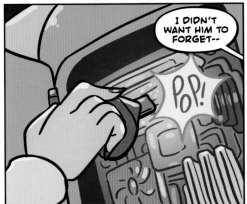

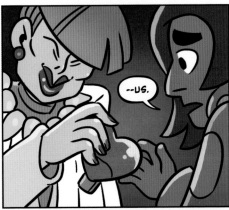

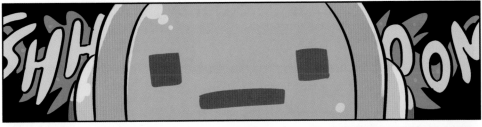

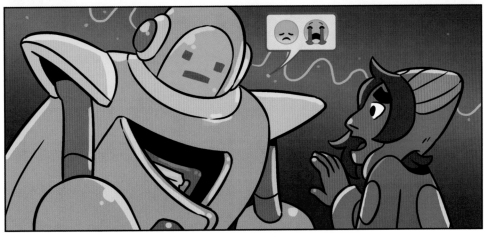

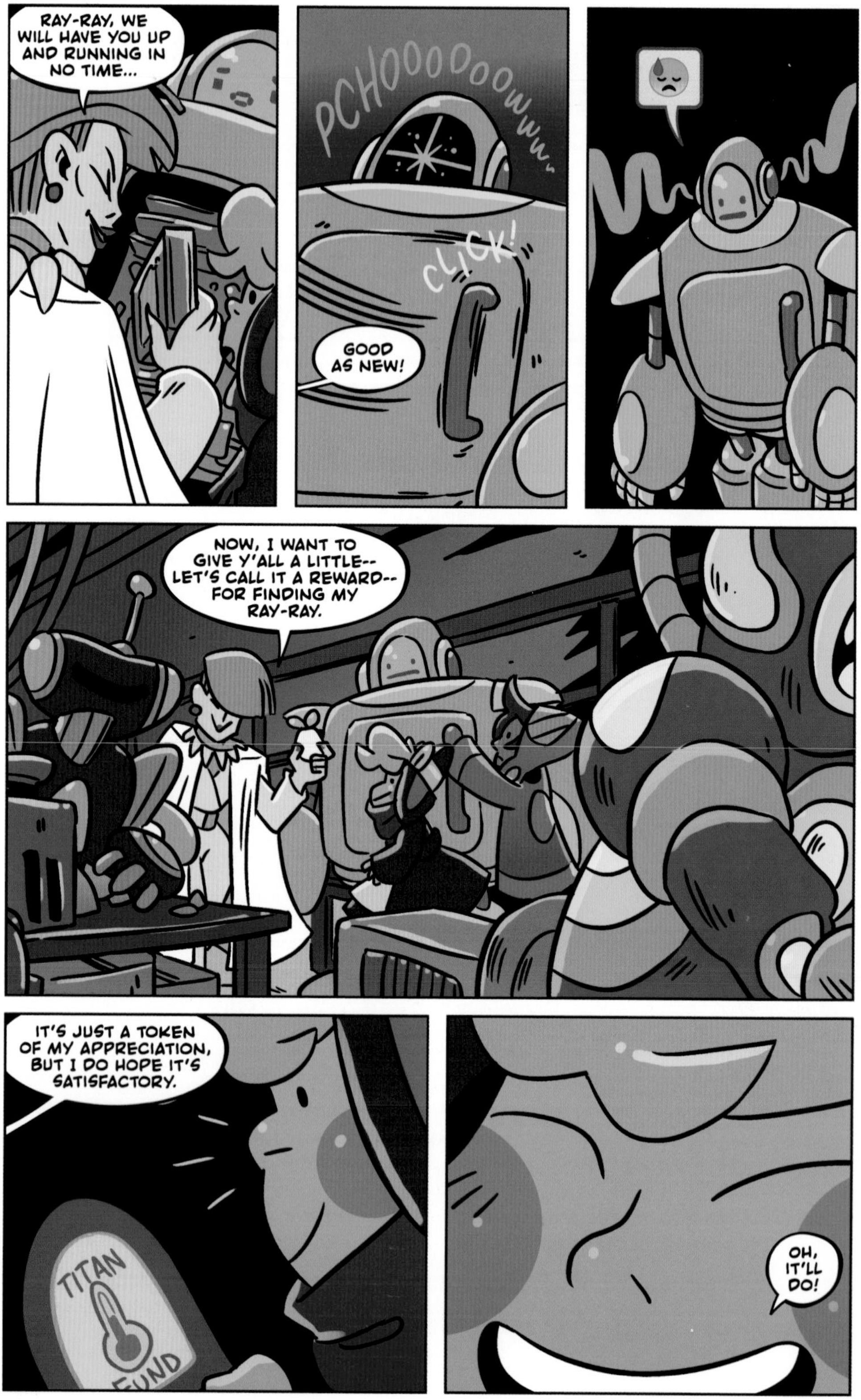
RAY-RAY, WE WILL HAVE YOU UP AND RUNNING IN NO TIME...
PCHOOOOOOOWWWW
CLICK!
GOOD AS NEW!
NOW, I WANT TO GIVE Y'ALL A LITTLE-- LET'S CALL IT A REWARD-- FOR FINDING MY RAY-RAY.
IT'S JUST A TOKEN OF MY APPRECIATION, BUT I DO HOPE IT'S SATISFACTORY.
TITAN FUND
OH, IT'LL DO!

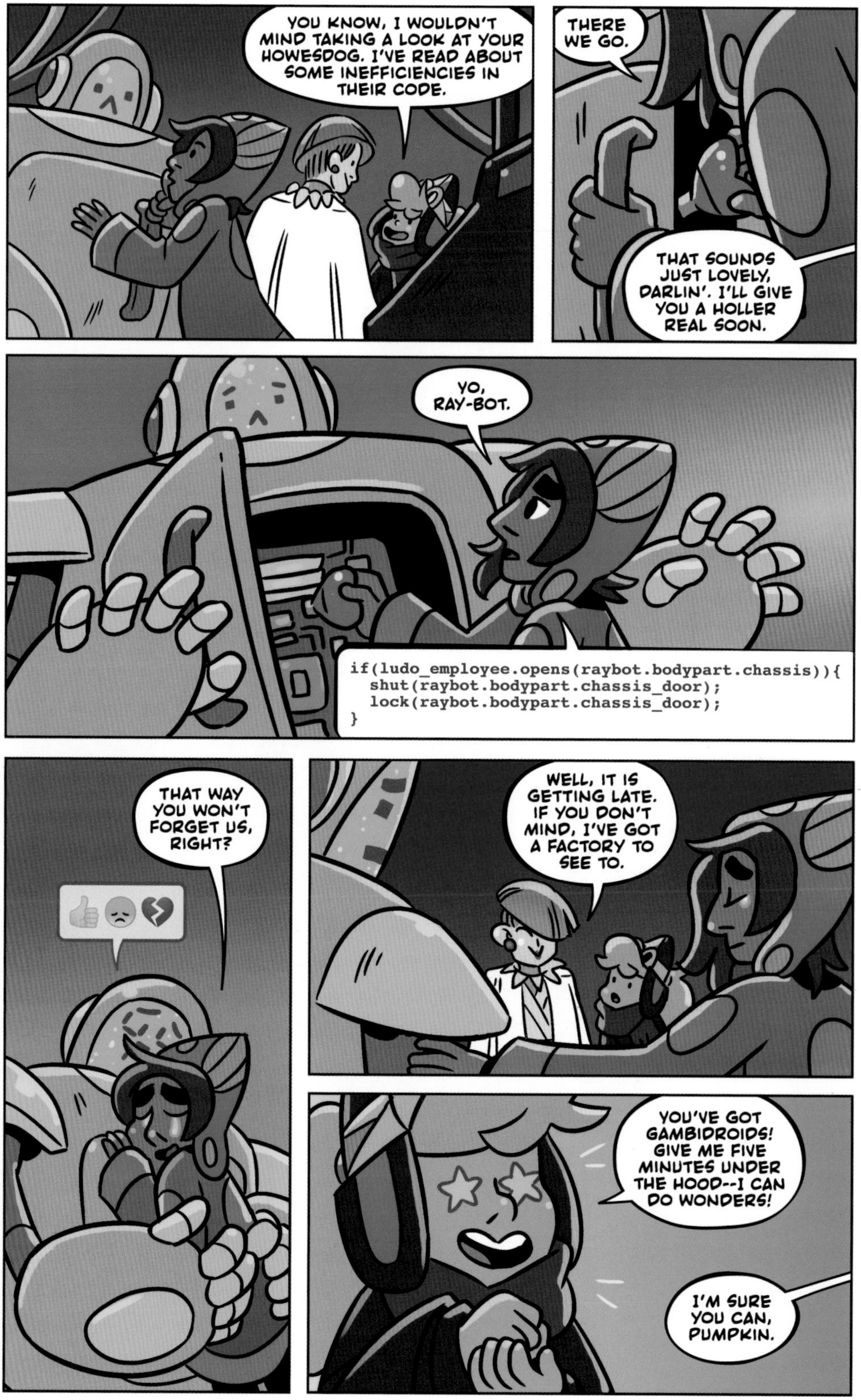
YOU KNOW, I WOULDN'T MIND TAKING A LOOK AT YOUR HOWESDOG. I'VE READ ABOUT SOME INEFFICIENCIES IN THEIR CODE.
THERE WE GO.
THAT SOUNDS JUST LOVELY, DARLIN'. I'LL GIVE YOU A HOLLER REAL SOON.
YO, RAY-BOT.
if(ludo_employee.opens(raybot.bodypart.chassis)){
shut(raybot.bodypart.chassis_door);
lock(raybot.bodypart.chassis_door);
}
THAT WAY YOU WON'T FORGET US, RIGHT?
WELL, IT IS GETTING LATE. IF YOU DON'T MIND, I'VE GOT A FACTORY TO SEE TO.
YOU'VE GOT GAMBIDROIDS! GIVE ME FIVE MINUTES UNDER THE HOOD--I CAN DO WONDERS!
I'M SURE YOU CAN, PUMPKIN.

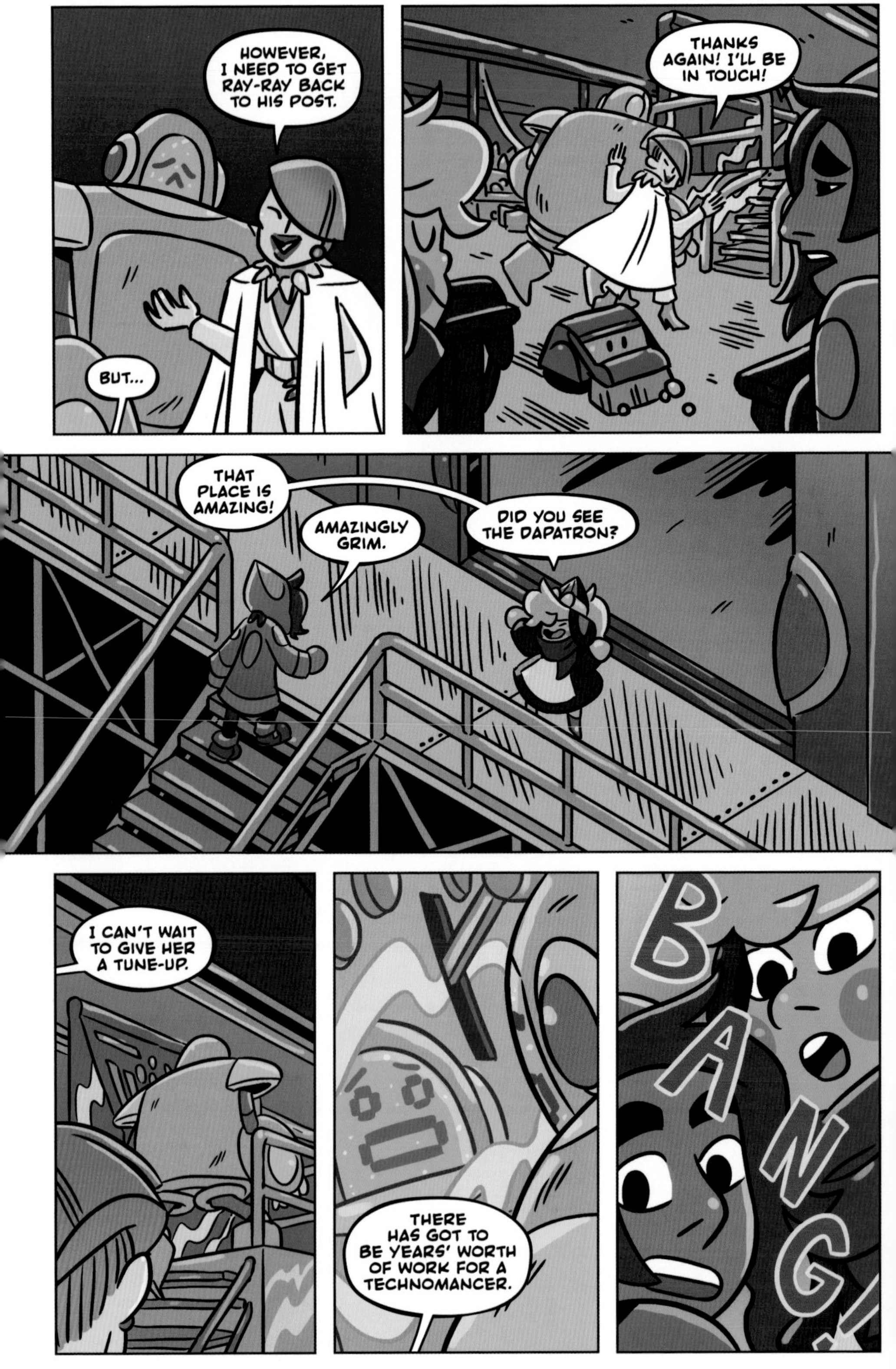
HOWEVER, I NEED TO GET RAY-RAY BACK TO HIS POST.
BUT...
THANKS AGAIN! I'LL BE IN TOUCH!
THAT PLACE IS AMAZING!
AMAZINGLY GRIM.
DID YOU SEE THE DAPATRON?
I CAN'T WAIT TO GIVE HER A TUNE-UP.
THERE HAS GOT TO BE YEARS' WORTH OF WORK FOR A TECHNOMANCER.
BANG!

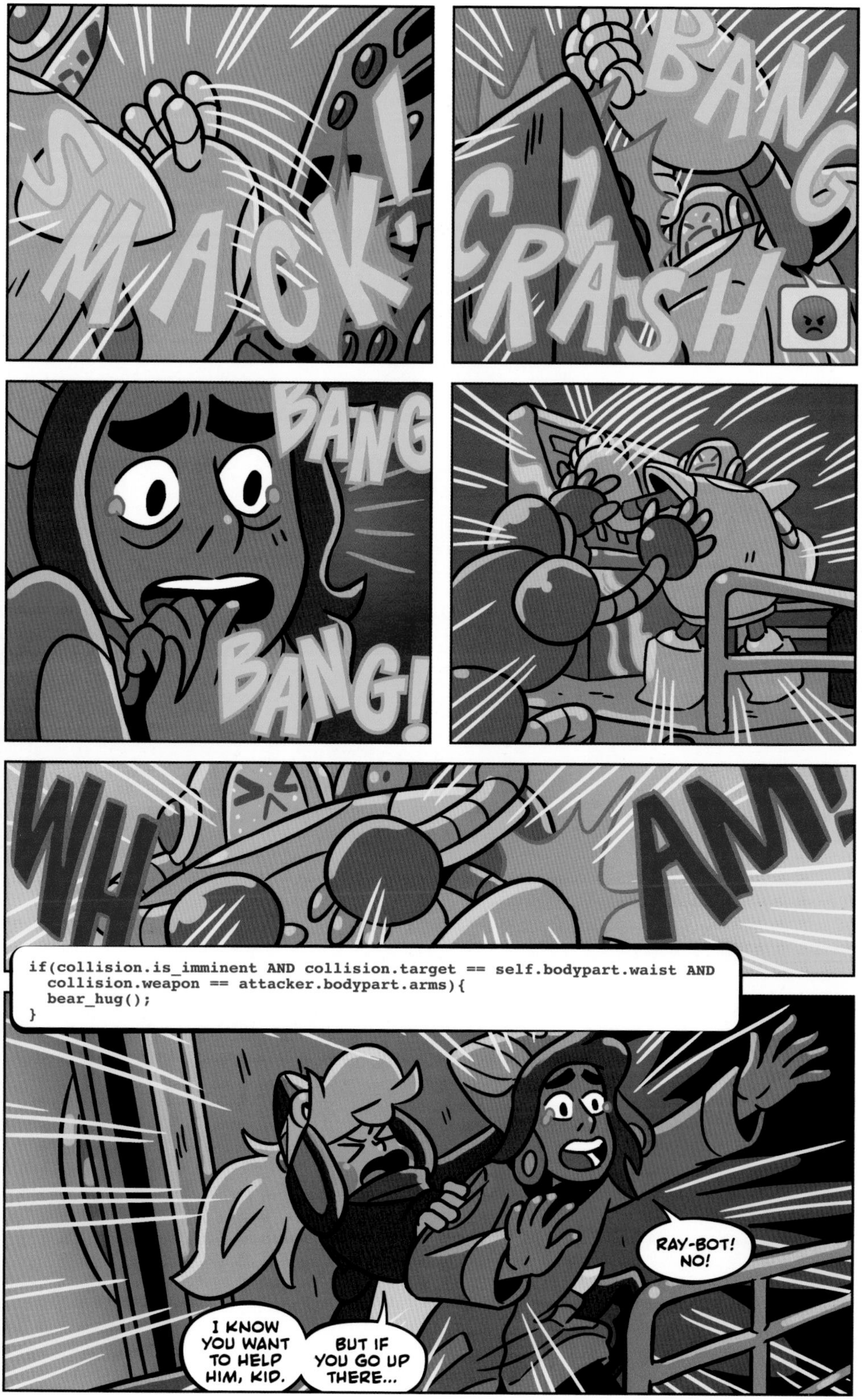
SMACK!
BANG
CRASH
BANG
BANG!
WH
AM!
if(collision.is_imminent AND collision.target == self.bodypart.waist AND
collision.weapon == attacker.bodypart.arms){
bear_hug();
}
RAY-BOT! NO!
I KNOW YOU WANT TO HELP HIM, KID.
BUT IF YOU GO UP THERE...

YOU'RE GONNA GET HURT.

NO, NO, NO.

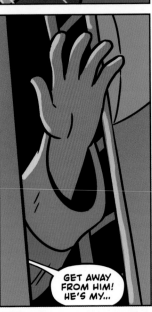

GET AWAY FROM HIM! HE'S MY...

...FRIEND.

DA-DOOOMM

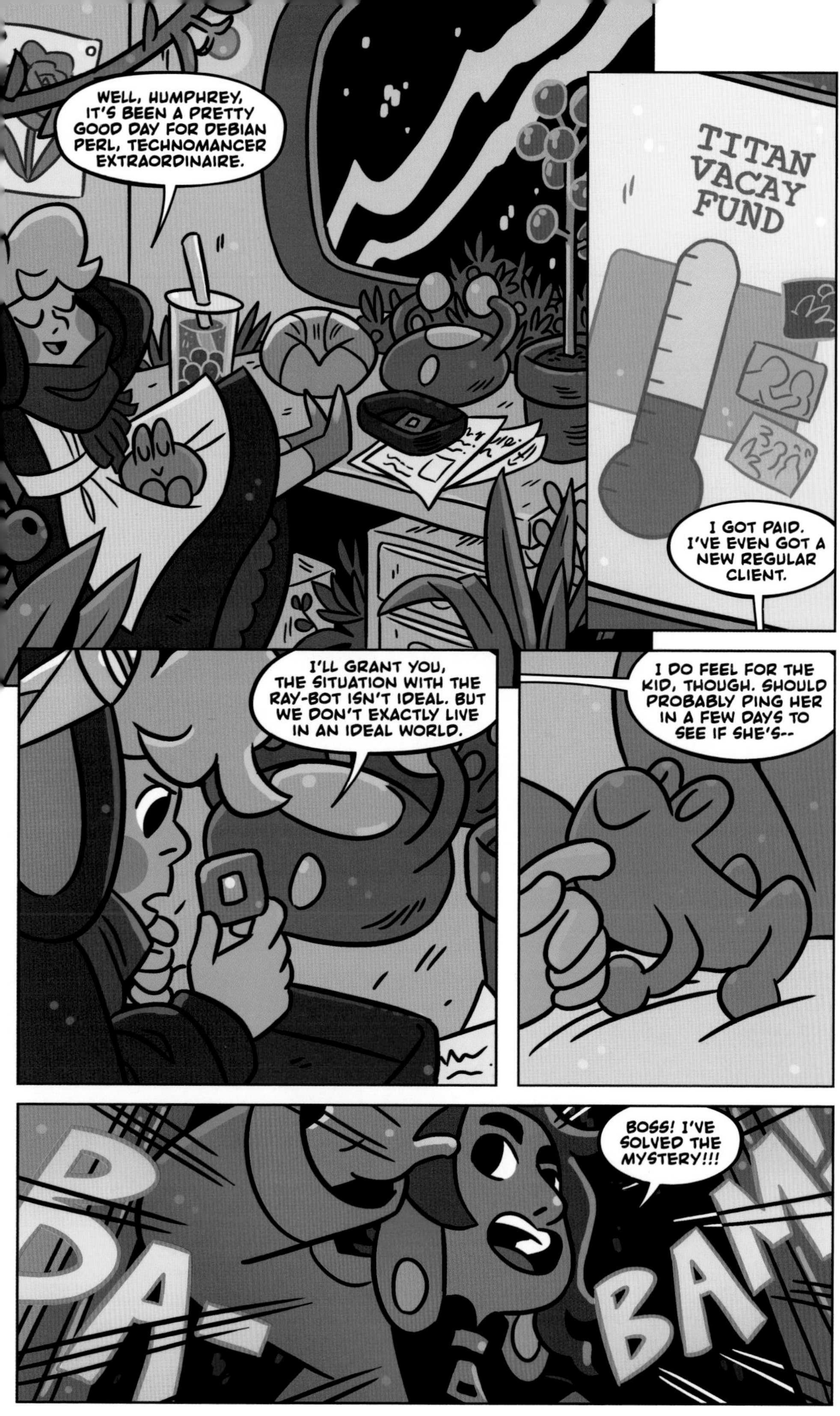

WELL, HUMPHREY, IT'S BEEN A PRETTY GOOD DAY FOR DEBIAN PERL, TECHNOMANCER EXTRAORDINAIRE.
TITAN VACAY FUND
I GOT PAID. I'VE EVEN GOT A NEW REGULAR CLIENT.
I'LL GRANT YOU, THE SITUATION WITH THE RAY-BOT ISN'T IDEAL. BUT WE DON'T EXACTLY LIVE IN AN IDEAL WORLD.
I DO FEEL FOR THE KID, THOUGH. SHOULD PROBABLY PING HER IN A FEW DAYS TO SEE IF SHE'S--
BOSS! I'VE SOLVED THE MYSTERY!!!

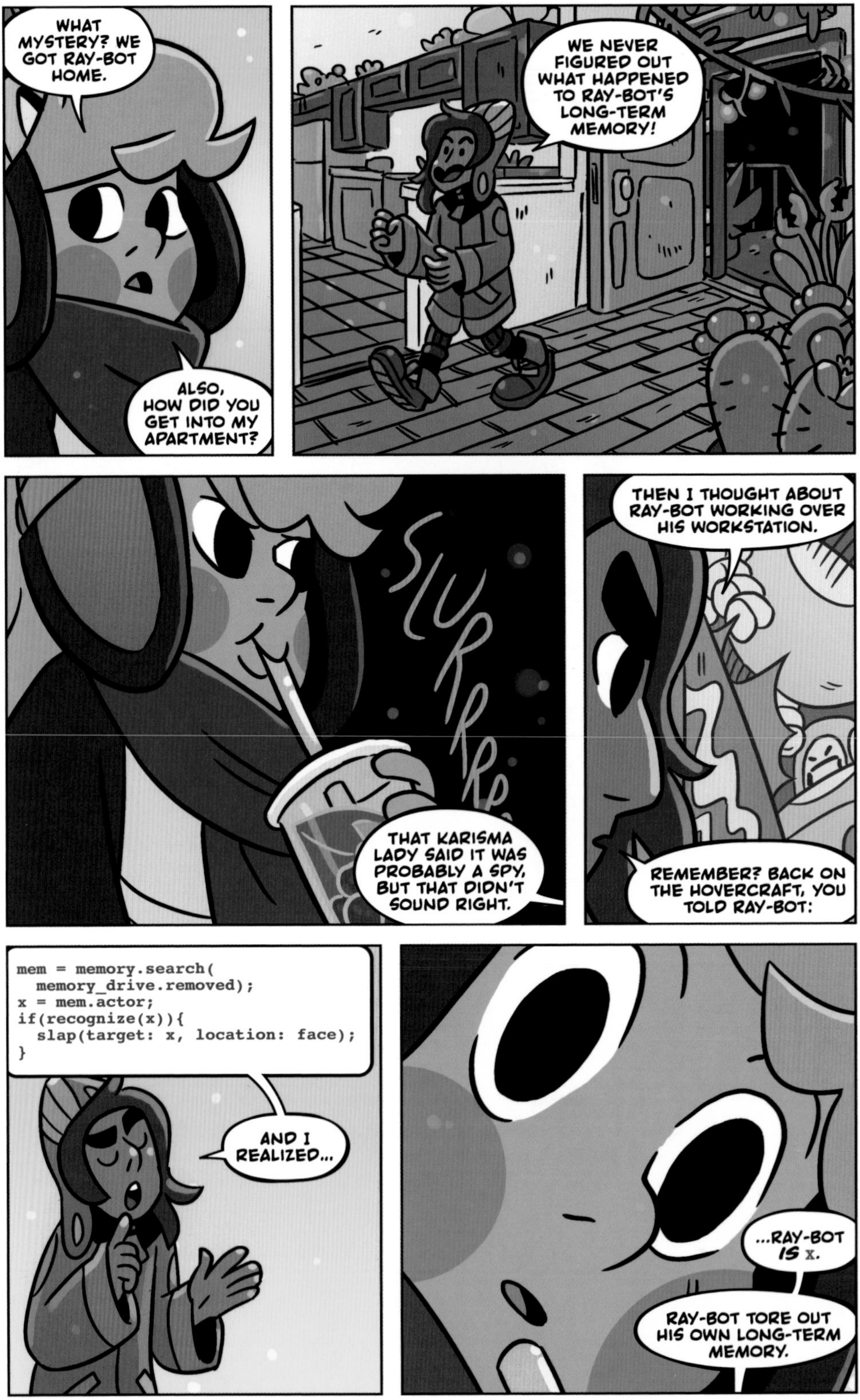
WHAT MYSTERY? WE GOT RAY-BOT HOME.
ALSO, HOW DID YOU GET INTO MY APARTMENT?
WE NEVER FIGURED OUT WHAT HAPPENED TO RAY-BOT'S LONG-TERM MEMORY!
SLURRRP
THAT KARISMA LADY SAID IT WAS PROBABLY A SPY, BUT THAT DIDN'T SOUND RIGHT.
THEN I THOUGHT ABOUT RAY-BOT WORKING OVER HIS WORKSTATION.
REMEMBER? BACK ON THE HOVERCRAFT, YOU TOLD RAY-BOT:
mem = memory.search(
  memory_drive.removed);
x = mem.actor;
if(recognize(x)){
  slap(target: x, location: face);
}
AND I REALIZED...
...RAY-BOT IS x.
RAY-BOT TORE OUT HIS OWN LONG-TERM MEMORY.

HE CLEARLY HATES IT AT LUDO. HE'S BEEN GIVING ORDERS, WATCHING ALL THOSE OTHER BOTS SUFFER.

PLUS, HE WAS PROBABLY OVERHEATING FROM ALL THE WORK!

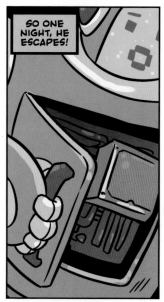

SO ONE NIGHT, HE ESCAPES!

AND TO COMPLETELY SEVER HIS TIES TO HIS OLD LIFE...

HE REMOVES HIS OWN MEMORY DRIVE!

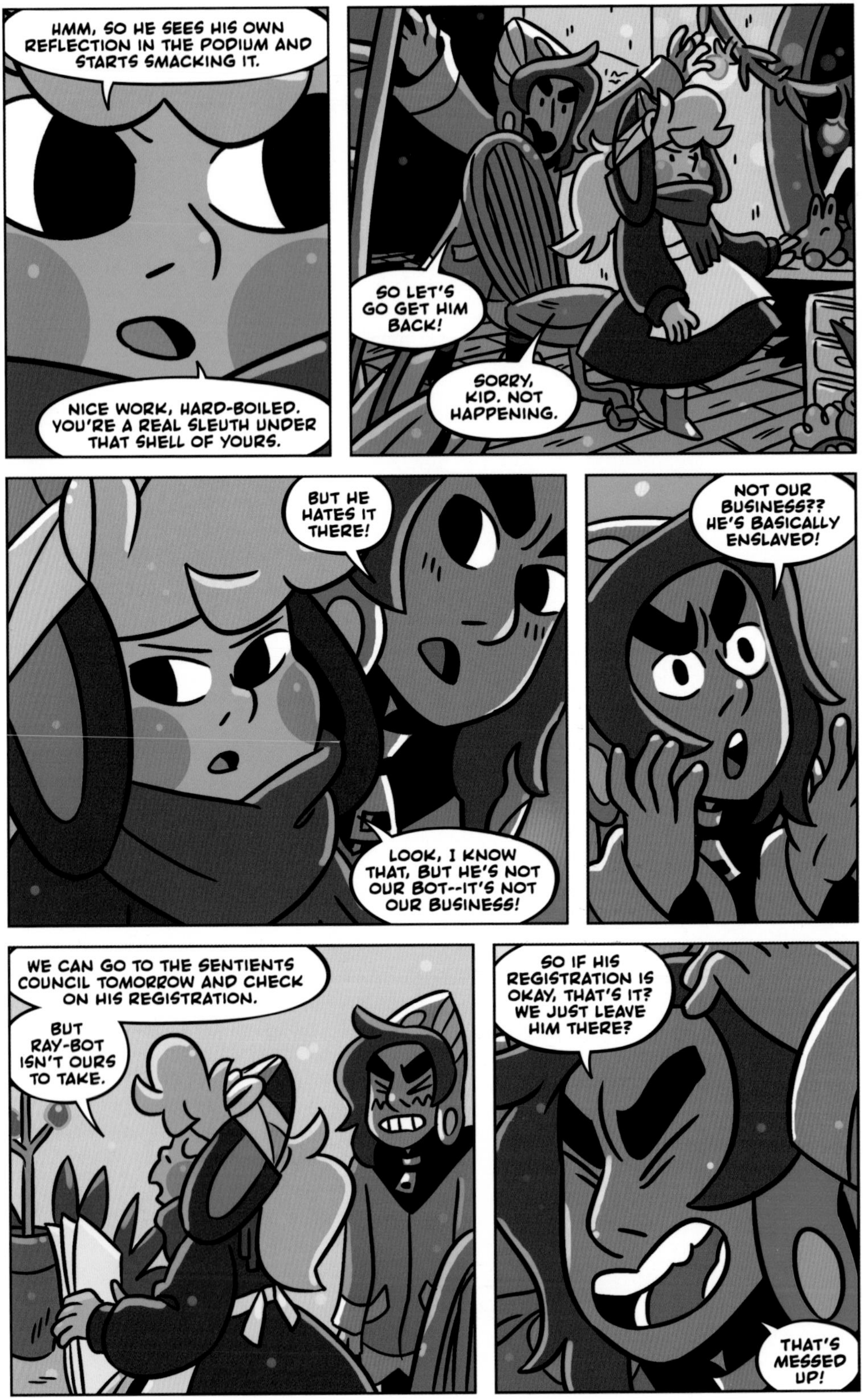
HMM, SO HE SEES HIS OWN REFLECTION IN THE PODIUM AND STARTS SMACKING IT.
NICE WORK, HARD-BOILED. YOU'RE A REAL SLEUTH UNDER THAT SHELL OF YOURS.
SO LET'S GO GET HIM BACK!
SORRY, KID. NOT HAPPENING.
BUT HE HATES IT THERE!
LOOK, I KNOW THAT, BUT HE'S NOT OUR BOT--IT'S NOT OUR BUSINESS!
NOT OUR BUSINESS?? HE'S BASICALLY ENSLAVED!
WE CAN GO TO THE SENTIENTS COUNCIL TOMORROW AND CHECK ON HIS REGISTRATION.
BUT RAY-BOT ISN'T OURS TO TAKE.
SO IF HIS REGISTRATION IS OKAY, THAT'S IT? WE JUST LEAVE HIM THERE?
THAT'S MESSED UP!

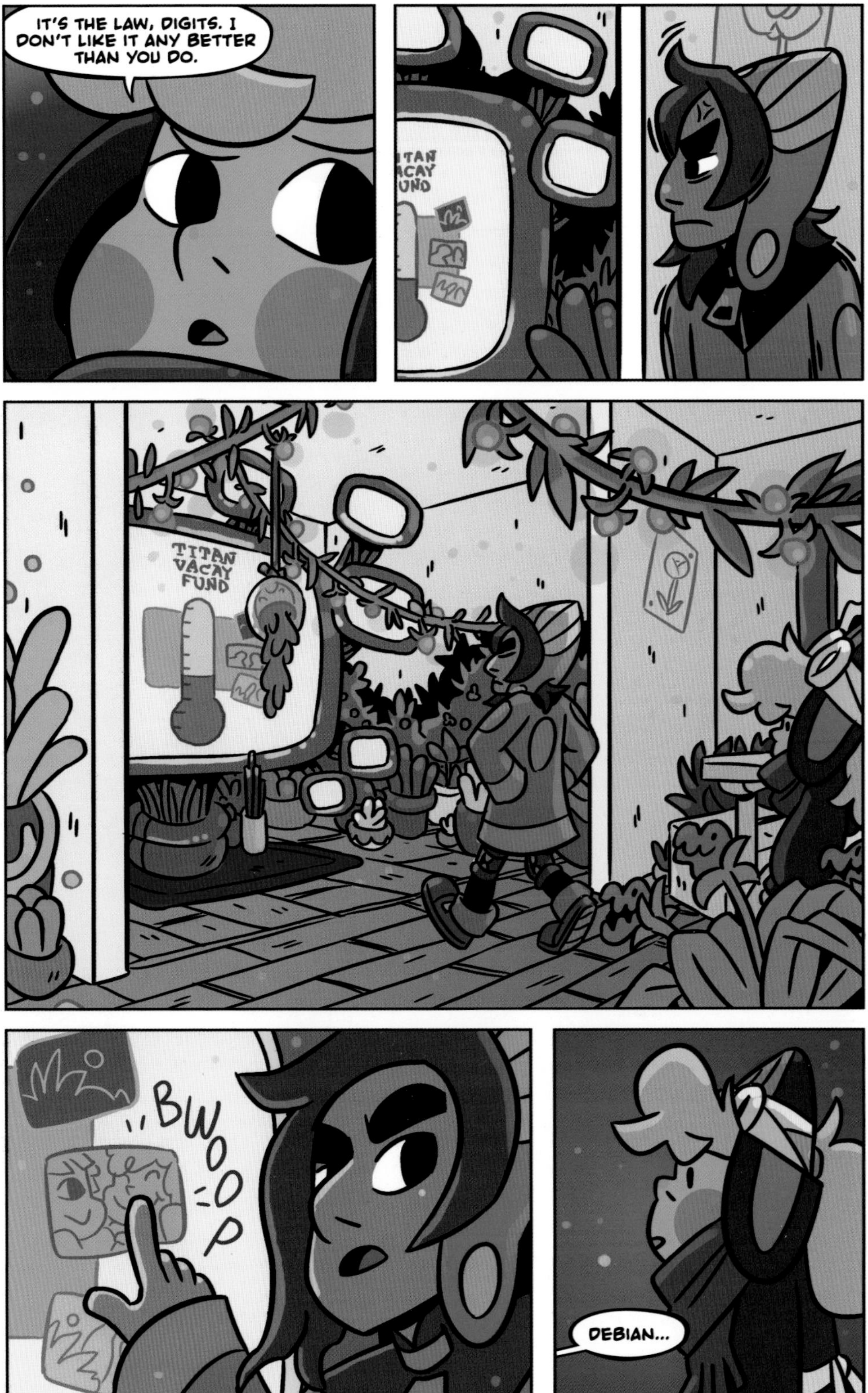
IT'S THE LAW, DIGITS. I DON'T LIKE IT ANY BETTER THAN YOU DO.
TITAN VACAY FUND
TITAN VACAY FUND
BWOOOP
DEBIAN...

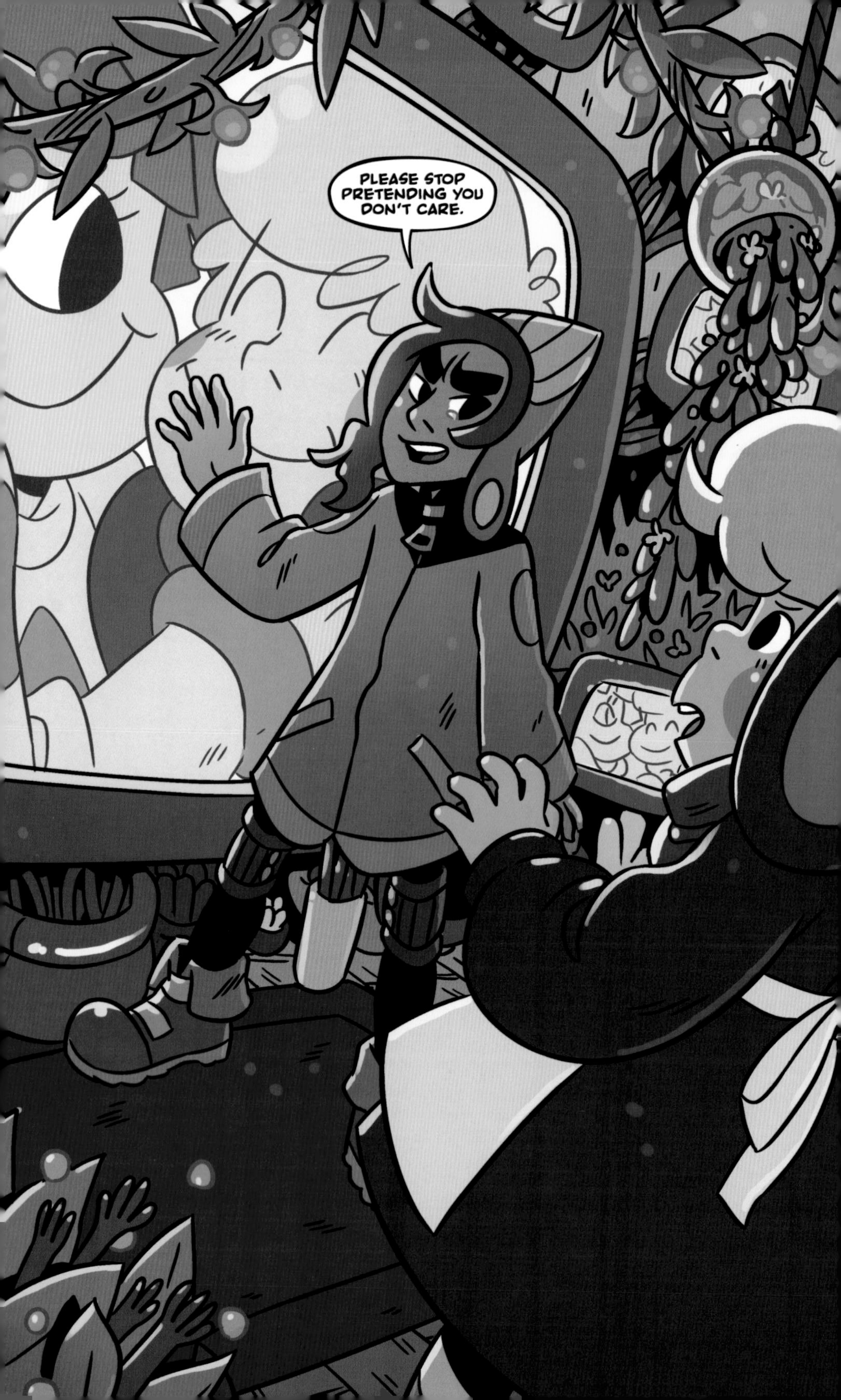
PLEASE STOP PRETENDING YOU DON'T CARE.

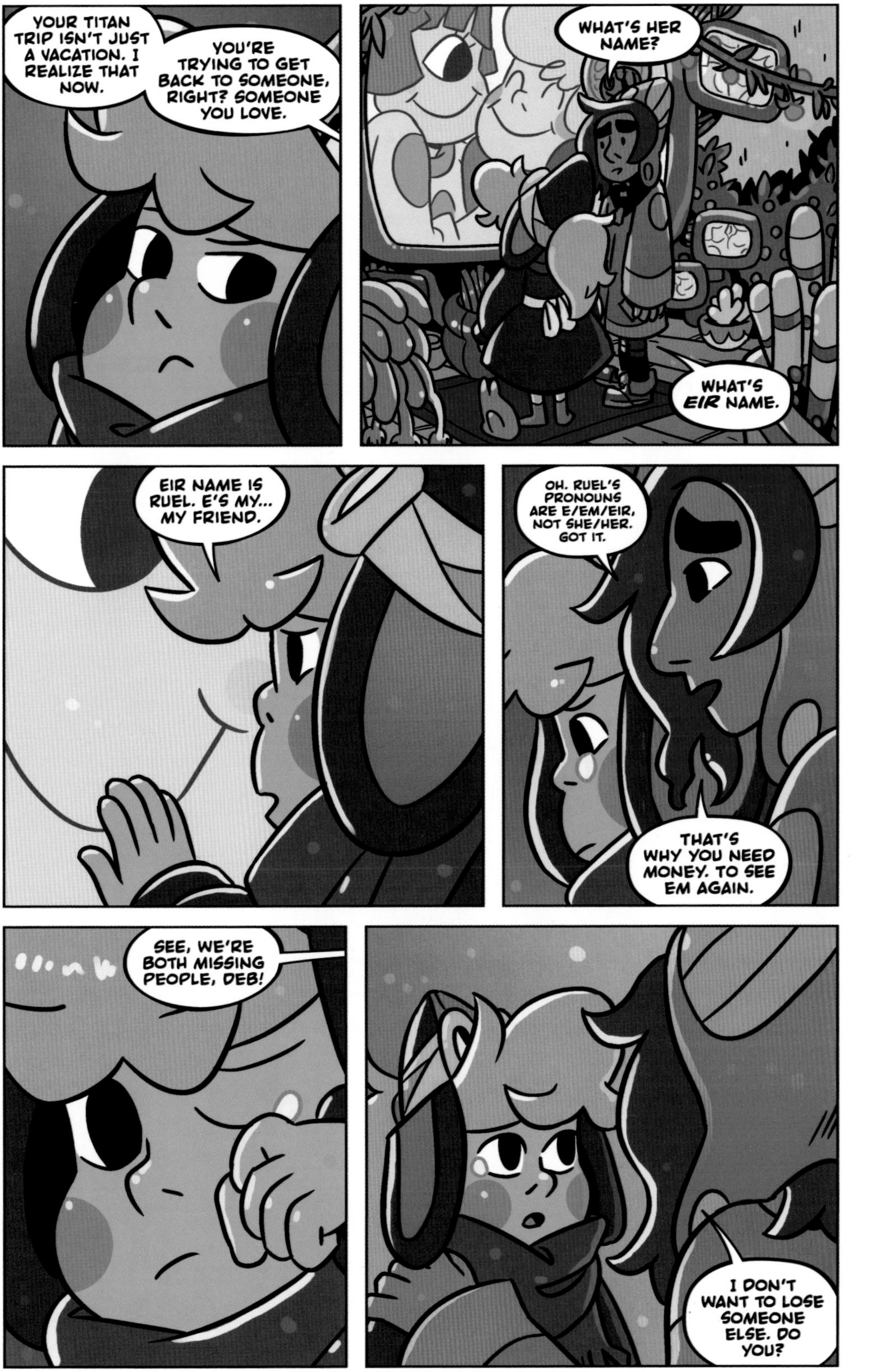
YOUR TITAN TRIP ISN'T JUST A VACATION. I REALIZE THAT NOW.
YOU'RE TRYING TO GET BACK TO SOMEONE, RIGHT? SOMEONE YOU LOVE.
WHAT'S HER NAME?
WHAT'S *EIR* NAME.
EIR NAME IS RUEL. E'S MY... MY FRIEND.
OH. RUEL'S PRONOUNS ARE E/EM/EIR, NOT SHE/HER. GOT IT.
THAT'S WHY YOU NEED MONEY. TO SEE EM AGAIN.
SEE, WE'RE BOTH MISSING PEOPLE, DEB!
I DON'T WANT TO LOSE SOMEONE ELSE. DO YOU?

BWOOOOOP~

LET ME GET MY COAT. AND A FLASH DRIVE.

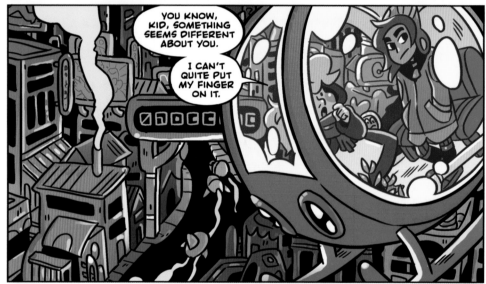

YOU KNOW, KID, SOMETHING SEEMS DIFFERENT ABOUT YOU.

I CAN'T QUITE PUT MY FINGER ON IT.

I'VE GOT IT! YOU DON'T HAVE YOUR EGG!

OH. THAT.

I HAD IT ON AFTER WE LEFT THE FACTORY.

WHILE I WAS TRYING TO FIGURE OUT WHAT WAS GOING ON WITH RAY-BOT...

PEOPLE WERE BLOWING UP MY EGG! I GOT FLOODED WITH NOTIFICATIONS!

Z

I COULD BARELY HEAR MYSELF THINK.

YOU HAVE NO IDEA HOW DISTRACTING THESE THINGS CAN BE!

DO TELL.

SO I PUT IT BACK IN SLEEP MODE, AND I THOUGHT ABOUT WHAT YOU SAID AT YOUR APARTMENT.

Z

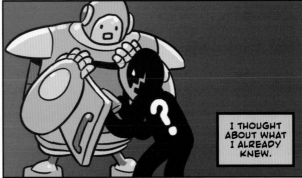

I THOUGHT ABOUT WHAT I ALREADY KNEW.

AND THEN THE ANSWER JUST CAME TO ME.

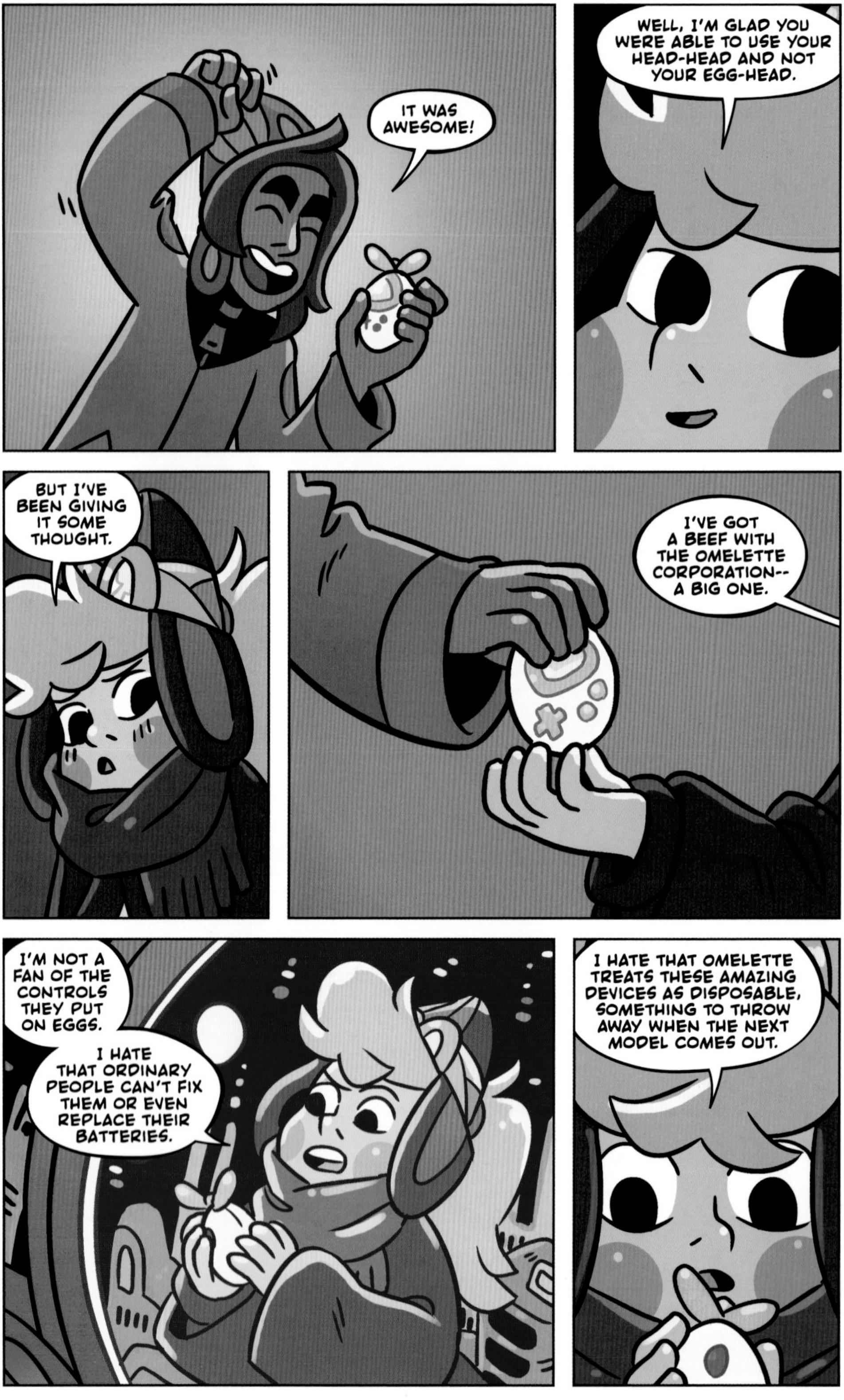
IT WAS AWESOME!
WELL, I'M GLAD YOU WERE ABLE TO USE YOUR HEAD-HEAD AND NOT YOUR EGG-HEAD.
BUT I'VE BEEN GIVING IT SOME THOUGHT.
I'VE GOT A BEEF WITH THE OMELETTE CORPORATION-- A BIG ONE.
I'M NOT A FAN OF THE CONTROLS THEY PUT ON EGGS.
I HATE THAT ORDINARY PEOPLE CAN'T FIX THEM OR EVEN REPLACE THEIR BATTERIES.
I HATE THAT OMELETTE TREATS THESE AMAZING DEVICES AS DISPOSABLE, SOMETHING TO THROW AWAY WHEN THE NEXT MODEL COMES OUT.

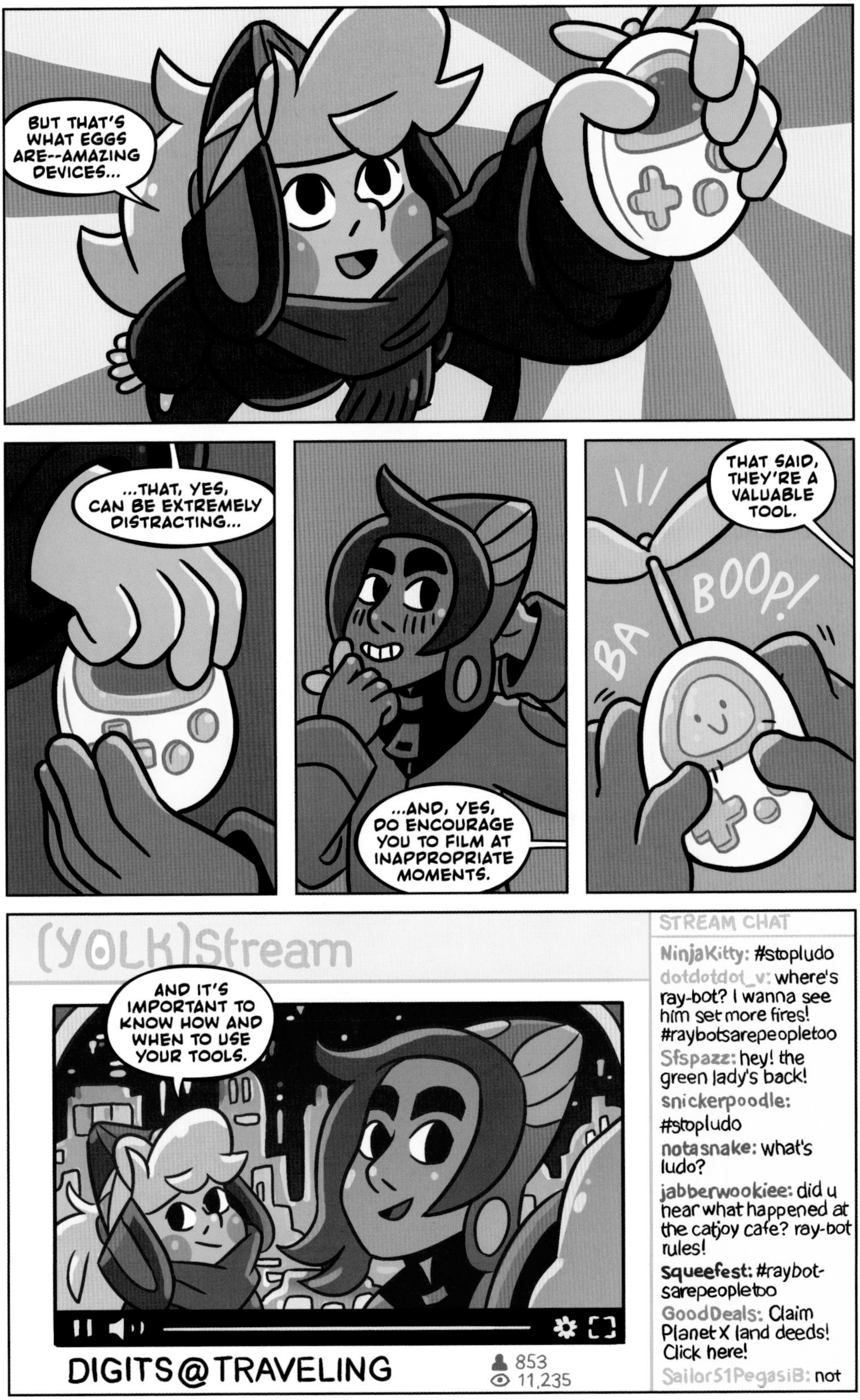
BUT THAT'S WHAT EGGS ARE--AMAZING DEVICES...
...THAT, YES, CAN BE EXTREMELY DISTRACTING...
...AND, YES, DO ENCOURAGE YOU TO FILM AT INAPPROPRIATE MOMENTS.
THAT SAID, THEY'RE A VALUABLE TOOL.
BA
BOOP!
(YOLK)Stream
AND IT'S IMPORTANT TO KNOW HOW AND WHEN TO USE YOUR TOOLS.
DIGITS@TRAVELING
853
11,235
STREAM CHAT
NinjaKitty: #stopludo
dotdotdot_v: where's ray-bot? I wanna see him set more fires! #raybotsarepeopletoo
Sfspazz: hey! the green lady's back!
snickerpoodle: #stopludo
notasnake: what's ludo?
jabberwookiee: did u hear what happened at the catjoy cafe? ray-bot rules!
squeefest: #raybot-sarepeopletoo
GoodDeals: Claim Planet X land deeds! Click here!
Sailor51PegasiB: not

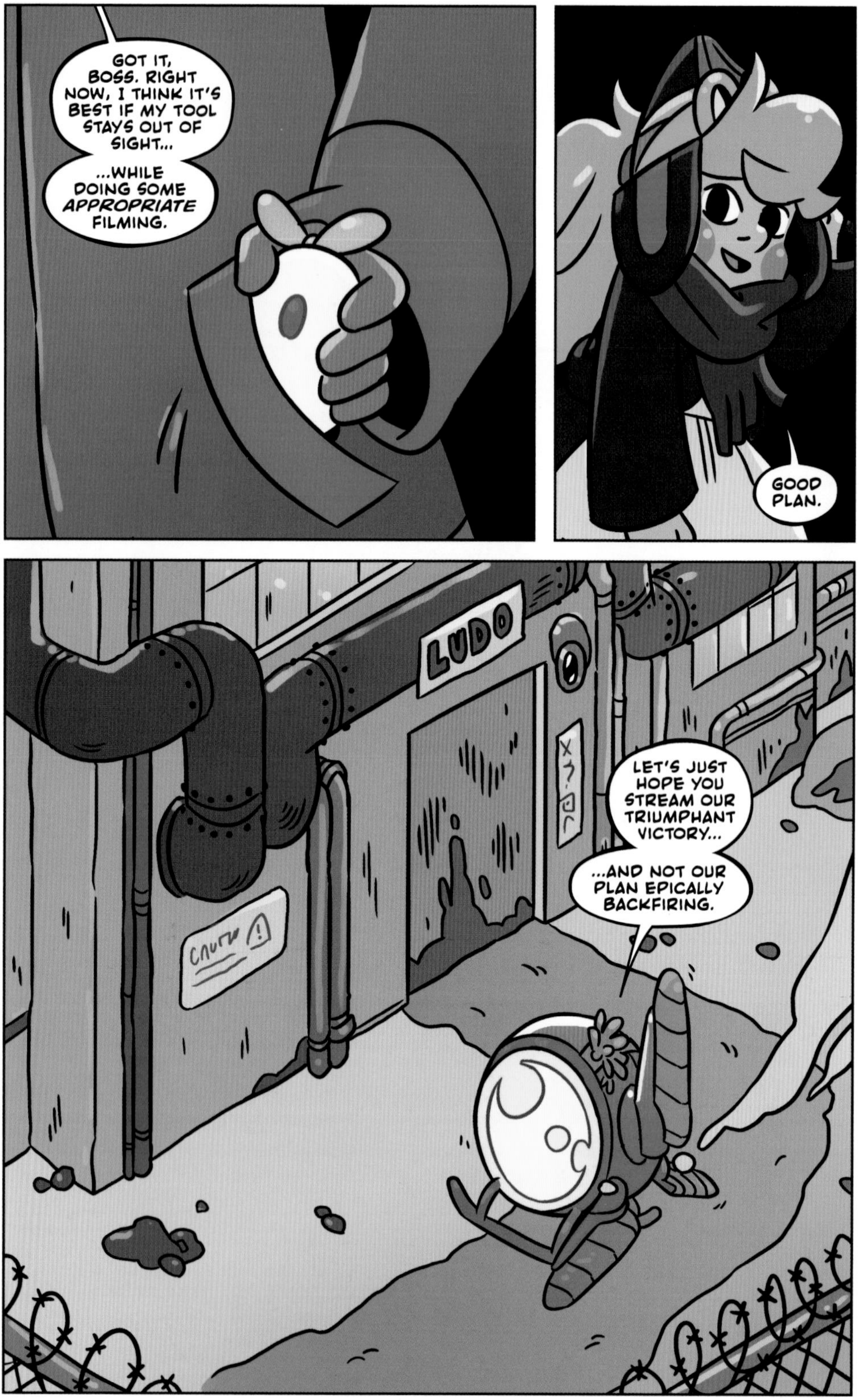
GOT IT, BOSS. RIGHT NOW, I THINK IT'S BEST IF MY TOOL STAYS OUT OF SIGHT...
...WHILE DOING SOME *APPROPRIATE* FILMING.
GOOD PLAN.
LUDO
LET'S JUST HOPE YOU STREAM OUR TRIUMPHANT VICTORY...
...AND NOT OUR PLAN EPICALLY BACKFIRING.

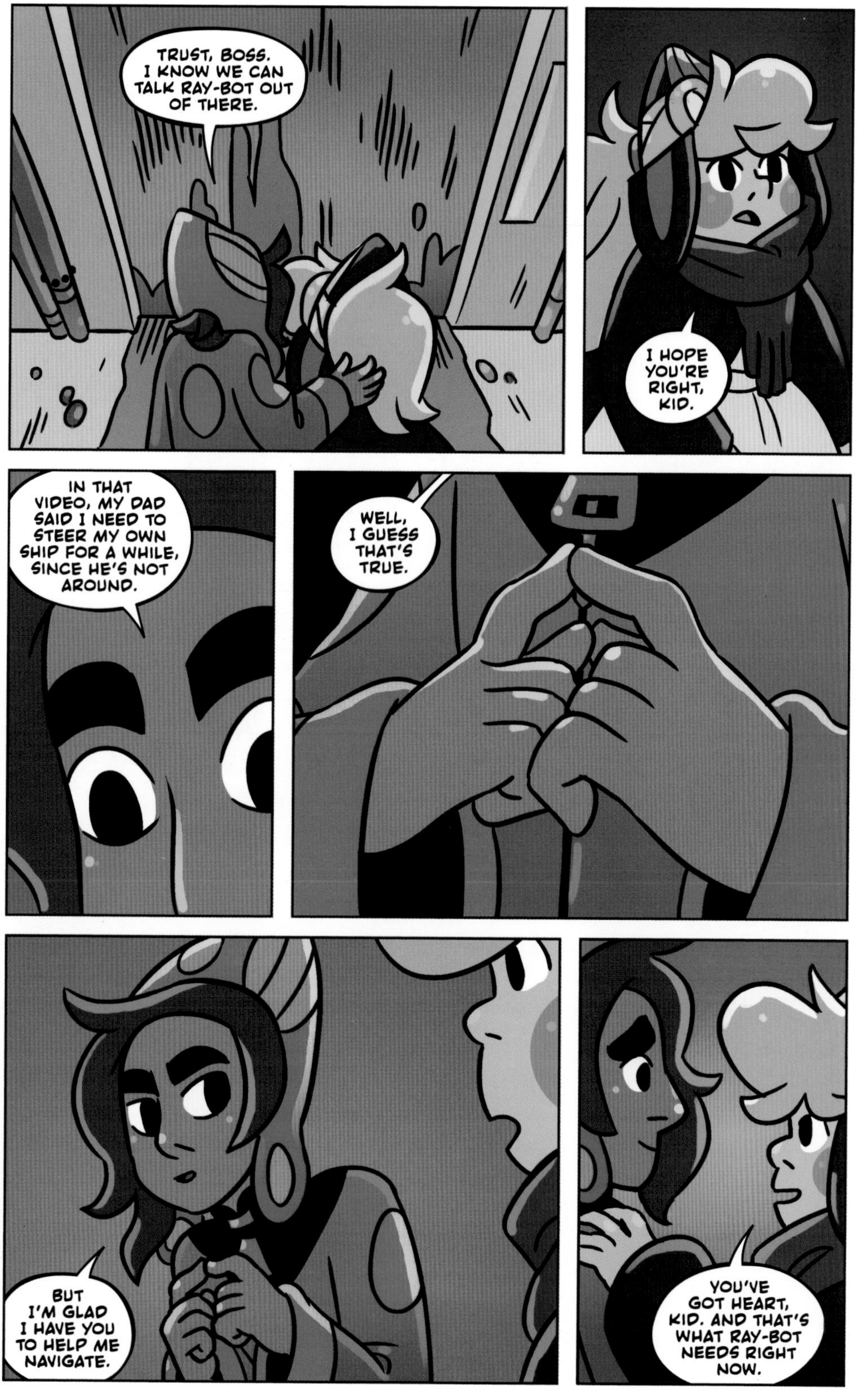
TRUST, BOSS. I KNOW WE CAN TALK RAY-BOT OUT OF THERE.
I HOPE YOU'RE RIGHT, KID.
IN THAT VIDEO, MY DAD SAID I NEED TO STEER MY OWN SHIP FOR A WHILE, SINCE HE'S NOT AROUND.
WELL, I GUESS THAT'S TRUE.
BUT I'M GLAD I HAVE YOU TO HELP ME NAVIGATE.
YOU'VE GOT HEART, KID. AND THAT'S WHAT RAY-BOT NEEDS RIGHT NOW.

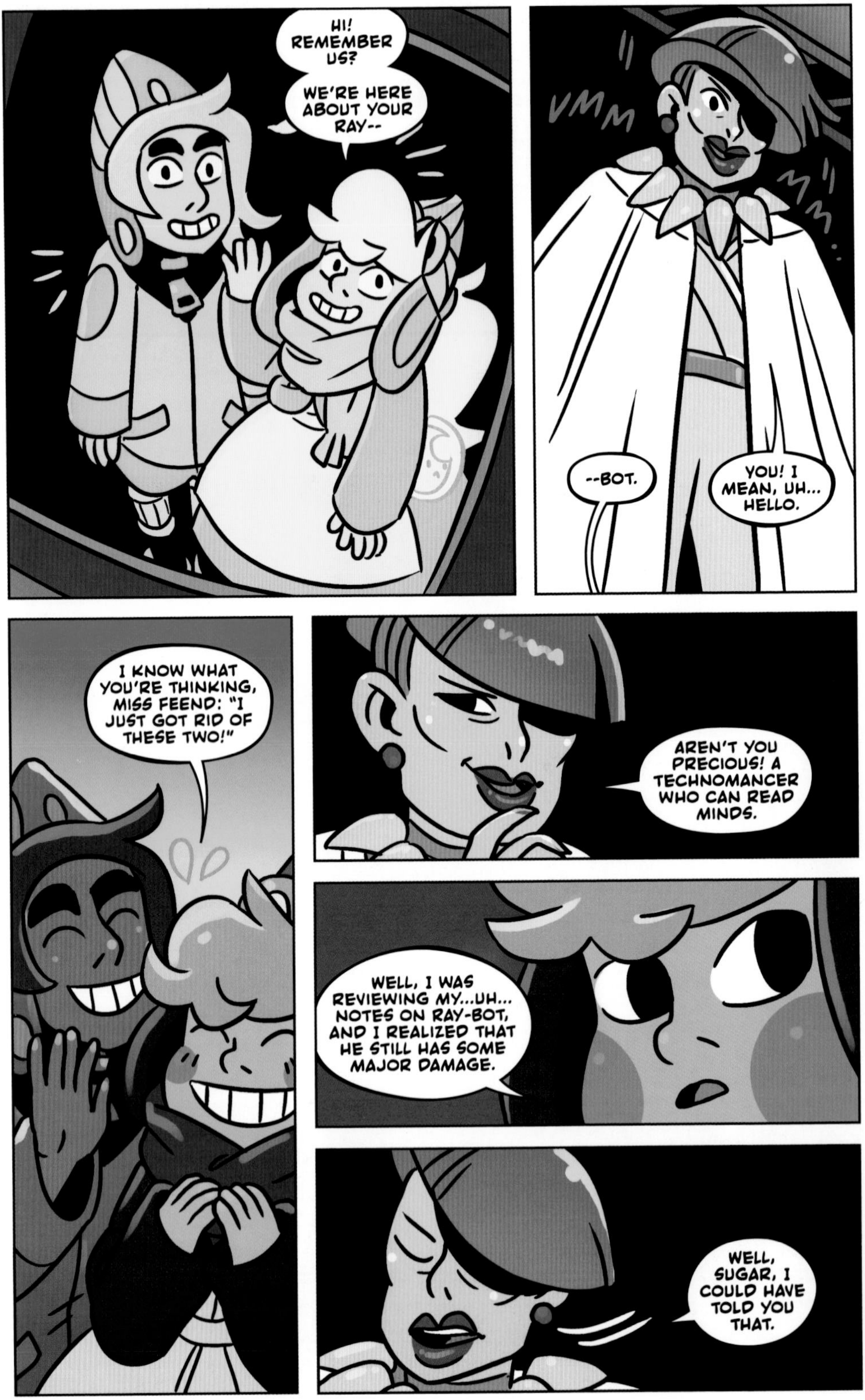
HI! REMEMBER US?
WE'RE HERE ABOUT YOUR RAY--
VMMM
MMM
--BOT.
YOU! I MEAN, UH... HELLO.
I KNOW WHAT YOU'RE THINKING, MISS FEEND: "I JUST GOT RID OF THESE TWO!"
AREN'T YOU PRECIOUS! A TECHNOMANCER WHO CAN READ MINDS.
WELL, I WAS REVIEWING MY...UH... NOTES ON RAY-BOT, AND I REALIZED THAT HE STILL HAS SOME MAJOR DAMAGE.
WELL, SUGAR, I COULD HAVE TOLD YOU THAT.

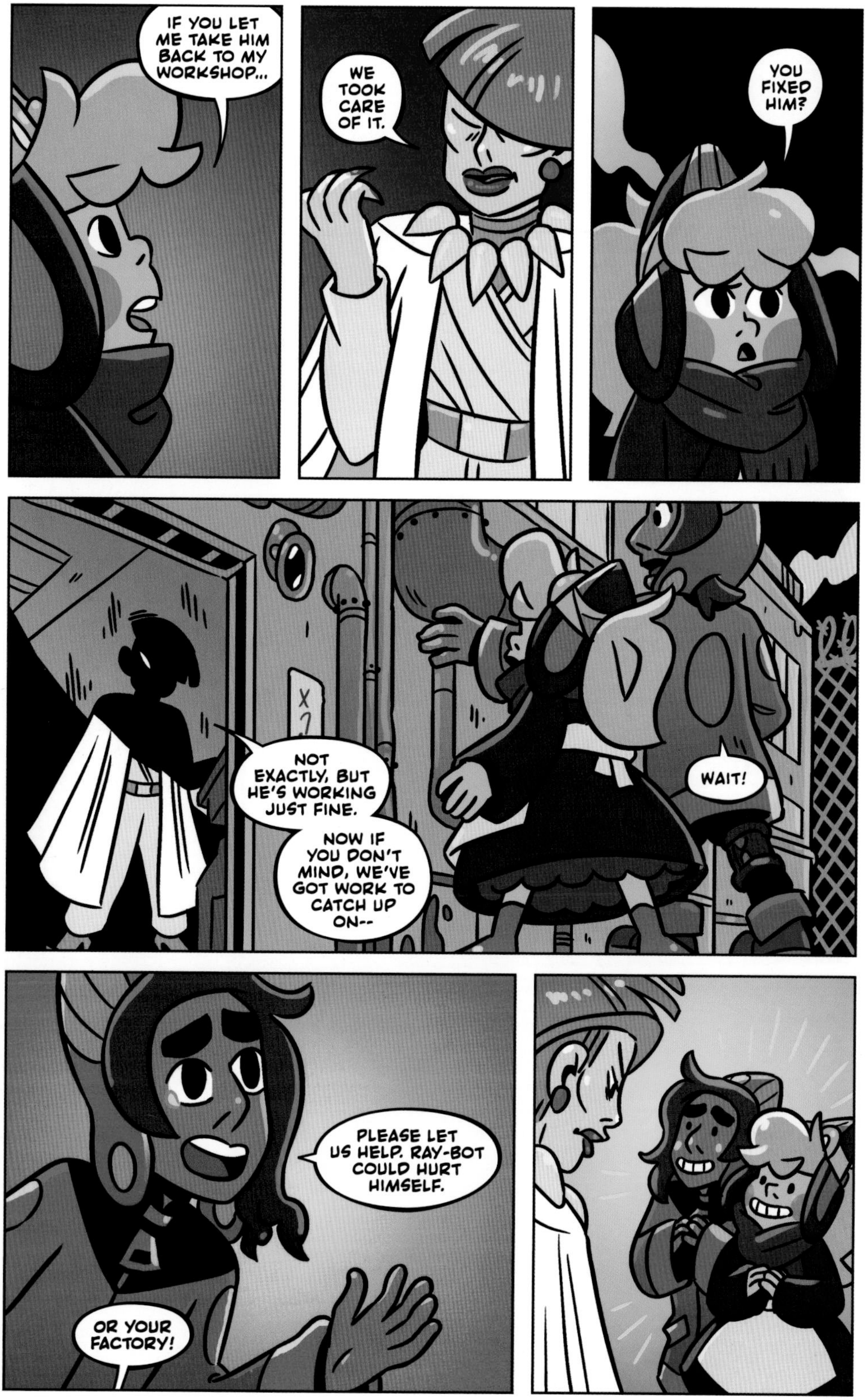

IF YOU LET ME TAKE HIM BACK TO MY WORKSHOP...
WE TOOK CARE OF IT.
YOU FIXED HIM?
NOT EXACTLY, BUT HE'S WORKING JUST FINE.
NOW IF YOU DON'T MIND, WE'VE GOT WORK TO CATCH UP ON--
WAIT!
PLEASE LET US HELP. RAY-BOT COULD HURT HIMSELF.
OR YOUR FACTORY!

YOU'RE BARKING UP THE WRONG TREE, YA HEAR? SEE FOR YOURSELF.

THEN YOU BOTH HAVE TO SKEDADDLE.

OF COURSE.

SO, HOW DID YOU HANDLE RAY-BOT'S PROBLEMS IF YOU DIDN'T ACTUALLY FIX HIM?

I'LL BE HONEST WITH YOU GALS: IT WAS THE DARNDEST THING I'VE EVER SEEN! RAY-RAY KEPT HAMMERING ON HIS STATION AND WE COULDN'T FIGURE OUT WHY.

WHEN WE TRIED TO OPEN HIS CHASSIS TO SEE WHAT WAS WRONG, WE COULDN'T GET IN!

FORTUNATELY, WE FOUND A WORK-AROUND.

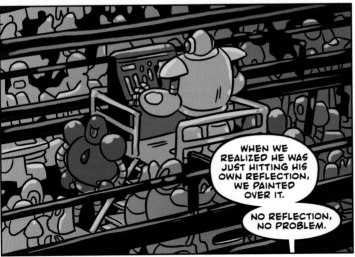

WHEN WE REALIZED HE WAS JUST HITTING HIS OWN REFLECTION, WE PAINTED OVER IT.

NO REFLECTION, NO PROBLEM.

RAY-BOT!

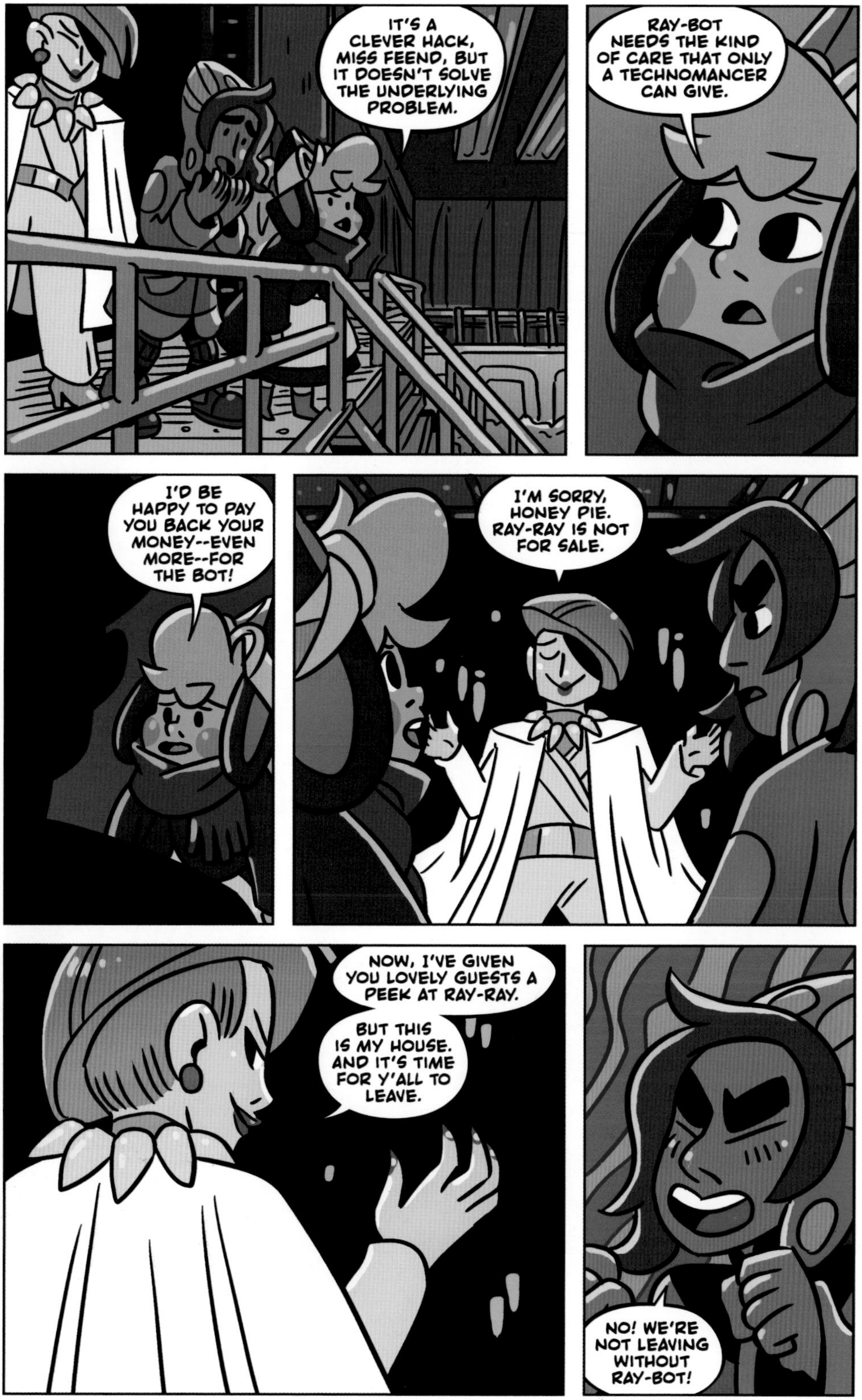
IT'S A CLEVER HACK, MISS FEEND, BUT IT DOESN'T SOLVE THE UNDERLYING PROBLEM.
RAY-BOT NEEDS THE KIND OF CARE THAT ONLY A TECHNOMANCER CAN GIVE.
I'D BE HAPPY TO PAY YOU BACK YOUR MONEY--EVEN MORE--FOR THE BOT!
I'M SORRY, HONEY PIE. RAY-RAY IS NOT FOR SALE.
NOW, I'VE GIVEN YOU LOVELY GUESTS A PEEK AT RAY-RAY.
BUT THIS IS MY HOUSE. AND IT'S TIME FOR Y'ALL TO LEAVE.
NO! WE'RE NOT LEAVING WITHOUT RAY-BOT!

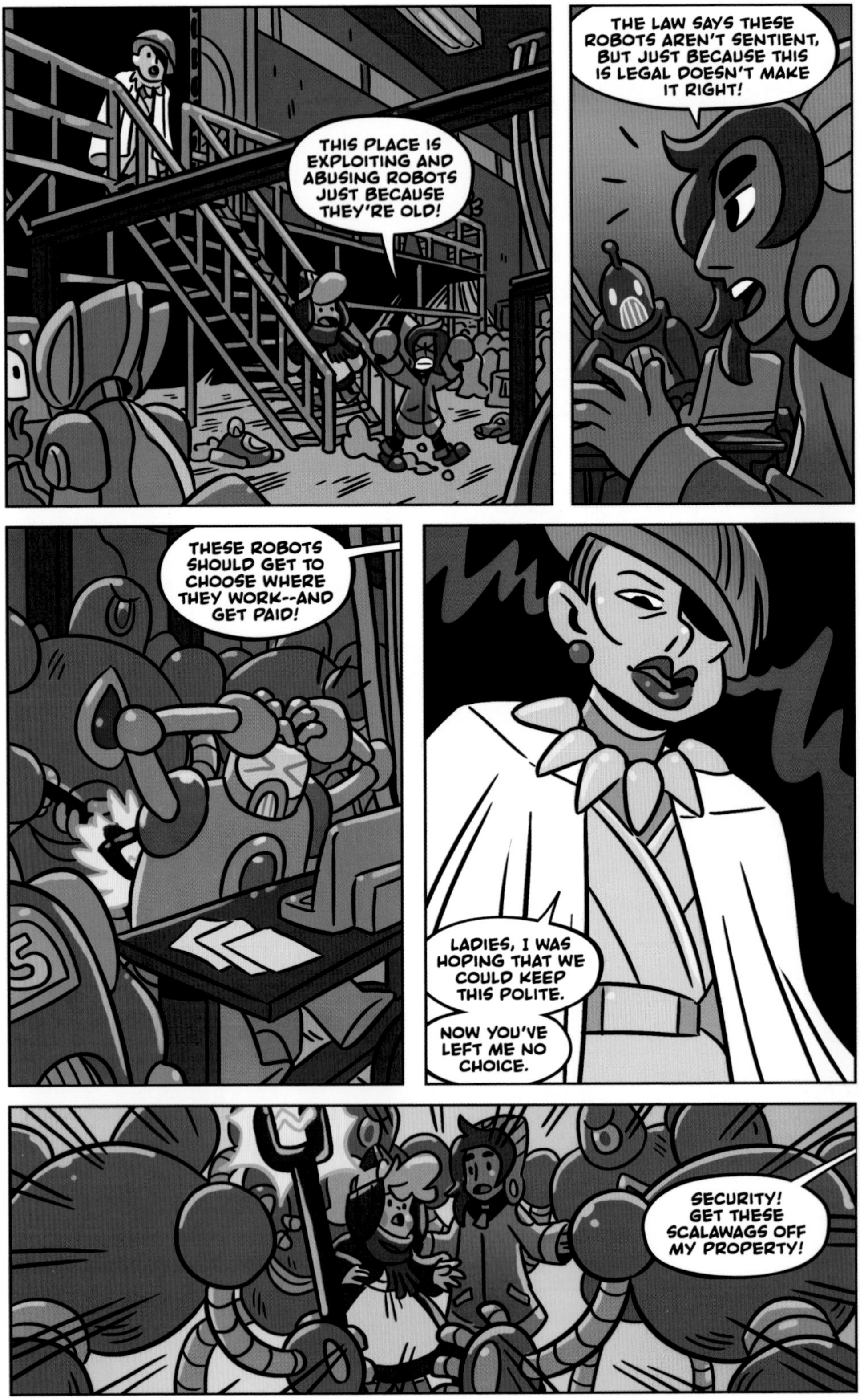
THIS PLACE IS EXPLOITING AND ABUSING ROBOTS JUST BECAUSE THEY'RE OLD!
THE LAW SAYS THESE ROBOTS AREN'T SENTIENT, BUT JUST BECAUSE THIS IS LEGAL DOESN'T MAKE IT RIGHT!
THESE ROBOTS SHOULD GET TO CHOOSE WHERE THEY WORK--AND GET PAID!
LADIES, I WAS HOPING THAT WE COULD KEEP THIS POLITE.
NOW YOU'VE LEFT ME NO CHOICE.
SECURITY! GET THESE SCALAWAGS OFF MY PROPERTY!

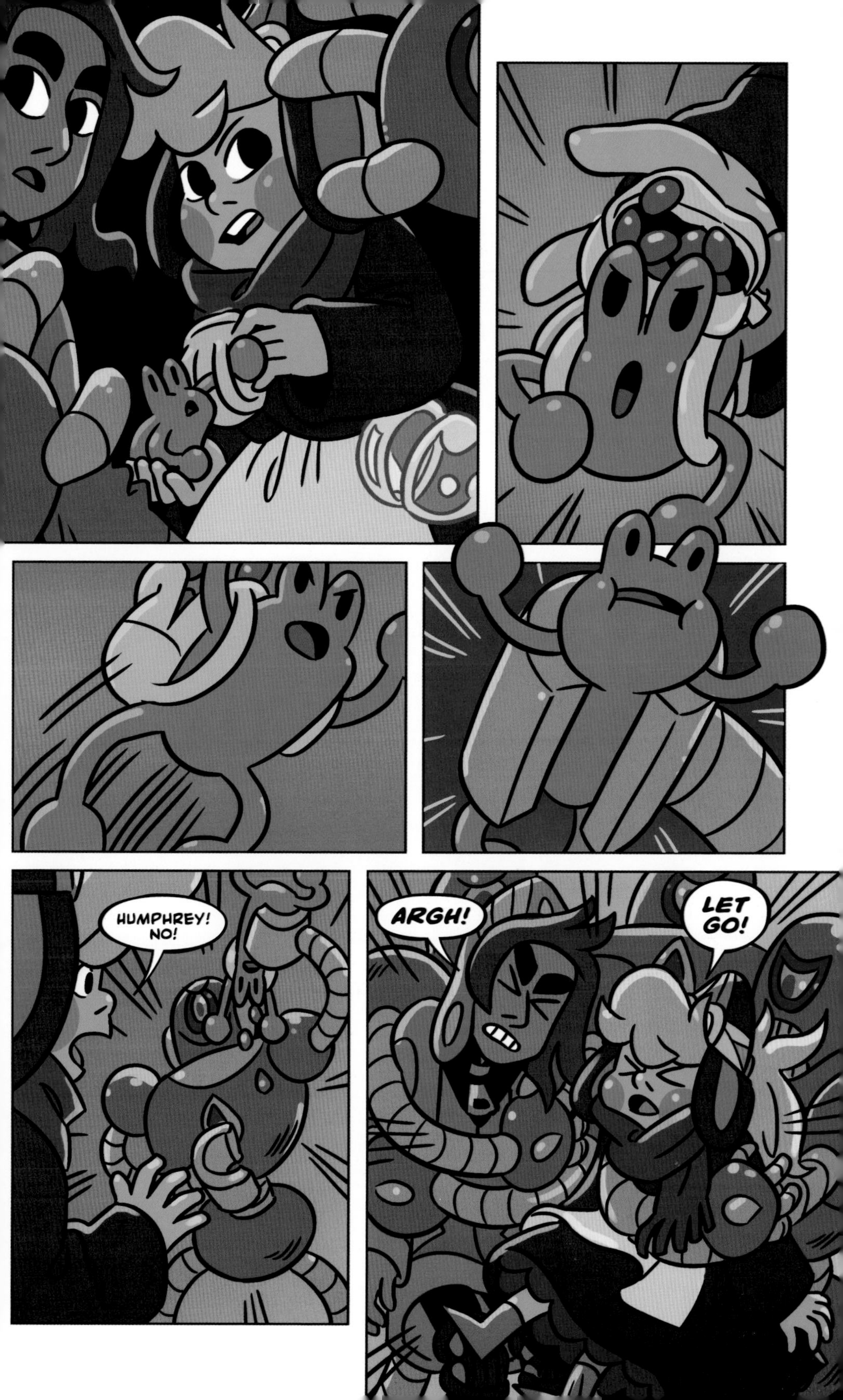
HUMPHREY! NO!
ARGH!
LET GO!

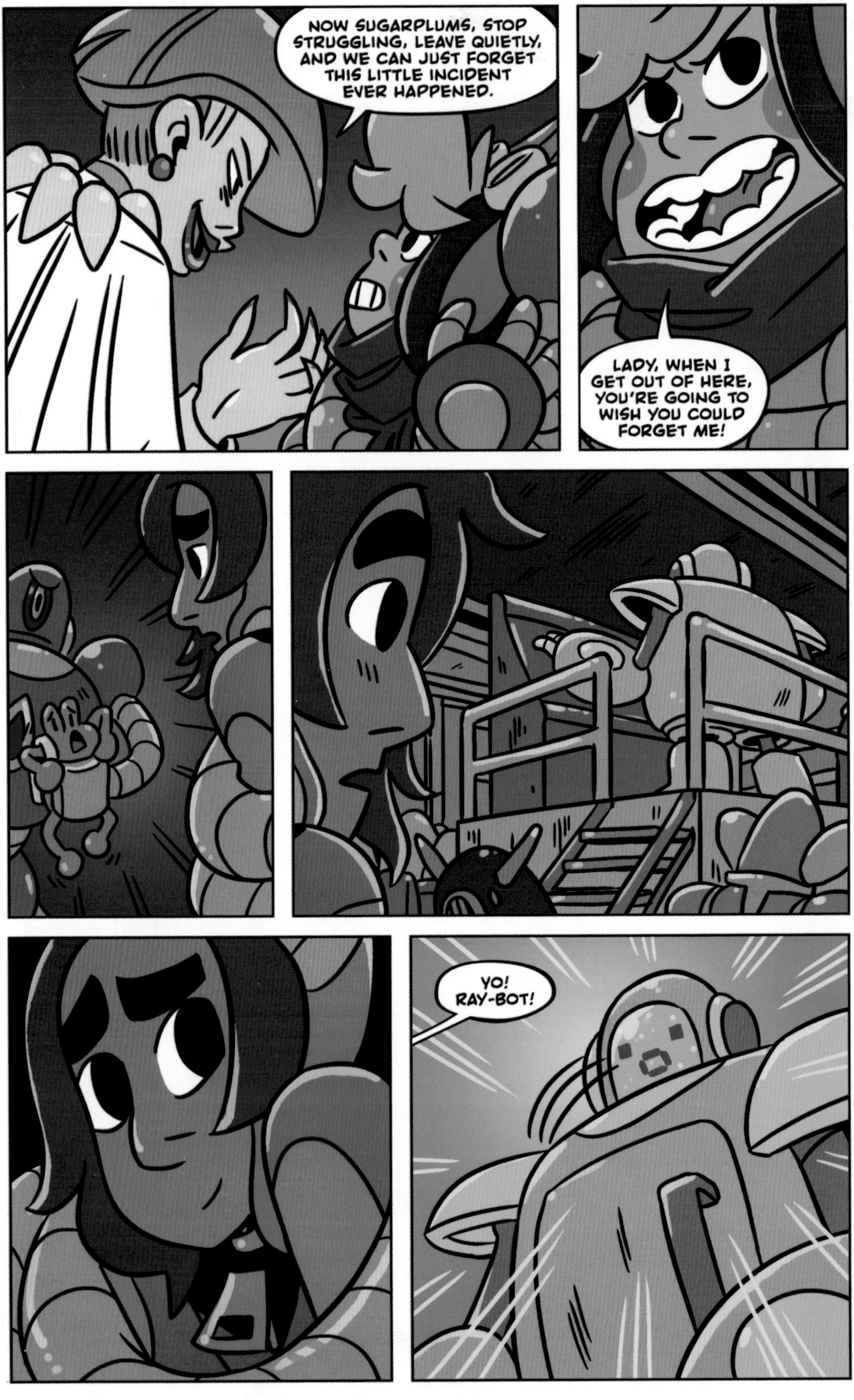

NOW SUGARPLUMS, STOP STRUGGLING, LEAVE QUIETLY, AND WE CAN JUST FORGET THIS LITTLE INCIDENT EVER HAPPENED.
LADY, WHEN I GET OUT OF HERE, YOU'RE GOING TO WISH YOU COULD FORGET ME!
YO! RAY-BOT!

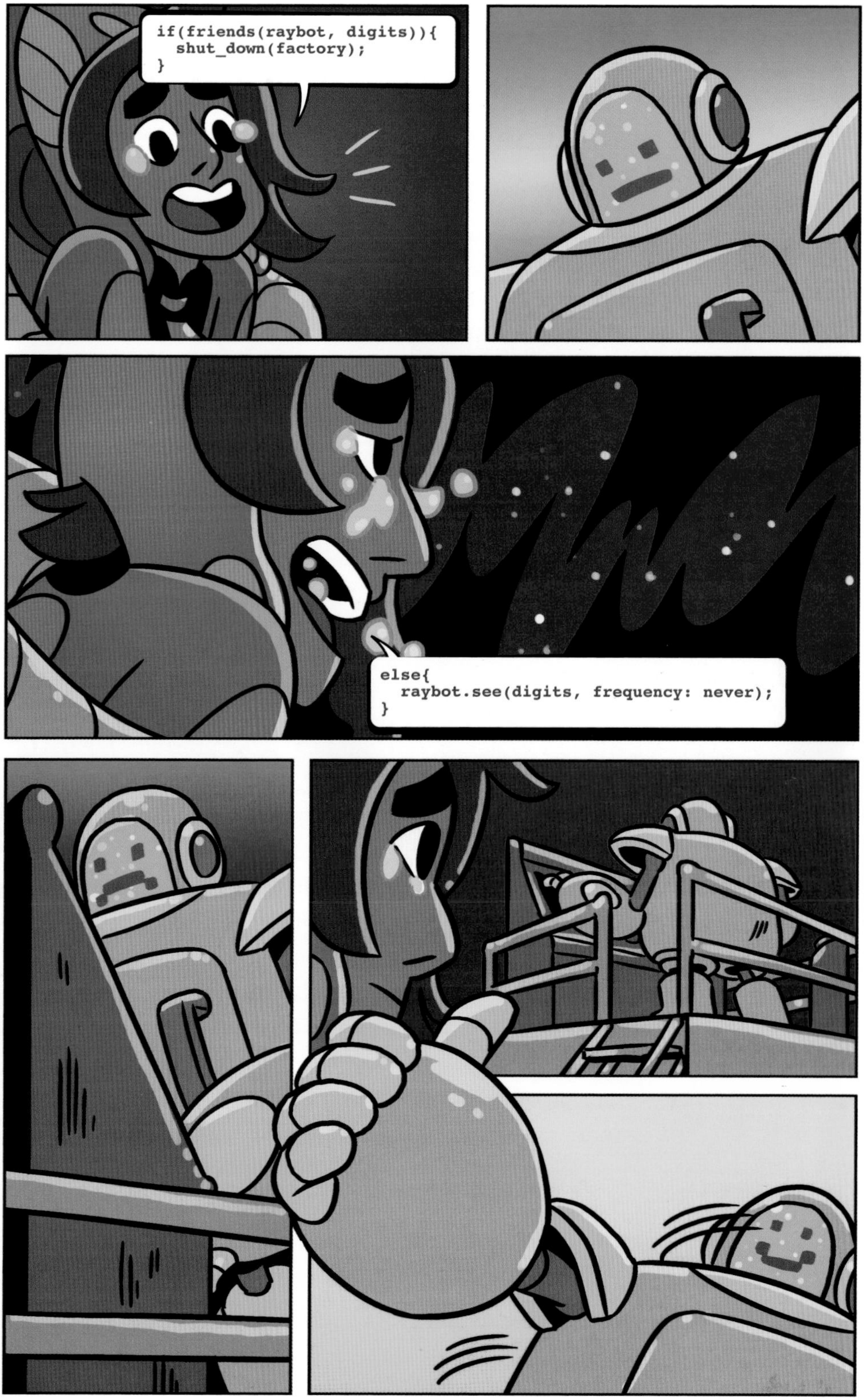
if(friends(raybot, digits)){
shut_down(factory);
}
else{
raybot.see(digits, frequency: never);
}

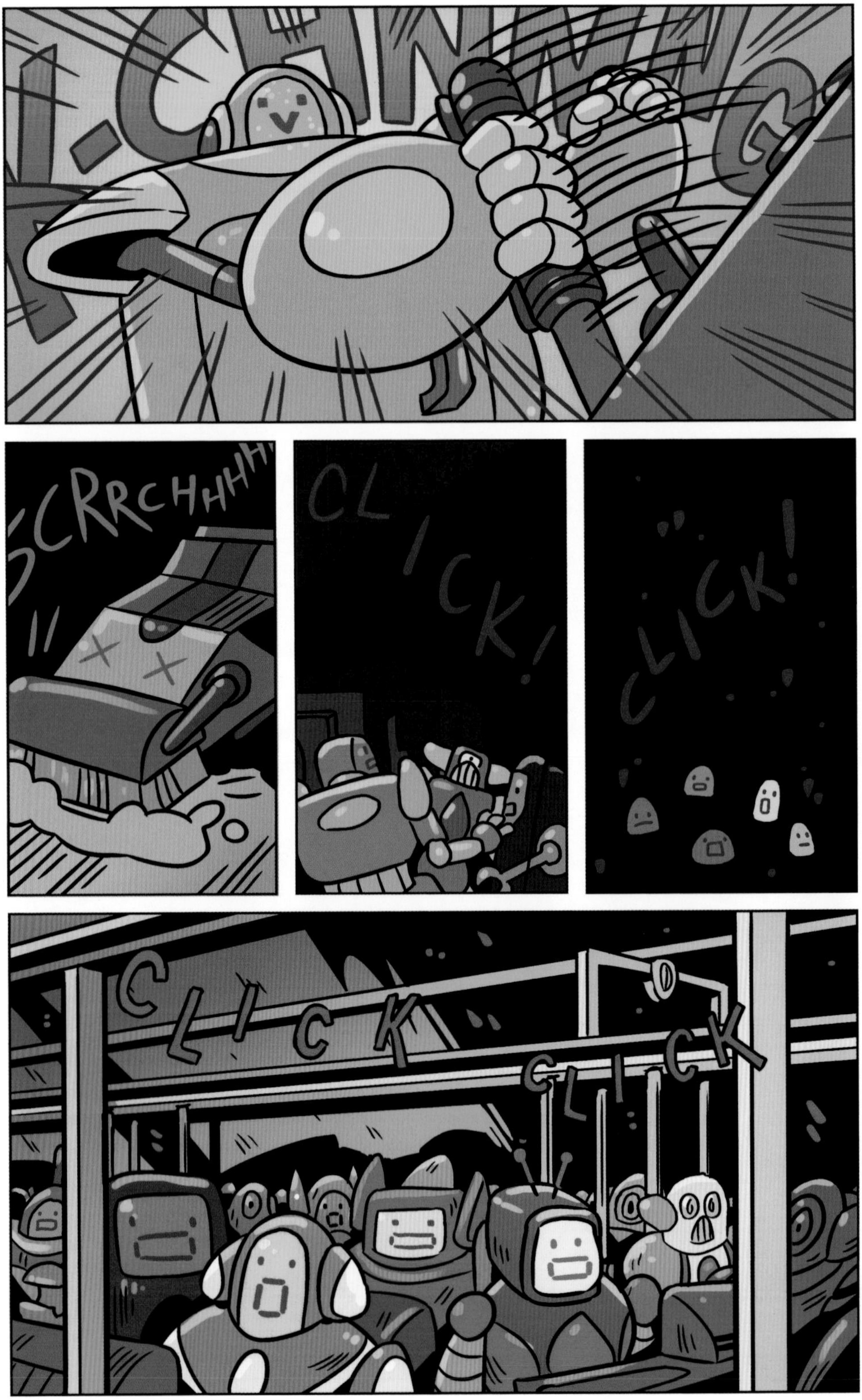
SCRRCHHHH
CLICK!
CLICK!
CLICK
CLICK

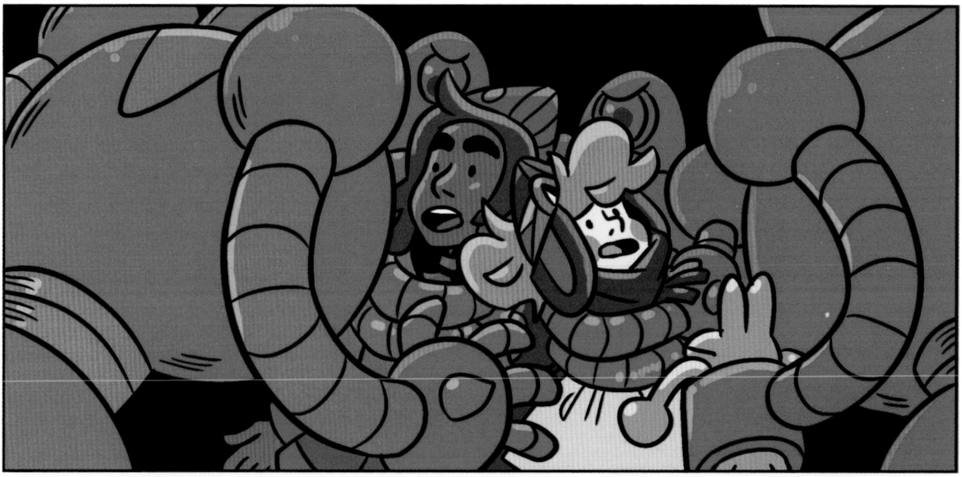

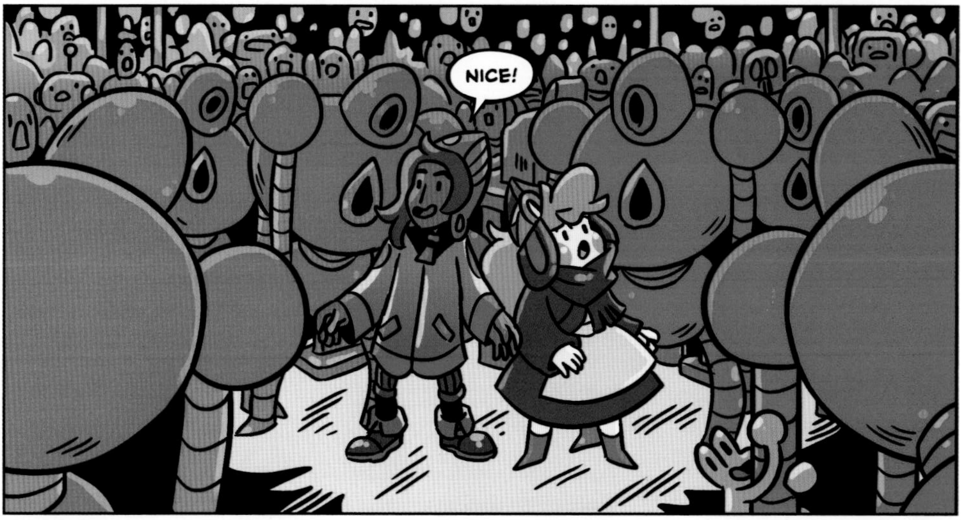
NICE!

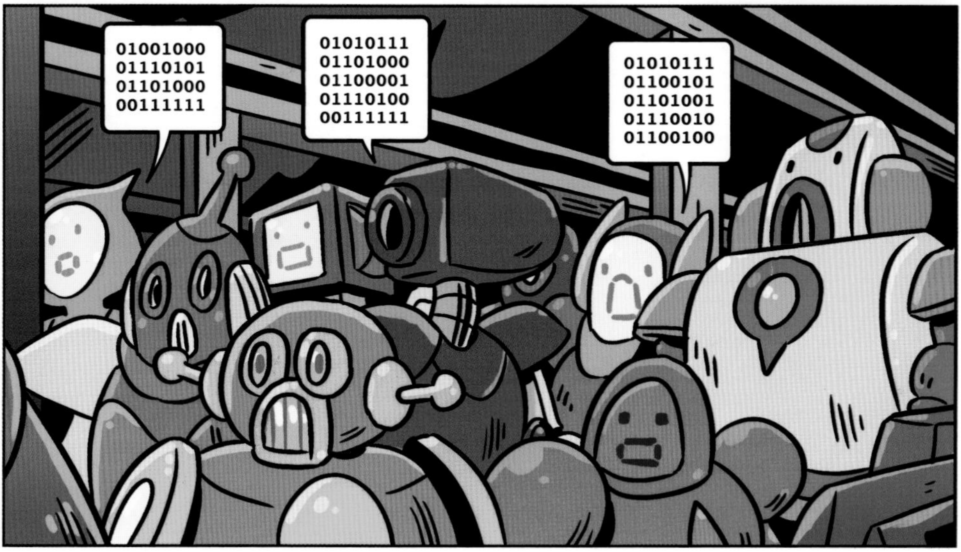
01001000
01110101
01101000
00111111
01010111
01101000
01100001
01110100
00111111
01010111
01100101
01101001
01110010
01100100

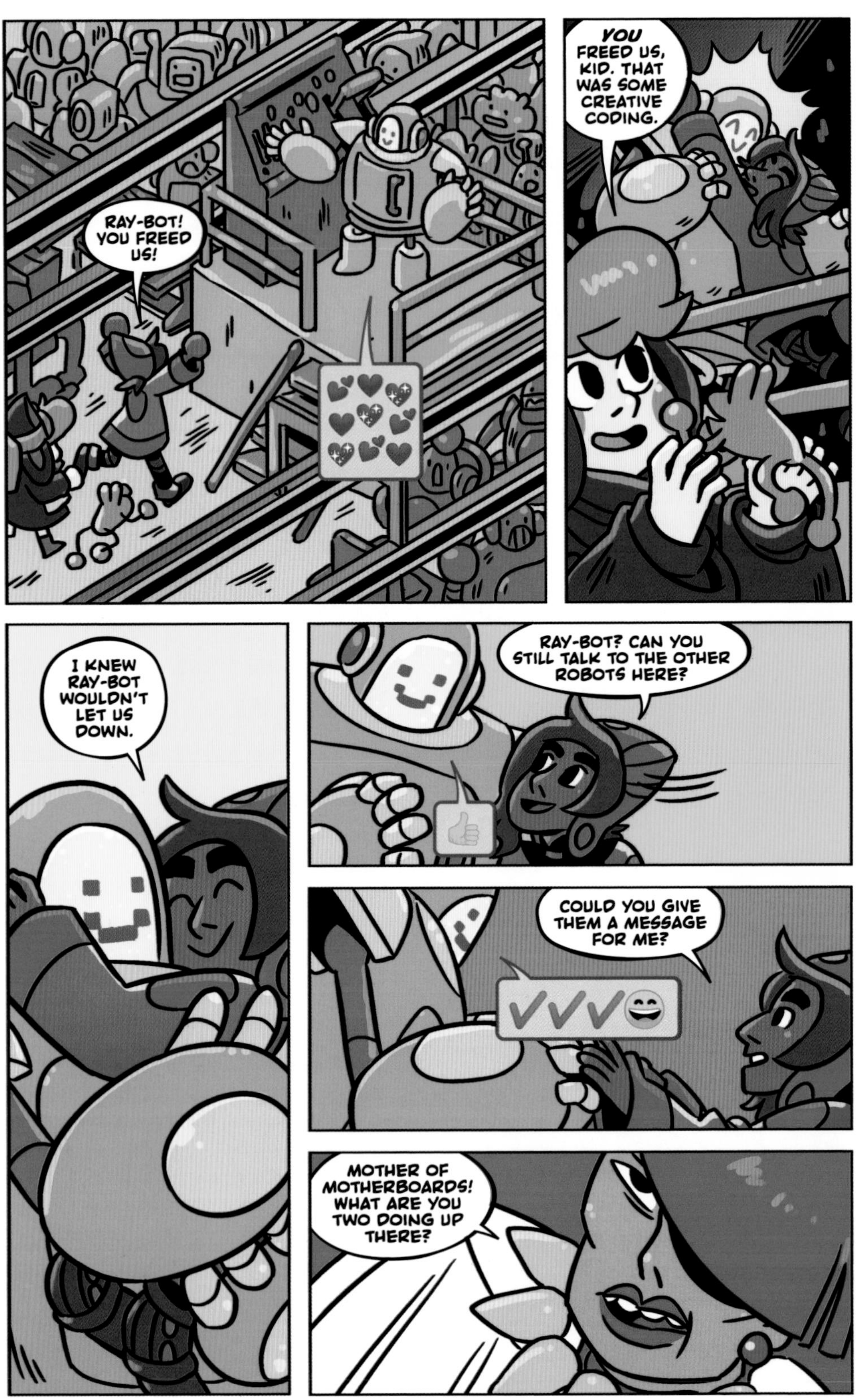
RAY-BOT! YOU FREED US!
YOU FREED US, KID. THAT WAS SOME CREATIVE CODING.
I KNEW RAY-BOT WOULDN'T LET US DOWN.
RAY-BOT? CAN YOU STILL TALK TO THE OTHER ROBOTS HERE?
COULD YOU GIVE THEM A MESSAGE FOR ME?
MOTHER OF MOTHERBOARDS! WHAT ARE YOU TWO DOING UP THERE?

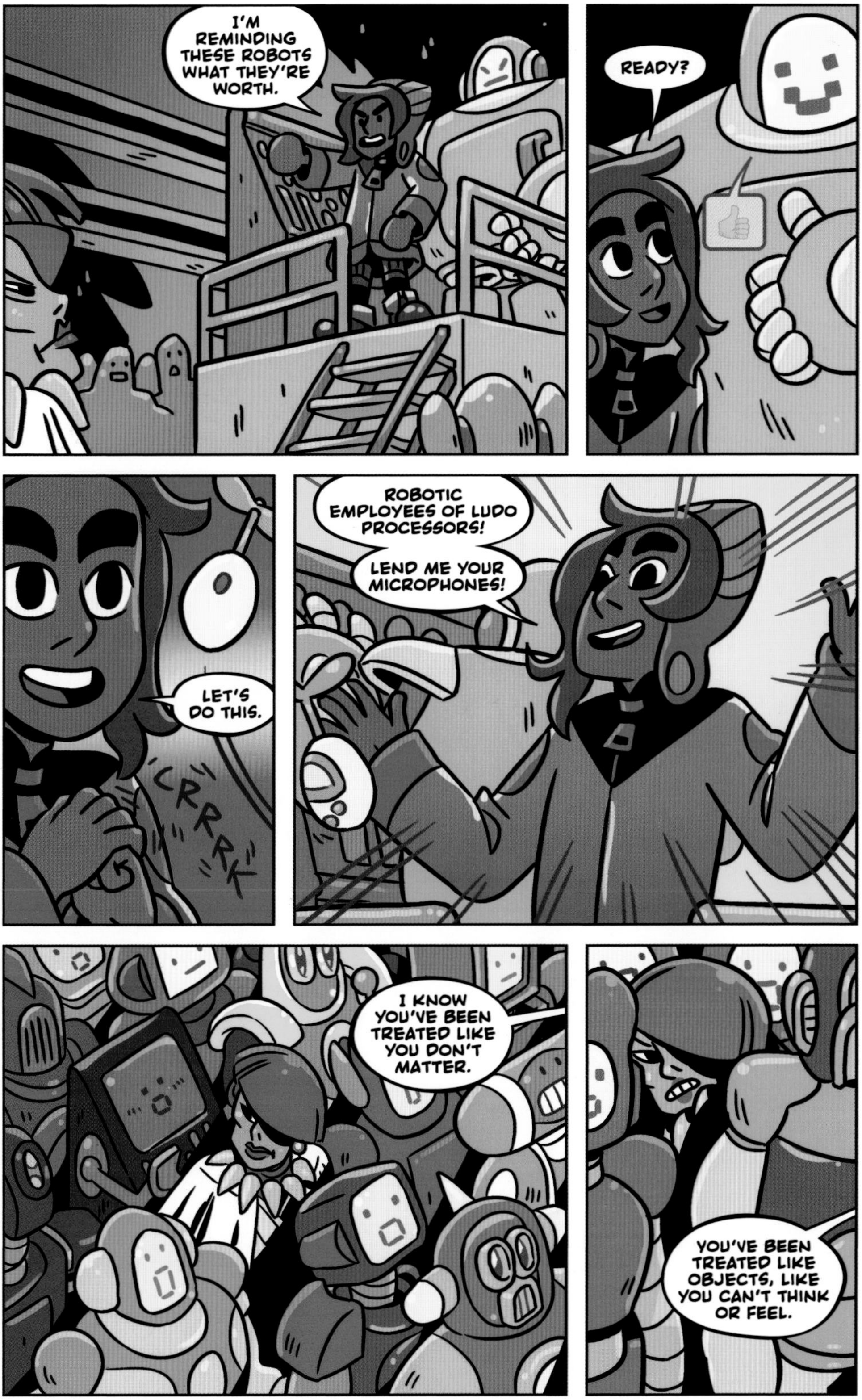
I'M REMINDING THESE ROBOTS WHAT THEY'RE WORTH.
READY?
LET'S DO THIS.
CRRRRK
ROBOTIC EMPLOYEES OF LUDO PROCESSORS!
LEND ME YOUR MICROPHONES!
I KNOW YOU'VE BEEN TREATED LIKE YOU DON'T MATTER.
YOU'VE BEEN TREATED LIKE OBJECTS, LIKE YOU CAN'T THINK OR FEEL.

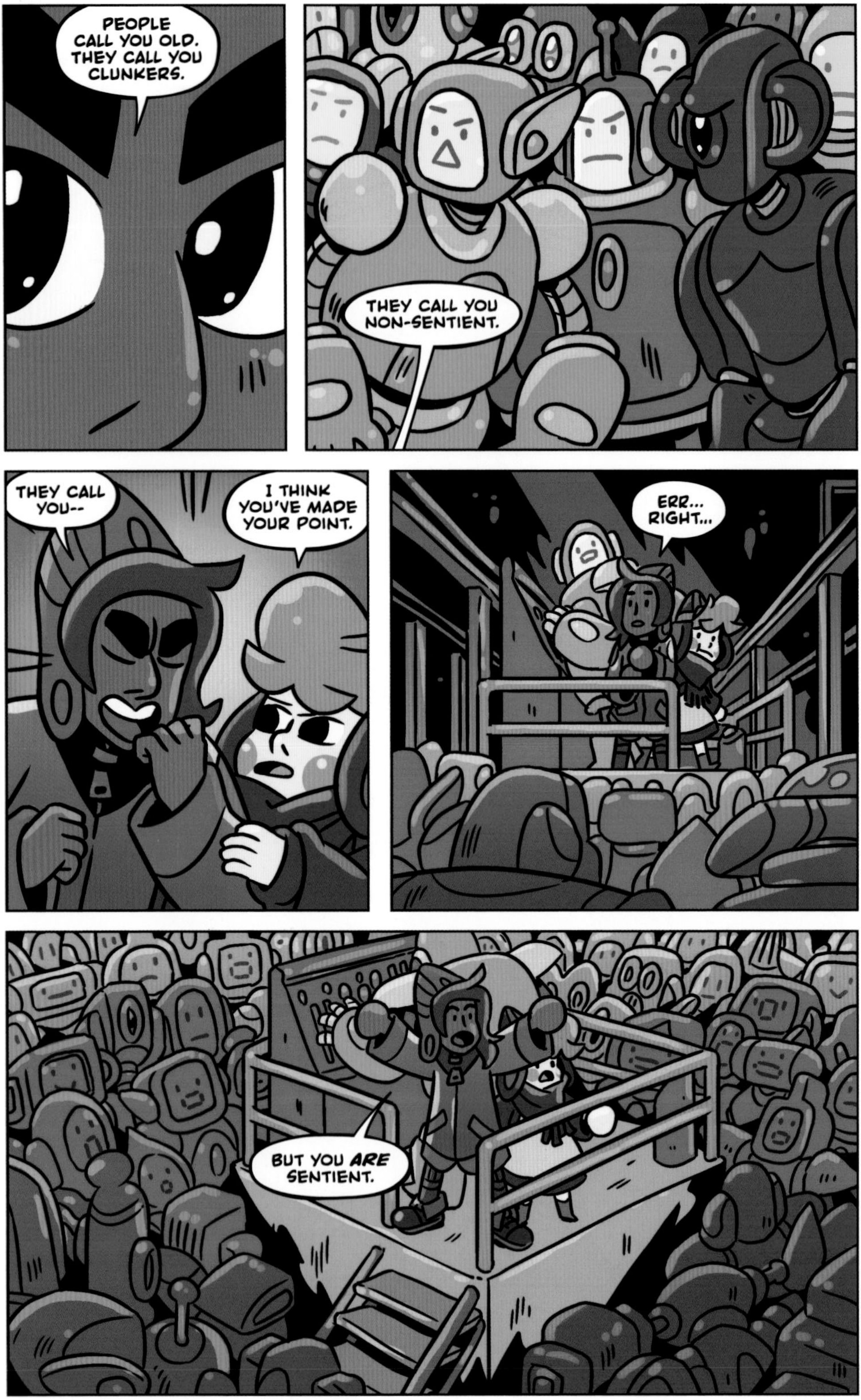
PEOPLE CALL YOU OLD. THEY CALL YOU CLUNKERS.
THEY CALL YOU NON-SENTIENT.
THEY CALL YOU--
I THINK YOU'VE MADE YOUR POINT.
ERR... RIGHT...
BUT YOU *ARE* SENTIENT.

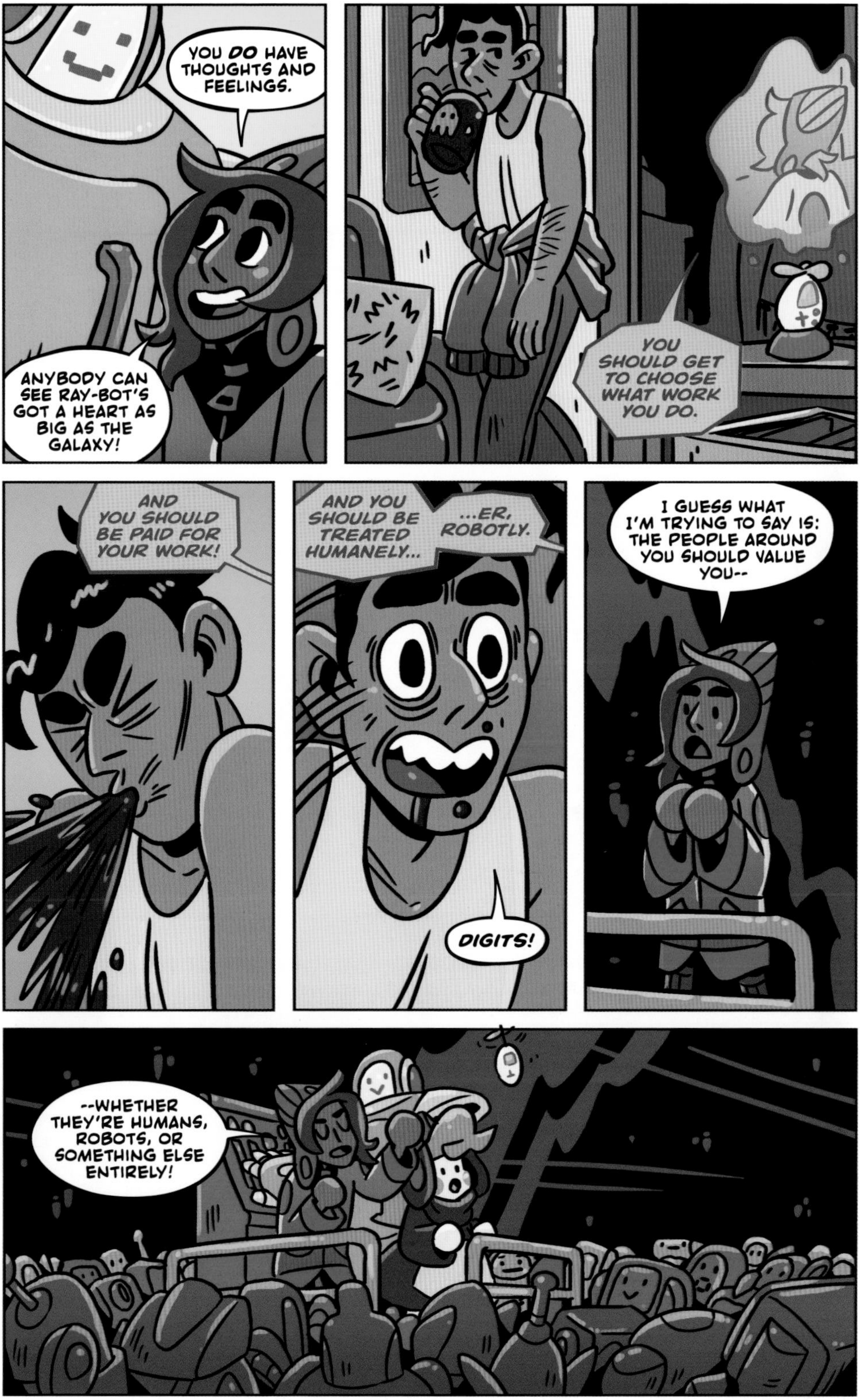
YOU DO HAVE THOUGHTS AND FEELINGS.
ANYBODY CAN SEE RAY-BOT'S GOT A HEART AS BIG AS THE GALAXY!
YOU SHOULD GET TO CHOOSE WHAT WORK YOU DO.
AND YOU SHOULD BE PAID FOR YOUR WORK!
AND YOU SHOULD BE TREATED HUMANELY...
...ER, ROBOTLY.
DIGITS!
I GUESS WHAT I'M TRYING TO SAY IS: THE PEOPLE AROUND YOU SHOULD VALUE YOU--
--WHETHER THEY'RE HUMANS, ROBOTS, OR SOMETHING ELSE ENTIRELY!

WAS THAT OKAY?

I'M A TECHNOMANCER, KID, NOT A MOTIVATIONAL SPEAKER.

01011001 01100101
01110011 00100001

YEAH, I GUESS IT WAS OKAY.

01011001 01100001
01111001 00100001

BACKUP POWER

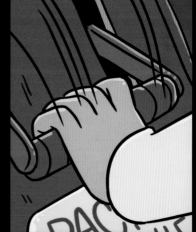

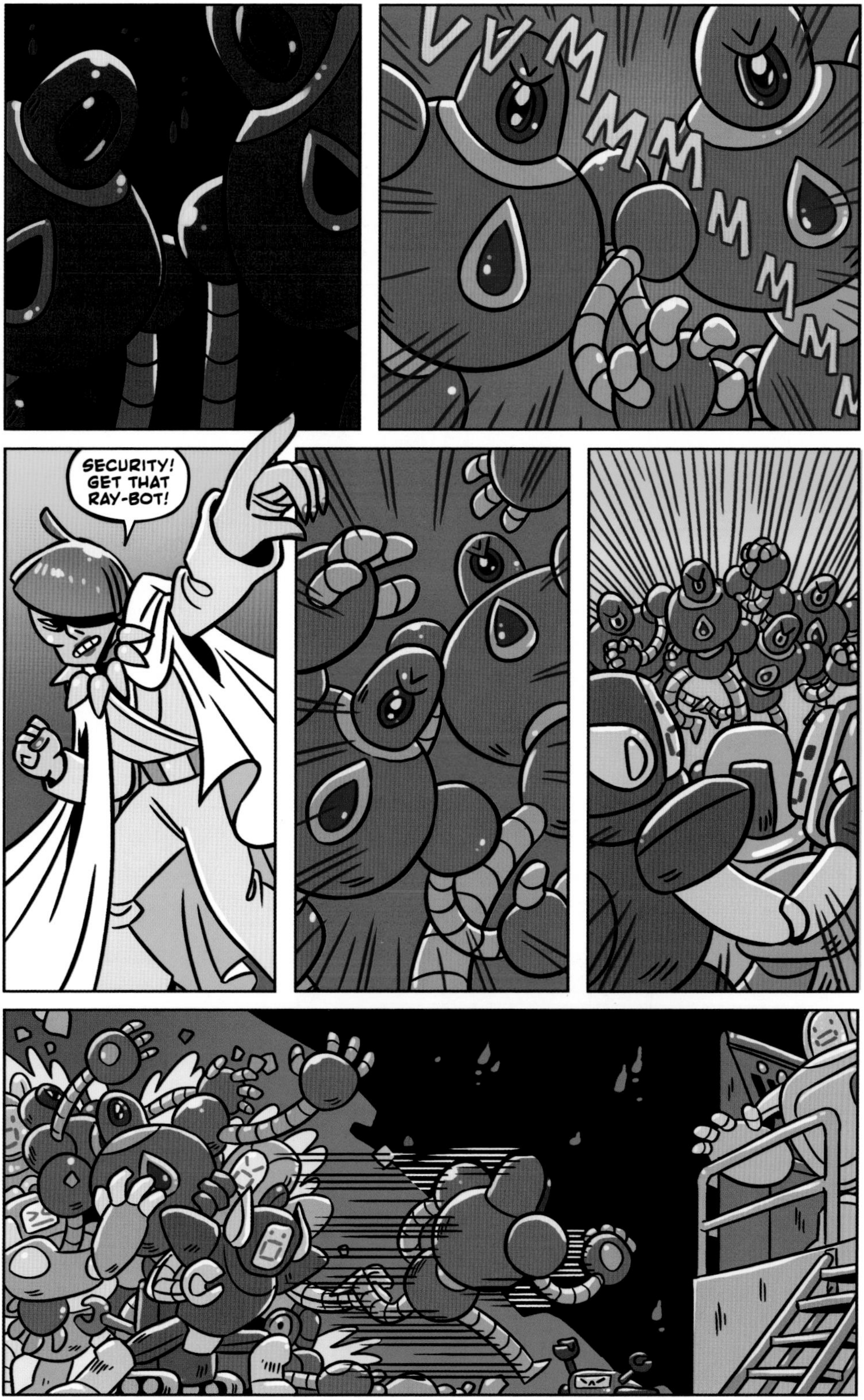
VVMMMMMMMMM
SECURITY! GET THAT RAY-BOT!

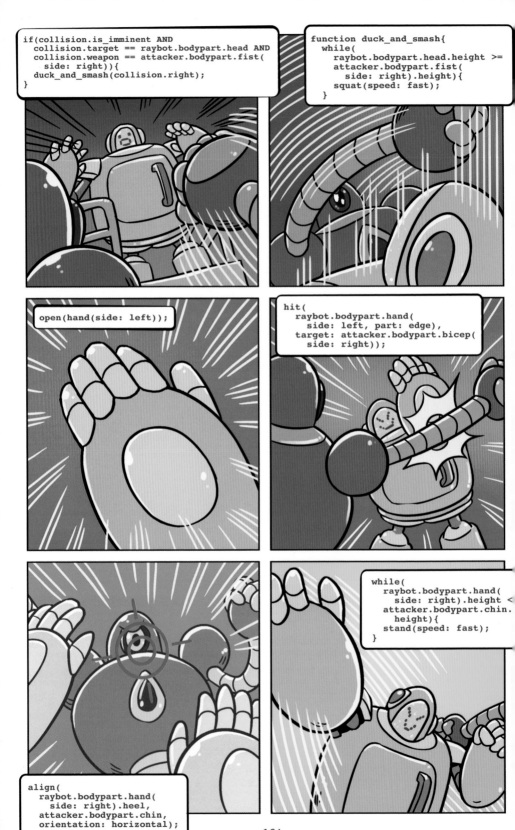

```
if(collision.is_imminent AND
   collision.target == raybot.bodypart.head AND
   collision.weapon == attacker.bodypart.fist(
      side: right)){
   duck_and_smash(collision.right);
}
```

```
function duck_and_smash{
   while(
      raybot.bodypart.head.height >=
      attacker.bodypart.fist(
         side: right).height){
      squat(speed: fast);
   }
```

```
open(hand(side: left));
```

```
hit(
   raybot.bodypart.hand(
      side: left, part: edge),
   target: attacker.bodypart.bicep(
      side: right));
```

```
while(
   raybot.bodypart.hand(
      side: right).height <
   attacker.bodypart.chin.
      height){
   stand(speed: fast);
}
```

```
align(
   raybot.bodypart.hand(
      side: right).heel,
   attacker.bodypart.chin,
   orientation: horizontal);
```

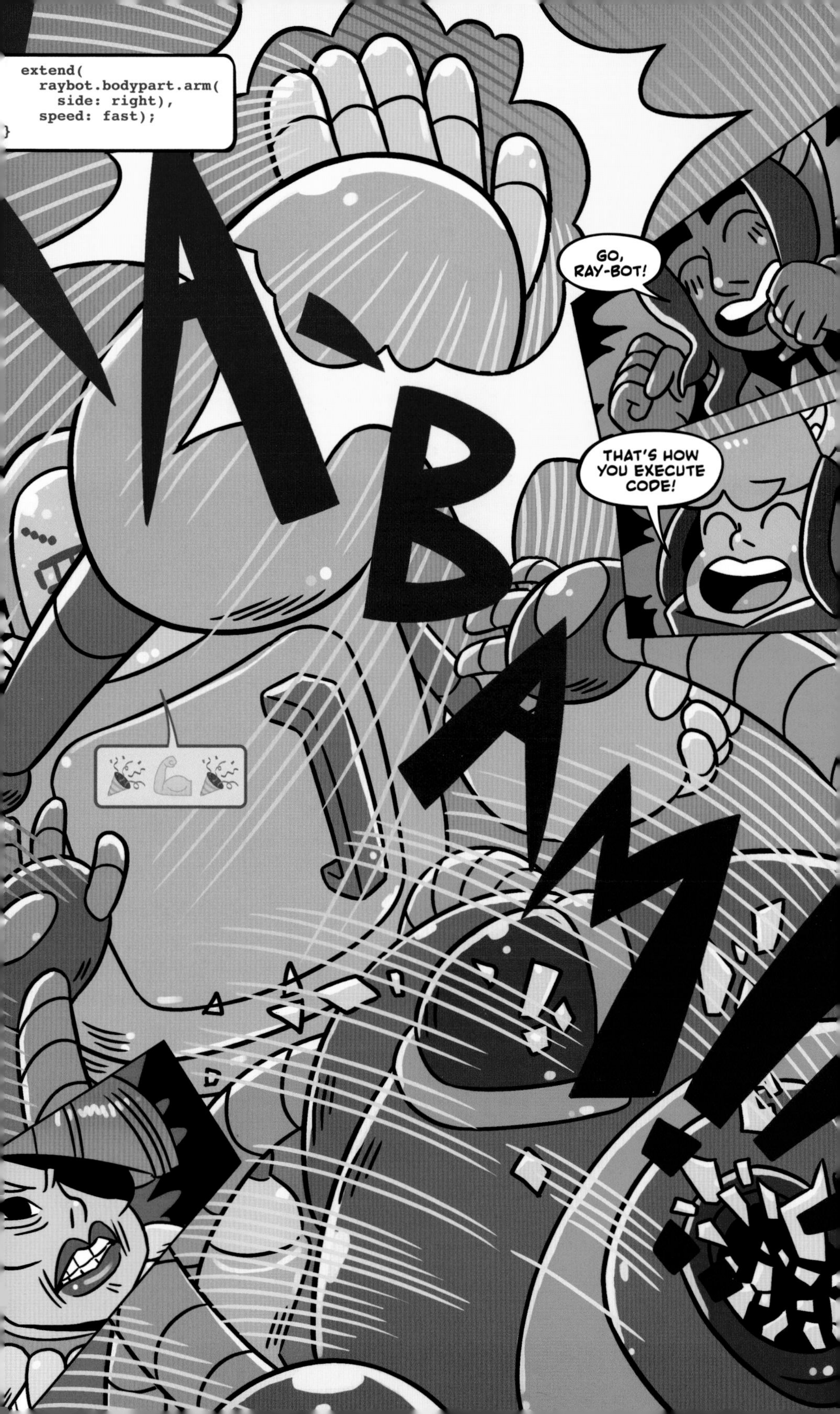
extend(
raybot.bodypart.arm(
side: right),
speed: fast);
}
KA-BAM!!
GO, RAY-BOT!
THAT'S HOW YOU EXECUTE CODE!

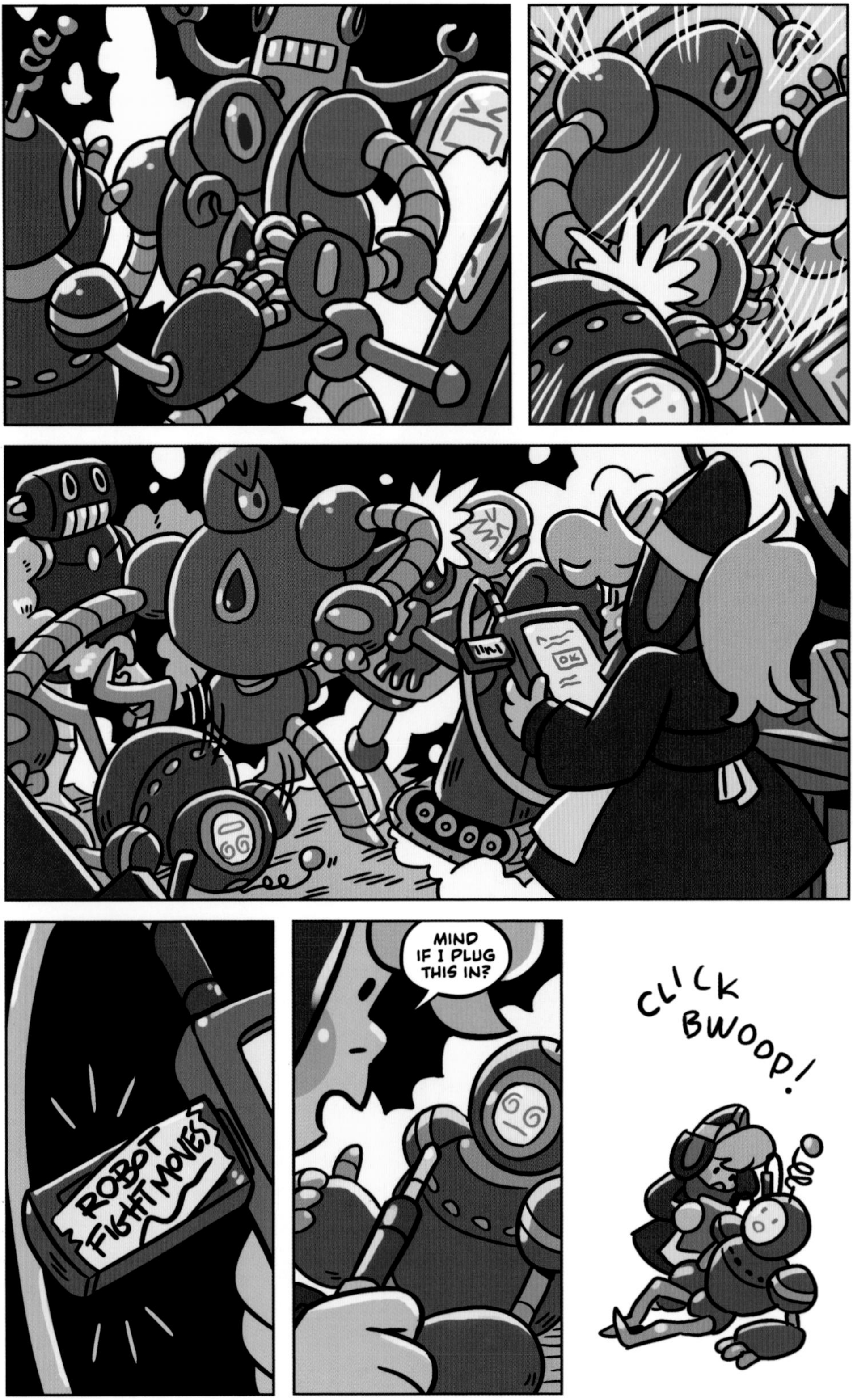
ROBOT FIGHT MOVES
MIND IF I PLUG THIS IN?
CLICK
BWOOP!

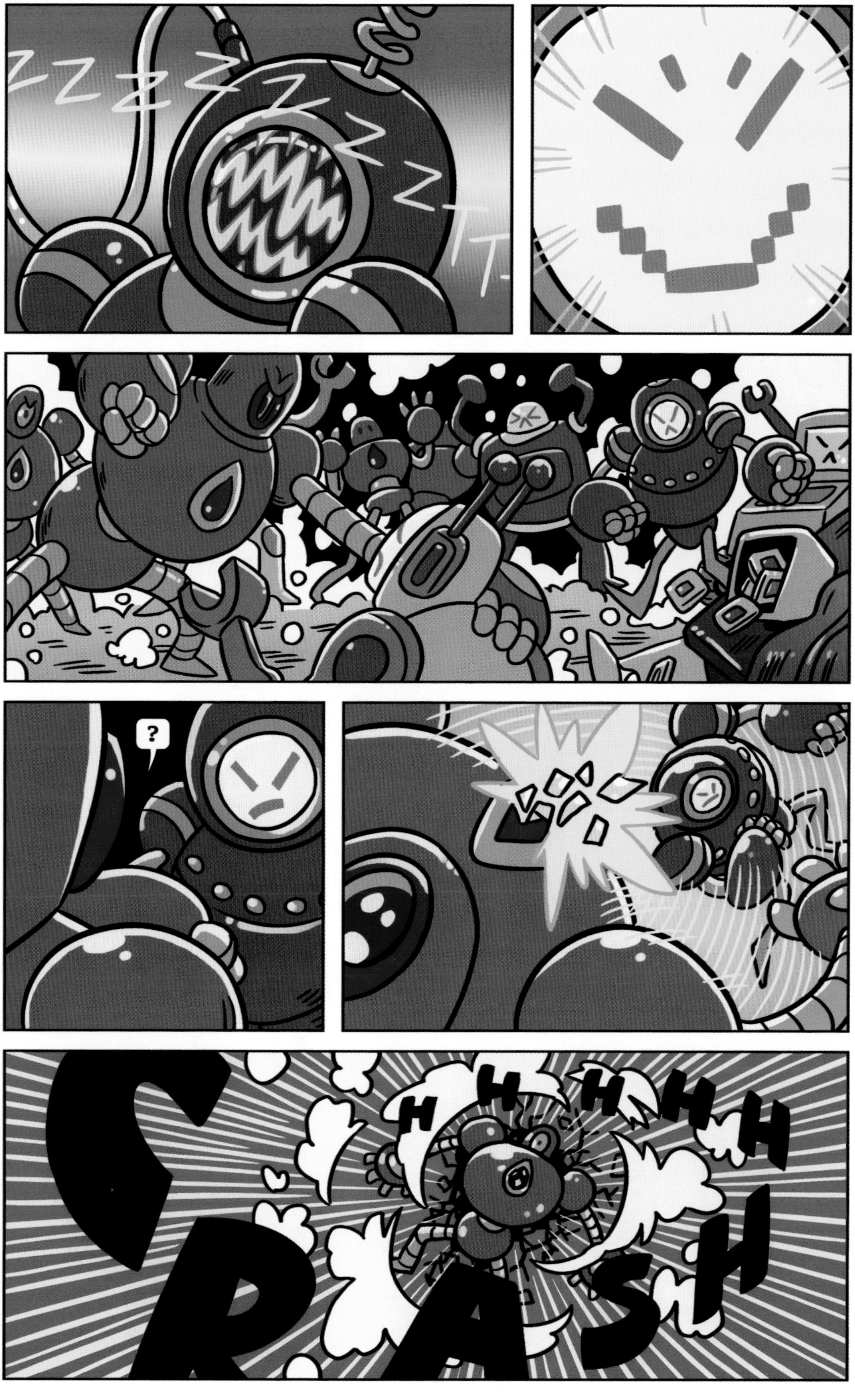
ZZZZZZZZZZZZTT-
?
CRASH
HHHHHHH

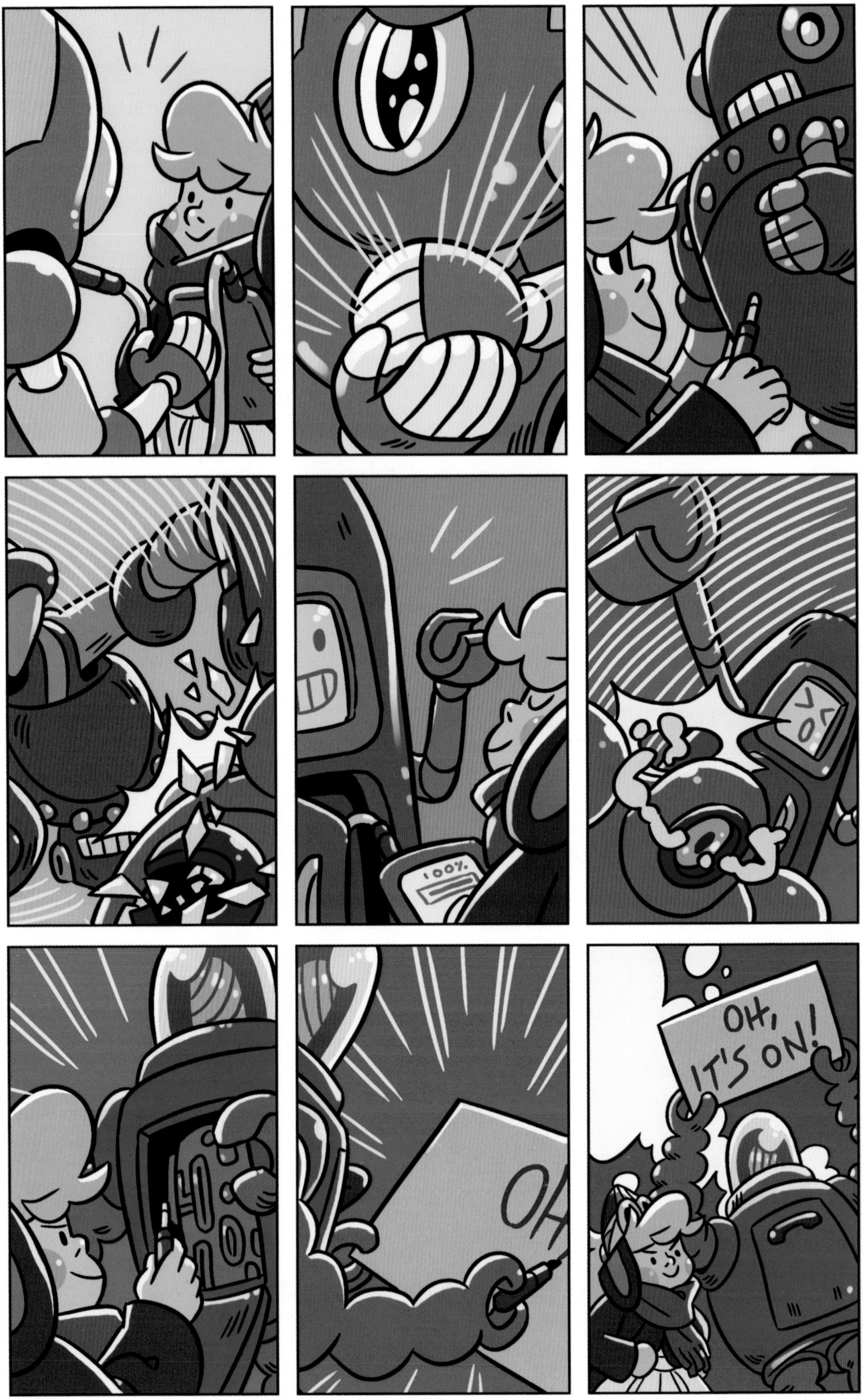
100%
OH
OH, IT'S ON!

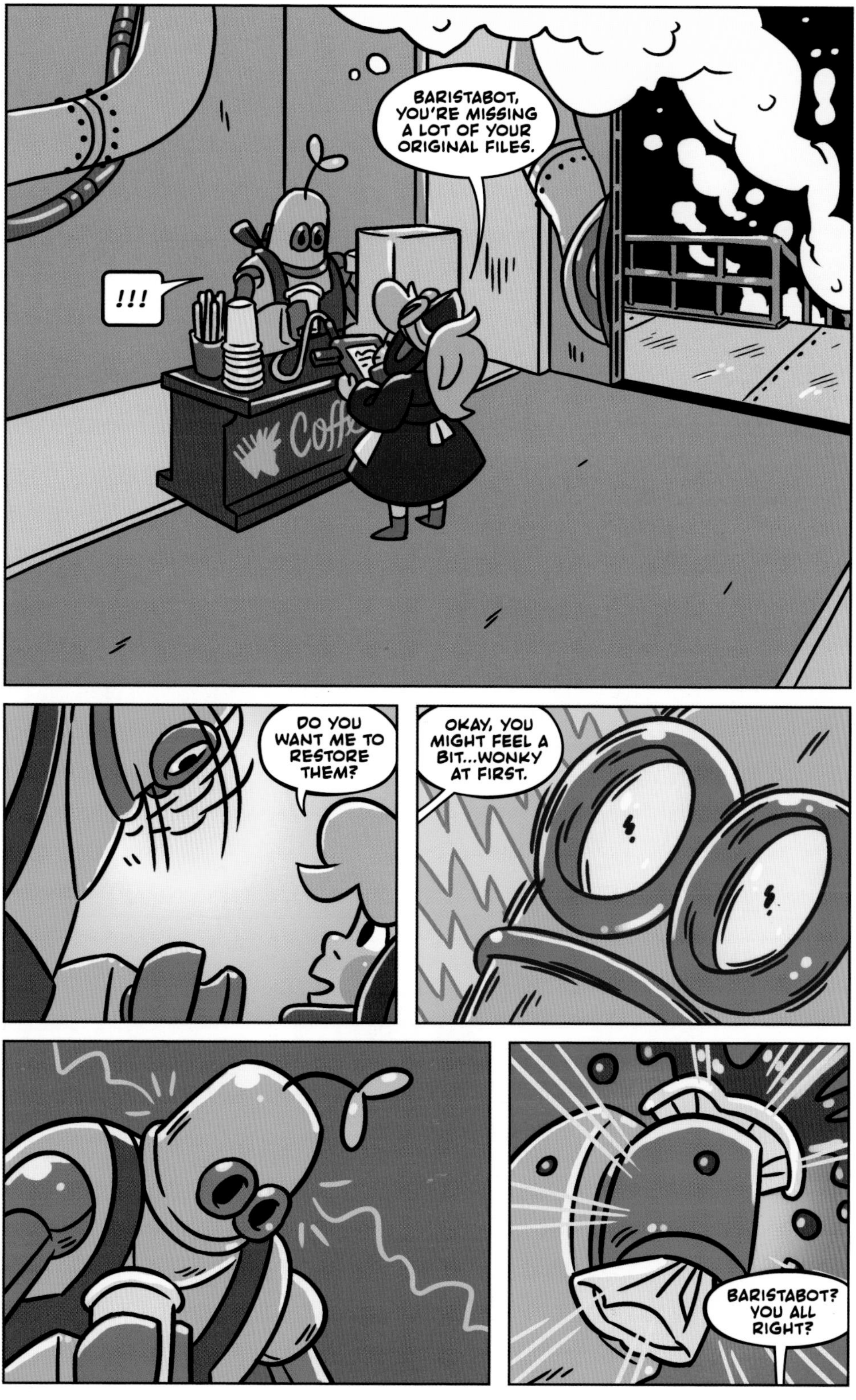
BARISTABOT, YOU'RE MISSING A LOT OF YOUR ORIGINAL FILES.
!!!
DO YOU WANT ME TO RESTORE THEM?
OKAY, YOU MIGHT FEEL A BIT...WONKY AT FIRST.
BARISTABOT? YOU ALL RIGHT?

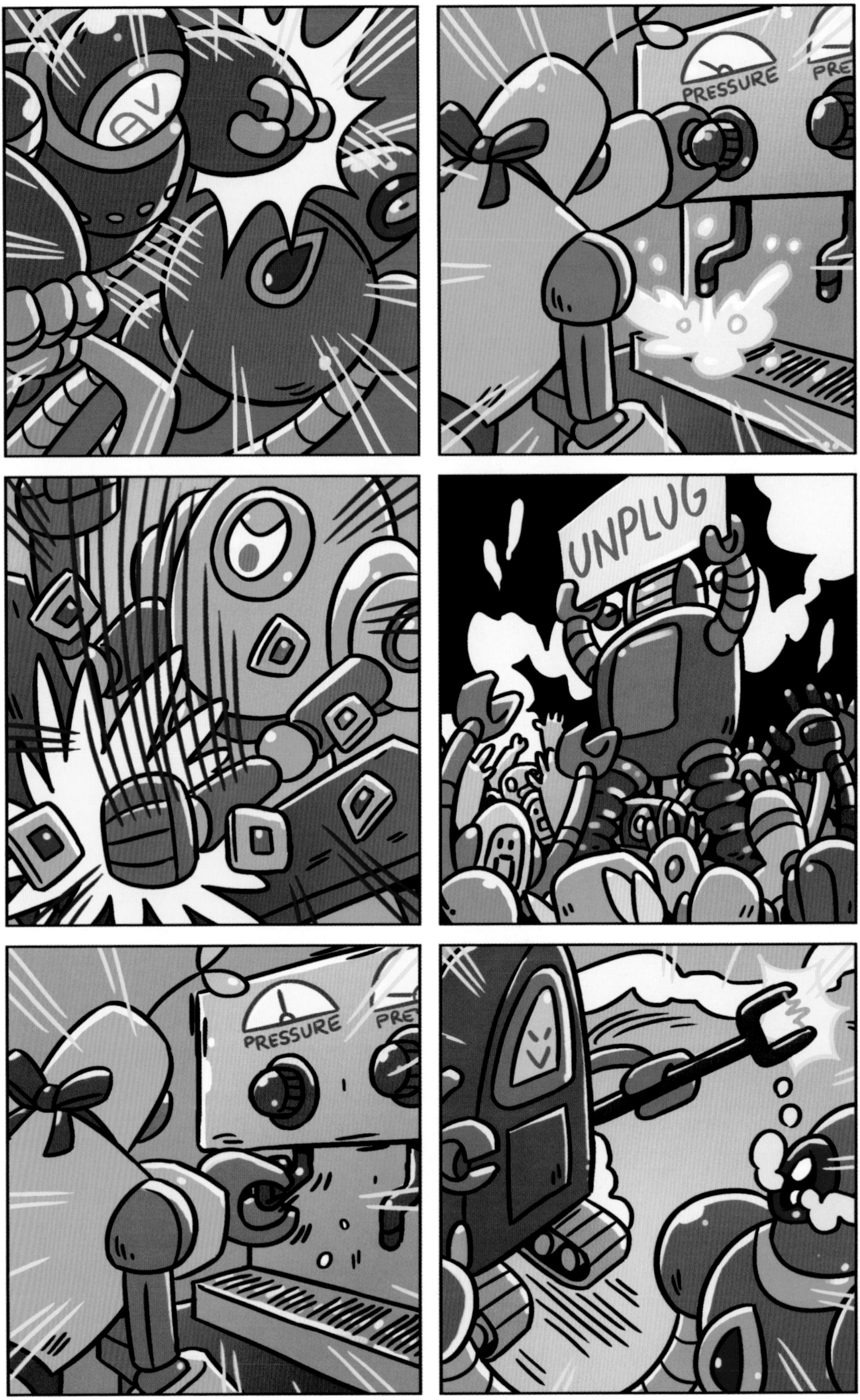
PRESSURE
UNPLUG
PRESSURE

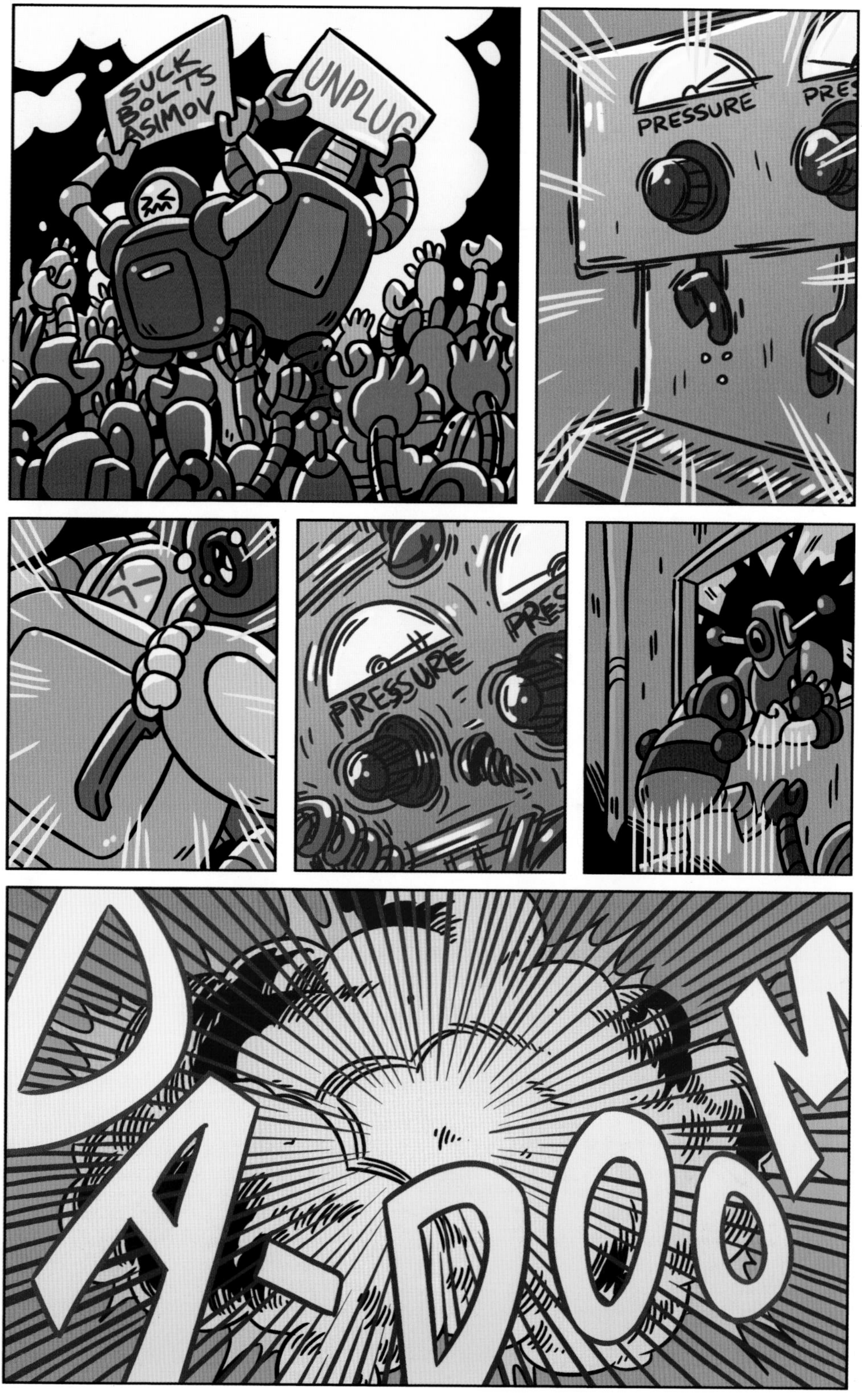
SUCK BOLTS ASIMOV
UNPLUG
PRESSURE
PRESSURE
KA-DOOM

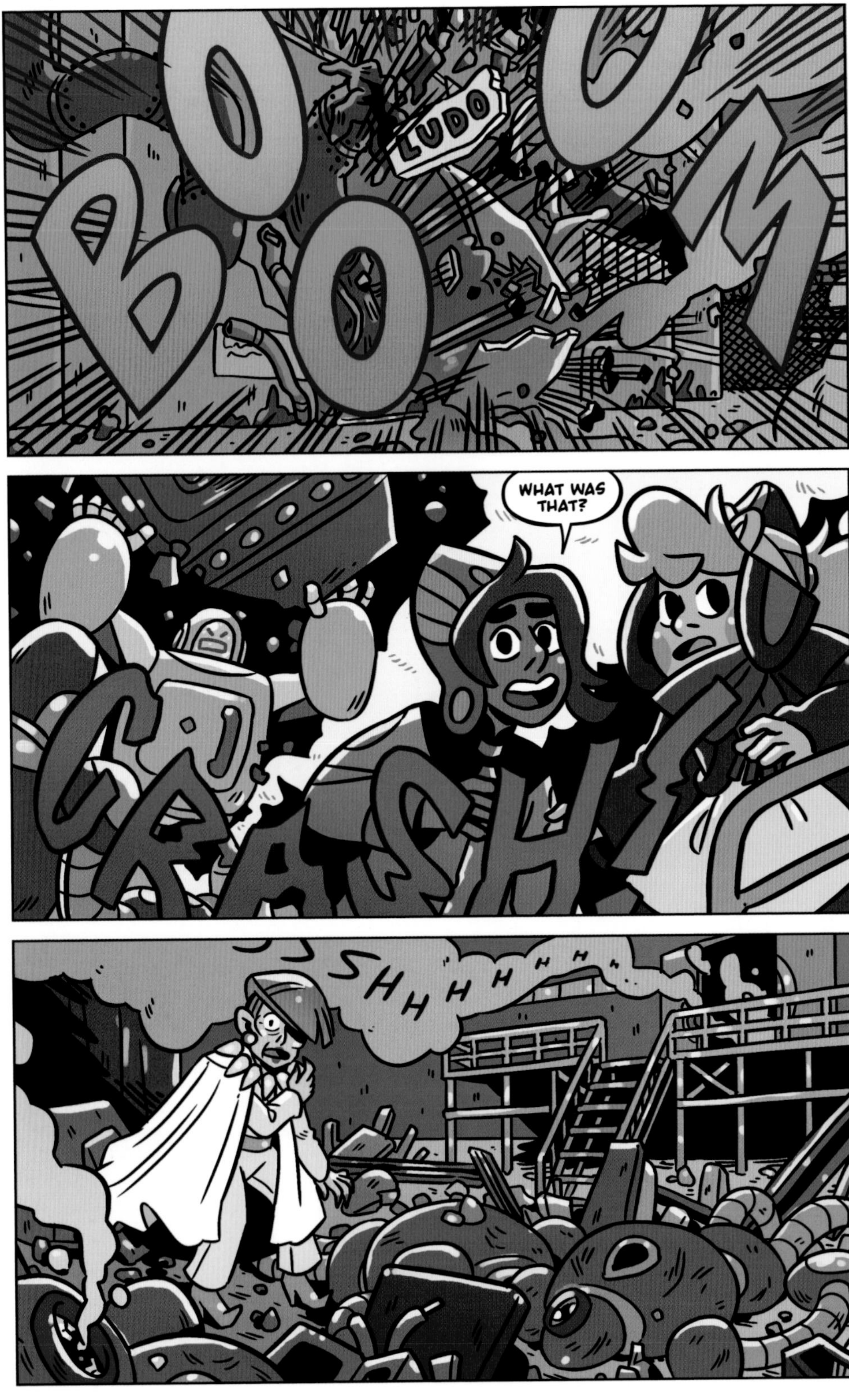
BOOOM
LUDO
WHAT WAS THAT?
CRASH
SHHHHHHH

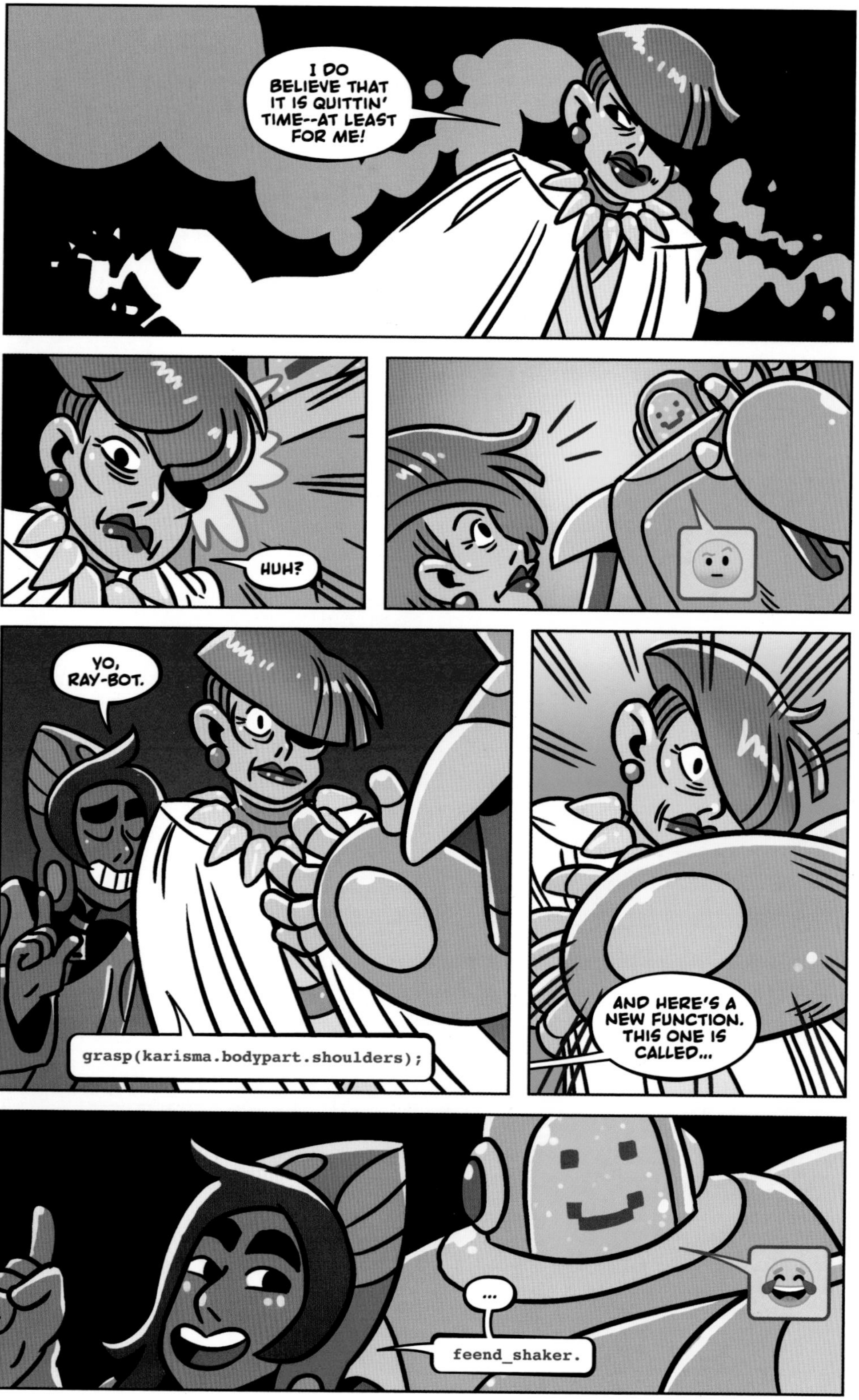
I DO BELIEVE THAT IT IS QUITTIN' TIME--AT LEAST FOR ME!
HUH?
YO, RAY-BOT.
grasp(karisma.bodypart.shoulders);
AND HERE'S A NEW FUNCTION. THIS ONE IS CALLED...
...
feend_shaker.

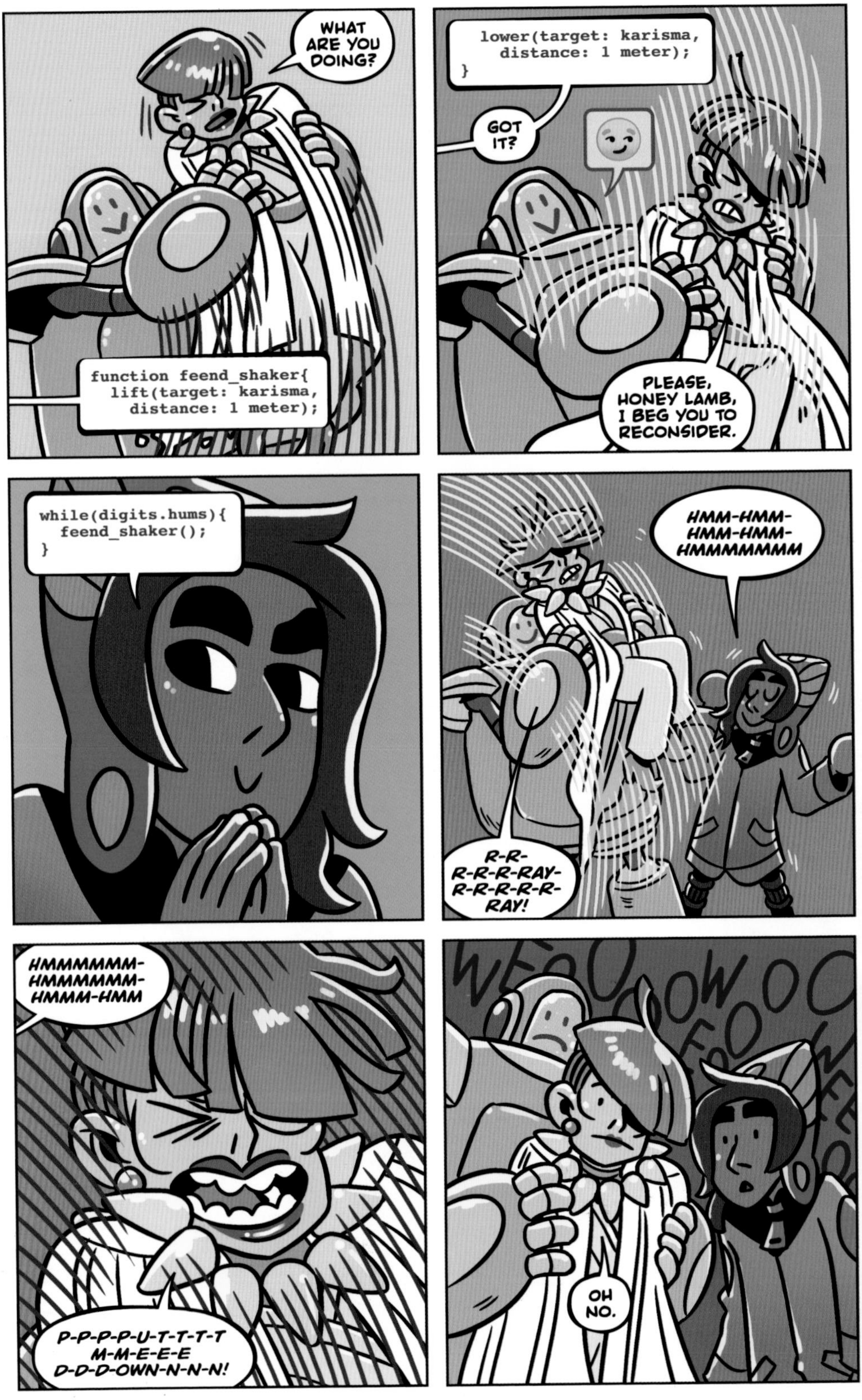
WHAT ARE YOU DOING?
function feend_shaker{
lift(target: karisma,
distance: 1 meter);
lower(target: karisma,
distance: 1 meter);
}
GOT IT?
PLEASE, HONEY LAMB, I BEG YOU TO RECONSIDER.
while(digits.hums){
feend_shaker();
}
HMM-HMM-HMM-HMM-HMMMMMMM
R-R-R-R-R-RAY-R-R-R-R-R-RAY!
HMMMMMM-HMMMMMM-HMMM-HMM
P-P-P-P-U-T-T-T-T M-M-E-E-E D-D-D-OWN-N-N-N!
OH NO.

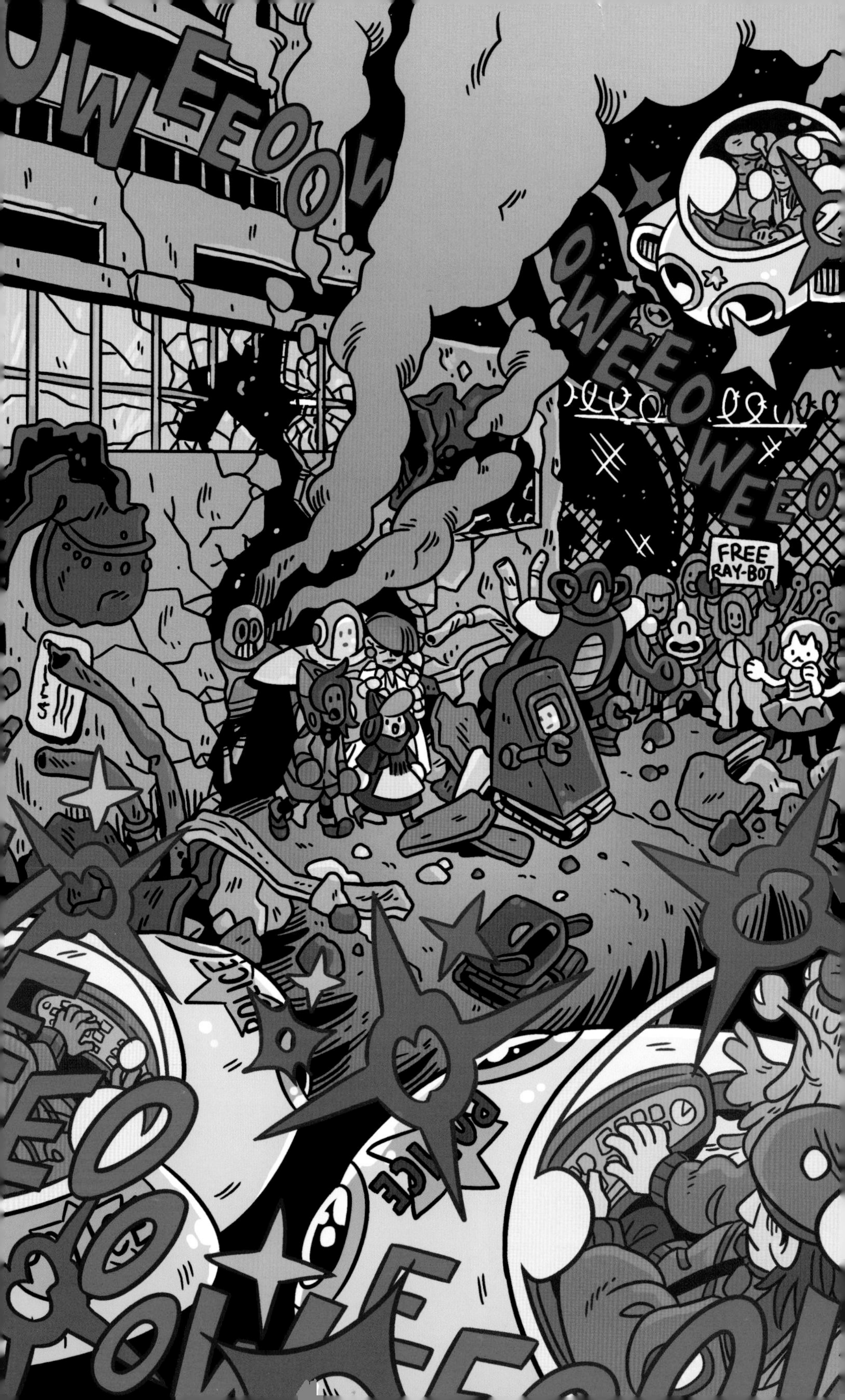
FREE
RAY-BOT

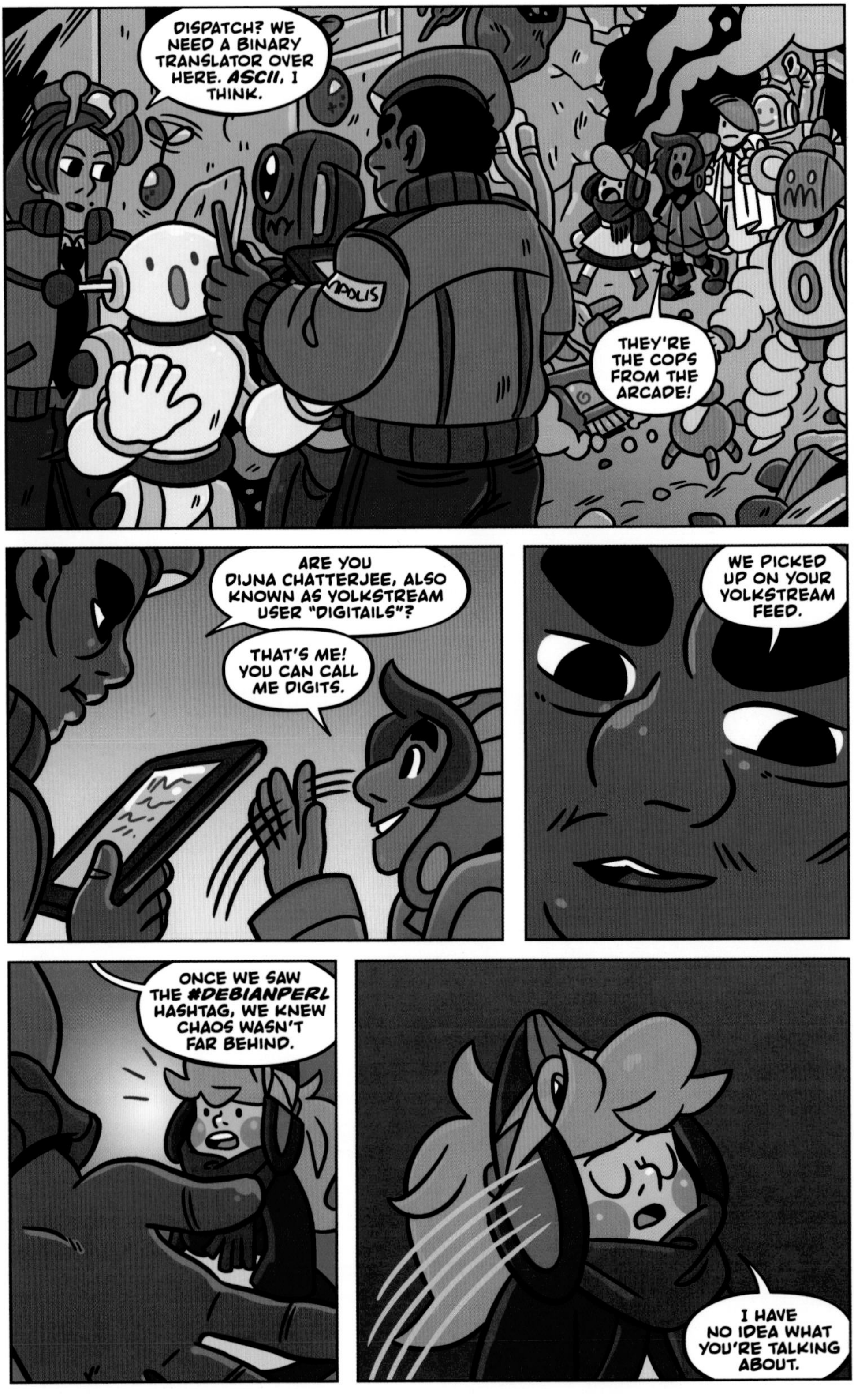
DISPATCH? WE NEED A BINARY TRANSLATOR OVER HERE. ASCII, I THINK.
THEY'RE THE COPS FROM THE ARCADE!
ARE YOU DIJNA CHATTERJEE, ALSO KNOWN AS YOLKSTREAM USER "DIGITAILS"?
THAT'S ME! YOU CAN CALL ME DIGITS.
WE PICKED UP ON YOUR YOLKSTREAM FEED.
ONCE WE SAW THE #DEBIANPERL HASHTAG, WE KNEW CHAOS WASN'T FAR BEHIND.
I HAVE NO IDEA WHAT YOU'RE TALKING ABOUT.

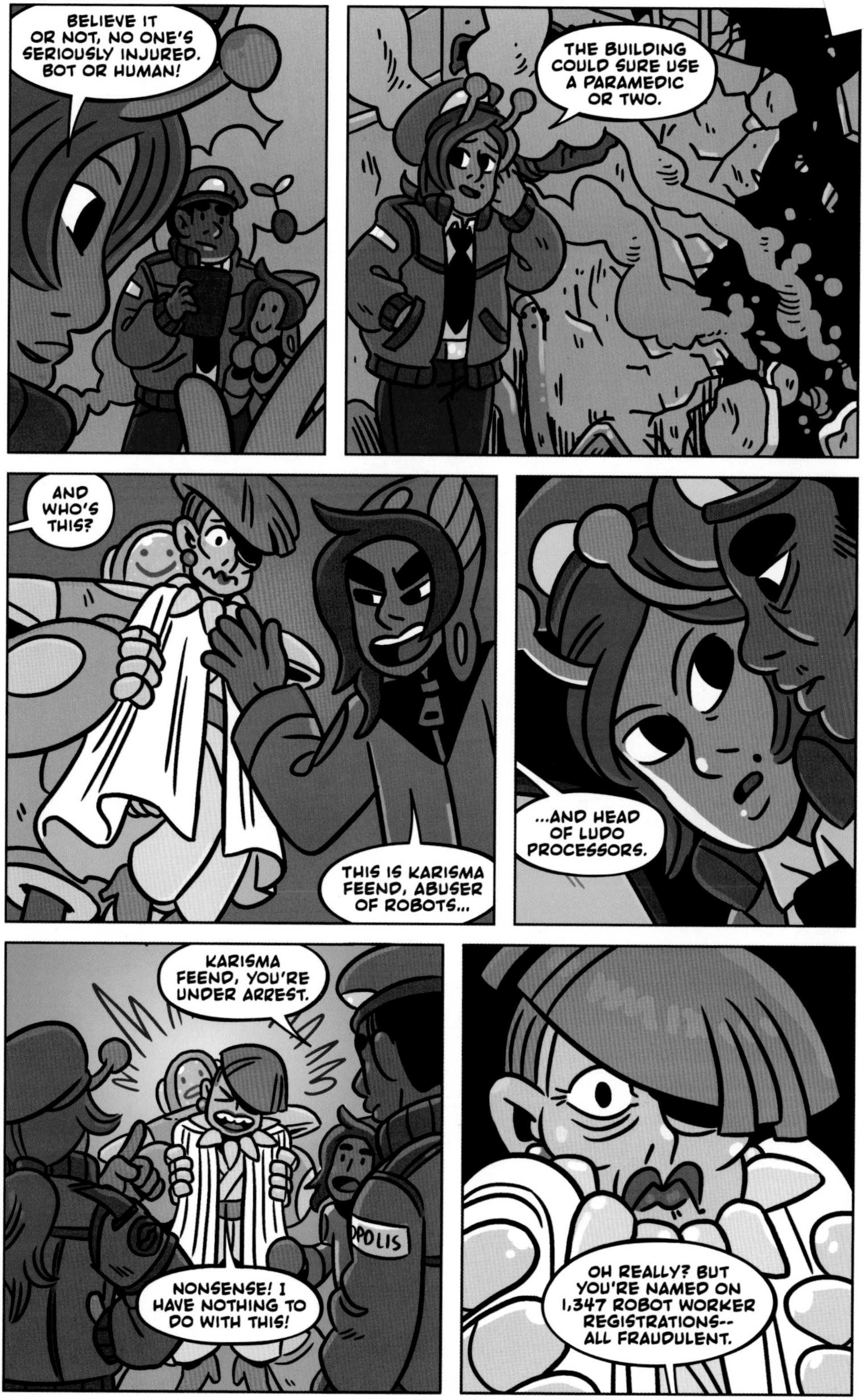
BELIEVE IT OR NOT, NO ONE'S SERIOUSLY INJURED. BOT OR HUMAN!
THE BUILDING COULD SURE USE A PARAMEDIC OR TWO.
AND WHO'S THIS?
THIS IS KARISMA FEEND, ABUSER OF ROBOTS...
...AND HEAD OF LUDO PROCESSORS.
KARISMA FEEND, YOU'RE UNDER ARREST.
OPOLIS
NONSENSE! I HAVE NOTHING TO DO WITH THIS!
OH REALLY? BUT YOU'RE NAMED ON 1,347 ROBOT WORKER REGISTRATIONS--ALL FRAUDULENT.

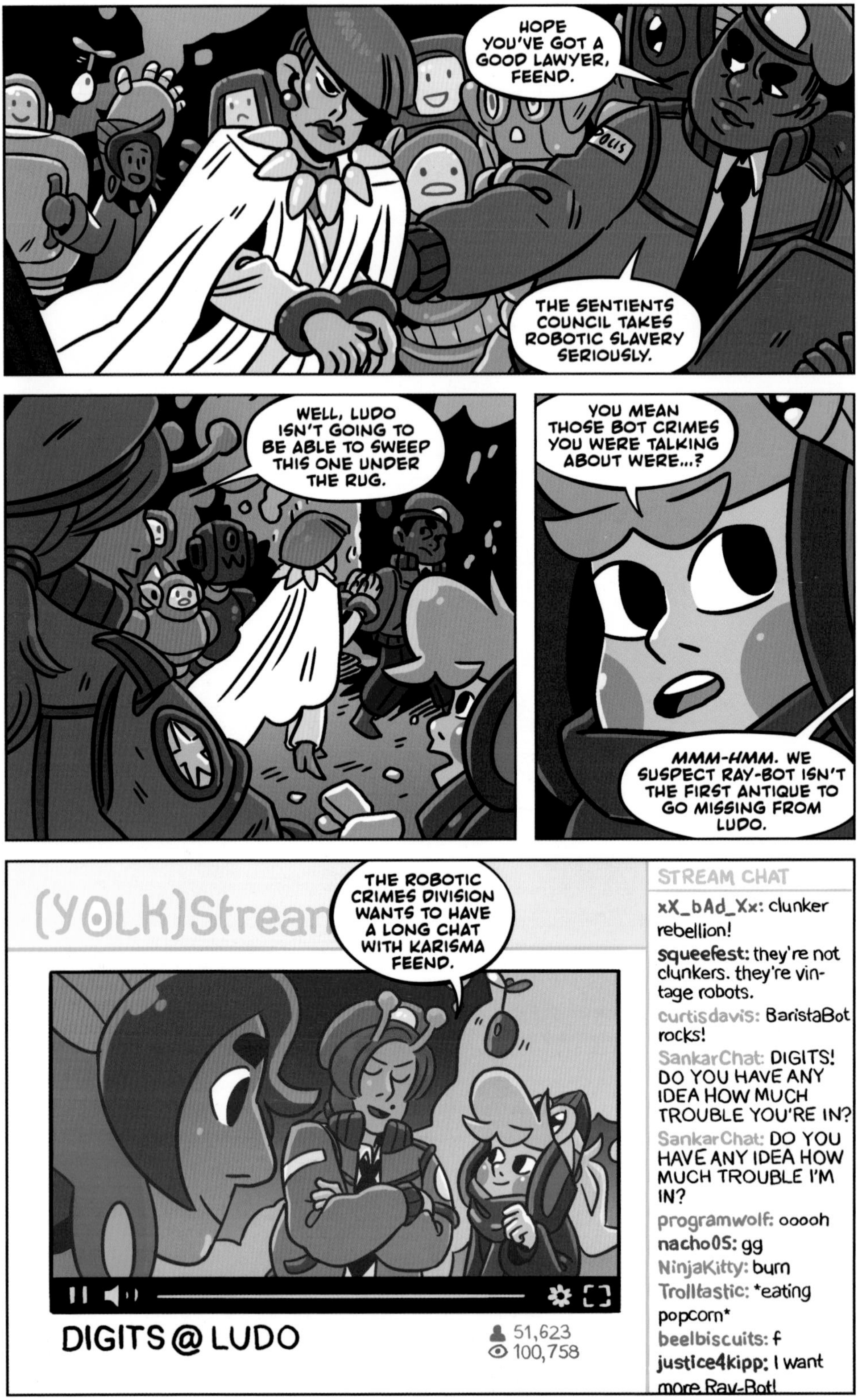
HOPE YOU'VE GOT A GOOD LAWYER, FEEND.
THE SENTIENTS COUNCIL TAKES ROBOTIC SLAVERY SERIOUSLY.
WELL, LUDO ISN'T GOING TO BE ABLE TO SWEEP THIS ONE UNDER THE RUG.
YOU MEAN THOSE BOT CRIMES YOU WERE TALKING ABOUT WERE...?
MMM-HMM. WE SUSPECT RAY-BOT ISN'T THE FIRST ANTIQUE TO GO MISSING FROM LUDO.
(YOLK)Stream
THE ROBOTIC CRIMES DIVISION WANTS TO HAVE A LONG CHAT WITH KARISMA FEEND.
STREAM CHAT
xX_bAd_Xx: clunker rebellion!
squeefest: they're not clunkers. they're vintage robots.
curtisdavis: BaristaBot rocks!
SankarChat: DIGITS! DO YOU HAVE ANY IDEA HOW MUCH TROUBLE YOU'RE IN?
SankarChat: DO YOU HAVE ANY IDEA HOW MUCH TROUBLE I'M IN?
programwolf: ooooh
nacho05: gg
NinjaKitty: burn
Trolltastic: *eating popcorn*
beelbiscuits: f
justice4kipp: I want more Ray-Bot!
DIGITS @ LUDO
51,623
100,758

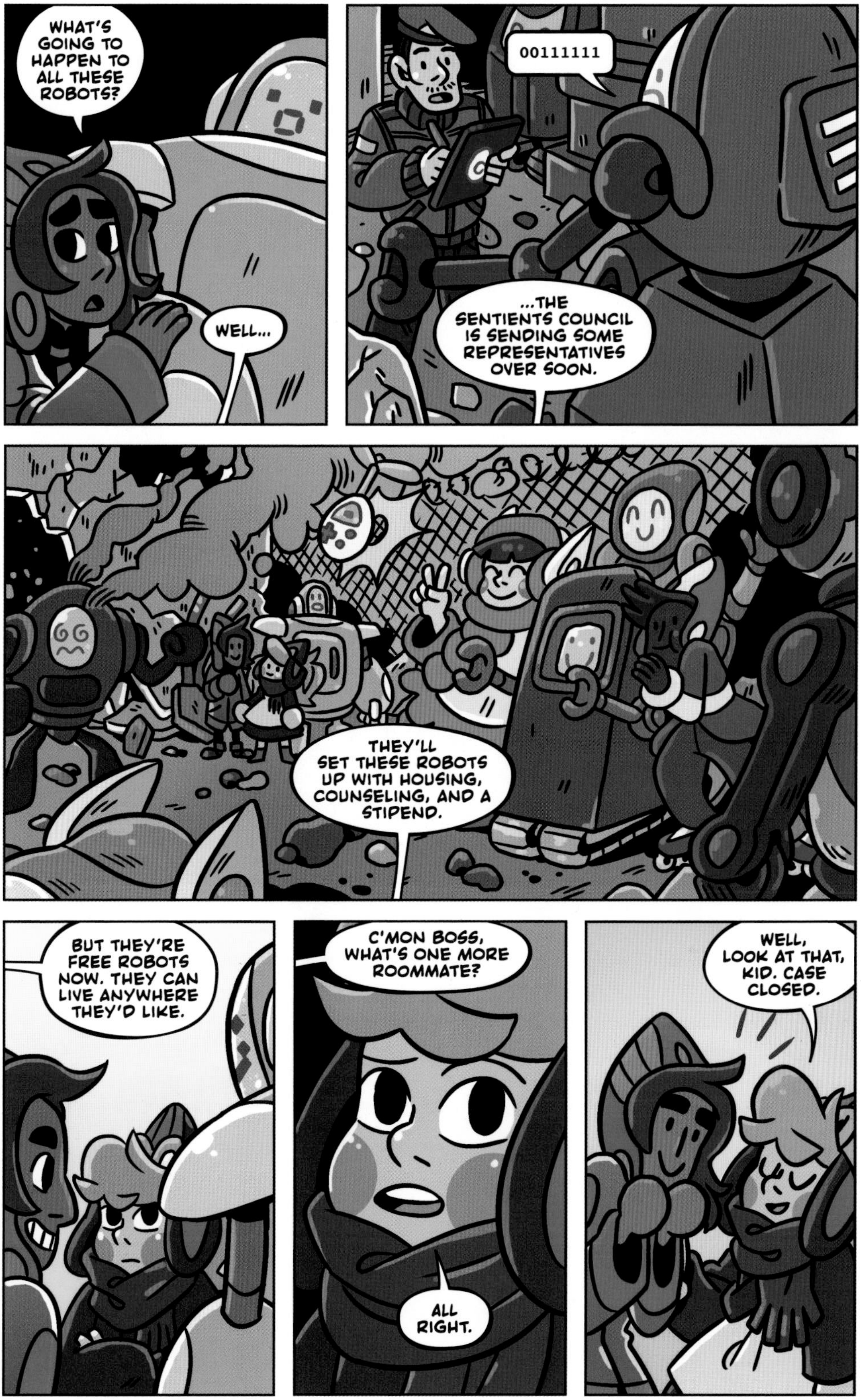
WHAT'S GOING TO HAPPEN TO ALL THESE ROBOTS?
WELL...
00111111
...THE SENTIENTS COUNCIL IS SENDING SOME REPRESENTATIVES OVER SOON.
THEY'LL SET THESE ROBOTS UP WITH HOUSING, COUNSELING, AND A STIPEND.
BUT THEY'RE FREE ROBOTS NOW. THEY CAN LIVE ANYWHERE THEY'D LIKE.
C'MON BOSS, WHAT'S ONE MORE ROOMMATE?
ALL RIGHT.
WELL, LOOK AT THAT, KID. CASE CLOSED.

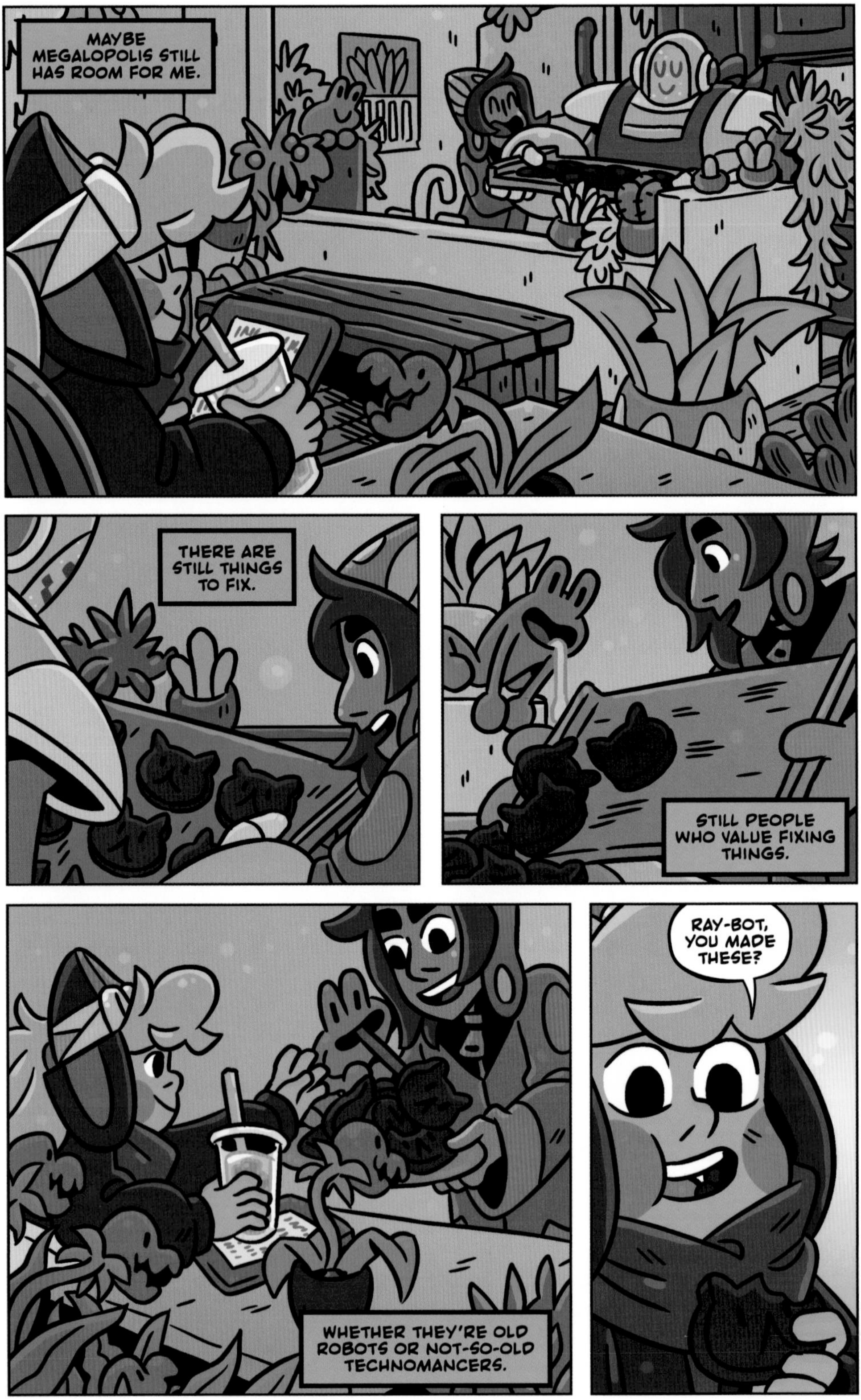
MAYBE MEGALOPOLIS STILL HAS ROOM FOR ME.
THERE ARE STILL THINGS TO FIX.
STILL PEOPLE WHO VALUE FIXING THINGS.
WHETHER THEY'RE OLD ROBOTS OR NOT-SO-OLD TECHNOMANCERS.
RAY-BOT, YOU MADE THESE?

HE SEEMS TO KNOW A LOT MORE STUFF SINCE HE GOT HIS MEMORIES BACK.

NO MORE WALKING INTO WALLS FOR YOU!

AND YOU'RE OKAY WITH THAT?

WE COULD REMOVE IT IF YOU WANT. OR I COULD ERASE SOME OF YOUR MEMORIES...

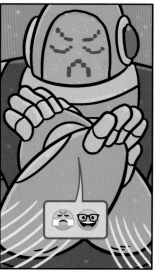

ALL RIGHT, RAY-BOT. LET ME KNOW IF YOU CHANGE YOUR MIND.

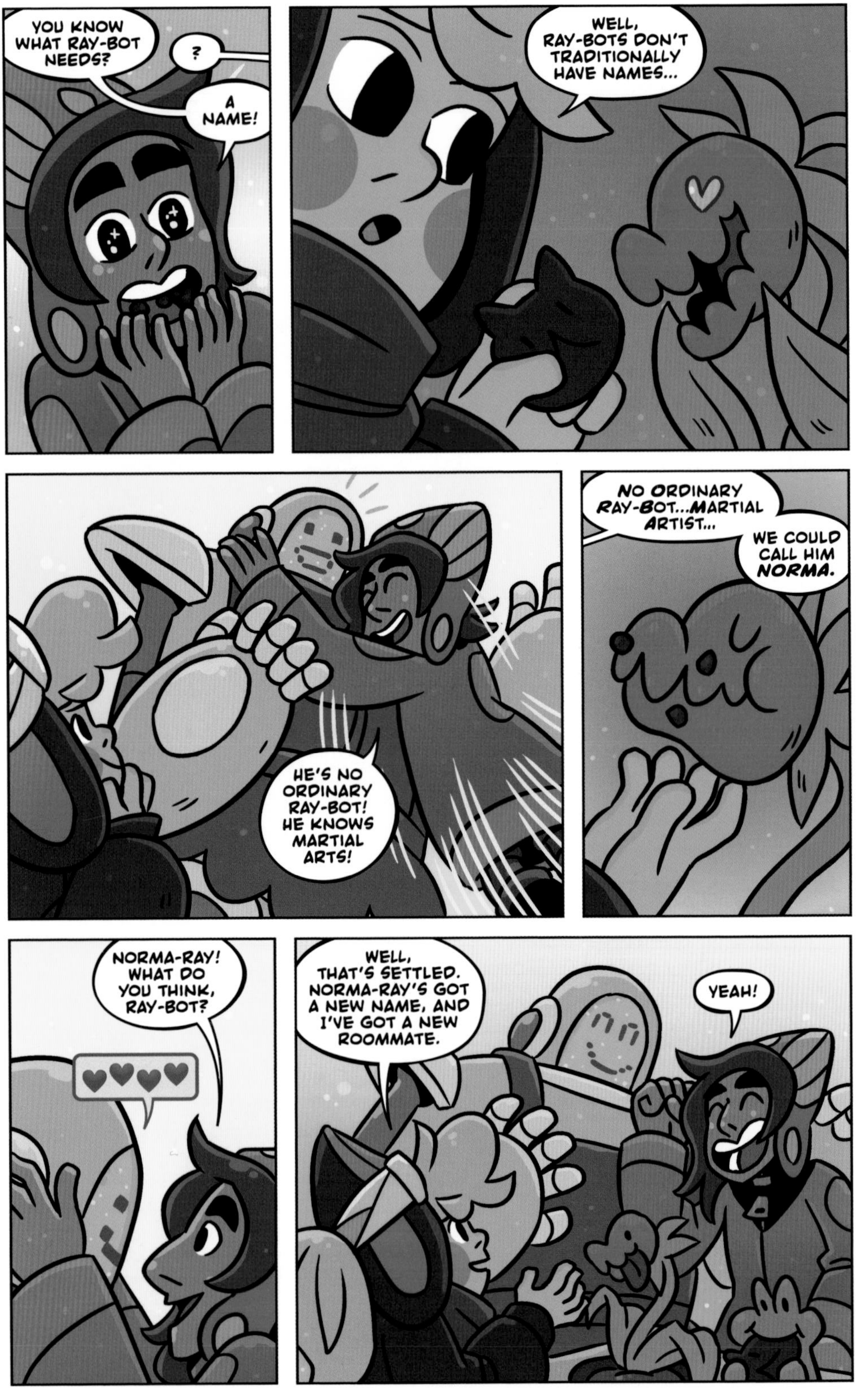
YOU KNOW WHAT RAY-BOT NEEDS?
?
A NAME!
WELL, RAY-BOTS DON'T TRADITIONALLY HAVE NAMES...
HE'S NO ORDINARY RAY-BOT! HE KNOWS MARTIAL ARTS!
NO ORDINARY RAY-BOT...MARTIAL ARTIST...
WE COULD CALL HIM NORMA.
NORMA-RAY! WHAT DO YOU THINK, RAY-BOT?
WELL, THAT'S SETTLED. NORMA-RAY'S GOT A NEW NAME, AND I'VE GOT A NEW ROOMMATE.
YEAH!

SORRY ABOUT YOUR VACATION MONEY.

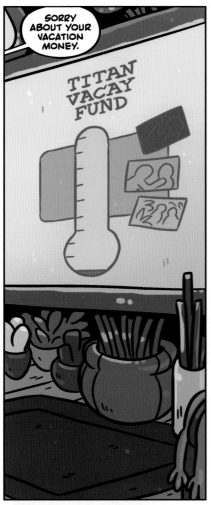

TITAN VACAY FUND

WELL, OUR LITTLE ROBOT REVOLT DID NEARLY BLOW UP A CITY BLOCK.

ROBOT SLAVE LABOR EXPOSED
OMELETTE CONTRACTOR DISAVOWS

THE SENTIENTS COUNCIL DID PROMISE TO HIRE ME TO TUNE UP OUR NEW FRIENDS.

IT'S NOT A TON OF CASH, BUT TECHNOMANCERS CAN'T BE CHOOSERS.

WELL...

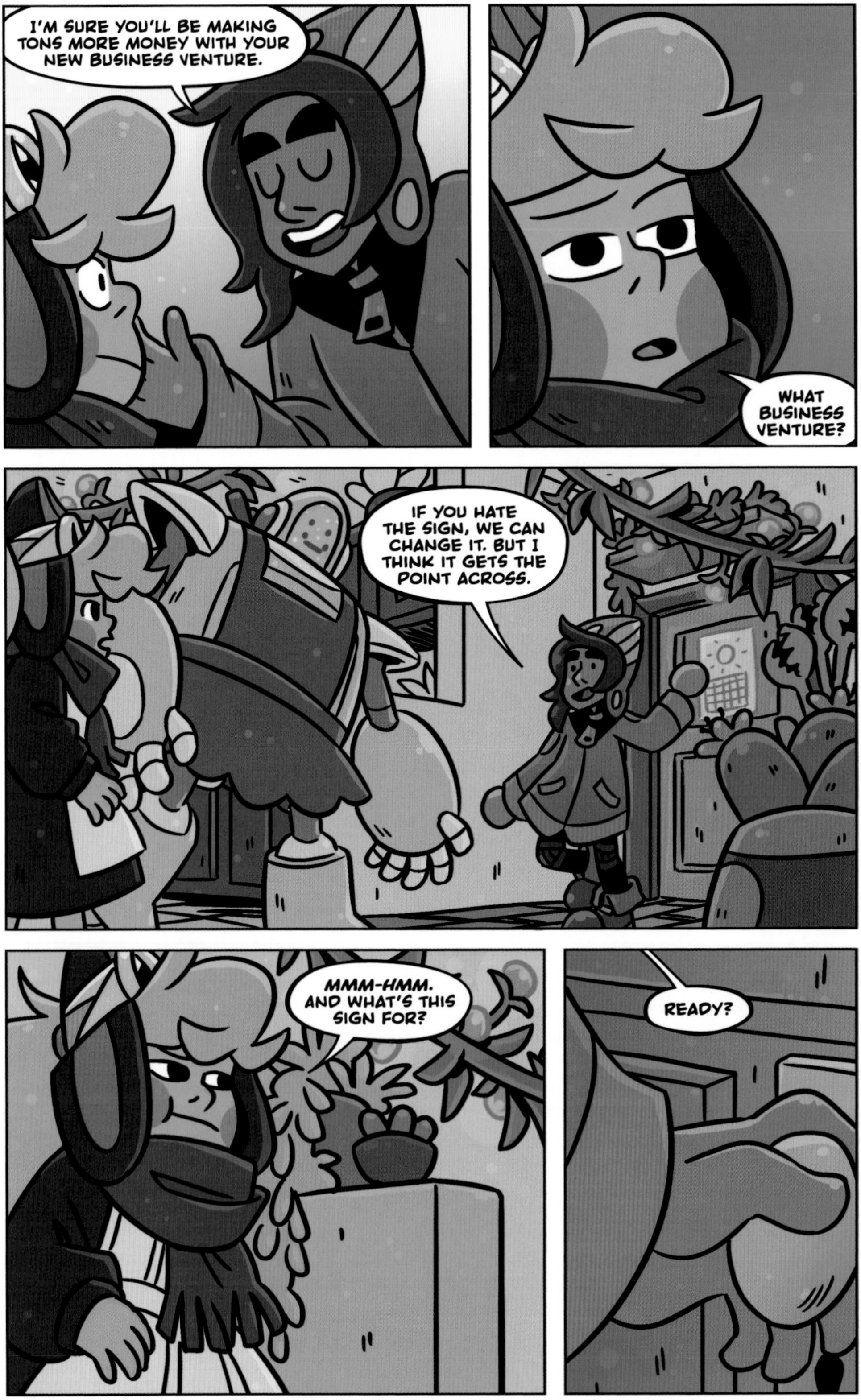
I'M SURE YOU'LL BE MAKING TONS MORE MONEY WITH YOUR NEW BUSINESS VENTURE.
WHAT BUSINESS VENTURE?
IF YOU HATE THE SIGN, WE CAN CHANGE IT. BUT I THINK IT GETS THE POINT ACROSS.
MMM-HMM. AND WHAT'S THIS SIGN FOR?
READY?

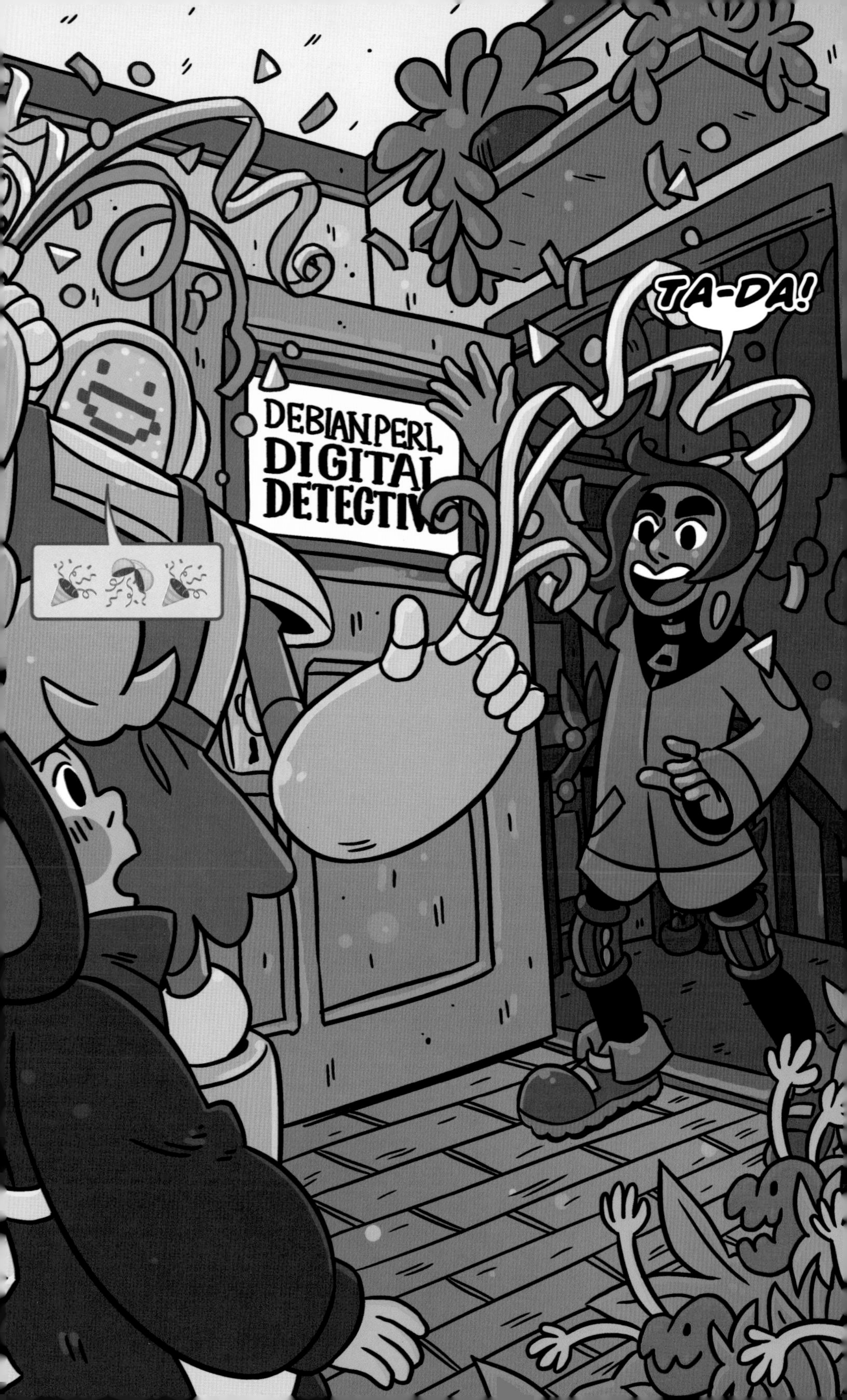
DEBIANPERL
DIGITAL
DETECTIV
TA-DA!

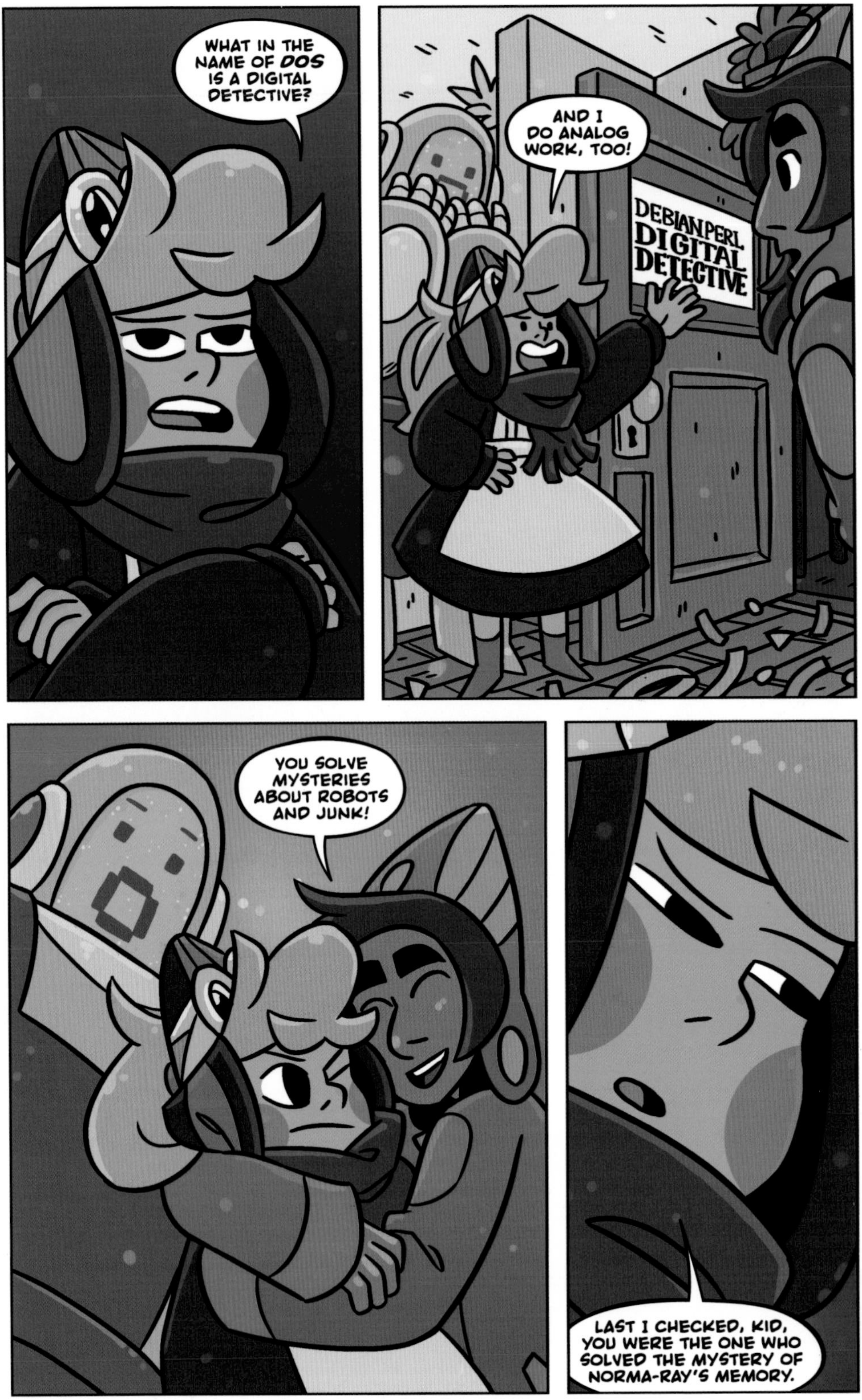
WHAT IN THE NAME OF DOS IS A DIGITAL DETECTIVE?
AND I DO ANALOG WORK, TOO!
DEBIANPERL DIGITAL DETECTIVE
YOU SOLVE MYSTERIES ABOUT ROBOTS AND JUNK!
LAST I CHECKED, KID, YOU WERE THE ONE WHO SOLVED THE MYSTERY OF NORMA-RAY'S MEMORY.

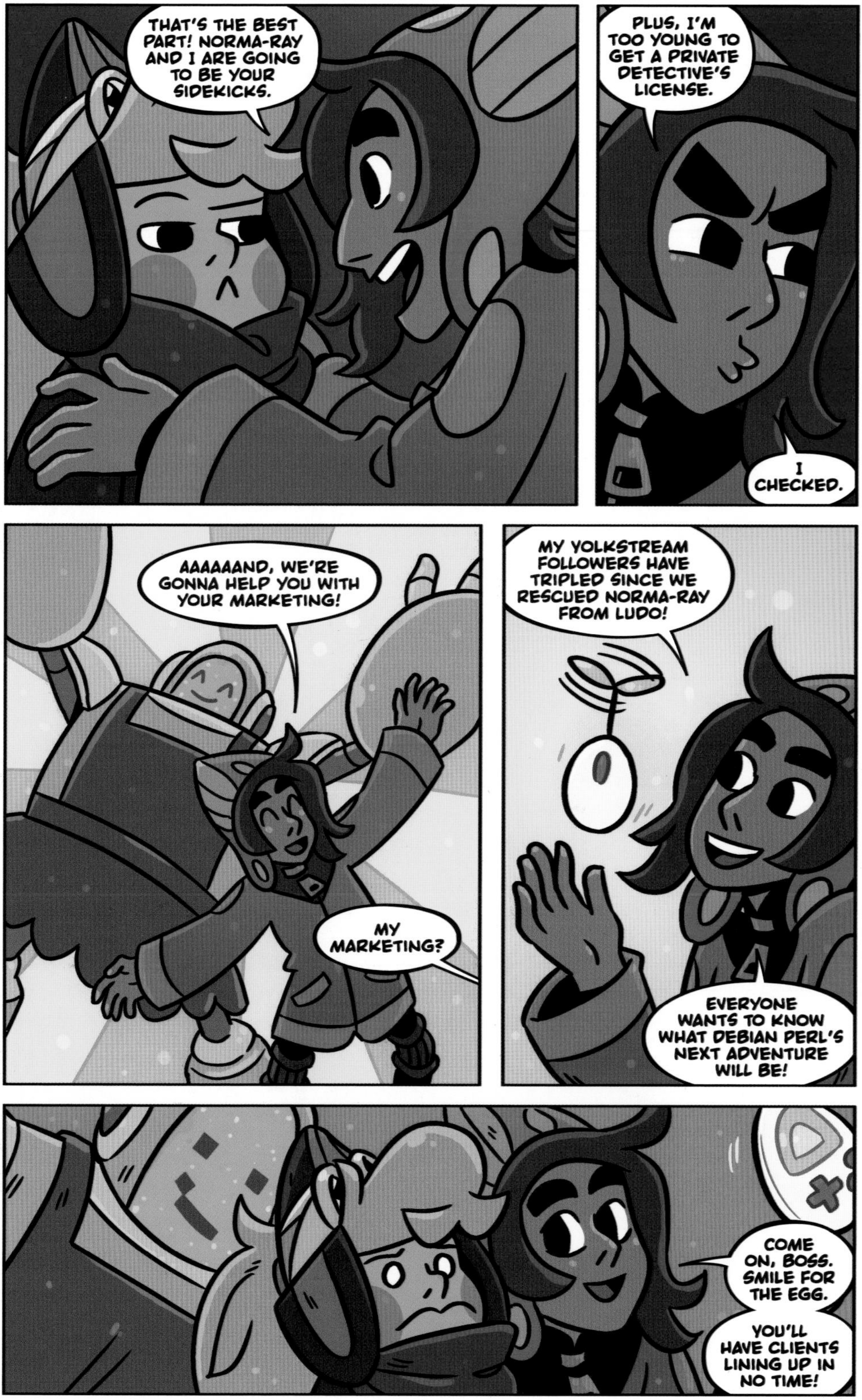
THAT'S THE BEST PART! NORMA-RAY AND I ARE GOING TO BE YOUR SIDEKICKS.
PLUS, I'M TOO YOUNG TO GET A PRIVATE DETECTIVE'S LICENSE.
I CHECKED.
AAAAAAND, WE'RE GONNA HELP YOU WITH YOUR MARKETING!
MY MARKETING?
MY YOLKSTREAM FOLLOWERS HAVE TRIPLED SINCE WE RESCUED NORMA-RAY FROM LUDO!
EVERYONE WANTS TO KNOW WHAT DEBIAN PERL'S NEXT ADVENTURE WILL BE!
COME ON, BOSS. SMILE FOR THE EGG.
YOU'LL HAVE CLIENTS LINING UP IN NO TIME!

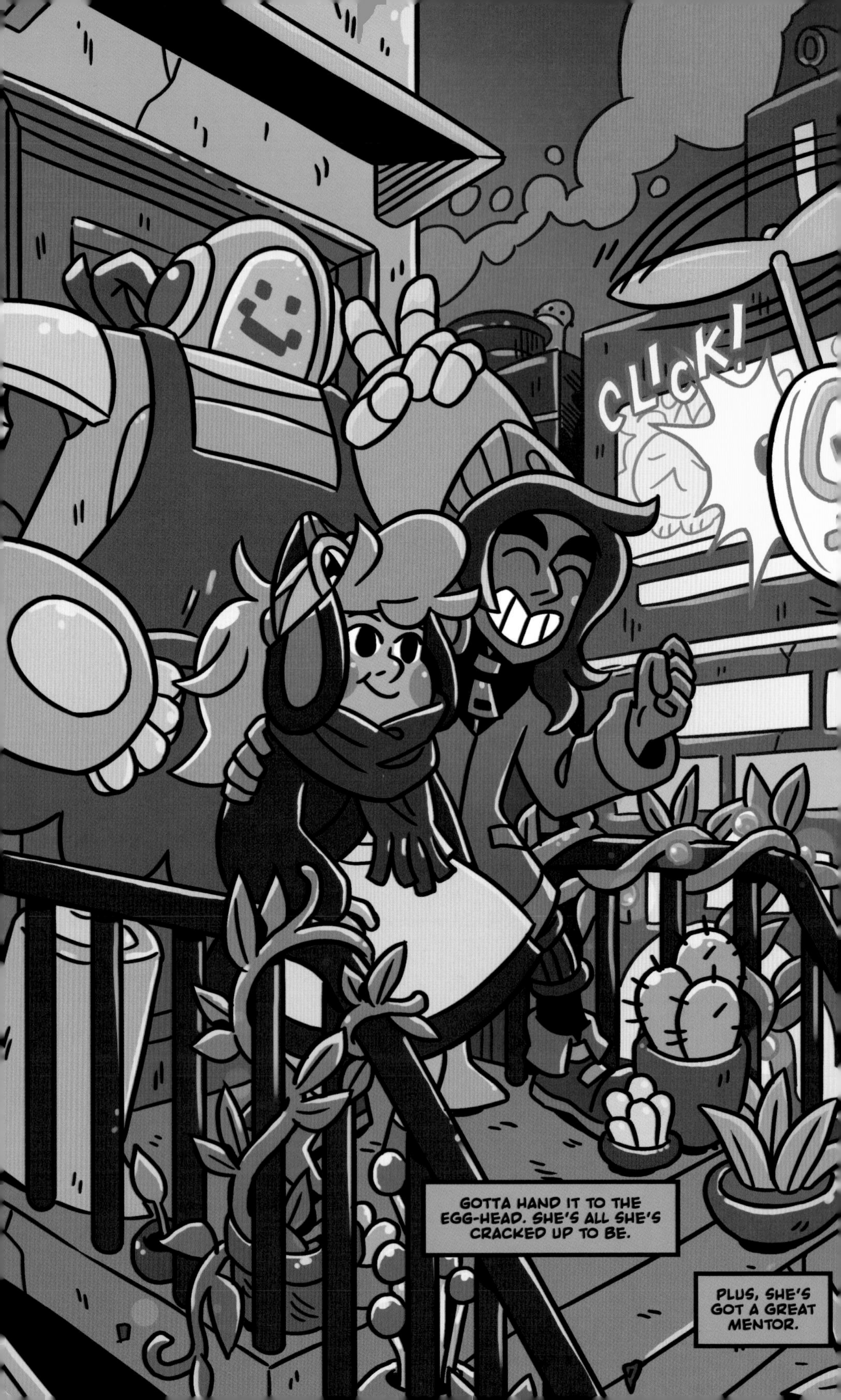
CLICK!
GOTTA HAND IT TO THE EGG-HEAD. SHE'S ALL SHE'S CRACKED UP TO BE.
PLUS, SHE'S GOT A GREAT MENTOR.

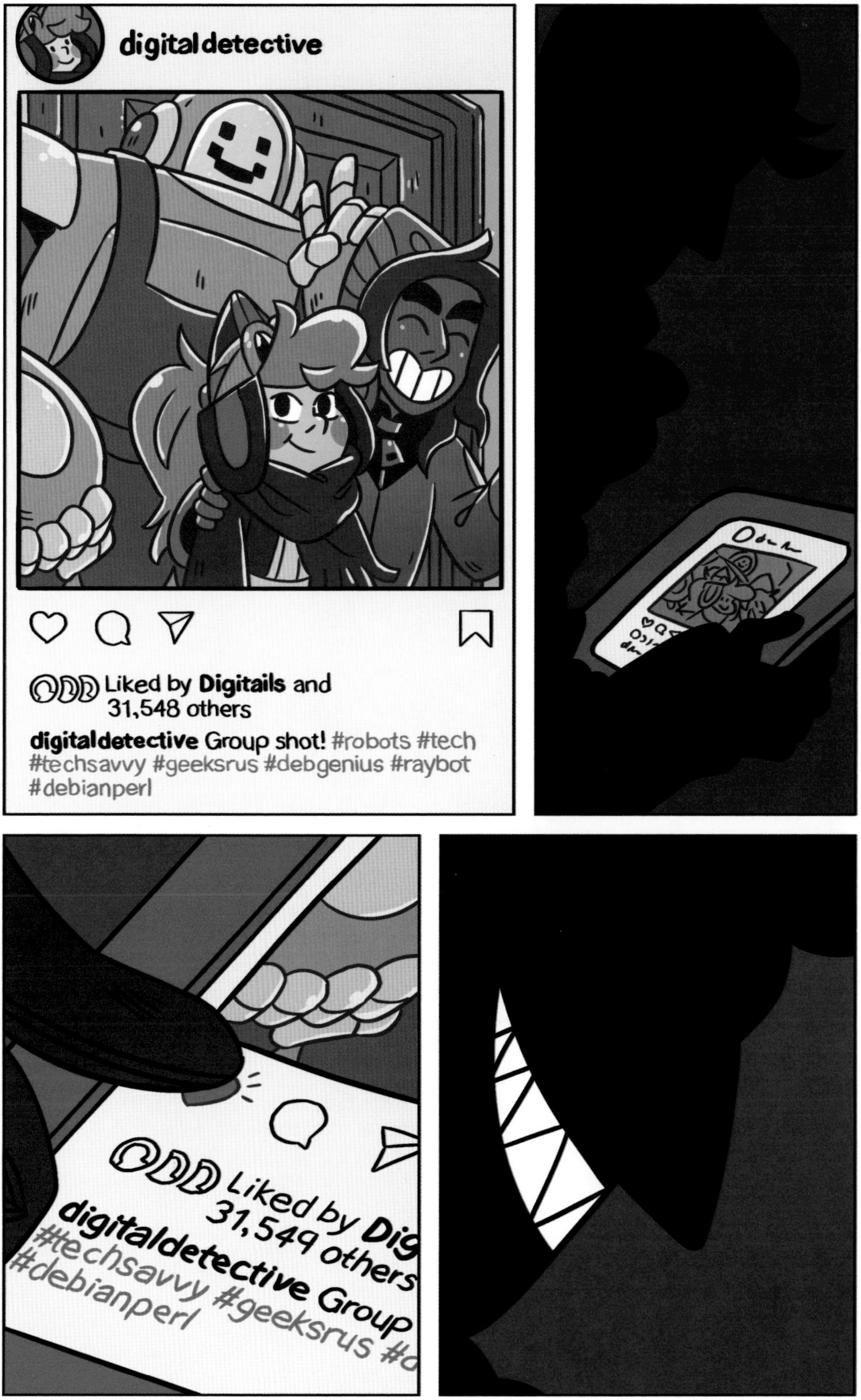
digitaldetective
Liked by Digitails and 31,548 others
digitaldetective Group shot! #robots #tech #techsavvy #geeksrus #debgenius #raybot #debianperl
Liked by Dig
31,549 others
digitaldetective Group
#techsavvy #geeksrus #d
#debianperl

LINGERING QUESTIONS and other things you might want to investigate!

What exactly is coding?

Coding is the process of taking an idea and turning it into instructions a computer can follow. We call these little bits that tell computers what to do **code.**

Small bits of code can make robots move or even do kung fu. But code can also be used to move data, like what to show on a computer screen, or the information on a website. Pretty much if it happens quickly and automatically, someone probably coded it!

```
move(direction: forward,
  distance: 6 squares);
turn(direction: right);
```

Why does code look the way it does?

Code is the way people tell computers what to do; it has to be very exact so the computer knows exactly what we mean. Since computers process using math and people process using language, it ends up looking a bit like a mix between the two.

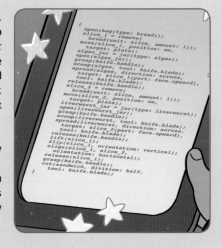

Code, as we think of it, has only been around for about sixty years. Compared to written language, which is thousands of years old, it's a tiny baby, so it's definitely still going to change!

{
open(bag(type: bread));
slice_1 = remove(
bread(unit: slice, amount: 1));
move(slice_1, position: on,
target: plate);
algae_jar = jar(type: algae);
open(algae_jar);
grasp(knife.handle);
scoop(algae, tool: knife.blade);
spread(algae, direction: across,
target: slice_1(part: face.upward),
tool: knife.blade);
release(knife.handle);
slice_2 = remove(
bread(unit: slice, amount: 1));
move(slice_2, position: on,
target: plate);
liverwurst_jar = jar(type: liverwurst);
open(liverwurst_jar);
grasp(knife.handle);
scoop(liverwurst, tool: knife.blade);
spread(liverwurst, direction: across,
target: slice_2(part: face.upward),
tool: knife.blade);
release(knife.handle);
lift(slice_1);
flip(slice_1, orientation: vertical);
align(slice_1, slice_2,
orientation: horizontal);
release(slice_1);
grasp(knife.handle);
cut(sandwich, division: half,
tool: knife.blade);
}

```
if(door.is_closed){
  open(door);
}
```

What is a coding language? Which one is the best? Why are there so many?

A coding language, or **programming language,** is a specific way to give a computer instructions. The original programming languages just told the machine exactly what to do using math statements (divide this, multiply that). It's hard to imagine, but computers were originally made mostly to do math!

As computers have gotten faster, we've been able to write programs in a language that's easier for humans to read. We've also found common operations we use a lot (like repeating sections of code in loops), and built those things into programming languages to make code simpler and our lives easier. Different languages develop from people trying to solve different problems in the world and in computers, and since there are a lot of ways to think about problem solving, there are a lot of languages!

Which one is best depends on each situation and the likes and dislikes of the people coding, but our team's own resident technomancer mostly uses Python and C++.

Is Norma's code a real programming language?

Norma's code is something called **pseudocode,** a made-up language used to talk about code without using any specific coding language. Programmers use these languages all the time when they're discussing solutions.

Although there's no computer that can operate on Norma's code right now, there certainly could be.

Is Norma's hardware real?

Norma's motherboard and other components are based on real computer parts! If you understand how Norma's motherboard works, then you have an idea how real computers work.

While real computers don't have feelings like Norma does (at least that we know of!), a computer's parts work the same way Norma's do:

Norma's Read-Only Memory (ROM) tells us who Norma is.

Norma's Central Processing Unit (CPU) tells us what Norma can do and how quickly.

Norma's Long-Term Memory tells us what Norma has seen and done.

It's the same with a real computer!

What is DOS?

DOS was an operating system popular on old computers in the 1980s and 1990s. It was pretty simple compared to operating systems today (picture a black screen with lots of big text on it), but a lot of people learned computers on them, so we have a warm, fuzzy feeling about it.

Of course, code tends to live a long time, so there are definitely still computers running DOS today.

Are there really technomancers?

There have always been people who like to solve problems and fix things; Deb is one of those, but specifically with technology. Today's equivalent might be a hybrid of a hacker, inventor/maker, and handyperson. Deb is a person who likes to understand how things work, so she appreciates anyone who likes to similarly "geek out" on something that interests them, even if it's not programming.

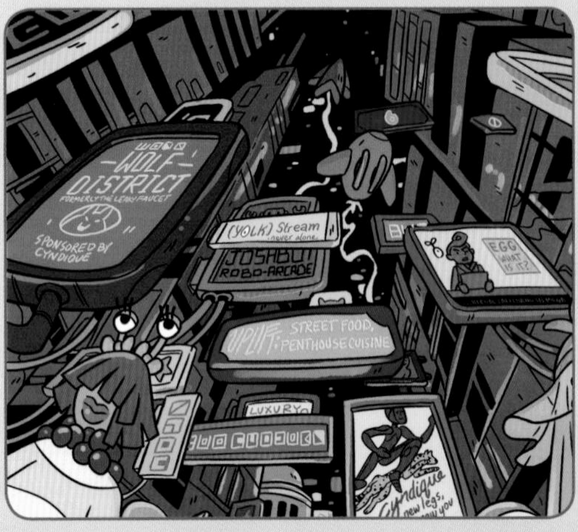

WOLF DISTRICT
FORMERLY THE LEAKY FAUCET
SPONSORED BY CYNDIQUE
(YOLK) Stream
never alone
JOSHBOT ROBO-ARCADE
EGG WHAT IS IT?
STREET FOOD, PENTHOUSE CUISINE
LUXURY
Cyndique
new legs,

Where is Megalopolis?

It's a coastal city in North America, and based on our home city of Oakland, California. Everything around Megalopolis is also an homage to the greater Bay Area. Nearby cities will likely be featured in future books.

Is Humphrey a robot?

We don't know! We suspect he is a frog whom Deb rescued with robotic implants, which would make him a cyborg. But only Deb knows for sure. #cyfrog

Are Deb's plant-robot hybrids real?

We don't think anyone has quite managed to make Deb's robotic plant vines, at least not yet. (Around the office, we call them the "Audreys," after the singing plant in *Little Shop of Horrors*.) But there are scientists working to combine plants with robotics. MIT biohacker Harpreet Sareen has created a wheeled robot-plant hybrid called Elowan. When the plant part of Elowan is too hot, too cold, needs sunlight, or is otherwise uncomfortable, its leaves and stems send out electrical signals. The

robot part of Elowan picks up those signals and drives to somewhere more comfortable. Deb owes a lot to these botany-robotics pioneers!

Why do you need a license to own a cat in Megalopolis?

Several decades before Digits was born, Megalopolis experienced an ecological disaster, and cats were part of the problem. Cats were preying on small animals that were vital to the city's ecosystem, so Megalopolis put strict controls on cats. People who want to get a cat have to apply for a special license, and cats must be kept indoors. Most people follow these

rules, but some folks (like Gigo Geiger) secretly keep unlicensed cats around.

What's the deal with Deb? Is she part plant?

Yep! There are a handful of plant people in Megalopolis. They need plenty of water and sunlight.

Why does Deb eat meat if she's a plant person?

Many species of plants actually eat meat! Venus flytraps, for example, catch insects and spiders in their snapping leaves, and pitcher plants can trap and eat small mammals!

Deb prefers to get her sustainably cloned meat products from the grocery store, however.

I want to read other stories about coding! What do you recommend?

There are lots of books that combine fictional stories with real-world coding and computational problem-solving! We've really enjoyed the *Secret Coders* books by Gene Luen Yang and Mike Holmes, *Hello Ruby* by Linda Liukas, *Lauren Ipsum* by Carlos Bueno, *Computational Fairy Tales* by Jeremy Kubica, and the *Girls Who Code* books—those aren't just for girls!

Now I want to code like Digits! What do I do next?

Ask your local librarian for resources about coding. There are videos, websites, languages... it all depends on the way you like to learn and the things that interest you. There's no wrong way to learn, get started, and (just like Digits) make some mistakes!

GLOSSARY

AI - Artificial intelligence. The intelligence seen in computers (as opposed to living creatures). Currently, techniques for artificial intelligence include machine learning, which uses complex algorithms to "train" a computer to perform functions that otherwise would be too hard to code. See page 49.

algae - A group of plant-like organisms that mostly live in water (seaweed, for example). See page 51.

analog - Allowing a full range of values, like the radio frequency on an old dial radio or the images on a film camera. Often used in contrast to modern electronics built on binary systems. See page 186.

ASCII - A standard way to encode text, using the integers 0 to 127 to each represent one character. See page 176.

Isaac Asimov - (1920–1992) Professor of biochemistry and science fiction writer. Known for his robot-related stories and his definition of the "three laws of robotics," a flawed security constraining what robots are allowed to do. See page 171.

assign - To set a value to a variable. See page 118.

automaton - Any moving, self-operating machine made to look like a human being; another word for robot. See page 22.

binary - Allowing only two values, like on or off, yes or no. Most computer systems today are built on electronics that process binary values. See page 176.

buses - Systems that move data within a computer. See page 39.

chip - A component of a computer used for processing or memory. These are made as flat pieces of a semiconductive material, like silicon, and appear in a motherboard. See page 99.

chlorophyll - A green chemical in plants, algae, and certain bacteria that allows them to absorb light energy. See page 96.

Arthur C. Clarke - (1917–2008) Inventor, undersea explorer, and science fiction writer. He wrote three "laws" that acted as guidelines for predicting the future of science and technology. His third law is the most famous: "Any sufficiently advanced technology is indistinguishable from magic." See page 100.

clock speed - A measure of the speed with which a computer processes data, defined by the number of cycles its processor completes a second. See page 32.

code - The instructions that tell computers what to do, or the act of writing those instructions. See page 51.

coder - A person who writes code. Also called a "programmer," or more formally a "software engineer" (usually when the person designs the code in addition to writing it). See page 47.

CPU - Central processing unit; the main part of a computer that processes data, (performing operations like add and multiply). See page 31.

DOS - A classic operating system popular in the 1980s and 1990s. Think white or green text on a black background. See page 21.

e/em/eir - Pronouns used by someone who identifies as non-binary (neither a woman nor a man) in terms of gender. These are alternatives to "she/her/hers" and "he/him/his." Other pronouns for a non-binary identifying person could be "they/them/their." See page 141.

function - A group of instructions given to a computer, typically given a name like **make_sandwich** or **clean_house**. See page 17.

glucose - A sugar chemical that organisms use as a source of energy. It is made by plants and algae through photosynthesis. See page 94.

hacker - An expert coder. Sometimes used to refer to a person who tries to get around computer security. See page 42.

hafnium and tantalum isomers - Substances used to make nuclear reactors; also referenced as something more valuable than gold (like Deb's word). These cost about $17,000/gram, while gold costs about $42/gram. See page 21.

hard drive - A part of a computer that holds data on a physical disc (like a Blu-ray does). This data is retained even if the computer is disconnected from power. See page 74.

hardware - All the physical components of a computer (as opposed to software). See page 31.

heatsink - The part of a motherboard that helps it distribute heat to its environment, preventing it from getting too hot and malfunctioning. See page 38.

hovercar - A car that drives on air instead of roads. Mostly theoretical. See page 24.

hovercraft - Any hovering vehicle. See page 71.

"if" statement - A statement that uses a conditional to decide whether or not to run a block of code. For example, "if" the door is closed, open the door. ("if" not, don't!) See page 68.

input/output controller - Part of a computer that controls how it interfaces with the outside world. For example, receiving images for visual input or outputting movements to robot arms. See page 38.

Mary Jackson - Born Mary Winston (1921–2005). Mathematician, aerospace engineer, and NASA's first African American engineer. See page 47.

jailbreak - To bypass the restrictions of a device set by the manufacturer. See page 45.

Hedy Lamarr - Born Hedwig Eva Maria Kiesler (1914–2000). Austrian American actress and inventor of the technology on which Wi-Fi, GPS, and cell phone signals are based. See page 90.

liverwurst - A debatably tasty sausage favored by Debian Perl. See page 51.

long-term memory storage - A piece of hardware that stores computer memory it needs for longer than its current power cycle. A hard drive or flash drive are both examples of long-term memory storage. See page 39.

loop - A portion of code meant to be repeated. See page 73.

malware - Programs made to harm a computer by spying on it or otherwise using it to do something the owner would not want. See page 45.

microcode - Code embedded in a computer's hardware, perhaps to manage the operations of a CPU. See page 69.

motherboard - The skeleton of a computer's processing hardware, used to interconnect all the pieces. See page 38.

overclock - Make a computer process data faster than the default settings provided by the manufacturer by overriding its clock speed. See page 32.

photosynthesis - The process of converting light energy to chemical energy (food). Most plants and algae and some bacteria perform photosynthesis. See page 95.

platinum - A silverish, white metal, from the Spanish *platino* ("little silver"). Used here as something more valuable than gold (like Deb's word). Because platinum is very dense, it takes more of it to create a similar item in gold; hence that item would cost more. See page 21.

programming language - A specific set of instructions used to write code. Like spoken languages, there are many of these and each of them expresses instructions in different ways. See page 52.

prosthetic - An artificial body part, such as a leg, nose, or heart. See page 7.

random-access memory (RAM) - Quick-access data storage that is restricted in size and is not retained when the computer is disconnected from power. See page 26.

read-only memory (ROM) - Data storage that can be used but not changed. Often used to store computer software that does not need to change over time. See page 39.

reboot - Turn a computer off and on again. See page 26.

soldering iron - A tool that uses heat to fuse metals. See page 127.

Titan - One of Saturn's moons. Titan is the second largest moon in the solar system—larger than Earth's!—and is the only other celestial body known to have rivers, lakes, and oceans. See page 5.

Alan Turing - (1912–1954) British mathematician, philosopher, theoretical biologist, and code-breaker during WWII. Sometimes referred to as the founder of computer science. See page 84.

variable - A value in a program that can change and is associated with a name. See page 118.

"while" loop - A loop that repeats as long as a certain condition is true. See page 72.

walled garden - A closed environment controlled by the owner of an operating system. A walled garden could restrict allowed apps or operations for a computer system to what the manufacturer or operating system creator allows. See page 43.

MEET THE KNOW YOURSELF TEAM

Helmed by renowned computer scientist Tim Howes, and staffed by cartoonists, writers, and designers, Know Yourself Inc. is an Oakland, California-based company that makes comics and toys that prioritize story and play (while imparting knowledge along the way). We create the toys and comics we wish we had as kids, and media that sparks the imagination. Enter new worlds at **www.knowyourself.com.**

Melanie Hilario has lived on planet Earth since the late 20th century. When she's not co-writing graphic novels with level-5 nerds, she's teaching other humans how their bodies move. During the rest of her waking hours, she fights gravity in ballet class, practices force production at the kung fu studio, tackles an infinite reading list, and binge-watches police procedurals. She lives and works in Oakland, California. Sometimes, she sleeps.

Lauren Davis is a carbon and tortilla chip-based lifeform living in Berkeley, California. Lauren worked for several years as an associate editor at the science fiction blog i09, where she thought about *Star Wars* at a professional level. She enjoys making silly comics, listening to audiobooks, and contemplating the implications of robot consciousness. Her favorite arcade game is Bubble Bobble.

Katie Longua is an artist and magical girl. She's been publishing her own comics for over ten years, including the award-winning series *RÖK*, *Her Space Opera*, and *Space Trash*. Her love of bright colors and quirky designs works its way into everything, including art, fashion, and life. She lives in a haunted house with her partner Josh and a small army of transforming robots. You're definitely pronouncing her last name wrong.

ACKNOWLEDGMENTS

Debian Perl: Digital Detective exists in this dimension because of many incredible humanoids:

Our amazing colleagues at Know Yourself, who shaped this book in ways great and small: Marilyn Perry, Sarah Hawkinson-Patil, Amber Padilla, Adi Patil, Liko Hudson, and Babylyn Schick.

One of our favorite comic geeks and botanists of all time, Betsy Gomez.

Our A++ VP, Samuel Sattin, who fearlessly led us to Lion Forge.

Tim Howes, our CEO and Head Nerd, who got *very into* writing Ray-Bot's pseudocode.

Our own resident technomancer, Sean Marney. Invaluable for his unique skill set as a computer scientist, programmer, comics maker, and storyteller; he's joining us as a writer on book two. Thank DOS!

In addition to the book's existence, the gorgeous colors of Megalopolis are because of the talented Brittany Currie. Letterer extraordinaire Deron Bennett made every bit of text beautifully clear and readable. Justin Hall was kind enough to read a draft of our script and gave us a gem for the end of the book. You're a real peach, Justin.

The three of us are extremely fortunate to have the support and expertise of Andrea Colvin and Grace Bornhoft of Lion Forge. A petabyte of gratitude for believing in this project, in us, and in our extremely unorthodox imaginations.

Lauren, our Researching Maven and Slayer of Plot Holes, thanks her husband, Bill, and all her pals in the CCA Comics community who helped her become a better comicker.

Mel, our Dialogue Doctor and Frequent Over-Indulger in Punnery, thanks her husband, Sam, her kung fu family, her writing cohorts from across the space-time continuum, and her exceptional co-creators for their skills, sentience, and general super-awesomeness. {the_best = you_guys}

Katie, our Official Rainbow Unicorn and Most Sparkly Visionary of the Future, thanks her partner, Josh, who kept her alive through many late nights of inking; her family, who was crazy enough to let her go off to art school; as well as Isotope Comics, without which she never would have started on this comic journey. Also anyone who ever bought a mini-comic from me . . . is this getting to be too much?

Lauren: No, it's perfect.
Mel: You just need semicolons. We got this.
Katie: I just want to thank all the weird people who bought my comics. And this comic.
Lauren and Mel: We love all the weird people. They're our people.

♥ Lauren, Mel, & Katie

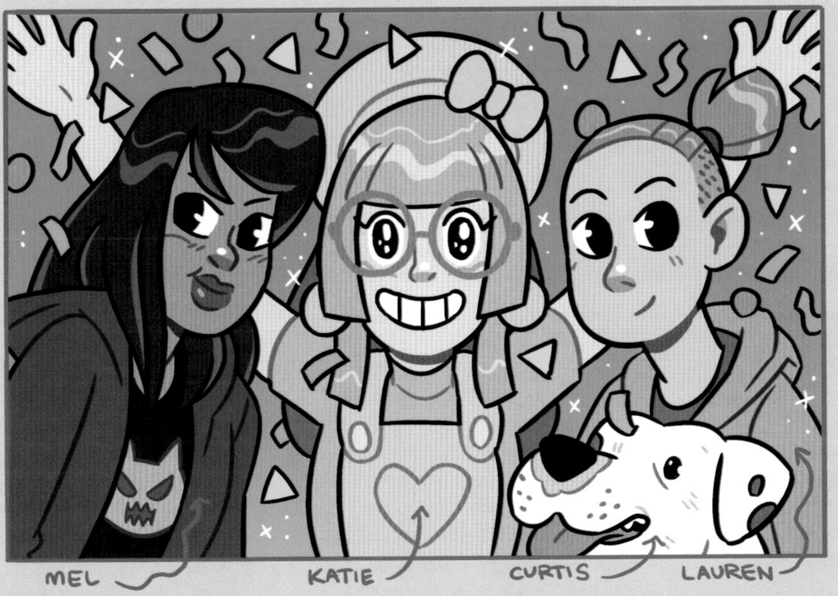
MEL
KATIE
CURTIS
LAUREN

CARACAL™

KNOWYOURSELF™

Written by MEL HILARIO AND LAUREN DAVIS

Illustrated by KATIE LONGUA

Colors by BRITTANY CURRIE

Letters by ANDWORLD DESIGN

Technomancer: SEAN MARNEY

Debian Perl: Digital Detective Book One, The Memory Thief, published 2019 by The Lion Forge, LLC. © 2019 The Lion Forge LLC and Know Yourself, PBC. CARACAL™, LION FORGE™ and its associated distinctive designs are trademarks of The Lion Forge, LLC. Know Yourself™ and its associated distinctive designs are trademarks of Know Yourself, PBC. All rights reserved. No similarity between any of the names, characters, persons, and/or institutions in this book with those of any living or dead person or institution is intended, and any such similarity which may exist is purely coincidental. Printed in China.

Library of Congress Control Number: 2019936686

ISBN: 978-1-5493-0332-6

10 9 8 7 6 5 4 3 2 1